D0838931

BLOOD TRADE

A SEAN COLEMAN THRILLER

To Garland.
Thanks & enjoy!

JOHN A. DALY

John A. Daly

BQB

Blood Trade: A Sean Coleman Thriller
© 2015 John A. Daly. All rights reserved.

Published in the United States by BQB Publishing Company
www.bqbpublishing.com

Printed in the United States of America

ISBN 978-1-939371-69-0 (p)
ISBN 978-1-939371-70-6 (e)

Library of Congress Control Number: 2015937918

Book design by Robin Krauss, www.bookformatters.com
Cover design by Dave Grauel, www.davidgrauel.com

Also in the Sean Coleman Thriller series from John A. Daly

From a Dead Sleep

Praise for John A. Daly
and *From a Dead Sleep*

Some writers are thoughtful. Some have style. John Daly has both. When I read his work, it's time well spent.

—Bernard Goldberg,
New York Times **bestselling author of** *Bias*

An epic thriller with a memorable, unorthodox main character . . . a riveting read . . .

—Colorado Country Life Magazine

A fast-reading suspense book that surprised me so much, I had to finish it in one sitting.

—Alice de Sturler
of the American Investigative Society of Cold Cases

A thriller that packs a punch! This was a very exciting debut novel from John A. Daly. This novel packs a lot of jaw-dropping action into its well-structured narrative—a narrative that gives life to the myriad of characters that inhabit its pages and provides plenty of plot twists and turns to keep you glued to the pages.

—Reading, Writing, and Riesling book blog

I loved this book. The suspense had me sitting on the edge of my seat . . . The author did a fabulous job with the setting details—I could picture every touch, smell, sight that the characters went through . . .

—Yawatta Hosby, author of the novel *One by One*

From a Dead Sleep is a page-turner, an exciting, well-written thriller with a solid back story and more than enough plot twists to keep you guessing.

—Marilyn Armstrong, Serendipity book blog

I totally enjoyed reading John A. Daly's *From a Dead Sleep*. The author used creative writing techniques that make this a mystery/suspense that is very different from other books in this genre . . . The author also does a wonderful job of creating characters and scenes that are quirky, yet believable . . . I highly recommend this entertaining story.
                                        —Paige Lovitt, Reader Views

John pens *From a Dead Sleep* in a well-written plot filled with mystery, suspense and drama. Between his well-developed characters and all the twists and turns within the story line, you will find yourself having a really hard time putting the book down . . . I know I did! Highly recommended for all mystery and suspense fans. I give *From a Dead Sleep* a five-star rating.
                          —Susan Peck, My Cozie Corner book blog

[An] exciting murder mystery that keeps the reader wanting more. A well-written novel that shows one man's flaws and how he redeems himself to the town and ultimately himself. I love a good mystery and this one is one that definitely deserves a read by the mystery lover.
                          —Kathleen Kelly, Celticlady's Reviews

I love mysteries and I love thrillers. This book was both of those things for me . . . I highly recommend this book for anyone who loves suspense, thriller, action novels . . . and yes, there is a little bit of romance in it. I am giving it five stars because, honestly, I couldn't put it down once I picked it up . . . it deserves FIVE STARS.
                     —Becca Wilson, Manic Mama of 2 book blog

John Daly's *From a Dead Sleep* is an engaging page-turner with likable characters . . . Daly delivers a twist and the famous words of Sir Walter Scott will be playing in the background, "Oh, what a tangled web we weave / When first we practice to deceive!" . . . If you're looking for a good mystery or are trying to break out of a reading slump, I highly recommend John Daly's *From a Dead Sleep*. Just a bit of warning: don't start this right before you go to bed, you won't be able to put it down.
                                        —Literary, etc. book blog

An unconventional hero that readers come to like if not love. Plenty of twists and turns will keep readers glued to their seats.

—Cayocosta72 book reviews

Wow, this book will keep you on the edge of your seat . . . The story takes twists and turns that you just simply won't see coming. This is a very exciting mystery and you won't want to put it down . . . John Daly's writing style is a refreshing one. And I must say that when I finished reading this book I wanted to read more by this author. I highly recommend this book to anyone who enjoys a well-written mystery, full of suspense and drama.

—Chris Condy, Recent Reads book blog

Dedication

To my wife, Sarah, who's always been my biggest supporter.

January 16th, 2002
Wednesday

Chapter 1

H e kept his distance from her car, letting up on the gas pedal just long enough to release her rear bumper from the imposing beams of his headlights. The evening had already been awkward enough. The last thing he wanted was for her to think he was following her back to her apartment to begin a new round of arguing.

If the traffic weren't so sparse, it wouldn't have been a worry. He would have just faded into a sea of other beams and she never would have even known he was still there. It would have spared him the mental torment of worrying about what might be bouncing off the walls of his twenty-year-old daughter's head as she glanced into her rearview mirror. He'd already caught her doing it twice.

Andrew Carson didn't have an appetite for more drama. He had no interest in further badgering Katelyn about wasting her time and energy on a *loser* boyfriend who had no ambition and didn't treat her right. He certainly hadn't the stomach to listen to more details of how blissful his ex-wife's life was with her new husband, either. Katelyn clearly liked her new stepfather, which made the repeated mention of him even harder to swallow.

All Andrew wanted right then was to clear his head and get over to the 24-hour Walmart to pick up some supplies for an accounting conference down in Colorado Springs the next morning: last minute items, like printer paper and binders for his presentation of a new software line. The late night detour to the store had been planned in advance, but he'd failed to mention the side-trip to Katelyn during dinner.

He sat in gratuitous silence that soon grew cumbersome under the intermittent glare of overhead street lamps. The muteness let his mind race with odd thoughts and regret. He leaned forward and twisted an illuminated radio knob, then went for the tuner. He found an unfamiliar song that was winding its way through a long, lonely guitar solo. It seemed to fit his mood, so he returned his hand to the steering wheel.

A light drizzle that had been sprinkling down across his windshield began shaping into fine flakes of snow, much like what he'd observed the night before from the upstairs bedroom window of his bare house as he laid awake in bed, unable to sleep.

He lifted his hypnotic gaze from the back of Katelyn's car and met his own dim reflection in the rearview mirror. He looked as tired as he felt. Above his brows dangled the bangs of his long and wavy dishwater-blond hair. He knew that most men his age would kill for such a dense mane. He mused that it was one of the few things beyond his job that he now had going for him in life.

Quickly approaching the adulthood milestone of a half century, his appearance often led others to speculate that he was younger than he was—perhaps not even a day over forty. He kept himself fairly trim, too, which added to the perception.

He certainly didn't *feel* young, however. For the most part, he had physically recovered from the automobile accident that had crushed his leg two years ago, so it wasn't his health that weighed on him. It was the emotional toll. Though his body was nearly mended, his marriage couldn't be. For someone once so content with every aspect of his life, the strange new world of solitude and self-doubt felt like a persistent opponent intent on keeping him off a game he had forgotten how to play.

Brake lights flared brightly in front of him, and his attention swept back into focus on the road. Katelyn's right blinker began pulsating. He smirked at the sight, knowing he needed to make the same turn.

He sighed. "Just another mile or so, sweetie, and then you'll be rid of me for the evening."

A years-old memory of how he used to read stories to his daughter before putting her to bed at night flickered through his head. It brought the slightest of curl to his lips, but the expression soon returned to one of sadness. It was good that they drove separate cars to the restaurant. He couldn't imagine riding back with her in close quarters after how they'd left things. Who knows what else would have been said?

He watched her veer onto the side exit, which led down a mild slope to the waiting interstate below. He was following her maneuver with his gaze when an unexpected sight grabbed his attention. A cloudy cloak of what appeared to be fog suddenly engulfed her automobile.

His eyes absorbed the transformation of her taillights from clearly defined rectangles to a pair of red blurs inside the fog. He found himself pressing his foot down heavier on the brake pedal that he had already been pumping to make the turn.

As best he could tell, Katelyn wasn't at all fazed by the billow that surrounded her. She even seemed to be picking up speed, prompting Andrew to speculate that she may have decided to use the opportunity as a proverbial smoke screen to put some distance between them.

His car entered the swell, and once inside, an odor of thick exhaust and burnt rubber poured in through his slightly cracked window. He quickly realized that he wasn't inside a dense fog but rather the product of some form of combustion. The cloud was thicker to his left where plumes of it rose up from the bottom of a steep gully off the shoulder of the road. He sat up in his seat and peered out his window over the edge of the slope to try and determine its source. What he saw was another set of taillights. They pointed upward toward the top of the hill. An automobile had gone over the embankment and crashed front first at its bottom.

"Christ," he muttered.

He quickly checked his mirrors before veering over to the opposite shoulder of the road, away from the ledge. He came to a stop about thirty yards past where the car had most likely gone over, skidding the last couple of feet along gravelly dirt. He flipped the transmission into park and twisted the ignition off.

Katelyn was already far off in the distance, speeding down the interstate, and most likely feeling relieved that he was no longer trailing her. It seemed that she hadn't noticed it was a car accident that had caused the cloud.

When Andrew opened his door, the cold and crisp January night air quickly flooded in along the open chest of his leather jacket. Guided only by a dim dome light, his hand found the brass handle of the wooden walking cane he occasionally used where it was wedged between the passenger seat and the center console. The slope of the road had a more than moderate angle to it, so the cane could be useful.

He knew from the lingering fume in the air that the accident had to have just happened. From the glance he had stolen, the drop-off was steep, but was probably no more than forty feet in depth. It didn't appear that the car had rolled. It possibly wasn't even totaled. No flames were present, which made him question if the thinning cloud was even actual smoke or a combination of exhaust, scorned pavement, and possibly steam from under the hood. There was definitely a stench of antifreeze in the air.

Even if the car was spared major damage, there was a decent chance that the driver was injured. Andrew felt obligated to help.

He stepped out of his silver Lexus LS and into the brisk darkness. He clearly remembered the night that he and his family had been in that accident two years ago on a remote road in the mountains where help hadn't arrived for thirty minutes. It had felt more like an eternity. It was a horrifying experience, especially for his teary-eyed, then teenage daughter, whose inability to pry her father free from the wreckage or wake her mother added to the chaos of the quandary. It was a night none of them would ever forget.

He wouldn't wish such torment on his worst enemy. If there was a chance he could spare someone else from such suffering and a sense of helplessness, he was at least going to try.

Feeling the tingle of cold moisture brushing across his face, he whisked his way out from under the dull light of a street lamp and walked across the road. Once on the other side, he began making his way back to the incline to the spot where he believed the car had gone over. He could hear no moans or cries for help, only some distant, oblivious traffic from the interstate below and the crinkle of patches of frozen grass that strayed up from cracks in the pavement beneath his feet.

The brake lights of the car below were no longer on, nor were the headlights. The darkness wouldn't let him make out the outline of the automobile or the shape of anyone who might have exited it.

"Don't go down there!" commanded a loud, unexpected voice from the night.

The abrupt order nearly caused Andrew to drop his cane. It hadn't come from below, but from above—further up the hill. He halted in his tracks. His head twisted back and forth as he struggled to pinpoint the voice's source.

A pair of headlights quickly flicked on and off about twenty yards up the road from him. There was another car, a van, hidden in what was left of the diminishing cloud. It was parked along the ledge of the embankment. The flash of the lights acted as a homing beacon, sent to Andrew from the van's driver.

He glanced down at what he could make out of the wreckage below before turning his gaze back to the parked van. He walked toward the vehicle, intermittently planting the tip of his cane into the gravel-laced shoulder as he did.

The van was a full-sized Chevy, a few years old. It looked to be white, and was possibly a work-van, though there was no company name visible on its side. As Andrew approached the vehicle, he could make out the driver's hand draped outside of the open window, motioning him to step in closer.

"The guy's crazy!" said the same voice, now nervous. "He was driving like a madman. The police are on their way."

Andrew reached the driver's side door and leaned forward to greet the man inside. Dim, blue light from the dashboard gauges offered little clarity, but enough for him to distinguish the contour of the man's face and body. He had curly hair under a dark baseball cap and a mustache with a crowded thickness that seemed a bit outdated for the current styles. He wore thick-framed glasses with even thicker lenses and looked to be of average weight and height. He was dressed in a dark sweatshirt and jeans.

"What's going on?" asked Andrew.

"I think he's drunk. He was all over the road up there," replied the man, nudging his head in the direction of the highway. "He took the turn way too fast and went over the edge." He held what looked to be a cell phone up for Andrew to see and explained that he had already been talking on it with a dispatcher to report the erratic driving when he witnessed the crash.

Andrew nodded. "You keep saying *he*. Are you sure it's a man?"

There was some hesitation. "I'm just assuming," the man finally said. "I guess I don't know."

"Okay. How long has the driver been down there?" Andrew asked. He twisted his head again toward the wreckage.

"Just a few minutes. Not long."

"You haven't gone down there to check on him? Or her?"

"No!" The response was impulsively defensive. The man took a deep breath before continuing. "Listen, he was driving like a lunatic. He didn't care one bit about anyone else on the road, so I say we should just let him sit down there in his car until the police come. Let them deal with him. He doesn't deserve our help."

"But what if he's injured?" asked Andrew.

The man said nothing at first, and then shrugged his shoulders. "Better him than us."

Air left Andrew's lungs. He considered the man's attitude, but couldn't bring himself to share it. "Well, maybe he's crazy or drunk, or whatever," he said, "but he might also be injured."

The man blew a chilly exhale from his mouth in frustration. He shook his head. The lights from the dashboard danced across his glasses.

"I'm going to check it out," said Andrew. He turned his back to the driver, gripped his cane firmly in his hand, and readied to begin a careful descent down the hill. He had only made it a couple of steps across some snow-blanketed earth when he heard the man behind him sternly shout.

"Wait!"

Andrew's head snapped back in annoyance. "What?"

"He's trying to drive out of the ditch. Look!"

Andrew's eyes narrowed at the faint sound of tires skidding on grass and slush. He turned his attention back to the car below and noticed its white reverse lights now illuminated brightly. The hum of its engine could barely be heard. The wheels didn't sound as if they were gaining any traction as the back of the car only bobbed up and down slightly from the motion.

"He's not hurt," said the man in the van. He craned his neck to grab a better view around Andrew of the trapped motorist.

The car below suddenly jerked up the hill a foot or two. It didn't get far, but it was enough for the person inside it to step on the brakes to lock in the progress. After a few seconds, however, the car slid begrudgingly back to its original position. A muffled snarl of frustration came from below. It sounded like a man's voice.

"You see? He's fine," insisted the man in the van.

Andrew sighed in relief. "I guess you're right," he conceded. "He sounds pissed, not hurt." He felt some tension leave his body. He would have made his way down the steep hill with his cane, but he was now glad he wouldn't have to.

"I suppose you're a better man than me for wanting to help," said the man. He seemed more at ease now, too. "That's good. The world needs more Boy Scouts."

Andrew drifted back over to the window and smiled. "I was kicked out of the Scouts when I was twelve."

Both men laughed.

"So what brings you out on a school night?" asked the driver in a gamesome tone.

"Just a late dinner in town."

"By yourself?"

Andrew sighed. "That probably would have worked out better."

An uncomfortable muteness fell between the two, and Andrew silently scoffed at the strangeness of the conversation.

The flakes of snow that fell from the sky seemed as if they were growing in size. The frosty air made Andrew raise his cupped hands to his mouth and blow into them. He eyed his own car parked along the exit ramp as the whine of spinning tires again ascended from the bottom of the gully.

"There's no sense in you hanging out here man," said the driver. "He's okay. And like I said, the police are on their way. I'll catch them up to speed."

Andrew took a moment to digest the man's offer, and then nodded. "Yeah, I suppose there's no point in me sticking around out here in the cold."

No sooner did he finish his remark than he heard the unmistakable thud of a car door closing from down at the bottom of the hill. He turned his head and saw a dark, male figure in what appeared to be a snug white t-shirt climbing up the hill toward them. The climber looked to be a large man with broad shoulders. Deep grunts of effort bellowed from his mouth.

"Ah, shit!" The van driver suddenly appeared nervous again behind the thick lenses of his glasses. He leaned forward and began fiddling with something below his steering wheel. A second later, the engine cranked.

"Go!" Andrew thought he heard someone say from inside the van. It didn't sound like the driver's voice.

Andrew's eyes widened in curiosity. "What are you doing?" he asked loudly over the roar of the van engine.

The driver kept facing forward on the road, ignoring Andrew's query and his questioning gaze. A grimace etched across the man's teeth as he popped the transmission. Wheels spun for just a moment on the wet ground before the van lurched forward and took off quickly down the exit ramp.

Andrew felt the spray from the tires slap his face. His chest tightened as he struggled to comprehend the driver's bizarre reaction. Though largely concealed in the darkness, he knew that his reaction was clearly prompted by fear—fear of a confrontation with the large man who was now nearly at the top of the hill behind him—the man who Andrew was about to be standing with . . . alone.

The loudening racket of hands and feet digging into frosty earth suddenly stopped. Andrew could feel warm breath bearing down on the back of his tense neck as the rest of his body turned ice cold. He swallowed before slowly turning his head to meet the eyes of the person standing behind him.

It wasn't the man's darkened eyes, however, that greeted Andrew's line of sight. It was his neck. The man was huge. He towered above Andrew, who had to lift his head to meet the man's opaque stare.

Andrew stumbled backwards a step, digging the tip of his cane into the ground after carving out some marginal distance between himself and the imposing stranger who hovered much too close for comfort.

The man didn't say a word, which made Andrew nervous. He wasn't sure if the man was just trying to catch his breath or if he was evaluating Andrew's reason for being there. He had short, dark hair and appeared to be Caucasian and somewhere in his mid- to late-twenties. His large biceps looked like upside-down tree trunks rooting out from his receding shirtsleeves. Half a dozen earrings snaked up the sides of each of his ears and a slightly larger ring looped through the bottom of his nose. The man should have been freezing with his bare arms and thin shirt providing no insulation from the brisk temperature, yet he didn't seem too affected by the elements. The strong, repellent stench of alcohol skimming the air perhaps explained why.

Andrew forced himself to speak, hoping to assess whether the paralyzing anxiety that rushed through his skin was truly warranted. "Are you okay?" he timidly asked.

There was no reply. Only heavy breathing.

Andrew opened his mouth, searching for something else to say when the man suddenly spoke.

"Yeah. . . I'm fine." His voice was eerily deep and somewhat hoarse.

Andrew didn't feel any less on edge. "I saw the exhaust from your car," he sputtered out in a single breath. "From the road. I was worried you were hurt."

The man just glared. A moment agonized by before he nodded. He slowly turned to gaze at the sight of his disabled automobile below. A couple of cars quickly sliced along the interstate beyond it, with their headlights casting brief shadows along the overpass. The man's head twisted back to Andrew.

"Who was that guy who drove off?"

Andrew hadn't been sure that the man had even seen the

fleeing driver, but he apparently had. Based on the driver's abrupt departure, Andrew considered that the two men might have been engaged in some kind of late night road rage. "Just some guy who also saw your car," he answered, thinking it to be the most harmless response. He took a second before continuing. "He called the police to report the accident. Help should be here soon."

The man's body tensed at the word *police*. Andrew questioned whether he should have offered up that information. He had done so as a way of incapacitating any hostile intentions the man may have been weighing in his mind.

The man's stoic presence suddenly shifted to one of worry, even though he tried to conceal the change.

Andrew watched him clench his fists until his large arms trembled slightly.

"Can you give me a ride to Denver?" he asked. "I need to get to Denver."

Andrew bit his lip and swallowed. Denver was over an hour's drive south. The man was trying to leave the scene. Andrew suspected, based on the alcohol he could smell, that he was trying to avoid a DUI charge. He seemed more glazed than drunk; his footing was solid and his speech wasn't slurred. Regardless, he clearly wasn't interested in waiting around for the police to arrive.

Feeling the weight of the situation pressing down across his shoulders, Andrew searched for an excuse to decline the request—one that wouldn't provoke a physical confrontation with the large man.

"Listen, I'm not headed to Denver, and besides, I'm just about out of gas."

"I'll pay you for the gas," said the man. "We'll stop at the next gas station."

Andrew's pulse picked up. He felt the situation quickly spiraling out of his grasp. He speculated that the man was not going to take *no* for an answer. In the developing tension, he strained to hear the hopeful sound of faint police sirens. There was none.

"Come on," urged the man. "Do me this favor, all right?"

Anxious indecision jetted through Andrew's veins like electricity through a wire. He weighed different tactics in his mind, but none felt promising. If he said no, the man might get angry, toss him down the hill, and take his car from him. Maybe the car stuck at the bottom of the hill was stolen and that was why the man didn't have any qualms about leaving it behind. If he said yes, he was trapping himself in a situation that he might not be able to get out of. The guy could be an axe murderer for all Andrew knew.

He repeatedly glanced up at the highway above, yearning to find the headlights of another car making its way down the ramp toward them. It would give him a chance to wave down some help and inject a buffer into the situation. Not a single automobile had passed down the road since the driver in the van had abandoned him. Andrew was on his own.

His mind raced, desperate to avoid a physical confrontation with the giant man. An idea filtered into his head. "I have a tow rope in my car!" he spewed. "I can pull you out of that ditch with it."

Though he was sure that the man's first priority was leaving the scene, Andrew banked on his preference to do so in his own car. If he'd stolen the car, however, that might change things. Andrew prayed that wasn't the case. It was best not to give the man too much time to dwell on the proposal. "Wait here," he said. "I'll be right back with my car."

Andrew spun away from the man and began walking briskly down the shoulder of the road. He had begun his career in software sales. Taking away the luxury of choice was a classic professional maneuver from a seasoned salesman, and he used that now. Andrew kept his stride even over the cold ground, with only a hint of his typically more pronounced limp. He was wary of advertising any sign of weakness to the more physically endowed man. It made him feel like a small, injured animal fearful of distinguishing itself to a stalking predator.

Even with his back to the man, he could sense the stranger's imperialistic eyes scrutinizing his every step and movement. He discreetly brushed his hand along his front pants pocket, panicking for a moment when he didn't feel the bulge of his car keys inside. He breathed again when he found them in the other pocket. He rehearsed a drill in his mind—quickly hop in the driver's seat of his car, crank the engine, and leave the confused stranger behind in a cloud of exhaust as he tore down the interstate alone.

He had no intention of helping the man out of this predicament. He didn't even have a rope in his car. He wasn't sure exactly what kind of situation he had come upon there on that exit ramp in the middle of the night, but he was certain that if he didn't cut things loose right now, he'd undoubtedly end up paying some kind of price.

As he put more distance from the man, he started to feel more at ease. His mind flew through his drill again.

The faint shift of gravel and the intermittent scuffing of wet pavement behind him caught his ear.

Andrew's heart sank.

As nonchalantly as possible, he bent his head over his shoulder for a glimpse. The man was walking after him—quickly.

Andrew's head snapped back around to face his Lexus, holding the lingering image of the pursuing man in his mind. Obviously, the stranger suspected he was being deceived or had made up his mind that he wasn't going to accept the proposal. The Lexus wasn't far away, but to Andrew it seemed frighteningly distant.

He crossed the street, stealing another glance at the stranger under the motion of checking for oncoming traffic. The large man was moving in faster now, displaying sternness and aggression with each lunge forward. A metallic rattle reached Andrew's ears, something like keys in the man's pocket or a wallet chain riding his hip. Andrew considered demanding that the man stay put and wait for him to back his car up, but he doubted the suggestion would be heeded.

He held out the small remote on his keychain and pressed a button to pop the trunk, hoping that seeing the trunk lid spring open would convince his pursuer that he was retrieving a tow rope. The move didn't faze the stranger.

Andrew concentrated on the steadiness of his footing; he couldn't afford to trip or lose his balance along the sloped pavement. He wouldn't stand a chance of getting away.

By the time he reached his car and tucked his fingers under the handle of the driver's side door, his arms were trembling.

The stranger's footsteps erupted into a near sprint. The metal rattling sound turned wild.

Andrew's eyes bulged and his chest stiffened. He yanked his door open. The man was bearing in fast, too fast for Andrew to slide inside his car, close his door, and lock it before he was reached.

He gripped the brass handle of his walking cane and quickly raised it hand over hand until his fingers clasped it around its base.

"Hey!" the man shouted from just a few feet away.

Andrew felt the wisp of the man's hand slide along his shoulder. He clenched his teeth, choked back on the cane, and swung it into the large man like a lumberjack axing down a tree. The sickening thud of metal landing on flesh and the crack of splitting wood echoed, drowning out Andrew's strenuous grunt. The cane connected with the man's forehead. The streetlamp added new visibility, highlighting the man's face as it contorted in shock. The man went down.

Andrew knew he'd gotten a clean, wicked shot in, but wasn't in any less of a hurry to get away. He dropped what was left of his shattered cane and slid inside his car. His rapid heartbeat nearly tore a hole through his chest. He yanked the door shut and snapped the lock. His hand shook uncontrollably as he managed to slide the right key into the ignition, twisting it so hard it nearly broke off. He popped the gearshift into drive and mashed his gas pedal to the floor. His tires spun madly along the road before gripping, sending him rocketing forward onto the off-ramp.

He roared in adrenaline-fueled triumph. He looked back and forth from the road in front of him to his rearview mirror, searching for the man sprawled out along the road behind him. He didn't find him. The night was too dark.

Air funneled up from his lungs and out his mouth as he worked to calm down. He flipped on his headlights. As his eyes went back to the road where the ramp met the interstate, he noticed the white van parked on the shoulder. The stranger from the hill who had abandoned him hadn't gone all that far.

A brief temptation to pull over and give the man a tongue-lashing for leaving him on his own entered Andrew's mind, but he ignored the taunt. He was done. The police would be there soon. They'd sort it all out.

The way Andrew saw it, he had tried to perform a good deed, and his reward was that he had nearly gotten attacked and his car stolen.

"Never again," he muttered.

———

Andrew's headlights lit up the overhanging branches of a long row of Nannyberry trees as he rounded a bend. Just a few months earlier, those branches had been dense with small white flowers. Now, they were completely bare other than with the thin blanket of accumulating snow that lined them.

Through a mesh of steady, large flakes, the Lexus glided up the short, wet drive to the entrance of the long, illuminated sign framed by a decorative concrete wall. It read "Hunter's Cove." Andrew had lived in the Greeley, Colorado, subdivision for years.

He slowed the car down to coast between a pair of oversized pine trees on either side of the subdivision entrance and then sped back up. He passed by several large, upper-scale homes with tall, arching facades lurching high above. In summertime, the residents' wide, well-kept yards were all cast in the same deep and attractive shade of green, their lush landscaping having evolved from an unspoken ongoing competition among homeowners. Concrete fountains, koi ponds, artistically trimmed hedges and shrubs—all were purposefully exuberant in their nature. Under the even sheet of snow, they now all looked the same.

The lengthy arch of Andrew's garage came into view from behind an eight-foot-tall hedge that divided his property from his neighbor's lot. With the press of a button, he commanded the steady rise of the garage door. As he waited in the driveway of his home, it suddenly occurred to him that he had never stopped at the store for supplies. He shook his head in frustration; his thoughts had been solidly preoccupied with the scene back at the off-ramp. He'd have to get up a little earlier than planned in the morning and make the stop on his way down to Colorado Springs. He pulled the Lexus inside the garage.

The interior was nearly bare. No tools draped along pegboards and no rakes or shovels hung from prongs. Not even a lawn mower. Andrew always hired out whatever yard and maintenance work that needed to be done around the house. He had never been much of a handyman and had little interest in learning such skills. He was a numbers guy.

When the broad glare of headlights vanished as he turned the knob, he was left alone in the dark. The bulb in the garage-opener above had burned out months earlier and he hadn't cared enough to replace it. The only assisting light came from a streetlight a couple of doors down and what little glow stemmed from his car interior light as he stepped out of the vehicle. He took a moment to let his eyes adjust to the night, losing himself for a second at the sight of faint flakes falling gently to the earth. Their delicate landing was a display of poetic profoundness.

He felt alone, fighting an adolescent urge to call someone—

anyone—and tell them of the strange, harrowing event that had taken place that night. He somberly accepted that there wasn't a single person left in his life who would even care. It was as if he was one of the flakes falling from grace outside, and upon impact, disappearing into nothingness.

He breathed in the cold air and stood with glazed eyes for a few moments longer before a broad, unexpected gust of wind brought him back to his senses. He turned toward the inside garage door, but as he did, he heard a muffled thump. It was quickly followed by a creaky groan of unsettlement that seemed to emit from his car.

He turned back to the Lexus and listened carefully. All that was heard now was some intermittent ticking from the engine. With his eyes narrowed, he took a breath and was about to unlock the door when he was halted by another noise. This time, it sounded like tapping metal.

He carefully walked to the rear of the car where the faint tapping continued and grew a bit louder. There in the dull light from the streetlamp he noticed the trunk wasn't completely closed. The gusting wind caused it to bob slightly up and down.

A smirk slowly curled along his face at the thought of his last-ditch attempt back at the off-ramp to convince his deranged pursuer that he was trying to help him and not escape from him.

"Tow rope," he whispered.

He had popped the trunk with his remote key before things got physical and it had remained unsecured the rest of the trip home. He slid his fingers under the edge of the trunk door and lifted it up in order to give it a good slam back down. He felt the sudden force of a sharp object plunged viciously into him just below his ribcage even before the trunk light exposed the large figure inside.

Andrew's eyes swiftly swelled and his mouth gaped in shock, but he couldn't breathe. He dropped the trunk and his hands instinctively went to his gut. He felt warm blood ooze freely between his fingers from the brutal stab. His face felt numb. A second thrust from the trunk sent another jolt through his body. This time he felt the object pierce just under his chest.

He staggered backwards, wobbly legs trembling. Wide-eyed, he watched in horror as a man's large arm pushed open the trunk from inside. The light exposed a menagerie of tattoos along the arm—most recognizable was one of a large swastika.

The man he'd clubbed at the bypass now climbed out of the trunk. Clasped in his hand was a large switchblade. Blood dripped from it.

Andrew wanted to run, but he couldn't breathe and his legs weren't responding. He didn't remember falling backwards, but he suddenly found himself sprawled out on his back along the frozen driveway. His fluttering eyes gazed up through the surreally peaceful white flakes that fell from the sky to his face. Among those snowflakes, he found himself gazing into the eyes of his tattooed attacker.

"You should have given me a ride, shitberg!" the man grunted out. He wiped his mouth with the back of his arm.

Unable to find his breath, Andrew's body felt frozen as the man slowly and methodically approached him. To Andrew, he looked eight feet tall. Cloaked in relative darkness, his presence was sinister, almost mythical—a grim soul cast in the mold of an angel of death.

The man flicked his wrist so that his fingers were clasped over the top of the knife instead of under it.

Andrew saw him grip the handle, readying to plunge it down into his chest to finish the job.

Andrew's lips moved in a silent plea for help, but he heard no sound escape his mouth. He thought of his daughter and all of the things he wished he had told her—the pride he had in her and all that she meant to him, the love that would last beyond the grave.

The evil hovering above him seemed to glare down into the trenches of his very soul, as if recognizing his every thought. Andrew knew that this sadistic man would be the last image he would see before he left this earth.

But as his vision grew blurry and his pulse winded down, he sensed another presence close by. He hoped it was an angel watching over him, ready to guide him to the afterlife. He mouthed a garbled prayer. The presence, however, wasn't that of a spirit.

A bright flash of blue light and the juiced sound of something electric sizzled nearby and then Andrew's attacker's body buckled under a crippling force. He barked out an incoherent sound that was higher in tone than expected from someone his size. He staggered to the side before dropping to a knee. The blue light lit up the driveway a second time and the man's body contorted into an unnatural pose and then collapsed face first to the cement.

Andrew wasn't sure what had happened; his mind rushed back to the life draining quickly from his body. His lower lip quivered uncontrollably. He could no longer turn his head at all. His limbs were cold, nearly numb. He could see his left arm rise in the air as if it were reaching for something that wasn't there.

He realized it wasn't he who was holding his arm up, but someone else. A man. The man's hand was wrapped around it, supporting it.

A face came into view over Andrew, hovering just inches above. The night kept it mostly unseen, but Andrew was sure he could read concern and compassion etched across it through the thick lenses of the man's glasses. The man's mouth was moving, but all Andrew could hear was a buzzing noise that no one other than the dying could hear.

"Poor bugger," a voice with an accent spoke.

The comment didn't come from the man who held Andrew. It came from a shadowy figure that he now noticed standing a few yards away with his hands hugging his hips. There were two men hovering above, not one.

Andrew felt a wild, impulsive urge to grab onto whatever life he could manage to cling to and his fingers went to the face of the man who held him. They ran along his glasses and then found a mustache, a thick one. Only, it wasn't real. He tore half of it from the man's face. It dangled in the air, swaying in the wind above the man's lips.

It was the last thing Andrew Carson saw.

Chapter 2

"Were you born or have you ever lived in or received medical attention in any of the following countries since 1977: Cameroon, Central African Republic, Chad, Congo, Equatorial Guinea, Niger, or Nigeria?"

Sean Coleman glared in irritation over the narrow, neatly kept desk at the woman who had asked him the awkward question. She was a large, top-heavy individual in her sixties. Her hair was short and nearly as white as the short-sleeved shirt she wore. Thick, black, wing-tipped glasses rested upon the edge of her round nose and her deadpan eyes suggested that she was in no mood for whatever guff she predicted from the man now silently judging her.

"Jesus. Are you kidding me?" asked Sean. His big body shuffled around uncomfortably in the orange fiberglass chair that would have been too small for even an average-sized adult. "I was just in here two days ago. You asked me these exact same questions then. Do you *really* think that sometime in the past two days I visited a witch doctor in some half-assed, bamboo hut in Africa?"

The woman's eyes rose to the ceiling and she folded her thick, flabby arms in front of her chest. His rant wasn't the first agitated outburst she'd had to contend with in her line of work. She sank back into a heap in her towering metal swivel chair. It let out a painful growl from the movement. Though she was short, her chair let her hover about six inches above Sean.

She replied in a restrained, seemingly rehearsed tone. "Mr. Coleman, it's our policy. We have to ask the same questions every single time you donate. I don't like it. You've made it clear that *you* don't like it. But that's the policy, and you should know that by now."

He slowly gave a curt shake of his head, a grunt escaping his lips. He scoffed at what he considered nothing more than a waste of time inside a building he would have rather not been in in the first place. He lowered his gaze to his right hand as he peeled a cotton ball from the tip of his index finger. The inside of it was stained crimson from where his skin had been pricked to draw a blood sample. He'd passed his test for an adequate protein level.

"Fine," he said abruptly. "Next question."

"I still need you to answer the last one."

"No! I've never been to any of those places!"

His raised tone stole the glance of a young man in a lab coat who negotiated his way through a tight hallway behind the woman. The man eyed Sean's appearance, taking note of the large, silver badge that hung proudly on Sean's gray uniform shirt.

"Hi. How are you?" Sean said loudly with wide, mocking eyes.

The man looked away and continued on by.

The woman behind the desk took a breath, leaned forward in her chair again, adjusted herself, and tapped a single button on the keyboard in front of her. The reflection in her glasses let Sean see a line of green text change on the small computer monitor that fed her questions. He could also see his own face in the reflection. It revealed that he needed a shave.

She proceeded with the questioning. "Have you ever had sex with another man, even once, since 1977?"

Sean's eyes narrowed and his face twisted into a sneer so sharp that it could have been mistaken for a symptom of physical pain. "Why the hell would you even ask me that? Do I come across as gay to you?"

Her shoulders dropped as if she were a puppet whose strings had just been cut. An exhausted sigh spewed from her, followed by a low mutter of something to herself. She removed her glasses, planted her elbows firmly on her desk, and eclipsed her face with the palms of her hands.

Minutes later, Sean was back in the building's intensely lit lobby, seated among a motley crew of men and women that ran the spectrum of age, ethnicities, and hygiene practices. His large body was positioned tightly between a short Hispanic woman who was knitting and a thin boy dressed in a raggedy t-shirt and jeans who couldn't have been older than nineteen. Sean looked like a giant beside them. His six-foot-five-inch frame and broad shoulders towered above the others, forcing both the woman and the boy to tilt their bodies away from him at unnatural angles.

Sean was largely oblivious to the sporadic conversations that carried on around him as he contemplated the significance of the year 1977 from the scripted interview he had just endured. That specific year was used in a number of the questions, which left him to ponder what kind of global epidemic must have went down back then. He filed that mystery away in a mental cabinet of the things he'd one day look up on the World Wide Web—if he ever scraped up enough money to pay for an Internet service.

After selling his blood plasma at the bank for several weeks, he still hadn't quite gotten used to the stench in the air—a mix of iodine and bleach. The smell emitted from all corners of every room.

He noticed a new donor being processed at the front desk. She was an older Arabic-looking woman with a younger woman, apparently a daughter, who was translating instructions from the receptionist into whatever foreign tongue they spoke. Both women wore burkas that covered their hair and bodies.

Sean felt some tension in the air from a few people in the waiting room. Cautious stares. Whispering. Only a few months had passed since the September 11 attacks, so the sight of a couple of individuals clad in Muslim attire in a public area didn't go unnoticed. He wasn't sure if the blank expression the mother's face wore came from the inability to understand what she was being told or from despondency over a misfortune in life that brought her to where she was now.

He understood such misfortune. Less than a year ago, he would have never envisioned himself sitting in such a place—a purgatory-like holding dock where people were forced to contemplate their financial failings before being strapped to a bed and drained of a liquid component in their blood for cash. A lot had happened in a year. A sober year, at that.

The money was good, though, as everyone sitting in the lobby knew. Forty dollars for the first donation of the week, fifty for the second. He was often amused that he was labeled a "donor" and that he was there to "donate" something. These were terms that implied he was giving something away for free, purely out of the kindness of his heart. He wasn't. Still, it was wording that the employees there were clearly trained to use and use often, probably as a way to help the clientele feel more positive about themselves.

No one was setting aside two hours of their life to come there and *donate* anything. Despite all of the posters decorating the lobby that educated participants on how their plasma was used to save lives, people were there for the money. All of them.

For Sean, the practice had become a lifeline to help his fledgling security business stay afloat. Up until six months ago, he had merely worked as a contracted guard for the company. At that time, his uncle, Zed Hansen, owned it. Hansen, however, had been killed back in July. An unfortunate encounter with an unhinged drug dealer, believed to have also killed two U.S. border security guards years earlier, ended Zed's life. Much to Sean's surprise, his uncle had left the company's assets to him in his will. The company wasn't some fancy home-security outfit where a guy strapped to a headset monitored alarm systems from his computer and alerted the police when necessary. No, Hansen Security was hands on, meaning a little roughing up might be required when the moment called for it. Typically, jobs consisted of walking the grounds of a property or serving as some intimidating muscle at an event.

Sean could have sold off the assets and shut down the business, but he felt that carrying on the company was not only an opportunity for him to move forward in his life but also a way to honor his uncle, whom he deeply missed. Zed Hansen was a good man, like a father to Sean, whose real father abandoned him when he was a child. Even though Sean didn't always have faith in himself, his uncle had always had confidence in Sean. Zed kept him on his payroll, even during the dark days when Sean struggled with alcohol and his inner demons. Sean's reputation as a town drunk who engaged in the occasional public fistfight had cost Zed potential business, but his uncle had always stood by his side. He was a loyal supporter.

Sean's demons from those days hadn't all left, but he managed to keep them at bay. He hadn't had a drink since Zed's funeral. It wasn't always easy to stay on the wagon, but he hadn't fallen off yet.

What he didn't know at the time of his inheritance was that Hansen Security hadn't been doing as well as he had believed. Profits were razor-thin and his uncle owed the bank a good amount of money. Sean's name was a detriment to the business. In a small town, reputation and associations were magnified. Several loyal customers just didn't trust him, and with good reason. He was the black sheep of his hometown of Winston, Colorado, a small, rural community deep within the Rocky Mountains. It was more than just his label "town drunk." People knew Sean to be a mean-spirited bully, an unreliable lush with a security badge, a man who couldn't "keep his shit together."

It didn't help matters that he was also the brother-in-law of Winston's Chief of Police, Gary Lumbergh. Because of that, the standards were set higher for Sean than for most residents.

While his uncle had managed to earn the respect of just about everyone he had ever met, few people respected Sean Coleman. Longtime clients went elsewhere for their security needs.

When 9/11 hit and the economy tanked, the situation had only worsened.

Still, Sean managed to generate some work since Zed's death, usually in spurts, but he often had to travel farther than he liked for jobs. On lucky days, he'd pick up stints in Lakeland—a thriving gambling town that sat about seven miles north of Winston; that's where he was now. Most jobs, however, were way outside of Winston. He knew he couldn't afford to hire extra help, so he filled all duties himself, a laboring task even for a company as small as his. Diana, his sister, helped when she could. She did the accounting work for free when she wasn't playing the role of caregiver for their mother.

Their mother was another area of Sean's life where he had dropped the ball. At the time of her stroke, he was deemed too incompetent by the rest of family to look after her. Diana and Gary uprooted their lives in Chicago and moved to Winston to pick up the slack. Sean was grateful for what his sister and her husband had done, though he had never actually told them that. It was a bigger sacrifice for Gary than anyone. He gave up a prestigious career as a big-city police lieutenant to become a small-town police chief. Sean suspected that Diana secretly enjoyed living the slower-paced, Winston lifestyle that she'd grown up in, but her days were about to get much busier in the upcoming months. Thus, Sean was thankful for whatever bookkeeping help she could lend him in the meantime.

When the sound of his name grabbed his attention, he stood and made his way through the maze of occupied, interlocked seats and entered the long familiar hallway. At the end of the bright corridor hung a long, vertical mirror, which he interpreted each time as a cruel joke, a way of forcing people to take a thorough, pensive look at themselves before it was their turn to take the needle.

He couldn't help but notice that the man staring back at him looked different than he used to—healthier. He had lost some weight in recent months. His once protruding gut had shrunk and the outline of his body no longer looked like he was wearing a spare tire around his waist. His pants were now looser and he even had to wear a belt. Had he realized sooner how much weight his habitual drinking added to the scale over the years, he might have given up beer earlier.

At least, that's what he tried to convince himself. He knew it probably wasn't true.

He had recently given his dark hair a short buzz cut, which gave him a leaner appearance. At the age of thirty-eight, he was almost satisfied—for the first time in a long time—with how he looked, though he noted how bloodshot his tired hazel eyes were.

He rounded the next corner and entered a large room. In it were roughly thirty reclined beds. Almost all were occupied by people. The beds lined broad walls in the shape of a rectangle. Sean's eyes met those of a young, blond man with a thin frame and pointy shoulders. Clad in a white lab coat that looked a size too large, he used a nodding motion to direct Sean over to an open bed in a back corner.

Sean took a seat on the vinyl-upholstered recliner, then sprawled out along it until his wide back sank in comfortably. His boots dangled over the edge of the raised footrest.

A half-dozen, twenty-inch television screens hovered just below the ceiling at moderate angles, letting the room's occupants enjoy a movie that Sean couldn't identify. It was something with Will Smith. The volume was muted, as it always was, and the people watching it wore earphones to listen. Sean rarely chose to listen to whatever was playing. He never liked the feeling of wires wrapped around his neck or face. Too constrictive. Too unnatural.

He wasn't much of a reader either, so he typically elected to people-watch. He'd convinced himself that it was good trade practice, a way of honing his instincts as a security guard. He often studied people and worked on reading their mannerisms, predicting how they might react under different situations.

He also found the practice mildly entertaining on a personal level. He enjoyed speculating on people's origins, backgrounds, and occupations.

As he began pumping his fist to build up a vein and let the blood in his arm flow more freely, he chose his first target. It was a short, stubby man dressed all in black, sitting directly across from him in another recliner.

Though some faces in the room looked familiar from past visits, this man's did not. He was mostly bald up top with a few long strands of brown but graying hair that had been combed over his head in a futile attempt to conceal his scalp. He wore tinted glasses with round frames and looked to be in his fifties. There was a paperback book propped up in front of him. He held it with his free hand while blood was drawn from his other arm.

Like everyone else in the room, the man's blood was pumped through a long, clear tube and into a centrifuge machine that sat on a cart beside him. The machine had a spinning component inside that helped separate out the plasma from blood. The contraptions always emitted a dull humming noise, and Sean could hear several of them murmuring around the room.

A semi-clear, cylinder-shaped container hooked in front of the machine was nearly filled to the top with the man's juice. It was the color of light rust. The quantity meant he was nearly finished.

Sean closely studied the man's appearance. His eyes traced the contour of his reclined body, taking note of his monolithic outfit choice. His short-sleeved dress shirt, pleated pants, and shoes were all black. The only variation was in the color of his socks, which were a dark burgundy. At first, it looked like the man was wearing dress shoes, but upon closer scrutiny, Sean determined them to be conservative tennis shoes. The man wore no wedding ring. The book he was reading was called *Turn the Tables*, but Sean couldn't make out the picture or artwork featured below the cover's title. The man's fingers covered all of it.

The gears in Sean's head began to grind away.

Though the man was wearing tennis shoes, he purposely had chosen a pair that was entirely black and would have appeared to be dress shoes to the casual observer. This suggested that the man was going for a professional-looking appearance. He possibly spent a lot of time on his feet and wanted to wear comfortable shoes.

His ensemble resembled that of a uniform, not an official government uniform by any means, but rather that of a company dress code. Whatever the man's line of work was, he most likely dealt directly with the public.

His plasma was a bit darker than most people's; usually it was the color of straw. This was a possible indicator of dehydration. In conjunction with his tinted glasses, he possibly worked outside. But it was wintertime, and in the winter, dehydration would more likely come from overactivity or the consumption of alcohol.

The most interesting clue was the book he was reading: Turn the Tables.

Sean cupped his chin in his palm and glared at the man so intensely that if he had happened to look up and meet the larger man's stare, he probably would have feared for his life.

Puzzle pieces bounced off the walls inside Sean's skull for a minute or two before they all began to fall into place. A sly smile developed at his lips and he crossed his arms in front of him with confidence.

"I've got your number, bub," he muttered.

"Sean Coleman," an emotionless female voice called out from a clipboard a few feet away.

"Yeah." He transferred his gaze over to a woman dressed in light-blue scrubs that he had come to know only as Jessica, according to her name tag. She was one of the regular blood drawers that stuck needles in people's arms and fired up the machines next to them to start the extraction process.

Jessica appeared to be in her mid-thirties and was thin, with a light complexion and long red hair that had a natural wave to it. The shade of her hair had always intrigued Sean. It was deep in color, as if dyed, yet there was stark pureness to it. It was unique. Though she never wore makeup, she was attractive. She had a firmly contoured face with high cheekbones, and he imagined that she would probably have a pretty smile, though he had never actually seen it.

There was always an aura of sadness surrounding Jessica, at least as long as he had been coming to the plasma bank. Her shoulders drooped and her eyes never lit up. She rarely engaged in small talk with her colleagues and was mostly all business when it came to dealing with donors.

He wondered at times if she had lost someone on 9/11 or perhaps had a husband stationed in the Middle East. There was no ring on her finger, though.

Despite her standoffishness, he sensed her to be a kind person inside. She had a gentle, nurturing touch. She was attentive, and when her warm hands slid the metal into Sean's arm, he never felt the prick of needlepoint.

She wrote something across a clipboard before hooking it alongside his bed. She then reached over him to snatch a Velcro blood-pressure cuff that dangled from a horizontal bar mounted to the wall behind him. He watched her as she leaned in close, her long red hair nearly brushing against his forehead. He subtly inhaled, seeking her scent, searching for a hint of perfume. He found none.

Seconds later, the cuff was tight around his dense bicep as the machine inflated it.

Like her, he wasn't much for small talk, but he felt a nagging urge to share his impromptu forensic analysis with someone. Maybe he'd even be able to impress her and get her to notice him a bit more.

"You see that guy over there?" he asked with a confident head jerk.

"What?" she replied, as if his words awoke her from a daydream. Her focus narrowed on him and she leaned in to meet his gaze.

Sean's heart nearly skipped a beat once her pretty green eyes found his. "The guy lying on the bed across from me. Do you see him?"

She nearly recoiled in confusion. She stole a quick glance at the man in black before her eyes swept back to Sean. "Yes," she said hesitantly. "Is something wrong?"

"No. Nothing's wrong. I'm just . . . I'm curious if you know what he does for a living. Is that information on his chart?"

Wrinkles formed on her forehead as she glared at him in bewilderment. "Are you serious? Are you trying to make a joke or something?"

"No. I'm not making a joke. Are you not allowed to tell me what his job is, due to confidentiality?"

Her jaw dropped open. She looked as though she wanted to say something but couldn't immediately find the words. A few seconds later, they finally came out. "Mr. Coleman, of course I know what his job is. Are you trying to be—?"

"Wait!" he said in a little louder voice than he intended, causing her to flinch. "Don't tell me!"

Her eyes went to the ceiling. She clearly had little tolerance for whatever game she felt Sean was playing.

Still, he was certain he was about to draw her in with a stellar display of deductive reasoning. "He's a card dealer at one of the casinos, isn't he?"

Her face twisted into what he interpreted as a wince. She shook her head dismissively before removing the deflated band from his arm. She recorded a number on her clipboard.

"Am I wrong?" he asked with a blank expression.

She ignored his question, her sharp movements suggesting that she had lost all patience with him. Either that, or she believed he was teasing her.

With a cotton swab, she rubbed iodine in a circular motion along the crevice between his forearm and bicep. It felt colder on his skin than it normally did, just like her demeanor. She removed a thick needle from a sealed bag, attached it to a long, thin, plastic line and shoved the needle into his flesh without a warning.

His body tensed, and he grimaced. This time, the needle hurt.

"What's your problem?" he asked as she quickly pressed a few buttons on the centrifuge machine.

She didn't answer him, instead writing another number or two down on a clipboard before storming off.

As dark-red blood began to creep its way up through the line secured to his arm, he watched her disappear into a small room in the corner. It had several large windows, so he could see her sit down in front of the computer. She began entering data.

He didn't understand her reaction at all. He struggled to dissect what he had said that offended her.

A series of high-pitched beeps from across the hallway suddenly grabbed his attention. The man in black was finished with his extraction. When another assistant approached the man to begin unfastening the needle from his arm, the man laid his book down on his lap.

It was then that Sean realized how completely wrong he had been in his estimation. With the book no longer obscuring his view, a white clerical collar at the top of the man in black's shirt revealed itself. Sean's stomach dropped.

"Ah, shit!" he snarled loudly enough that the man's head lifted.

He scowled at Sean in disapproval.

"Sorry, Father."

It suddenly made sense to Sean why Jessica acted as she did. She hadn't taken into account that Sean's low position in his bed kept him from seeing the man's collar. To her, it was quite visible and quite obvious. She probably thought Sean was making some tasteless joke at the expense of a man of God.

He had come across like a creep.

When the man in black stood up, Sean peered at the cover

of the book he held. Below the title, *Turn the Tables*, was an artist's rendition of the famous *Cleansing of the Temple* narrative where Jesus had overturned the tables of the money changers in the synagogue. Sean shook his head.

In her trips in and out of the backroom over the next hour or so, Jessica didn't make eye contact with Sean. Not once. If she had, he would have signaled her over and settled the misunderstanding. He wasn't sure himself why it was so important that he set the record straight. The *old* Sean Coleman wouldn't have cared about offending anyone or saying something unpopular. The *old* Sean Coleman would have blown off her attitude. Today's Sean Coleman cared.

Maybe it had something to do with his failed relationship with his ex-girlfriend, Lisa. The two had met each other under turbulent circumstances six months earlier, and their unconventional romance had never quite found its legs. She lived two states away in Las Vegas, and with phone conversation being their primary means of communication, their partnership was perhaps doomed from the start.

He had never been a man of great verbal eloquence. Words often left his mouth differently than the way he intended. All parts of his life suffered from it. It didn't help that Lisa was a recent widow who needed more comfort and compassion than could be given over a phone. His awkward pauses and long minutes of silence had perhaps been interpreted by her as indifference.

When the plasma extraction was complete and Sean's machine let off its own series of beeps, a young man in scrubs attended to him. In just a matter of minutes, the needle was free from Sean's arm and the puncture covered with cotton and gauze. A lot of beds were empty by then. The larger one's body mass was, the longer the process took, so several people who'd come in to donate after Sean had already been wrapped up and sent on their way.

Jessica was still in the backroom. A shade was pulled across the window, but he knew she was there.

When he was all set, he stood up with the ticket he had been given to cash in back at the front desk, but he wasn't ready to leave quite yet. He waited until the handful of remaining attendants was ministering to others before he cautiously walked over to the backroom. When he was certain no one else was watching, he twisted the knob on the door that led in and quickly entered.

The bright light from the larger outer room flooded into the small, darkened office and Jessica's body jolted forward. In a clear panic, she feverishly clicked buttons on the computer mouse as she nervously glared at the monitor in front of her.

On the monitor, Sean noticed the words *The Denver Post* written in a large, bold black font. Underneath the text was a close-up photo of a man in his forties or fifties with thick sandy-blond hair. His arm was wrapped around a young, attractive woman in her early twenties with long brown hair. Sean recognized neither of them but was familiar with the longstanding *Denver Post*. Jessica had been reading an online version of the statewide newspaper.

The web browser window hosting it disappeared and Jessica spun around in her chair to face whoever it was that had just stepped into the room. Tears were streaming down her cheeks and her eyes were red. She had been crying, but her expression was a mix between despair and alarm, which suddenly changed to fury when she realized it was Sean.

"What in the hell are you doing back here?" she snarled loudly, leaping to her feet. "You can't be back here! This room is for employees only!" Her chest heaved in fury with each deep breath. Her lower lip quivered as she stared at him, her eyes demanding an explanation.

"Why are you cry—?" he asked calmly.

"Don't worry about it!" she snapped. "Why are you in here?"

"I needed to tell you something."

"What?"

"I didn't know that man was a reverend, or a pastor . . . or whatever he is."

Her thin eyebrows narrowed and her head shook erratically. "Mr. Coleman, I have no idea what you're talking about. I just know that you need to leave. Now!"

"The man lying in the bed across from me. The one I thought was a casino dealer. I wasn't trying to make some joke. I just couldn't see his collar. His book was in the way."

Her face went blank for a few seconds before her eyes began blinking with recollection. "*That's* why you came in here?" She placed her hands on her hips and suddenly looked a bit more composed, though still angered. Her breath steadied. "Mr. Coleman, if I had a dollar for every time a donor made some nonsensical remark to me, I could have retired by now. Don't worry about it."

She wiped one of the long, flowing tears from her face and shook her head as her gaze dropped to the floor. When her attention returned to him, she reiterated that it was time for him to leave.

"Are you going to tell me why you're crying?" he asked.

She shook her head. "No, because it's none of your business."

He let a grunt escape, nodding ever so slightly. He turned around and opened the door.

He closed it softly behind him and made a beeline to the hallway that he had entered through earlier. After sliding a brown farmer-style jacket on, he stood impatiently at the front desk as the receptionist counted out the money he was due in ten-dollar bills.

Seconds after he nestled the money away in his front pocket, he was out in the parking lot where light snow fell from the sky. He saw his breath in the chilling temperature. Few cars were left in the lot. Most had a small American flag dangling from their antennas in a show of national solidarity in the 9/11 aftermath that still hung over the country.

A light dusting of white covered his '78 Chevy Nova, concealing its ancient pale-blue paint job. He walked over to it and cleared the windshield with a broad sweep of his arm. The glass hadn't yet begun to ice up, so he was spared scraping.

The car's spent shocks groaned under his weight as he plopped down in the driver's seat. When he slammed his door shut, the snow that had been covering his side window fell to the ground. He twisted his key in the ignition. The engine reluctantly fired up and the screeching of worn wiper blades drowned out whatever dull noise was coming from the radio.

Sean glared up at the wide, bland GSL Plasma sign that hung above the building's entrance. His headlights illuminated it like a small billboard. After delivering a sharp scowl at the sign, he popped the Nova into gear and sped off onto a side street, skidding on the wet snow.

The clamor of the car's shot muffler echoed off of neighboring dim buildings as he fled into the night.

Chapter 3

B y the time Sean reached the Winston town limits, the snow had gotten much heavier. Between each swipe of a wiper blade, clumps of powder packed onto his windshield.

He felt his rear tires lose some traction as he crested a steep hill at the edge of the town square. A few pumps of the gas pedal kept him aligned on the road.

The whitened limbs of the large pine trees prevalent throughout the area bowed from the added weight of the elements. The tops of small buildings, closely clumped together, displayed a good four inches of buildup along their triangular arches.

The small business district of downtown Winston wasn't on Sean's way home, but a nagging question he'd held in his mind from the moment he'd left GSL urged him to take a detour.

There wasn't much going on in town that late on a weeknight. Bernard's Pawn had been closed for over an hour. So had French's Pharmacy and Benson's Hardware. The flickering neon "Open" sign hanging outside of the Winston Café hadn't yet been turned off, but as Sean drove by the restaurant's wide windows that faced the street, he saw chairs placed on top of half the tables. No patrons were inside.

Down the street, he noticed a couple of lights on inside the Winston Police Station. A Jeep was parked out in front. Police Chief Gary Lumbergh appeared to be burning the midnight oil on something. Apparently, not even shoulder surgery could keep him out of the office for a few days.

Sean milked the brakes as he approached the center of the

square—a small patch of snow-covered grass that could have been considered a little park if it were only a bit larger. Instead, it served as a lasting tribute to one of the town's most respected former citizens: Zed Hansen.

A life-sized, bronze statue of Hansen had been unveiled at the site just a few months earlier. It was a good likeness: his uncle's trademark straw cowboy hat sat proudly on his head; his long sideburns and goatee; a toothpick wedged between his teeth. Having been sculpted using a pile of pictures provided by Diana, it managed to capture Hansen's always dignified demeanor.

When passing through town, Sean would often steal a glance at the statue and chuckle at the sight of a random bird perched upon its toothpick. Birds were obsessed with the statue. It was often covered with white, runny excrement. One persistent swallow even tried to build its nest on top of Uncle Zed's squared chin. It drove Diana nuts, but Sean knew his good-natured, modest uncle would find the same humor in it that he did.

Three small spotlights lit up the effigy from the ground, and though most of the figure was covered with snow, its wide hat-rim kept the face fairly dry.

Just a few yards away, on the cobblestone sidewalk in front of the statue, were two metal newspaper vending machines. They were barely visible from the indirect light around the statue. The navy-blue machine dispensed copies of the *Denver Post*. The bright-yellow one belonged to the *Winston Beacon*. Both were coated with powdery snow.

The *Winston Beacon* was a local paper sold only in town. Its owner, Roy Hughes, had become somewhat of a nemesis of Sean in recent years. When Hughes, at the age of twenty, inherited the fledgling publication from his father, he decided that the only way to keep a sustainable level of readership was to turn a section of it into what was essentially a tabloid column. The regular piece entitled "The Winston Buzz" featured town gossip, often with an invasive, investigative reporting twist to maximize the shame of those Hughes chose to target.

Sean Coleman was by far Hughes' favorite victim.

Sean had a long history of being a drunk, a bully, and a man who had a knack for always making the wrong decisions at the worst possible times. Much of the town's citizenry didn't like him. Thus, Hughes felt legitimized in exploiting him for the purpose of lowbrow entertainment. It worked well with a readership that had an appetite for learning of Sean's failures. Hughes had backed off for a while following Zed's murder, but in recent weeks— possibly due to a decline in sales—he'd begun to ratchet things up again. Sean figured it was probably tough for a guy like Hughes to compete against the national news cycle with a war going on in the Middle East. Crucifying Sean was apparently his answer to that problem.

Sean pulled up to the curb and stepped out of his car, nearly taking a tumble after his foot slid on a patch of ice along the sidewalk. He fed a quarter into the blue machine and yanked open the door at its face.

"Fuck!" he snarled at the sight of an empty shelf inside.

Had the front of the machine not been covered with snow, he would have noticed that all copies of that day's *Denver Post* had been bought. *Or had they?*

He had long speculated that Roy Hughes occasionally emptied the competing paper's machine out with a single coin in hopes of compelling disappointed readers to purchase a copy of the *Beacon* instead. He had never caught Hughes in the act, but he hoped to one day.

Regardless, the empty machine riled him. He let its door slam shut and in frustration sent the *Beacon* machine to its side with a stiff kick. It crashed to the sidewalk with a metallic thud that echoed loudly through the cold night air. He nearly climbed back into his car and sped off for home when he found his eyes lifting to meet those of his uncle glaring down at him from above with a kind, permanently etched grin.

His chest inflating and contracting, Sean narrowed his eyes. He brought his visible breath under control and nodded slowly. He leaned forward, wrapped his ample hands underneath the yellow apparatus, and pulled it back up to its short, stilt-like legs. Uncle Zed would have never condoned vandalism.

With the snow now knocked from the front of the *Beacon* machine, he could see the front of the day's edition pinned behind the glass. His heart stopped. His own face was pictured just above the fold. The photograph had been taken at an odd angle, somewhere in an outside setting without Sean's knowledge. He quickly spun the machine to face the light so he could better read the unusually long headline featured above it.

"Guess Who's Selling His Sperm for Cash? A Case for Forced Sterilization?"

Sean's eyes widened to the size of silver dollars. His fists and teeth clenched and his body began to shake in rage. "Son of a bitch!"

It came out like a vicious howl. He lunged forward, wrapped his arms around the machine, and hoisted it up over his shoulder as if it weighed no more than a large stuffed animal. He lumbered out into the middle of the street, roaring obscenities, before arching his back and body slamming the machine to the pavement with every ounce of strength he could muster. The implosion sounded like a bomb had gone off. Glass shattering. Metal shrieking. Asphalt cracking.

Sean didn't remember getting back into his car, but he soon found himself in his Nova's driver's seat. He tore down Main Street, heading for the outskirts of town where Roy Hughes lived. He couldn't hear the cry of the car's muffler over the sound of blood boiling through his veins.

Hughes had somehow discovered that he was selling his plasma to make ends meet—maybe followed him to the bank one night. It was the only explanation; Sean had told no one of the practice that he found degrading.

The *sperm* angle was pure media sensationalism. He knew Hughes didn't simply get the story wrong. Hughes *knew* the truth. He just wanted to spice things up and magnify the potential for humiliation at Sean's expense. Hughes knew what *Beacon* readers wanted. They needed *massive* failure from Sean Coleman—big time embarrassment. And in the latest edition of the *Winston Beacon*, it was being served to them on a silver platter. A lawsuit would have been the logical recourse for such an act of defamation, but Sean wasn't the suing type. He settled scores with his fists.

All he had wanted to do was pacify a nagging curiosity. All he'd wanted to do was find out which news story had so upset Jessica, a woman he barely knew from the plasma bank. Instead, he was now roaring toward Roy Hughes' doorstep. He pictured himself dragging the pencil-necked reporter out into the snow and slamming both of the man's small hands in the metal door of his Nova. Hughes wouldn't be able to type anything more about Sean if his fingers were all broken.

"First Amendment, my ass!" Sean barked as he took a corner far too quickly for the road conditions. His rear tires swung forward, and he gasped as he felt the automobile slide out of control.

"Shit!"

He clenched his steering wheel and turned it sharply to try to regain some traction, but the move did no good. The car spun wildly, sending every stray item that littered the dashboard and console onto his lap. Headlights swept quickly across a thick grouping of snow-capped trees, setting them ablaze in white light as they drew rapidly near.

Sean straightened his arms and pressed his back deeply into his seat to brace for impact as his heart punished his chest. A wicked jolt brought all momentum to an abrupt halt, peeling him from the vinyl beneath him for a moment before he collapsed back down into a seated position.

Deep breaths spewed from his lungs as his large eyes surveyed the white, heavy branches that now draped over the hood of his car. Snow continued to fall in dense particles. He watched in silence as they landed on his windshield.

Once the glaze that coated his eyes began to evaporate, he formed a fist and angrily hammered it across the top of his dashboard. From under his seat, he retrieved a twelve-inch-long black Mag flashlight. He flipped it on, surprised the beam was strong as it was considering he couldn't remember the last time he had replaced its batteries.

He tugged on the inside door handle and was relieved that he could swing the door open without any problems. It was a good sign that the frame of his car was spared significant damage. He carefully pulled himself out into the cold and kept a hand on the hood for balance as he shuffled his way on uncertain footing to the front of the car.

His eyes winced to keep the snow and chilly breeze from bringing them to tears as he stood at the edge of a small ditch. Ducking under the thick limbs full of snow, he leaned around to the grill of the car and spotted no damage. He'd assumed he had struck the trunk of a tree head-on, but he hadn't. He'd stopped a couple of feet short of it.

He made his way to the other side of the car, where he discovered the real obstruction—a large, rounded rock just outside of the ditch at the shoulder of the road. His tire had nailed it squarely and was now completely flat.

"Dammit," he muttered.

The truth was that it could have been far worse. A new tire was at least a manageable expense; a new car was not. Even luckier was Roy Hughes.

Hughes had probably already turned in for the evening, being on an early-morning delivery schedule. He was probably fast asleep under warm, comfortable covers, smack dab in the middle of some dream about the next hit-piece he would run on Sean. He was safe, at least for now.

Sean popped his trunk and pushed aside piles of wadded up clothes, gear, and trash until he'd freed up enough room to pull out his spare tire and the metal jack underneath it. He recalled the day he had first learned to change a tire. His uncle had taught him the skill when he was around ten years old—the kind of training that normally would have been carried out by one's father. By then, Sean's father had already left.

"Patience. . ." Zed would tell Sean when he'd have trouble lining up the jack or threading the lug nuts back on correctly. "Patience is bitter, but its fruit is sweet."

Zed claimed to have come up with the quote, but Sean always suspected he was fibbing. Still, it begrudgingly seemed to be the right advice as Sean had worked on removing the flat back then. The irony of the scene wasn't lost on him. He half suspected that from high above, his uncle had had something to do with blowing out the tire.

Maybe it was the crispness of the air or the calmness that came with the solitude surrounding him, but he managed to regain his temperament and clear his head. His thoughts went back to Jessica.

He couldn't bring himself to understand quite why he had taken such an interest in her. She was largely a stranger—someone who hadn't given him any reason to care about her. Yet, the image of tears streaming down her face wouldn't leave his mind. He was determined to get a copy of that newspaper and figure out what had triggered the episode. And once Sean Coleman was determined to do something, he wasn't going to sleep until he got it done.

When he was finished changing the flat, he slammed the trunk shut and climbed back inside his car. The engine had been running the entire time, so the cab was almost sweltering from the forced air of the heater. He glanced at the small, plastic digital clock that he'd stuck to his dashboard years ago. It was nearly ten-thirty.

He wondered if someone in particular would still be awake.

Chapter 4

I t was late—too late to just walk up to the front of the small house and ring the doorbell. Sean slid around to the back, ducking under the leafless, drooping branches of aspens. He was careful to make as little noise as possible, even as the crunching of hardening snow accompanied every step.

As he approached the back porch, he detected a sound that resembled that of a dull, repetitive moan funneling out from behind the house's walls. He feared the person he had come to see was already fast asleep, snoring.

He crept across the wooden porch, nearly losing his breath when a loud creak halted him in his tracks. There was no audible reaction from inside, so he continued on until he reached the back corner of the house. There, a two-pane window with its curtains open was lit up from pulsating flashes of a television screen inside. Sean slid his body in under the windowsill and then steadily lifted his head up like a submarine periscope.

A subtle grin formed across his face when he spotted the image of a portly thirteen-year-old boy with short brown hair sitting at the edge of his bed. He was watching an old episode of *Magnum, P.I.* The boy was dressed in snug pajamas and his body was hunched forward as he sat Indian-style. He appeared to have a clipboard in one hand and a pen or pencil in the other.

Sean carefully tapped the back of his knuckles on the outside of the frosty window. "Toby!" he said as loudly as a whisper would allow him.

There was no reaction from the child. The boy seemed totally captivated by an action scene on TV featuring actor Tom Selleck clad in a bright Aloha shirt and inexplicably short shorts running across a sprawling green yard with a pair of black dogs chasing after him.

"Toby!" Sean spoke in a slightly louder, more forceful tone. He heard the moaning noise again. It was coming from the other side of the house. This time it was louder. He feared that he was beginning to stir Toby's mother, who would not at all view Sean as a welcome guest—not just at night, but *any* time.

Joan Parker was a single mother, doing her best to raise her son on her own, and if there was any negative influence that she didn't want anywhere near her boy, it was Sean Coleman. To her, Sean embodied everything she didn't want her son to one day grow to be. She knew Sean the same way much of town knew him, as a crass drunk who viewed life through a lens of bitterness. As far as she was concerned, he could bring nothing but harm to the development of her impressionable son.

Sean dropped to a knee in the snow and slid his back up against the side of the house, staying out of sight in case Joan happened to peer out a window. He waited for the noise to dissipate before climbing back to his feet and lifting his head up to Toby's window to get the boy's attention again.

The piercing brightness of a flashlight suddenly blinded Sean from just inside the window. Toby Parker let out a terrifying, high-pitched scream.

Sean's eyes bulged and he stood straight up, frantically putting his finger to his mouth to plead for the boy's silence.

"Oh! Hi, Sean!" spoke Toby through the glass in a demeanor so calm and contrary to the outlandish display Sean had just witnessed that Sean half-believed it was imagined.

"Toby!" Sean heard the boy's mother cry out in concern from the other room. "Are you okay?"

"Yeah, Mom!" the boy loudly replied, holding back laughter as he put his hand to his mouth. "I'm sorry about that. I just got scared by something on the television."

Sean remained hunched forward, his eyes shifting back and forth across the house, nervously bobbing up and down while trying to formulate what his next move should be.

"You're just watching *Magnum*, right?" she loudly asked.

Toby draped his head back over his shoulder. "That's right, Mom! You know how scary Doberman pinschers can be! They were bred to turn ferocious and aggressive on command, after all!"

Toby turned back to Sean with wide eyes. With a nod of his head, he silently mouthed, "Did you know that?"

Sean raised his shoulders and threw his hands in the air in bewilderment.

"Okay, well, just turn it off when it's over, okay?" Joan shouted from inside the house.

"Will do, Mamacita!"

Sean twisted his wrist in a rolling motion, and Toby figured out he was being directed to open the window. Once the boy had unlatched it, Sean helped him push the screenless pane upwards until the two stood face to face.

"Sean, why were you doing that thing with your hand?" the boy asked in a whisper. "My window slides up and down. You can't crank my window open."

Sean shook his head dismissively. "Whatever. I have a favor to ask."

Toby's eyes lit up with excitement. "I bet I know what it is!"

"I kind of doubt it," Sean quickly replied at a restrained volume.

"You need money, don't you?" Toby asked with an all-knowing smirk. "I have seventy-eight dollars I can give you. I saved it up from my allowance and Christmas money. I was going to use it to buy a Special Edition Space Station Erector set. You can build cranes, ships, and even robots, Sean! Robots!"

"Shh," hissed Sean, holding his finger up to his mouth again.

"Sorry," Toby said before continuing. "I'm not talking about a robot like R2-D2 or C-3PO. The picture on the box looks more like a cartoon robot like that one from the *Jetsons* named Rosie. Do you remember that show? *Meet George Jetson!* But I'd rather give the money to you, since we're buddies and buddies help each other out!"

Sean's face contorted in puzzlement. He was used to the boy's longwinded dialogue and tendency to shift from topic to topic in a single breath. He'd been told that it was a symptom of Asperger syndrome, a mild form of the mental disorder, autism, that Toby lived with. The premise of the oration, however, confused Sean.

"I don't want your money," he said. "Why would you even think that?"

"Well, I read in the paper that you've been donating your sperm. I kept asking Mom why you would do that, and she wouldn't tell me at first. Instead, she just kept telling me to stop saying that word."

Sean's hand clenched his forehead as Toby continued.

"After a bunch of times of asking her, she finally told me that there are people who pay a lot of money for sperm, so I used *deductive reasoning*," he said importantly, "to determine that you were doing it to make some extra money. Personally, I think it's neat that there will be a bunch of little Sean Colemans running around in a couple of years. Do you think you'll ever get to play with them?"

Sean glared back in scorn. He knew the boy was not at fault for the words that came out of his mouth. He was only responding to what he had read in the paper. But hearing the words leave his mouth angered Sean nonetheless.

To Toby, nothing of what he read about Sean Coleman ever changed the way he viewed the gruff security guard. In Toby's eyes, Sean could do no wrong. The boy was an unconditionally loyal cohort. He idolized Sean, much to the dismay of his mother. He did so for reasons Sean never fully understood. It didn't seem to matter how rude or dismissive he was to the boy at times. Toby was there for him, and Sean had come to discreetly value that relationship, living in a town in which he had few friends.

"Can you still get on the Interweb from the computer in your room?"

Toby laughed. "It's the *Internet*, silly. Sure I can. Did you want me to help you sell some things on eBay?"

"Toby, this has nothing to do with money, okay? I just need you to look up something for me."

Toby opened up his mouth to say something, but Sean quickly placed his hand over his lips, concerned the boy's mother would hear her son's voice that seemed to be rising in volume with each utterance.

"Just listen," Sean whispered. "Can you bring up the *Denver Post's* home page, or web page, or whatever it's called? There's an article on it that I need to read."

With wide, attentive eyes, Toby nodded his head. Sean removed his hand from the boy's mouth. Toby hustled over to a white wooden desk at the corner of his room.

Upon the desk were a thick computer monitor and a large keyboard. Toby pressed a button on the keyboard, which replaced an animation of flying toasters on the monitor with a bright, white screen. His hand latched onto the computer mouse and he began clicking and weaving from window to window until the digital sound of a phone dialing emitted from somewhere under the desk. It was followed with a low, screeching noise, and then what sounded like radio static.

Toby turned his head to Sean during the clamor and smiled, waving his hand in acknowledgment. Once the noises ended, Toby turned his attention back to his monitor and began typing on his keyboard. A page slowly loaded, and though Sean was a few yards away, he could make out the *Denver Post's* newspaper logo at the very top of the screen.

Sean cupped his hand to the side of his mouth and whispered to the boy to look for a picture. He described the photograph that he had seen on Jessica's monitor back at the plasma bank. Toby nodded his head and clicked from screen to screen, patiently waiting for each page to leisurely load—the hindrance of a slow connection.

Sean blew warm breath into his hands as the lowering temperature began to sink under his skin. His hair was now white from a thin layer of snow that had settled across it, and he noticed that snow was also entering the boy's room through his open window. Toby's shoulders rose and his arms pressed tightly to his body to ward off the cold as he continued to work the computer.

Several minutes went by with Sean's strained glare scrutinizing images on the screen that clearly weren't the one for which he was looking. When it came, slowly loading from the top of the photograph to the bottom, he noticed the unique shade of the man's hair first, then his smile, and then the girl beside him.

"Toby!" he whispered. "That's it! What does the article say?"

Toby nodded and his lips began working silently as his gaze flashed along the screen. The brightness from the monitor lit up his face as if he were holding a flashlight under his chin.

"It's about a man who's missing!" he said excitedly at an uncomfortable volume. His long eyelashes blinked erratically.

"What's his name?" Sean asked, softening his voice to urge Toby to do the same.

Toby's head spun back and forth from the computer to Sean.

"His name is Andrew Carson!" the boy answered emphatically, again too loud.

Sean's face twisted in frustration. He raised his finger to his mouth and clenched his teeth. It became apparent to him that there was virtually no chance of the boy relaying all details of the article to him without his mother hearing the commotion and being alerted to Sean's presence. He also didn't trust the boy to get the content of the article right.

"Can you move that thing over here, Toby?"

"Do you mean the computer?"

"Yeah."

"I sure can't, Sean. I would have to unplug all of the cords that go from the computer to the surge protector on the floor. If I did that, which I can certainly do, the phone cord wouldn't reach the jack in the wall, so there would be no Internet connection. Also, I would have. . ."

"A simple *no* would have been fine," Sean mumbled to himself, tuning out the rest of the boy's explanation. His eyes lifted to the window frame and intently traced its edges. He then peered down inside the room and noticed no obstructive furniture directly below. He raised his arms and pressed the palms of his hands along the bottom of the open window, pushing it open wider with a grunt.

"Toby, I'm coming in."

"Oh, neat!" The boy breathlessly stood up from his chair, looking as if he was about to pull out a tub of popcorn and enjoy the show.

The bottom of the window frame sat about five feet off the ground—just high enough to make it awkward for Sean to try and slide inside. He clenched his hands onto the windowsill and pushed his body upward just a few inches before ducking inside the window, doubling over, and letting his shoulders angle toward the floor.

He slid along his chest and then his stomach, pressing his sprawled out hands along the carpet. His body was almost entirely inside when he felt something tugging at the cuff of one of his pant legs. He briskly shook his leg to free himself from whatever he was hung up on. That's when he felt something give.

He fell to the floor hard, and when he did, he felt something else coming after him. He twisted his head just in time to see one end of a curtain rod swinging from its perch. He had somehow hooked a curtain tieback with his leg and now the entire window treatment was collapsing before his very eyes.

"Watch out!" Toby screamed.

The curtain rod swung into the side of a three-foot-tall dresser where a ceramic piggy bank, in the shape of an actual pig, exploded on impact. The rod crashed to the floor along with shrapnel from the bank and gobs of loose change, the clatter sounding like the jackpot payout of a slot machine.

Sean's breath left him when he heard the imposing sound of loud, heavy footsteps galloping from down the hallway outside the boy's room. He climbed to his knees, and after exchanging glances with Toby who also had a look of concern on his face, he glared at the door that was decorated with small posters and drawings. He knew there was no sense in trying to hide or escape. At any second, the door would swing open, the lights would flip on, and standing there would be the dainty frame of Joan Parker. Her eyes would search the room for about half a second before they found him, and then a hellfire of verbal fury would be unleashed—one that would likely wake up the entire neighborhood.

But when that door did swing open and that light did turn on, the sight presenting itself wasn't one that anyone could have expected. It was one of pure terror.

The first thing Sean saw was a long buck knife that looked monstrously large in the hand of the virtually naked man tightly clenching it. Every raw muscle in the man's body was recoiled and looked ready to explode under his dark, tattooed skin. Long, wild, black hair nearly covered his entire face. His wide, savage eyes burned through the strands.

Toby screamed. Sean reached for the back waistband of his pants, instinctively searching for the gun that he sometimes kept there. Nothing. He'd left it in the car. With his heart nearly beating a hole through his chest, he lunged to his feet and shoved Toby behind him as he grabbed the top of the nearby desk chair with his other hand. He brandished it in front of him in a defensive position.

"Coleman!" the man shouted out in astonishment.

Sean almost recognized the voice. Teeth clenched and arms locked in battle-readiness, he was prepared for physical confrontation.

The man held up his empty hand in a calming motion. The savagery in his eyes dissipated into anger. He was wearing only tight, gray underwear briefs. Old animal and military tattoos in green ink lined his arms and chest, the latter throbbing as precautionary adrenaline surged through him. "What the hell are you doing here?"

Sean's fight or flight mindset wouldn't let him process who the man was at first—only that he wasn't a stranger.

"Oh. Hi, Ron Oldhorse!" Toby explicably welcomed.

Sean's eyes widened and his mouth gaped open. "Oldhorse?" He suddenly pictured the man clothed in denim with his long hair tied back in a ponytail, the way he was used to seeing him.

Both men stared at each other, cautiously sizing one another up and down, struggling to understand the other's presence in the bedroom.

Sean knew Ron Oldhorse, but not well. The rumor was that he was formerly in the armed forces, but Sean didn't know for sure. All he knew was that the man lived as a hermit in the hills outside of Winston. Of Native American heritage, Oldhorse chose to live largely as his ancestors did, hunting for his own food and growing his own crops. He owned a bare-bones cabin with no modern conveniences that was so old and weatherworn that anyone who happened to stumble across it in the woods would probably think it was uninhabitable and had been abandoned decades ago.

Oldhorse had played an incidental but important role in bringing Alvar Montoya, the man who had murdered Sean's uncle, to justice. For that, Sean respected him, but he couldn't wrap his mind around why the man would possibly be standing before him now, looking the way he did.

"It's okay, Sean," said Toby. "You don't have to be scared. I just didn't know that Ron Oldhorse was coming over tonight. That's why I yelled. Mom's always telling me that I yell before thinking sometimes, and that I need to process things first." He swallowed quickly before continuing. "I actually thought I was making some good progress until tonight."

Both men, still breathing heavily in the awkwardness enveloping the room, held onto their weapons.

Sean frowned. "Why would he be spending the night, Toby?"

Lighter footsteps trounced down the hallway and then Joan appeared by Oldhorse's side, dressed in a dull blue robe. Her short, graying hair was matted to her head, framing angry eyes.

"You've got to be kidding me," Sean muttered, lowering his chair to the floor.

Joan slid under Oldhorse's outstretched arm and stood in front of him to face Sean. She was trembling in anger as she glared at him. Oldhorse lowered his knife to his side.

"Sean! Why in the hell are you here?" she screamed so loudly that the others winced.

Sean and Toby exchanged glances.

"Don't look at my son!" she snapped, commanding the attention back to her. "Why are you here?"

Oldhorse shook his head, taking a breath before he turned around and quietly left the room.

"I wanted him to look something up on the Interweb for me," said Sean.

"Internet," Toby whispered.

Sean ignored him.

"At eleven o'clock at night?" she wailed, throwing her hands up in the air and glaring a hole through Sean's very soul.

Sean's face soured and he found himself subtly nodding. "I guess you have a point there."

Her head cocked to an angle and her eyes blinked repeatedly, reflecting the audacity of Sean's words.

"But it was for something important!" he added up with some gusto in his voice.

"What, Sean? What was so important that you had to sneak in here and scare the hell out of my son in the middle of the night?"

"Me?" he sputtered. "I'm not the one who ran in here waving a knife around!"

"We thought someone had broken in!" she yelled, her nostrils flaring to the size of nickels as she tightened her fists. "What am I saying? Someone *did* break in! *You* broke in!"

Toby interjected. "Mom, I actually let him in and—"

"Shut up, Toby!" she bit out.

The boy's gaze went to the floor.

She ordered her son to close the window where the chilling breeze and blowing snow were still flooding into the room.

"Listen," Sean said. "He has an article up on the screen here that I need to read, and then I'll be gone."

"Oh, no," she quickly replied with her eyebrows raised authoritatively. "You're not spending another second inside my home. You're going to leave right now."

"Please. This will just take a couple of minutes."

"No!"

"Mom!" Toby interrupted. "I can just print out the article for him and he can take it with him. Can I do that?"

The expression on Sean's face twisted into one of perplexity. He looked to Toby, completely forgetting his mother for the moment. "Are you telling me you could have just printed that out on paper and handed it to me through the window?"

Toby nodded enthusiastically, his face wearing a wide smile.

"Why didn't you tell me that before I climbed inside?"

Toby raised his shoulders and answered, "I wanted you to see my room."

Joan's face contorted with perplexity, emulating Sean's as she twisted her head to glare at her son.

So painfully slow was the speed at which the printer-head glided back and forth across the sheet of paper it had been fed that it took all the strength Sean could muster not to prematurely yank it out of the machine. It gave him a chance to notice that Toby's pajamas had a pattern of dachshunds prancing along in rows. Sean used to own a dachshund. It also compelled Toby to show Sean the notes he'd taken on the episode of *Magnum, P.I.* he had been watching that night.

Sean just wanted to leave, especially with Joan hovering in the corner of the room like a buzzard training a scornful eye on the back of his head. She tapped one of her slipper-clad feet, which seemed to count down the seconds until the print job was done. Still, Toby's account of the investigative skills he'd taken away from the television episode forced Sean to fight back a smirk.

Sean had long fancied himself an amateur investigator—a man with a keen eye for detail and a knack for forming conclusions based on available evidence. Though there were often mixed results when it came to the accuracy of those conclusions, Toby believed Sean to be the real deal—an expert in the realm of examination and analysis. Sean had once told Toby that he gathered those instincts from watching crime shows on television, and the boy had clearly taken the remark to heart.

Once the second sheet of paper, a bit crinkled from fresh ink, finally slid onto the plastic tray attached to the printer, Joan's raised finger pointed Sean to the front door. Sean snatched the printed article and acknowledged Toby with the nod of his head before briskly making his way through the narrow hallway that led through the heart of the small house. Lots of pictures decorated the walls; all were either of Toby alone or the boy with his mother. They spanned several years.

Sean was outside of the front door in no time, standing on a small cement porch that revealed another man's footprints in the snow. The door quickly slammed behind him.

When Sean circled around to the front of a small garage that protruded out a bit from the house, he found Ron Oldhorse, now fully clothed in jeans and a homemade coat that looked to be made of buckskin. He stood in the driveway close to the garage door, smoking a cigarette that was dark in color, and definitely not store-bought. It was probably homemade as well.

"Is that you, Oldhorse?" Sean asked. "It's hard to recognize you with your pants on."

"Bite me," said Oldhorse.

"Is that a peace pipe?" Sean asked sarcastically.

"You wish," Oldhorse muttered. His voice exuded the same monotone depth Sean was accustomed to from their sparse dealings in the past.

Snow continued to fall from the dark sky above as Sean drew in closer. "So how long has this being going on?" he asked, still trying to wrap his mind around Oldhorse's relationship with Joan. To him, they were polar opposites. Joan was uptight, conservative, and very outspoken. Oldhorse was a socially inept free spirit who diligently kept to himself.

"A while," Oldhorse said before taking a smooth drag on his cigarette.

"Is it supposed to be a secret or something?"

Oldhorse said nothing, glaring out beyond Sean's shoulder with indifference.

He wondered if Oldhorse knew the answer himself or was just being aloof. He pivoted to stare out into the night in the same direction as Oldhorse. As a frosty breeze brushed along his face, Sean thought about Toby and what it might mean to him to have a man back in his home after so many years. Like Sean, Toby's father had abandoned him at a young age. Sean knew it had to be tough for Joan to raise a boy with autism on her own, but it was clear that she had done a good job thus far. He just hoped that she had thought through bringing someone like Oldhorse into their lives. After a few moments, he spoke. "That boy's special, you know?"

Oldhorse nodded his head and took another drag. "That's why his mother doesn't want you around him."

Sean let a conceding chuckle escape his lips. "I know," he said. "I guess that's what makes her a good mom."

About a minute went by without either man speaking a word. They just stood there in conjoined silence as delicate flakes of snow dotted their bodies.

"You need a ride?" Sean offered, aware that Oldhorse didn't own a car. "Or are you staying here tonight?"

"Staying here."

"All right." Sean headed for the car when Oldhorse unexpectedly spoke again.

"I'm meeting with Lumbergh in the morning."

It was unlike Oldhorse to prolong any form of small talk. From Sean's experience, a conversation with the man was typically like talking to a brick wall. It made no sense to Sean why his brother-in-law would need to talk to Oldhorse, a man who had no interest in town business whatsoever. He wasn't even sure the two had spoken since the Montoya shooting. He glanced back. "Lumbergh? Why?"

Oldhorse shook his head, his gaze still trained forward. He took another drag before saying, "Don't know. He left a note on my door. He wants to meet. I'll find out tomorrow."

Chapter 5

Police Chief Gary Lumbergh's exhausted eyes burned a hole through the thin computer screen that was propped up along the center of his redwood desk. His dark, thinning hair was uncharacteristically frazzled. A light green, button-up shirt that had been neatly pressed that morning now hung off his short, thin, 135-pound frame in a rumpled, dampened mess. Half of it was untucked, dangling over the edge of his pleated pants following a hasty trip to the restroom.

His left arm was suspended below his chest in a wide sling. It was an irritating but necessary companion following his recent shoulder surgery, glenohumeral joint reconstruction. He hoped it would be the last time he would have to come under the knife.

The past six months hadn't been easy for the chief. The hail of automatic gunfire that had left him with a collapsed lung, a broken humerus, and a family of lead lodged under his flesh was a memory he had hoped to one day leave behind. His small, damaged body, however, seemed determined not to let him forget.

He recalled sitting next to Oldhorse that fateful July day, drooped over in the passenger seat of a car as they sped down a twisty mountain road, desperate to make it to the hospital. He'd been a bloody mess, with cloth strips torn from an old sweatshirt holding his arm together. He'd been shot up badly by Alvar Montoya and was fading in and out of consciousness. He'd barely made it to the hospital alive.

As if the surgeries weren't reminder enough of that day, recent revelations were now playing a far more cruel game on his psyche. He had learned at the beginning of the month that Alvar's older brother, Lautaro Montoya, had escaped from a maximum security prison in Chihuahua, Mexico. He'd been serving time for drug trafficking on top of a murder rap for taking out a rival dealer. His escape route was an underground tunnel that he'd been working on over what local authorities believed was a span of two years.

"He was a committed man," the warden of the prison had told Lumbergh in a thick Spanish accent over the phone.

The tunnel, thirty-five inches in diameter, had extended over fifty yards. It led straight from a removable cluster of tile in the wall behind Montoya's cot to the open desert just beyond the outside prison walls. Left behind in the tunnel were several makeshift chisels and a sledgehammer, thought to have been supplied to him by a corrupt prison guard.

In Montoya's cell, a number of articles from Mexican newspapers detailing the death of his brother Alvar were found taped to a slab of cement. The shootout between Alvar and Lumbergh had been big news in Chihuahua. The Montoya family had a long criminal history throughout the area, much of it pertaining to violent, sadistic behavior including several suspected homicides. Most were never proven. With one brother behind bars and the other reported dead, celebrations ensued throughout numerous localities, and the tale of Alvar's slayer, Chief Gary Lumbergh of Winston, Colorado, spread like wildfire south of the border.

The discovery of the newspaper clippings in Lautaro Montoya's cell was information relayed to Lumbergh not by Mexican authorities but by a local journalist covering the story, who thought it important to pass along.

Lumbergh initially gave little credence to the journalist's concerns, but a week later, when he began receiving eerie calls at the office from a man speaking only a single word in Spanish before hanging up, the chief's worries intensified.

Marranito. Translated into English, it meant "baby pig."

The chief's attempts to trace the number back to an individual proved fruitless as the calls were placed from a prepaid cell phone. He was, however, able to determine that the phone had been purchased in a border town just south of Las Cruces, New Mexico. Anyone traveling from Chihuahua to central Colorado would pass through Las Cruces on Interstate 25.

Sitting alone in the silence of his office, with the past still on his mind, Lumbergh continued to punch buttons along his keyboard, using only his right hand. He'd been doing it for hours as his mind drifted into memories.

He stopped for a moment, sliding open the top drawer of his desk and latching onto a brown prescription bottle. His thin, slightly trembling fingers worked its lid in an awkward motion as he cradled the bottle against his chest. Using a technique he had mastered in recent months, he was able to twist off the lid and conquer its safety mechanism without having to use his other hand.

He popped a couple of mid-sized white and yellow capsules into his mouth, hesitating a moment before flinging a third one in. He then reached for the three-hour-old, half-empty mug of coffee that sat on a coaster on his desk. He washed the capsules down his throat in a single gulp and then used his tongue to pry the long-expired wad of chewing gum from the inside of his cheek. He brought it back to the center of his mouth and gnawed on it feverishly before glancing at a picture propped up on the corner of his desk. It was of him and his wife celebrating his recent thirty-ninth birthday at a local restaurant. Both wore broad smiles.

After returning the mug to its coaster, his hand went back to his computer mouse resting on the blue pad that had a digital image of a police badge emblem on it. He navigated to a couple of web browser windows he had opened earlier that night, logging back into various law enforcement databases whose connection sessions had timed-out.

His eyes surveyed a handwritten list of names from the top sheet of a notepad that lay on his desk. The word "Aliases" was written and underlined. Half of the names he'd already crossed out with a pencil. He typed the next unblemished one into an input field on the computer screen. A tap of the "Enter" key revealed multiple rows of thumbnail pictures: prison mug shots. All were of men with dark hair. Most looked of Hispanic descent. He clicked on one of the pictures.

"Tell me someone picked you up, *pendejo*," he muttered.

A sudden thud somewhere from the front of the building yanked his attention from his computer. His mouth slid open. His gaze zipped past the numerous plaques and awards that hung from his office wall—recognitions he had earned in his former life as a police lieutenant in Chicago. He felt like the accolades were taunting him as he swallowed some bile and quickly flicked off his desk lamp.

The lamp was the only light in the room other than that coming from his computer monitor, which he briskly turned off as well. He hurriedly rose from his leather office chair and reached into the brown leather side-holster stripped below his ribcage. He pulled out the Glock and relieved its safety, wincing from a jolt of pain that went up his opposite arm from the movement.

Quietly he moved to the open doorway of his office. There, he dropped to a knee before peering out into the darkened hallway of the police station, his gun pointed out in front of him with his arm straight and parallel with the floor. He scoped out the two solid wooden doors at the entrance that were closed and appeared still locked. His head then spun toward the back door of the building.

He made his way down the hallway, keeping low and scanning the interior of each side room in the small architecture. He scrutinized each nook and cranny, searching behind every desk and file cabinet until he was certain that he was the only one inside the building.

He slowly walked toward the entrance. Beads of sweat ran down the sides of his face as he stood straight and pressed his shoulder against one of the front doors. With the muzzle of his gun, he pulled back the shade that covered the door's window.

"Show yourself, you son of a bitch," he muttered. His heavy breathing left an imprint on the frosty glass.

A dim street lamp lit up the narrow parking lot in front of the station. The only car in the lot was his Jeep and the fresh snow revealed no new tracks. None from tires, none from shoes.

He patted his front pocket to make sure his keys were snugly inside, and then carefully unlocked the door, twisted the knob, and opened it up about an inch or two. The cry of dry hinges brought a wince to his face and he mouthed a silent obscenity. He crouched and slid his arm and head outside. Large flakes of snow fell from the sky, coming down in a steady stream, tapping his shoulder and head as his eyes carefully panned the outside area.

Nothing looked out of place until his gaze drifted far beyond the street and quiet nearby shops to the town square where the silhouette of Zed Hansen's statue stood. Beneath it, there had always stood two newspaper vending machines, but now there was only one; at least, only one that he could see from his distance. It was a peculiar discrepancy, but nothing that warranted immediate attention.

He took a few steps outside, searching for anything else that looked wrong as the cold, stewing wind pressed up against his body. He found nothing. Satisfied, he stepped back inside and closed the door behind him, then locked it.

He took a deep breath and let the silence settle back in. He slid the gun back into its holster and let his shoulders sink as the tension receded from them. Wiping dampness from the back of his neck, he made his way back down the hallway to his office, taking a moment to first adjust the thermostat along a wall.

A subtle tapping noise that would have otherwise gone unnoticed had things not been so quiet stole his attention. His face tightened. He craned his head toward the back door where the sound seemed to be coming. It was an intermittent noise, but it continued.

Aware that there was no outside light at the back of the building, Lumbergh retrieved a flashlight from his office. He lit it up and carefully made his way toward the back door. The percussion didn't sound as if anyone was trying to enter; more like something was brushing up against the door, possibly due to the strengthening wind.

He kept his gun holstered, not sensing danger, but instead complying with an urge to settle the nagging curiosity. Still, there was an eerie chill in the air that tensed his muscles—something frigid that didn't feel spawned from a draft outside.

He approached the door and glided the flashlight beam along its edges before twisting the lock on the doorknob at its side, then slid the deadbolt. He wedged the flashlight in his armpit and slid his hand around the doorknob. His fingers trembled under the ray of light.

With a twist and a pull, the door barely budged. Some frost and ice had built up around the doorframe. Gritting his teeth, he planted a foot against the wall and gave the door a hard tug.

When it flew open, the flashlight fell and crashed to the floor. It rolled along the tile in a semicircle, still illuminated, as a blast of cold air poured in.

"Come on," he mumbled as he lowered to one knee and retrieved the flashlight.

He guided the beam through the open doorway. An object hung directly at its center. It was the color of pale, human flesh.

He gasped and fell to his butt, biting his lip and dropping the flashlight. He quickly grabbed his Glock.

Holding his breath, he targeted the object and nearly shouted out a warning but then held back when his eyes more clearly interpreted its shape. The bottom of the object was partially lit up by the flashlight lying on the floor. Two animal hooves were revealed.

Keeping his gun trained on the object, Lumbergh quickly climbed to his feet and flipped on a nearby light switch. Though the light fixture was halfway down the hallway behind him, there was enough light to expose the horrific sight dangling in the wind before him.

It was a dead pig, hairless, strung up by a thick rope wrapped around its throat. Its limp body looked nearly frozen and it spun slowly in the wind. The animal's long tongue protruded sickly from its mouth, suggesting that it may very well have been strangled to death from the very rope that it now hung from. It wasn't fully grown. Young. Probably less than a hundred pounds.

Snow clung to many parts of its body. It had been there for a while, dangling outside the seldom-used door for at least a couple of hours, likely before Lumbergh had even returned to the office from his house after a quick dinner. He carefully slid past the animal to the small staircase that led to the alley behind the building. He found no footprints in the snow.

The concerns he had had over the past week were now substantiated; his fears were not unwarranted. The veiled threats he'd received were not part of some hoax. This was real.

Lumbergh was the "baby pig." He was a cop of small physical stature who until now was ignorant about the situation he had gotten himself into by killing Lautaro Montoya's older brother. Lautaro had arrived in Winston, and Lumbergh's family wasn't safe.

Chapter 6

S ean tossed a small, split log into the mouth of the old cast iron stove in the corner of the frigid room. In his other hand, he held a fried-chicken drumstick that had been sitting by its lonesome in the cardboard bucket at the back of his refrigerator for at least a week. He sank his teeth into it and enjoyed its spices as he watched the flames in the stove devour new fuel.

He had been fond of the stove from the time he was a child. On the few occasions when he and his sister got to spend the night over at their Uncle Zed's, the two children would sit in front of it for what seemed like hours with their arms wrapped around their folded legs as they warmed themselves and played silly word games.

The stove seemed much larger and more intimidating back then. With the steel door at its front missing, the fire inside almost made it look like one was staring down the Devil's throat. Diana used to worry that some sporadic cave-in of the wood inside would send a stray ember hurling through the air and onto one of them as they played. Sean had relished stoking that concern.

More than once back then he had faked getting burned, rolling around on the large woven rug that lined the wooden floor beneath the stove, screaming wildly. He once even brought his sister to tears. Zed always fought back a smile while denouncing Sean for his niece's benefit, but that curl along the side of his mouth was unmistakable. Sean recognized it, and his uncle knew he did.

The stove hadn't been moved from that spot in years. It still sat right at the edge of the small living area that led into the front office of Zed's old business. Sean owned the building now, and it became his new home after his uncle's death. The building was nearly paid off, with Zed having made the monthly mortgage payments for a couple of decades. Sean was thankful for this. Just eighteen more months and he'd have a big expense off his hands. Until then, he'd likely let the vampires at GSL Plasma continue to drain him of his blood.

Surrounded by the crisp scent of burning wood, he retreated to the old, well-used aluminum desk that was pressed up against one of the surrounding wood-paneled walls. He pulled the chain of the small lamp with a deep-green shade that sat on the desk and pushed aside a stack of bills and invoices that lay beside it.

He took a moment to unwrap the thick gauze strip that had held a cotton ball to his arm for the last few hours where the plasma needle had been removed. The puncture had probably healed about ten minutes after it had been wrapped, but often he'd forget it was there until much later in the night. He dropped the dressing in a wastebasket underneath the desk. From his back pocket, he retrieved the folded up *Denver Post* article that Toby had printed out for him. He straightened it out along the top of his desk and used the sides of his hands as steamrollers to marginalize the creases.

He sat down on a metal folding chair that creaked with dissent, his eyes squinting as he examined the article's content. He read of how a man named Andrew Carson had gone missing from his home in Greeley, Colorado, a week earlier. A picture of Carson and a young woman accompanied the article. A significant amount of blood was found at the crime scene, both in the garage of his house and on his driveway. It was "believed to be Carson's," as the *Post* writer put it.

There were signs of a physical altercation, though the details of that evidence weren't printed because the case was still active. The police believed he had been attacked as he arrived home from having dinner with his daughter, Katelyn, at a restaurant in Fort Collins that night. Katelyn was the young woman pictured next to Carson in the photograph. Robbery was not thought to be a motive, though the article didn't explain why.

Much of the piece detailed the exhaustive efforts taking place in search of the missing man, including the open-land areas that surrounded his neighborhood. Part of the article profiled Katelyn, a recent college graduate with a nursing degree who worked at a clinic in Greeley. The statements the *Post* printed from her were those of an understandably scared and distraught young woman who was desperate to have her father back.

"We argued the last time we talked," she was quoted. "I wish that hadn't been the case."

A picture on the second page showed Katelyn standing in what appeared to be a field, though the light snow that covered the land behind her didn't make that apparent. She was clad in a light-blue winter jacket and jeans as she organized a search party, pointing off into an unseen direction. Toby's color printer had really captured the redness of her wind-beaten face that showed her in the middle of barking out instructions to volunteers. Beside her stood two people described in the photo's caption as her boyfriend and her mother. The mother was noted to be Andrew Carson's ex-wife.

Sean smirked at the boyfriend's appearance. He was a dead ringer for the fictional character Harry Potter—thin, with floppy brown hair, circular glasses, and a scarf wrapped around his neck.

Sean was about to continue reading when his attention was caught by something in the picture that felt so familiar that it sent butterflies through his gut. A unique shade of red.

He yanked open a shallow desk drawer and snatched the old magnifying glass that his uncle had used when working on the weapons in his gun collection. He held the thick, circular lens in front of the photo and saw that the red was a woman's hair. He studied the face of the woman closely. It took him only seconds to determine that it was Jessica. She wasn't standing with Carson's family, but rather off in the background by herself, probably unaware she was being photographed.

He completed the rest of the article, and when he got to the very last sentence, he read that Katelyn Carson's mother Molly, her boyfriend Derek, and her cousin Jess were assisting Katelyn in her search efforts.

"Jess... Jessica," Sean said aloud. Jessica from GSL Plasma was the niece of the missing man.

He raised his head. His tired eyes stared forward at the wall in front of him. Below a high shelf of old, dusty country music records hung several pictures. Many were of his uncle showing off his hunting and fishing prizes or firing a rifle at a distant target. One toward the bottom of the wall revealed a younger Zed Hansen with dark hair and a darker mustache. He was down on one knee beside Sean as a child. Both were gripping a fishing line that was heavy from the weight of a large rainbow trout that dangled from an unseen hook somewhere below their interlaced fingers.

There was an unmistakable fountain of pride gushing from his uncle's eyes in the photo. The closer Sean looked, the more it seemed, however, that there was something else etched behind those eyes. It was as if his uncle was requesting something of him.

Zed was a man who had always gone out of his way to help others in need and he never asked for anything in return. However, at that moment, Sean experienced a sensation in his gut that Zed was indeed trying to call on his nephew's services from beyond the grave—perhaps in payment for leaving behind the means for Sean to build his own legacy. Those eyes were telling him to step up and do something good for someone else—someone who had also lost an uncle.

Elsewhere in Winston that night, Lumbergh had come to several conclusions about his past and his present. Not just his own present, but Diana's, too. The plan was to draw Lautaro out into the open. Lumbergh sent away his family and all nonessential employees at the police station for their own safety. Whenever Lautaro was set to strike, Lumbergh didn't want any innocent parties caught in the crossfire.

His line of work had already affected one innocent, albeit resilient, party. Lumbergh wanted to avoid more complications. He made the few calls he knew he had to.

He believed that Ron Oldhorse's military training would prove invaluable in bringing down Lautaro. Oldhorse had agreed. The chief and recluse shared a mutual benefit. Oldhorse made it clear he appreciated the large favor Lumbergh had done for him in the Montoya shooting aftermath. It was something that neither forgot, but also something that neither could mention.

Lumbergh had scrubbed Oldhorse's name from the official police report, eliminating all mention of him in the details of how Alvar Montoya died—as per Oldhorse's request. The truth was that while Lumbergh was indeed responsible for ending Montoya's life with a bullet between his eyes, he would have never had the chance to take the shot if it wasn't for Ron Oldhorse. Lumbergh let his mind wander along memories he dared not utter aloud.

Oldhorse had happened upon the shootout in the mountains just as Montoya was about to end Lumbergh's life. Lumbergh had been flat on his back, bleeding profusely and barely able to move, with his firearm on the ground just a few feet away. Montoya had been standing over him with his gun raised. An arrow that Oldhorse shot into Montoya's back from afar removed that advantage. Lumbergh had regained his pistol and ended things.

Lumbergh's teeth chomped harder on his chewing gum at the recollection. The omission had been a tough call for him to make. He was a man who had risen up the law enforcement ranks in Chicago to police lieutenant, in large part, by doing everything *by the book*. When Oldhorse had confided in him that there was a federal arrest warrant out for him stemming from an incident in South Dakota years earlier, however, Lumbergh had a serious decision to make. He could stick to the truth and watch the highly publicized event with federal implications result in the man who had just saved his life being hauled away in handcuffs, or he could withhold a superficial portion of the story in order to achieve a different type of justice for someone he was highly indebted to.

Oldhorse had instinctively reclaimed the arrow from Montoya's body at the scene, as he would have from an animal he had hunted down and killed. Lumbergh believed the deception would be easy to pull off while not damaging the case.

As far as the official record was concerned, Oldhorse happened upon the scene after the shooting had already ended. Thus, the news media was largely satisfied when given the story that it was a nearby hunter, who wished to remain anonymous, who assisted Lumbergh afterwards. Oldhorse escaped all of the celebrity that fell squarely on the shoulders of Lumbergh. It suited both men well, most of the time.

Lumbergh wanted to make certain no one without a badge got involved in his police work again.

Chapter 7

S ean awoke the next morning with a strong sense of purpose flowing through his veins. He'd slept well that night, which was a rarity. Typically, he tossed and turned in bed until the wee hours of the morning while his mind continually redirected him to a hundred different thoughts.

He'd sometimes dwell on the past. He'd think about the relationships he'd lost throughout his life, including the one with his father. Other times, he'd contemplate why it had always been so hard for him to capture the endearment of a woman—someone who could open her heart to him and see through his rough exterior to find something worth sticking around for. And then he'd worry that he *had* indeed found such a person in Lisa, yet managed to let the opportunity slip right through his fingers.

The crisp tune of Johnny Cash's "I Walk the Line" poured out through a pair of speakers stationed on opposite sides of the room. Sean had always liked the warm sound of vinyl, but the only records he owned were those that he inherited from his uncle. Sean didn't have an ear for country music, which was all Zed had listened to, but Johnny Cash never struck him as quite fitting into that genre. So, one of Cash's greatest-hits albums was the only one that wasn't still collecting dust on the shelf above Sean's desk.

Sean threw on an old gray sweatshirt that smelled clean and a pair of frayed jeans that didn't. After he laced up his hiking boots and buttoned his coat to the top, he pulled a ski cap down over his ears and made his way out the front door. He knew the record player would shut off by itself once the album wrapped up.

The Nova cranked a little rough because of the cold weather, but it eventually roared to life, and Sean spent the next ten minutes brushing snow and scraping ice off of the car windows amidst the freezing temperatures. The snow had stopped sometime during the night and now the bright sun lit up a winter wonderland of scenery outside of the Hansen Security office building.

Large evergreens stood like imposing white towers overseeing unblemished blankets of snow whose drifts had been chiseled into sleek shapes from the overnight winds. The dirt road at the end of his driveway had been yet to be traveled upon that morning. That was about to change as Sean climbed into his car and fiddled with the radio dial before popping the transmission into reverse.

He took things much easier than the night before, watching his speed, and pumping the gas pedal when needed. In just a matter of minutes, he was coasting through the downtown area where the streets were being carefully cleared by a plow on the front of an old pickup truck being driven by Alex Martinez.

Martinez was a college kid who Sean guessed was around twenty years old. He'd been working an internship at the Winston police station for a few months while taking criminal justice classes at a community college in nearby Summit County. Chief Gary Lumbergh was big on Martinez. Somehow, he saw promise in him as a future law enforcement officer. When Sean looked at the kid, however, all he saw was a "five-star kiss-ass," as he put it. Martinez's overeagerness to please and impress Lumbergh always made Sean squeamish.

Sean often observed Martinez performing what he called the "public monkey work" around town that no one else wanted to do. The kid wore a permanent smile across his face while he did it, too. It was a shifty smile as far as Sean was concerned. When Martinez's smile was paired with his disproportionately large nose, the kid's face reminded Sean of the mascot for the Cleveland Indians. It was that smile, along with the wave of a hand, that greeted Sean as the two passed on the street. Sean nodded his head subtly, not really returning the gesture.

"Lumbergh's bitch," he muttered as he listened to the truck's plow scrape packed snow from the pavement.

Only Lumbergh's Jeep and his lone officer's cruiser sat in the police station's cleared parking lot. Sean pulled in alongside the cruiser, watching shards of snow fall from the roof of the building as the subtle warmth of the sun began to strengthen.

It was hard to believe with the sun so bright that a large snowstorm was expected to come through the following night. Some Lakeland deejays had been talking about it on the radio. At least two feet of snow was the estimation, possibly more.

When Sean walked in through the front door of the police station, he saw no activity in the reception area to his right, which was unusual. He did, however, hear some voices from down the hallway creeping out from Lumbergh's office. The tone of the dialogue was low and restrained, and when Sean approached the office door, the talking stopped—seemingly in reaction to his presence.

Sean poked his head in through the doorway to see the alert eyes of three men staring back at him: Lumbergh, Ron Oldhorse, and Jefferson, Lumbergh's sole officer. They all looked anxious. Jefferson even had a thumb resting on the backstrap of his holstered firearm.

The display prompted a sneer from Sean. "What the hell's going on?"

When the men recognized him, the tension seemed to release from their bodies all at once. Shoulders lowered and the uniformed officer's hand dropped from his pistol.

"A little antsy this morning, aren't we, Jeffrey?" taunted Sean as he trained his gaze upon the officer. He lowered his eyes to the pistol. "Lumbergh doesn't actually let you keep bullets in that thing anyway, does he?" He knew Jefferson hated being called *Jeffrey*. Sean had called him that since high school.

"He sure as hell does!" Jefferson snapped back, taking Sean's bait.

Sean's assertion had clearly struck a nerve with the tall, lanky officer, whose handlebar mustache and bloated chest sometimes drew comparisons to a Civil War reenactor.

Lumbergh shook his head in irritation, displaying little patience for the bickering. "Can you give us a minute, Sean?"

"Why?" Sean quickly retorted. "Is this a secret club meeting?"

"Please, Sean. Just a minute."

Sean read exhaustion in Lumbergh's eyes. It was then that he noticed the rest of the police chief's appearance. His face was unshaven and his normally well-groomed hair was a frazzled mess. His eyes were red and glazed, and they blinked with sensitivity to the sunlight that was beaming into the room from the window beside him. He looked as though he hadn't slept in some time, though the clothes he wore appeared slept in.

He had never seen Lumbergh like this. The police chief was a man who always valued his appearance, priding himself on looking professional in a job he took very seriously. Yet today, he bore no resemblance to a "metrosexual." Sean had recently begun referring to him that way after hearing the term used on an episode of *Law & Order* and deciding it applied to Lumbergh.

Whatever conversation the men had been engaged in looked serious, and the mystery of what was behind it triggered Sean's curiosity. He would have pressed Lumbergh for an explanation, but he had come there to ask for a favor; pissing off the chief wasn't a great way to get what he wanted. He bit his tongue, nodded his head, and walked back to the small lobby. He imagined that the silence following his departure probably came from the shock experienced by all three men. Sean Coleman actually complying with a request from Lumbergh was almost unheard of.

Once the office door snapped shut, Sean quickly pivoted and entered through the doorway of the neighboring room. He carefully made his way inside, leaving the overhead light off and relying on the luster from the hallway to keep him from running into anything.

The musty, windowless room housed a number of thick oak shelves overflowing with town documents. The newer ones were stored in uniform, white-cardboard boxes. Many were probably case files. The older ones, likely tax records and court documents, were bound in tall leather books that appeared many decades old. They were pressed together in several tight rows.

He tiptoed (as best a man of over 250 pounds could) around the shelves and a long, solid wooden table before reaching the sidewall that adjoined Lumbergh's office. He placed his ear to it.

The wall was thin enough to hear the men's voices, though not clearly. The three had likely lowered the tone of their discussion, weary of Sean's nearby presence. Still, he made out snippets of dialogue—phrases like "back door" and "How could he get so close?"

As Lumbergh was talking, Jefferson erupted into a long coughing fit that pretty well drowned out the rest of what was said.

"Jesus, Jeffrey," Sean whispered in irritation. As best he could gather from what he'd heard, someone had either broken into the police department or vandalized it from the outside. When he heard the loud shuffling of a chair, he briskly lumbered his way back around the shelving and out the doorway to the front lobby. He softly closed the door behind him.

He stood in the lobby, pretending to gaze out the window on the front door. When no one immediately emerged from the office, however, he did take a moment to pay some attention to the outside world. He became transfixed on the brightness outside. It was almost blinding, with the sun reflecting off of the snow in dazzling brilliance.

From where he stood he could see that the yellow newspaper machine was vertical again, standing beside the blue one. Though it was quite far away, Sean could make out some of the damage he had done to it the night before. It was lopsided and warped, and he smirked as he mused over the expression that likely adorned Roy

Hughes's face the moment he showed up that morning to load it with papers.

Moments later, Lumbergh's office door opened up and both Jefferson and Oldhorse streamed out. They exchanged sober glances with each other before walking right by Sean, barely acknowledging him.

"Jefferson," said Sean, using the officer's full name. "Do you need a cough drop?"

The men stopped and the officer spun around.

"Do you have one?" Jefferson asked, his eyes wide.

"Yeah, I think I've got one right here," Sean replied, digging his hand into his pocket. He lifted his hand out, empty, but his middle finger stood up at full mast for Jefferson to see. "There you go," he said with a satisfying grin. "Feel better?"

Jefferson's eyes narrowed angrily.

Oldhorse fended off a smirk. "Come on," he muttered to Jefferson, who struggled to find a verbal comeback.

"You're an asshole," was the best he could blurt out.

The two men left through the front door.

Sean pondered why Oldhorse had been there in the first place. His involvement in a matter as simple as vandalism made little sense. All Sean could think of was that Lumbergh called on Oldhorse for his tracking skills, which were second to none. But with the area covered in snow, Sean imagined that *anyone* could simply follow footprints if there were any to be found.

Regardless, Lumbergh was now alone in his office, and Sean aimed to take care of some business. As he walked back down the hallway, he noticed for the first time that a collapsed steel folding chair had been placed up against the back door of the building. It was wedged there at an angle, as an extra lock, presumably to prevent entry.

He peered through the office doorway and found Lumbergh sitting at his desk with his head turned toward his window. The chief gazed through the glass as if he were lost in a deep thought. His eyes shifted to Sean once he entered.

"What do you need, Sean?" Lumbergh asked. He grabbed a couple of manila file folders from the top of his desk and shoved them into the top drawer.

"Everything okay?" asked Sean.

"Yes. Fine. What do you need?"

Sean took a deep breath. "What do you know about Andrew Carson, the missing person down in Greeley?"

Lumbergh's face twisted in confusion, as if he were having difficulty transitioning away from his previous thought. "Andrew Carson?"

"Yeah. He's the guy who went missing out in front of his house. Blood in the garage. Blood in the driveway."

"Okay. Sure." Lumbergh nodded and pulled himself deeper into his desk. "All I know is what I've read in the paper and seen on the news. That case is pretty far out of my jurisdiction."

"I know that."

"Why are you asking me about it then?"

Sean's eyes drifted to a corner of the room before a chuckle escaped his lips. He wasn't sure how to best formulate his words. When his gaze returned to Lumbergh, it was met with raised eyebrows. The chief was awaiting an answer.

"I know someone who's related to him," Sean blurted out.

"Okay. Is there some information they want to bring forth or something?"

"No. I was just wondering if there was any progress in the case. Any leads? Any suspects? Maybe something they're not reporting on in the papers?"

A wince formed on Lumbergh's face. "Sean, even if I was privy to that information, which I'm not, I couldn't give it to you."

"Why not?"

"What do you mean *why not?*" Lumbergh said angrily, leaning forward in his seat. "It's official police business. It's an active case. I can't just leak that kind of information out to people."

Sean's jaw squared as he glared at Lumbergh, scrutinizing him with his eyes. He shook his head slowly. Lumbergh gasped at the audacity of Sean's reaction, throwing his good arm up in the air and tilting his chair back.

The sound of the front lobby door being opened and closed grabbed both men's attention.

"The streets are all clear, chief!" the enthusiastic voice of Alex Martinez sounded out.

"The streets are all clear, chief!" Sean said in a mocking tone, not loud enough for the intern to hear him. "Kiss ass."

"Shut up, Sean," said Lumbergh. He shouted instructions for Martinez to record his time in a ledger posted at the reception desk and then added that he could take off for the day. He turned his attention back to Sean. "How many years have you known me now, Sean? What have I done during that time that gives you the impression I would just spill out confidential information from this office upon your personal request?"

Sean crossed his arms in front of him. In a scoffing tone, he replied. "Nothing, Gary. You've done absolutely nothing to show special treatment to the guy whose sister you're married to. I get it!"

He paced back and forth a bit, surveying Lumbergh as he did. He then raised his index finger and pointed it in the police chief's direction. "But you owe me!"

The chief's eyebrows formed upward arrows as he glared at Sean the way a parent would at a child who was about to make a reckless decision. He leaned forward in his chair. "Tell me you're not serious."

"You bet I'm serious," Sean answered, locking his arms in front of his chest. "Did you really think I was going to cash in a favor from the police chief of Winston by having him shovel my driveway or something? I cleaned up your shit. You owe me!"

The back legs of Lumbergh's chair scraped loudly along the tile as he pushed himself away from his desk and rose to his feet. The sound of Martinez exiting the building went unnoticed. "Sean, I can't tell you what's going on in an active case. It's against the law! And again, it's not my case! It's not my jurisdiction! I know nothing about it!" He forcefully pressed his finger to the top of his desk with every assertion.

"Bullshit!" Sean roared back. "Gary, you're a goddamned celebrity now! The Montoya shooting turned you into Super Cop! I saw the way the other police chiefs swarmed all over you at that convention Diana dragged me to last month—the one where they gave you that award! They just don't like you; they want to *be* you!"

"What are you getting at?" Lumbergh sneered.

"All you have to do is pick up the phone and call your counterpart over there in Greeley. I'm sure he'd be more than happy to spill the beans on everything that's going on over there." Sean could almost see the steam rising out of Lumbergh's ears as the chief's eyes pierced forward. He knew Lumbergh would regret the day he indebted himself to him, though the truth was that Sean had never intended on cashing in the favor. Still, he took some guilty satisfaction in watching the realization settle over Lumbergh's face that the day had finally come. He liked watching the "big city" former police lieutenant squirm in discomfort at the mercy of his far less polished brother-in-law. He knew Lumbergh to be a man of his word—a trait he perhaps valued even more than his commitment to professional protocol.

For the next five minutes, Sean paced back and forth from the hallway to the front of the chief's desk as Lumbergh did his best to engage in cordial small talk over the phone with someone at the Greeley Police Department. Lumbergh's sociable tone didn't at all mesh with the disdainful glare he kept trained on Sean during the conversation. Still, he sounded genuine enough.

"Oh, you saw that interview?" Lumbergh spoke into the receiver with a brief grin. "Well, I'm glad you liked it. They threw some interesting questions at me in that one. Like, '*What gun would you have ideally had with you during that shootout?*' Ridiculous."

Sean rolled his eyes.

Before long, Lumbergh brought up Andrew Carson, framing his query in the context of a similar unsolved case he had worked back in Chicago during his days as a police lieutenant. The details that he shared came out too naturally for Lumbergh to have made them up, Sean decided. They likely tied back to a real missing person's case, though the chief's mentioning of its possible relevance to Carson's was less than sincere. Lumbergh explained repeatedly to his law enforcement colleague that a connection between the two would be an enormous long shot and that manpower shouldn't be pulled off of other leads to pursue it.

"Oh, I can just log in to the mainframe?" Lumbergh said in surprise, quickly leaning forward in his chair with his eyes switching over to his computer monitor. He tucked the phone receiver under his jaw and nodded his head while the officer on the other end presumably fed him access information. Lumbergh punched in the keys slowly with his good hand.

"I really appreciate this," he said. "Hopefully, I can give you something in return."

He worked his computer mouse back and forth across the blue pad, clicking with fierce intent. When Sean attempted to join him on his side of the desk to share Lumbergh's view, the chief removed his hand from the mouse just long enough to snap his fingers loudly in irritation. He directed Sean back to where he was with an index finger and a scowl. Sean complied.

"Okay, I've got it," Lumbergh spoke into the phone, before thanking the officer and hanging up.

"What is it?" Sean asked. "What are you looking at?"

With his eyes glued to the screen, Lumbergh replied, "It's

information on the case. A little professional courtesy can often get you a long way."

"And a little celebrity probably doesn't hurt either," Sean said. "Can I see it?"

"No."

Sean watched the expression on Lumbergh's face shift numerous times, making it difficult to decipher what was going on in his brother-in-law's mind as he viewed the information.

"They've got a suspect—person of interest—they feel really good about," he finally said. "He already had a couple of warrants out for his arrest before Carson went missing. He's not in custody yet. They're still looking for him, but they think they've got the right guy."

"What's his name?" asked Sean.

Lumbergh shook his head. "No, Sean. It would jeopardize the case. I'll just tell you that they've got evidence that places the man at the crime scene."

"Fingerprints? DNA?"

Lumbergh offered no response.

Sean interpreted the silence as a *yes*. "Has Carson's family been told about this? That a suspect has been identified?"

"No. The department wouldn't do that. Not yet. They'd wait until they had the suspect in custody. They wouldn't risk his name being leaked to the press."

"Wouldn't the police *want* the press to run the suspect's name and ask for the public's help in finding him?"

"Not at this point," answered Lumbergh, shaking his head. "They have their reasons." Sean opened his mouth to speak, but Lumbergh cut him off. "Sean, I'm not telling you anything else, and you didn't hear any of this from me," he warned. "Do we understand each other?"

Sean shook his head.

"Listen," Lumbergh continued. "I only did this because I owed you. We're even now. Got it?"

Sean wanted the suspect's name and he wanted it badly. What he intended to do with such information, he wasn't sure himself, but the fact that it was on display a mere five feet away taunted him. He needed to see what was on that computer screen. "All right."

Sean nodded his head and thanked the chief, then turned and left the office, walking out into the hallway and adjusting his coat. He peered to the back wall of the building for a moment before pivoting to face Lumbergh again. "Do you want me to close the back door?" he asked, his demeanor one of casualness. "It's pretty cold outside."

Sean watched Lumbergh's eyes quickly bulge to the size of golf balls.

"The back door's open?" Lumbergh exclaimed before leaping to his feet.

"Yeah. Jefferson probably left it open. Want me to close it?" Sean spoke the words with forced poise, knowing full well that Jefferson had left the building through the front with Ron Oldhorse only minutes earlier. He knew Lumbergh knew that, too.

Lumbergh looked to be in a state of near panic. He snatched his gun from his holster and nearly hurdled himself over the corner of his desk. He knocked a pile of papers to the floor as he briskly moved in toward Sean.

"Get in here!" he muttered in a forced whisper, motioning Sean inside his office with the nudge of his head.

Sean quietly abided. He watched Lumbergh slide around him and out into the hallway, where he raised his gun and pressed his back up against the side wall.

Sean knew that whatever had previously gone down behind the office building had Lumbergh spooked, and spooked enough for him to drop everything and quickly respond to the claim of a door—which was essentially barricaded—now left wide open.

The moment Lumbergh was out of arm's length, Sean discreetly shut the office door behind him. He twisted the lock at the center of its knob. While Lumbergh slithered his way down the hallway, Sean hustled around to the front of the chief's computer and leaned forward on the desk to examine the information left up on its screen. He knew he only had seconds.

His eyes briefly studied the large blocks of dark text, filled with police lingo that Sean didn't recognize. He switched his focus over to a column of pictures from the crime scene—small pictures with underlined labels of "Click to enlarge" below each one. As described in the newspaper article, there were large splotches of blood on the cement. It was more blood than Sean would have guessed, immediately leading him to believe that the police likely considered Andrew Carson to be dead.

Just as Sean tapped the Page-Down key he found at the right side of the keyboard, he heard the fierce rattle of the office doorknob.

"Shit," he muttered, keeping his eyes on the screen.

"Sean!" Lumbergh yelled at the top of his lungs. He then spewed such vulgar and vile language that Sean could hardly believe it had come from between his brother-in-law's lips. "Get away from that fucking computer! Now!"

Sean stole a quick glance at Lumbergh through the door window. Lumbergh's twisted face and enraged eyes made him look absolutely deranged. Sean tried his best to ignore the commotion and centered his focus again on the computer screen. There were numerous mug shot photos of an unsavory-looking man with short dark hair and a neck as thick as a fire hydrant. There was an unsettling bitterness in the suspect's eyes in every shot. Some pictures appeared older than others, featuring the man with varying lengths of hair. Sean clicked on the one that looked to be the most recent.

The man's face was decorated with hardware. Multiple earrings rode all the way up to the top of his ear, one through his nose as well. A separate photo of what looked to be the man's arm revealed a flesh canvas of interlaced tattoos. At the center was one of a swastika.

Sean searched for a name and he found one in boldface. "Norman Booth."

Sean's body suddenly jolted at the vehement explosion of broken glass as Lumbergh's elbow smashed through the office door's window. Large shards crashed to the floor, splintering into smaller pieces upon impact.

"Jesus!" Sean barked before leaping to his feet, astonished by the severity of Lumbergh's action.

Lumbergh's hand punched through the remaining fragments. He unlocked the door and swung it open violently, nearly cracking the drywall behind it. He stormed in, once again grabbing his gun from his holster—this time pointing it directly at Sean.

"Get away from the computer!" he snarled slowly, decisively, as the air rushed through his nostrils and his chest heaved.

"Okay. Jesus!" said Sean, raising his palms out in front of him, feeling as if he was suddenly dealing with an utterly unhinged man that he had never met before. He stepped out from behind the desk and inched himself along its edge, following Lumbergh's eyes with his own. "What's wrong with you?"

"You picked the wrong day to fuck with me, Sean!" Lumbergh growled. "Now get the hell out of here!"

Lumbergh's hand shook erratically as a thin stream of blood crept its way down across his knuckles. A couple of drops fell to the tile floor.

Sean kept his eyes on Lumbergh, refusing to turn his back on him. He carefully walked in reverse through the office door. The only noises heard in the eerily tense room were of the two men breathing and the broken glass that crackled beneath Sean's shoes. He slowly lowered his hands down as the chief lowered his firearm.

When Sean reached the hallway, the two men glared at each other.

"You need help, Gary," Sean stated with a pointed finger. He then turned around and quickly left the building.

Chapter 8

The image of the crazy grimace that stretched across Lumbergh's face lingered in Sean's mind the entire trip up to Lakeland. So did the scowl on the mug of Norman Booth—the suspect on the chief's computer screen.

Sean knew Jessica's regular schedule. At least he thought he did. On those days when he didn't have a security job lined up, he'd head over to GSL in the afternoon when foot traffic was light, and get through the plasma-drawing process a bit faster. Jessica would always show up around one o'clock. He'd watch her from his bed if he happened to have a view of the clerical area. She'd walk in, never smiling, and hang her coat on a hook along the wall before beginning her duties.

Sean sat for some time in the parking lot, and by the time the digital clock that clung to his dashboard hit 1:35, he had begun to convince himself that she had taken the day off. It was certainly possible she was again assisting in the search efforts for her uncle. Still, he decided to give it a few more minutes.

He tapped the steering wheel impatiently as warm air that smelled like dust poured out of the vents he had positioned toward his face. He leaned across to the passenger's side of the car, pinched the glove compartment open, and pulled out of it a granola bar that was wedged in between years of registration and insurance forms. It had been there for some time, too. He tore off its wrapper in a flash and let it fall to the floor among other trash and discarded items. He devoured the cold-hardened snack in four large bites, barely tasting the chocolate chips.

He wondered how close Jessica was with her uncle and if their relationship was at all similar to the one he had shared with his Uncle Zed. Was he a mentor to her? Someone she admired? Maybe they weren't tight at all and merely saw each other once a year, around the holidays.

"Hell, for all I know, they hated each other," he said out loud.

When he heard the sound of a car engine approaching from the road, he used the edge of his hand to scrape away frost from his side window. He spotted Jessica's long red hair through the glass of a white Chevy Cavalier that pulled erratically into the parking lot.

Sean switched off the ignition and climbed out of his car, immediately feeling the bite of the cold. The temperature was warmer than earlier, but couldn't have been any higher than the twenties.

His stomach felt tight as he approached Jessica's car, now parked at a space not far from the front of the building. Fears over how she would take his intervention into her life made him tense, but he felt he had something to offer her—even if it was something small. And maybe, just maybe he could convince her of the one thing he had never been able to convince Lisa of—or *anyone* for that matter: that he cared.

Jessica ascended out of her car quickly, her hair a bit frazzled and her purple coat unbuttoned. She was wearing sunglasses. Her thin hand gripped the handles of a brown purse whose strap she didn't bother to toss over her shoulder. She was clearly in a hurry to get inside.

"Jessica!" Sean shouted.

Her head spun toward him, her face blank. She was probably expecting to find a co-worker who was on the way inside as well. Instead, she found a tall, large man who raised his hand in a timid greeting.

It seemed she had trouble recognizing him at first. She raised her hand to her forehead, using it as a visor to marginalize the bright glare of the sun, which Sean's large frame was partially eclipsing. Her scrutinizing eyes appeared to be tracing the outline of his body. He knew that at any second she would realize who he was.

When he was within only a few yards, he opened his mouth to speak, but all that came out was a loud yelp when he felt his foot catch a patch of ice under the snow. He lunged forward to solidly plant his other foot and keep his balance, but it found ice as well.

As he crashed down to the unforgiving asphalt, he caught an image out of the corner of his eye of Jessica instinctively reaching out her hand to try and grab his. She was unsuccessful, only managing to lose her sunglasses when they fell from her face.

Sean lay there for a moment, sprawled out along the snow-covered blacktop and digesting the bitter sting of embarrassment, before climbing to his feet.

Once he lifted his head to meet Jessica's distressed eyes, he watched her face twist in sour recognition of who he was. Her shoulders drooped as if she was carrying a twenty-pound dumbbell in each hand. Her gaze rose to the sky and her breath appeared to leave her lungs in a heap. She was clearly not excited to see him.

"You're forgiven, okay?" she said in an agitated voice as he stood upright.

"What?" he replied. Indiscriminate patches of snow gripped the front of his pants and coat.

"That's why you're here, isn't it?"

His eyes narrowed.

"You know," she began, constructing her impending statement in her mind before continuing, "I'm sorry I was short with you the other day, but you've got to get over it. Are you really this sensitive?"

He scoffed at the suggestion that he was sensitive. He was a lot of things, but *sensitive* wasn't one of them—not in any traditional sense of the word, anyway. He realized she was referring to the communication problem they had had from the previous night.

"I'm over it," he said bluntly.

Before he could continue, he noticed what appeared to be a sharp discoloration under her left eye—a mixture of black and green. It looked like a shiner. She also seemed to have some mild swelling on the left side of her lip. He was sure it wasn't there the previous night.

"What happened to your face?" he boldly asked.

She tilted her head and countered him with a denouncing glare. "I fell on the ice, but not as gracefully as you just did." She clearly read the suspicion etched across his face, so she continued. "Don't worry, Mr. Coleman. No one's abusing me. I really did just fall."

He nodded his head in acceptance.

"Why are you here then?" she asked. "You've already donated twice this week. You're done."

He took a moment to breathe, and then said, "I want to talk to you about Andrew Carson."

Her eyes froze on his. All expression slowly drained from her face. Her mouth gaped open and her complexion turned as white as the snow that garnished the scenery around them. Her purse fell from her grip and landed on the ground beside her sunglasses.

It was a reaction even more dramatic than what Sean had envisioned. "Your uncle, right?"

Her eyes danced in multiple, random directions, seemingly losing their sentience, as her lower lip began to quiver. When she aimlessly took a few steps backwards, Sean grabbed onto her arm, fearing she was about to topple over.

She nodded her head. "You know about my uncle?" she said, her eyes squinting as she glared at him.

"It's okay, it's okay," he said, trying to determine if she could stand without his assistance. "I caught you off-guard here. I'm sorry. I'm just trying to help."

It seemed as though every new word that left his mouth drew an added level of confusion from Jessica, so he started from the beginning. He explained to her how he had seen the *Denver Post* article over her shoulder in the back office and noticed how much it had upset her. He told her that he'd later read it, saw her picture, and figured out who Carson was to her.

"I have a law enforcement connection," he said. "He says they're making good progress on the case and that they have a suspect in Andrew's disappearance."

She still appeared to be in partial disarray, now leaning on her car for support with her hands on her knees. She stared at the ground and forced herself to take a couple of deep breaths. "I'm sorry," she muttered. "When you first brought up his name like that, I thought that..." She hesitated, glancing up at him.

"You thought what?" he asked, his face now displaying confusion.

"That *you* had something to do with his disappearance."

"Excuse me?"

Jessica shook her head, letting her gaze fall to the ground again. "I'm sorry. It just sounded like you were going to demand a ransom or something."

Squinting, he let the choice of words he had used bounce around his mind. "We don't communicate well, do we?"

She let out an unexpected spasm of laughter, and then held her hands to her face where tears began to stream. She asked if the suspect was in custody and Sean answered no. He explained that the police were looking for him, and that they were confident they had the right guy.

"They have no idea where my uncle is, do they?" she asked.

"No," he replied, taking from her tone that she had already accepted that she'd probably never see him alive again.

"Do you know the suspect's name?" When he said nothing, she looked up at him through moist eyes and asked again.

"No," he finally answered, knowing such information could spell bad things for Lumbergh and also jeopardize the investigation. "I don't know anything else."

She nodded. He could read the skepticism in her eyes.

"Well, thank you, Mr. Coleman," she said. "Thanks for letting me know. My family will appreciate hearing that progress is being made."

He nodded. "You're welcome."

She squatted down to pick up her purse and sunglasses, prompting Sean to try and help, too, though he was too slow. She brushed a strand of her long, bright hair behind her ear as she rose back up to her feet.

"Let me know if you hear anything else, okay?" she asked reservedly.

"Okay. Do you have a phone number?" He tried not to sound too eager.

"Just call GSL. I'm at extension 106. If you leave a message on my voicemail, I'll get it."

He opened his mouth to speak, but before he knew it, she had already turned her back on him and was heading toward the front door of the building. He thought she might turn around and glance back at him as she stepped inside, but she didn't. She disappeared through the door.

Sean turned to the sun and stared up at the blue sky above, feeling the warmth press against his face while the rest of his body still felt cold. He closed his eyes. The sun's hospitality almost seemed to be commending him for doing a good deed, though he found himself questioning if he had done much of anything at all.

He worried that bringing marginal comfort to someone he barely knew risked further straining his already labored relationship with Lumbergh. At least he hadn't given out the name.

He strolled back to his car in no particular hurry, taking some guilty satisfaction in believing he had at least changed Jessica's impression of him. He had left her better than he had found her, or so he worked to convince himself.

He propped open the driver's side door of the Nova, which was heavy from the frosty weather, and slid inside. The car's shocks made a faint buckling noise as he did. When he peered into his rearview mirror to check the traffic on the street behind him, he found his own eyes staring back at him. Their hazel depths expressed a nagging discontent that he tried to look away from but couldn't. He *hadn't* done enough. Not yet.

Instead of twisting his key in the ignition, he leaned to his side and began wading through all the food wrappers, receipts, and crumbs that lined the floorboard until he found the newspaper article that Toby had printed out for him. It had slid off the passenger seat earlier.

He traced his finger from paragraph to paragraph until he spotted the residential address where Andrew Carson had gone missing. He opened his glove compartment and dug through a collection of old street maps, many of which he had inherited from his uncle's business, until he found one for Greeley, Colorado.

When he rose back up above his steering wheel and glanced out his windshield, he spotted Jessica. She was standing outside, a good distance off at the back corner of the plasma building. He only had a partial view of her. Snow-covered limbs from a nearby tree that sprung out from an island in the parking lot obstructed his view. If it weren't for the color of her hair, he probably wouldn't have even noticed her at all. He watched her gaze back and forth across the parking lot in a sweeping motion, and he wondered if she was looking for him. Did she have more to say?

He thought about stepping back out and waving to her, but when she pulled a cell phone from her purse and began punching numbers on it, he stopped himself.

Wrinkles formed on his forehead as he sat still, letting his curiosity captivate him as Jessica held the phone tightly to her ear. It made sense that she would want to quickly call her family and fill them in on the news Sean had told her, but her body language didn't seem right for that. She wasn't carefully relaying information to whomever she was talking to. She seemed upset. Panicked. She tossed her free hand up in the air as she spoke.

What Sean saw didn't resemble calmness or relief. It looked like desperation.

Chapter 9

The afternoon traffic heading east along Interstate 70 wasn't bad. It rarely was during that time of the week. Fridays were the day when scores of travelers made their way west up from Denver to the high country for a weekend of skiing or snowboarding. They'd pour into the resort towns, gallivanting around in their turtleneck sweaters, drinking hot chocolate throughout the day, and boozing it up at night. Few people were headed in the opposite direction, so Sean met little resistance on his way down to the suburbs.

From Denver, I-25 to Greeley wasn't quite as forgiving. Sean had beat rush hour, but some unexpected construction and inexplicable pockets of congestion left him snarling and pounding his fist against the steering wheel a number of times. By the time he reached the Greeley city limits, it was bearing down on four in the afternoon. He began to doubt that his trip had been worth the trouble. The narrow winter day would begin to turn dark in just over an hour and he had feared that the search parties looking for Andrew Carson may have already given up for the day.

A camera man from a local news network, who was tethered to an attractive woman reporter in front of Carson's house, directed Sean to an open field area about a half mile away. That's where the volunteers would be doing one final sweep.

Minutes later, Sean was trouncing down a steep gully through a collection of about sixty bundled-up men and women of different ages. Some were carrying homemade walking sticks made from broom handles and tree branches, using them to poke through shrubs and lumps in the snow. A few were wearing orange vests.

"Okay, let's get together and try one more stretch while we still have enough light!" a female voice sounded off in the distance. "Bring it in! Bring it in!"

About halfway through her shouted instructions, Sean figured out who was speaking. She had long dark hair and was wearing a blue winter coat. When he drew closer to her alongside several others, he recognized her as Katelyn Carson, Andrew Carson's daughter. She looked just like she did in the picture he had seen in the paper. Next to her was her boyfriend. He looked the same, too. His shoulders rode high, his arms were pressed to his sides, and his hands were jammed in his pockets, as he tried to keep warm. The sour expression underneath his fogged-up glasses suggested that he'd been ready to leave for some time.

Sean watched Katelyn divide up groups of people to set off in different directions along the open prairie. She came across as a natural leader, or perhaps she had just gone through the routine so many times that it now felt like second nature.

Upon receiving their marching orders, people began peeling away from the larger crowd. Sean suspected that Katelyn herself would likely join the last group, so he subtly moved himself to the edge of the congregation.

She must have noticed that Sean was a new face because once she had finished delegating, she looked at him and said, "Thank you for coming out today, sir. We appreciate it."

Sean nodded.

"You need a stick?" she quickly asked him.

Before he could open his mouth, she grabbed a broom handle that her boyfriend had pinned under his arm while his hands were in his pockets. She handed it to Sean.

The boyfriend's eyes bulged from the imposition and his head quickly swiveled toward her. He looked as if he had just been woken from a daydream.

"If you're cold, go wait in the car," she told him with an eye-roll, her statement laced with irritation.

He opened his mouth to say something, but she quickly turned her back on him, directing the rest of the group to follow her as she set out for a shallow ravine to the west. The boyfriend just stood there, unsure of what to do or say. Everyone else accompanied Katelyn, and the boyfriend eventually turned around and began making his way back to the nearby residential neighborhood where Sean had parked his car next to several others.

The area looked like it had already been thoroughly surveyed. There were footprints in the snow just about everywhere. Sean knew that one more sweep wouldn't turn up anything, and he suspected Katelyn knew that as well. But just as he had become invested in the mystery of what had happened to Andrew Carson, he understood that the last thing a missing man's daughter could do was sit helplessly by while the investigation was left solely in the hands of law enforcement. She had to do something—anything—to help.

Sean knew more than she did about her father's disappearance. He knew the specific suspect the police were looking for. But that information didn't make it any less likely that Carson's body was lying outside in some ditch in the snow, waiting to be found. It just meant that the guy who could have dumped him there had a name.

He watched Katelyn and the others poke their sticks into the snow whenever they came upon a large lump or some other discrepancy in the terrain of the land. He followed suit.

Every couple of minutes, he found his gaze drifting up to meet Katelyn's face. Though she and Jessica didn't look much alike, he recognized the same shared sense of despair in her eyes. That alone displayed a certain resemblance between the two.

After a while, Katelyn noticed Sean's attention turned to her, and she brought herself to answer his gaze with a polite smile. She walked up to him and formally introduced herself, extending her gloved hand and thanking him again for his help. Her face was red, likely burned that color from the frigid winds she had been working through in the past days.

"I'm Sean," he told her. "Sean Coleman." He wondered if his name would mean anything to her, thinking Jessica might have mentioned it over the phone after their conversation back at GSL. She must not have, because the introduction drew no recognition.

"Where are you from?" she asked him in a hoarse voice after wiping her nose with the back of her glove. She seemed to have a cold.

"Winston, Colorado. It's a little town south of Lakeland."

"Wow. You've came a long way," she said, tilting her head and displaying a tone of gratitude. "Well, we appreciate it."

"No problem," he answered. "I kind of know your cousin. I wanted to help out."

"Jess?" she said.

"Yeah."

"Well, great. My family is very grateful for all the help we've received."

She leaned into Sean—something he wasn't expecting—opened her arms, and wrapped them around him. She gripped him in a tight hug. He wasn't sure at first how to take the show of affection, but he soon found his own arms wrapped gingerly around her as well.

"Thank you," she muttered with sincerity in her voice, wiping a stray tear from her face after she pulled away.

He nodded.

The search went on for another twenty or thirty minutes, with nothing to show for it other than an old bicycle tire buried in the snow. Katelyn walked close to Sean and confided in him things that he wouldn't have expected one to tell to a stranger. She talked about how she had gotten in a huge argument with her father the night he went missing, and that she feared her raised, angry voice would be his last memory of her. She spoke of how her father was disappointed in the decisions she had made in her adult life, and how painfully hard it was to sometimes concede that he was right. It was clear from some of the early stories she told of her and her father that the two were as tight as could be when she was a child.

He mostly nodded as she spoke, feeling unequipped to offer any emotional counsel. That appeared to be all right with Katelyn, who seemed satisfied just being able to voice her scattered emotions to a fresh set of ears.

The group headed back to the hill at the base of the residential area and rendezvoused with the others. That's when Sean suddenly heard Katelyn shout out the name Jess. She was waving her arms back and forth in broad strokes, vying for attention.

Sean's head jerked up upon hearing the name. He didn't understand how Jessica could have been there when she was just beginning a shift at work right before he'd left for Greeley. There were bodies moving in every direction along the slope like busy ants marching over an anthill. He tried to follow Katelyn's line of sight to spot Jessica, but wasn't having any luck.

With butterflies bouncing off the inside of his stomach, wondering how she'd react to him being there, he guardedly walked over to Katelyn. Amidst battling conversations between members of the search party, he continued to scan the crowd as a tall teenage boy with wavy bleached-blond hair approached Katelyn. The two hugged before turning to Sean.

"Your friend showed up to help, Jess," she said with a smile.

Sean's head snapped toward the two of them like a weathervane in a sudden gust of wind.

Katelyn retained the smile on her face while the boy expressed a scowl of confusion that mirrored Sean's.

"Jess?" Sean said.

Katelyn's eyes narrowed and she turned her head to the boy beside her.

"Who the fuck is this?" Sean asked, his nostrils flared and teeth showing. The volume of his voice caused the two to jump.

"What?" Katelyn said, clearly taken aback.

"I don't know this guy, Katie," said the boy.

Sean shook his head. "I was talking about your *cousin*, Jessica. Not this guy."

Katelyn and the boy looked at each other, expressionless.

"What?" Sean said in frustration, throwing his hands in the air.

"I don't *have* a cousin named Jessica," Katelyn said. "Jess . . . This guy right here. He's my only cousin."

Sean was speechless. His mouth hung open like the lowered drawbridge of a castle. He quickly dug his large hand into his coat pocket and dragged out the *Denver Post* article. He unfolded it and presented it to the two of them, his thick hands shaking with anxiety.

"Right there," he said, pointing at the image of Jessica in the background of the photo. "Who's this woman?"

The two both leaned forward, tilting their heads to grab a closer look.

"Beats me," said the boy.

"I don't know," said Katelyn. "I think I remember her being here a few days ago, helping us search. I don't think I talked to her. We had a lot more people that day, and there was so much going on. I didn't get to talk to a lot of people who were here."

"Neither of you know this woman . . .? At all?"

They shook their heads *no* before exchanging confused glances again.

Sean felt the earth below his feet stir. The fading horizon off in the distance suddenly seemed slanted. Off. His eyes refused to focus on either individual's face for a few moments, his head lost in a cloud of questions.

"You probably just misunderstood her, man," said the boy he now knew as Jess.

Sean didn't respond, still standing there in an almost hypnotic trance.

"Well, thanks either way," said Katelyn. "I hope you get it sorted out."

Sean wasn't sure when it was that they had walked away, but the next time he glanced up, both of them were halfway to the parked cars above. Most everyone else had also left, leaving him by himself in the field. The wind began to pick up.

A sudden gust whipped against his face, leaving behind a stinging sensation that felt as though he'd just been slapped with an open hand.

In Sean's view, that was exactly what had just happened.

Chapter 10

From his snug, grimy jeans pocket, the man pried out a well-worn, diamond-shaped keychain. A single key dangled from it. At the center of the diamond's face was a piece of masking tape yellowed with age. The number three was written on it in black Magic Marker.

It was nighttime. The temperature had dropped rapidly and he could see his own labored breath.

He slid the key into the womb of the brass doorknob where he twisted it until he heard a click and felt the door give. When it swung open, dry, rusted hinges cried as if they were pleading for help. The light from a flickering neon-blue motel sign just a dozen yards away lit up the foot of a queen-sized bed covered in a thin bedspread that had probably once been white.

The small room inside was musty and warm, a climate brought on by the old baseboard heater beneath the lone window facing the parking lot. The heater emitted a continuous tapping noise, just as it had the night before when it kept him up late tossing and turning.

The cryptic scent of an artificial air freshener lingered inside. Its placement beside the heater was likely intended to conceal a fouler odor.

He tossed a heavy, graphite-colored, canvas backpack onto the bed. He stuck his head through the doorway and cautiously skimmed the outside parking lot for notable activity. He found none. He pulled his head inside the room and kicked the door closed behind him.

The uncovered overhead light sprung to life with the flick of a switch. It brought little clarity, however, with only one working bulb. An amateurish painting of an old abandoned sawmill in front of a mountain landscape decorated the wall above the headboard. It hung crooked.

The man sat down along the foot of the bed, the mattress springs groaning from his weight. He brushed some dust from his pants and then leaned forward, placing his elbows on his thighs and running his fingers along his scalp as he faced the floor.

After a moment, his eyes rose to meet his own reflection in the mirror on the wall in front of him. It hung above a sturdy dresser made of dark, polished wood.

Through dimness, he recognized the hate and vengeance that burned in his own eyes. He greeted it with a fiendish grin that nearly eclipsed the entirety of his face. The smile dissipated after he tugged at a rubber band that he wore around his opposite wrist, stretching it to its fullest extent and then releasing it into a painful snap.

He rose to his feet and methodically removed all of his clothes, folding each garment neatly before placing them in a tidy stack on top of the nightstand. He stepped inside the small adjoining bathroom whose pale walls seemed to be critiquing him once the lamp above exposed their dispassionate glare.

He lifted his eyes to the lamp and answered, "It has to be done."

Steam rose from the shower, which doubled as a bathtub. His feet were planted on the vinyl textured mat suctioned in place. The back of his head bumped against the steel showerhead each time he brought it up straight after soaping himself down. What sounded like the eerie whimpering of a hungry dog caught his ear. He didn't recognize that it was coming from his own mouth until it erupted into inconsolable sobbing that nearly knocked him down to his knees.

When the water shut off with a squeak, he stepped out of the shower and headed back to the main room, ignoring the rack of fresh folded towels on his way out. He plopped his sopping wet body down across the foot of the bed and leaned forward, twisting the knob of the medium-sized television that sat on top of the dresser. Snow across the screen lit up his face, casting his large, eerie shadow along the wall behind him.

He dug his hand under the flap of his backpack and pulled from it a black, unlabeled video cassette. He quickly fed it into the mouth of a VCR that rested on top of the television. He watched the digital clock on its display flash "12:00 am" for a few seconds before a picture came on and his wide eyes fell to the screen.

The picture—the top quarter of it tilted at a forty-five-degree angle—revealed some chaotic camera work among a large group of reporters. They shouted questions about the Alvar Montoya shootout over each other as their shoulders grinded together. Some of them impatiently shoved their way in front of others.

"Chief Lumbergh! Chief Lumbergh!" a female voice sounded out above the rest. "Can you tell us when you'll be returning to duty?"

When the camera-shot stabilized, the blurry face of Gary Lumbergh quickly came into focus. It nearly filled the entire screen before the camera zoomed back out and revealed the chief's arm wrapped around his wife. He was wearing a navy-blue polo shirt with a dark-green jacket draped over his opposite shoulder. The jacket only partially covered the sling and the cast that kept his arm elevated.

Lumbergh seemed to be in good spirits, chuckling at the question while Diana wore a broad, prideful smile.

"Oh, I'll be back soon enough," he spoke into the cluster of microphones that were held out in front of him. "Right now, I'm just ready to get back home and relax some more. The hospital food here at St. John's is better than everyone says, but I miss my wife's chicken parmesan."

Sporadic laughter belched out from some of the reporters. The man sitting naked on the bed parodied it with his own unhinged-sounding snicker. He then leaned forward and pressed the fast-forward button, speeding through the scene until the picture cut to another.

This time Lumbergh was standing in front of his house in Winston, again talking to a group of reporters, though not as many as before. Seemingly enjoying the camera's attention, a wide grin lined the police chief's face.

"I have another surgery scheduled for next week," said Lumbergh. "Afterwards the doctors will have a better idea as to whether I'll need more."

A few more taps of the fast-forward button showed the smile suddenly disappear from Lumbergh's face in response to the question. The man rewound the tape a few seconds to hear what was asked.

"Chief Lumbergh, there was news this morning through an anonymous source in the county sheriff's office saying that there are, quote, 'notable discrepancies' between your account of the shooting and the coroner's autopsy report on Alvar Montoya. How do you respond to that allegation?"

The sobriety in Lumbergh's eyes looked just for a moment like a mix of fear and anger.

His face turned deadpan.

"This is the first I've heard of this allegation," he replied. "I'm certainly willing to discuss this topic with the county sheriff if there are any facts that need to be ironed out."

A slew of other questions erupted from the small reporter pool, but Lumbergh raised his hand in departure, offered the cameras an uneasy smirk, and told them that he was done answering questions for the day.

Just as the chief turned his back to the reporters, the man rewound the tape again back to when the question was posed. He watched the expression on Lumbergh's face transform, and then did so over and over again at the touch of a button.

With each viewing, he felt the hostility further descend into his soul. That deep sense of betrayal tortured his body, as if he were strung to a wooden post and lashed repeatedly with a bullwhip. His arms and head trembled, nostrils flaring with each anguished breath.

He lunged forward and clenched his hands around the VCR, violently yanking it from the television. Sparks flew out of the outlet as its cord was stripped from the wall. The television screen turned back to snow. He hurled the VCR across the room. It crashed into a small table lamp sitting in the corner. Shrapnel from its base exploded in several directions.

"*Mentiroso!*" he screamed with all of his might, clenching his fists as air jetted out through his nose.

The broad shadow cast on the wall from his quivering body looked as if it was on fire.

His neck slowly twisted in the direction of the bed and his eyes transfixed on the large, heavy backpack that lay there.

He repeated again, "It has to be done."

Is it getting lighter? Still so dark in the room, but I think it's getting lighter. How long was I asleep this time? Could it be morning? I'm weaker, just like they said I'd be . . . The drugs. I'm too weak to lift my head from the bed and look at the clock. It's better not to move anyway. When I hold totally still, it's like the rest of it's not real; just a bad dream. It's when I move that the nightmare comes to life. The tubes tighten around my face and neck. My stomach turns sick. The pain starts again.

I've forgotten how it used to be. I've forgotten what it's like to feel warm. To feel free.

The clicking of the clock seems louder than before . . . louder than I've ever heard it. Is it telling me my time's almost up?

Sometimes, I'll open my eyes and find her standing over me. Her eyes are so sad, but she makes herself smile. She does it for me. I love her smile. I'm going to miss her smile.

Chapter 11

Sean sat there for what seemed like hours, upright in his recliner and staring into the dancing flames inside the opened cast iron stove across his living room. He didn't remember turning his television on, yet there it was, alive in the corner of the room with its volume turned down all the way. He paid it little attention. Though his body was idle, blood raced quickly through his veins and muddled thoughts bounced off the inside of his head like numbered balls in a lottery machine.

He had stopped back at GSL on his way back to town, but Jessica had already left for the night. He'd asked the receptionist for Jessica's phone number, and then her home address, but both were met with authoritative lectures about the company's privacy policy. All he could get was a last name, and that was only because the shift manager let it slip when he walked over with his chest puffed out and asked Sean to leave.

Landry. Jessica Landry.

Sean had then gone to a gas station two blocks away from GSL. He asked politely to use their phone book. Once he got it, he quickly thumbed through the white pages, but found no listing in the area for anyone with the last name of Landry or close spellings. He'd spent the next thirty minutes sitting in his car in front of a liquor store with his hands clenched tightly to the steering wheel. His old instincts urged him inside, but his body kept him glued to the driver's seat.

Why would she lie to me? he pondered as the devil at the center of the stove breathed fire before him.

The question punished his soul. It made no sense. Jessica *had* to know Andrew Carson. The tears Sean had watched streaming down her cheeks in the back room at the plasma bank were real. He was certain of that.

He racked his mind, searching for an alternate explanation. *Could the two have been romantically involved? She and Andrew Carson?* It was little more than a stray thought at first, but as he further examined the notion, he realized that the premise could explain some things. It would justify Jessica's emotional reaction to Carson's disappearance and why she felt compelled to assist in the search. It would explain why Katelyn didn't know her. Maybe Andrew wanted to keep the relationship a secret, possibly being uncomfortable with the idea of having a love interest that was much closer in age to his daughter than to him.

But if that theory were true, why would she have lied to him about being Katelyn's cousin? What possible motivation would there have been to do so?

He leaned back in his chair, ignoring the recliner's mechanical plea. He closed his eyes and did his best to recall the details of his conversation with Jessica in the parking lot earlier that day. It was *he* who had drawn the family connection between Jessica and Carson—not she. However, she had absolutely corroborated it, and there had to be an explanation for that.

"You know about my uncle?" He remembered her exact words. She played up Sean's assertion. She didn't refute it.

The phone rang, waking him up from the contemplative spell he'd trapped himself in. When he picked up the receiver of the old rotary phone from his uncle's desk, he heard the voice of Diana. There was a sense of distress in her tone that quickly commanded his full attention.

"Sean, Gary asked me not to call you, but I'm getting really worried."

"What are you talking about?" he replied, eyes narrowing.

"There's something wrong. Something that's got him scared and he won't talk to me about it. He sent us out of town late last night. . ."

"Wait, wait, wait . . . You and Mom aren't in Winston?"

"No. We're staying with. . ." Diana hesitated for a moment. "Well, I'm not supposed to tell anyone."

"Bullshit," he said, wincing at the notion. "Where are you?"

She paused again, seemingly weighing the decision to answer, before explaining that they were staying with an old high school friend of hers whose name was familiar to him. She lived in Silverthorne, about twenty-five miles away.

"He seemed worried about our safety, Sean," she continued. "I've never seen him like this. Do you have any idea what's going on?"

He shook his head. "No. I saw him this morning and thought he was dealing with a break-in at the office. You're right. He wasn't himself. There must be more to it."

A brisk knock suddenly echoed off the front door of his shop. His head spun toward a window at the side of the house. When the phone's intrusive spiral cord slapped against his face, he held the receiver to his opposite ear.

Through a pulled blind he could see that an outside light had been triggered on by a motion sensor he'd helped his uncle install a couple of years ago. Sean had unexpected company.

"Diana, someone's here. Can I call you back?"

She relayed the phone number of where she was staying. He wrote it down on the small sheet of a notepad before saying goodbye and hanging up.

He glanced at a nearby wall clock. It was nearly ten thirty at night. Few people ever came to visit Sean, and even fewer showed up unannounced, especially so late at night. He made his way through the dark, narrow hallway until he stood at the small entrance of the building.

"Who is it?" he asked through the windowless door in a loud, agitated voice.

Moments crawled by before he received an answer. "Sean? It's Jessica from the plasma bank. Can I speak to you?"

His chest tightened. *What in the hell is she doing there?*

The night was pitch black, the temperature below freezing, and yet there she was, waiting on an unfamiliar doorstep outside a remote town she had likely never before passed through.

Had he not driven to Greeley that day and discovered what he had, butterflies likely would have been fluttering through his stomach. He'd assuredly be experiencing a desperate urge to quickly clean up his place and evaluate his personal appearance before letting her in.

Things, however, had changed dramatically since that afternoon. What would have been certain exuberance was replaced with suspicion—profound suspicion that stewed hostility in his gut.

A grunt escaped his lips before he unlocked the door and pulled it open.

The porch light poured down across Jessica's mane of scarlet hair in a way that immediately made her presence look warm and unaffected by the frigid weather. Her hair was down, freed from the restrictive ponytail that Sean had often seen it in. It flowed down the sides of her face and was longer than he would have guessed.

When their eyes met, a broad smile formed on her red lips, causing his heart to skip a beat. It was the first time he had ever seen her smile. Its brilliance lit her entire face.

She looked different in other ways, too. Her lips were painted and moist. Her eyelids dark. She was wearing makeup, and a burgundy-colored leather jacket and black denim pants that tightly hugged her legs, ending in black mid-calf boots.

As attractive as she looked, the stark change in her appearance and demeanor sent warning signals jolting up and down Sean's spine. There was an eerie awkwardness lingering in the cold night air—artificial in presence and cryptic in meaning. His mind struggled to predict what she was going to say, weary that whatever was about to leave her mouth would likely be less than sincere.

"Can I come inside?" she said in response to his scowl. "It's cold out here."

He stood there for a moment, revealing little emotion. "Sure," he finally said.

She stepped inside, and as she did, her sweet, alluring scent caught his notice. He had never known her to wear perfume from their past meetings at the plasma bank. It never before seemed to suit her, but clearly there was another side of Jessica that he was about to meet.

He noticed her car parked out front before closing the door behind them and sealing off the cold air that had spilled inside. He flipped on the inside light and watched Jessica's pretty face as her eyes wandered around the room that consisted of little more than a tall wooden countertop with a barstool behind it and certification papers adorning the walls.

"Do you live here . . .? Where you work?" she asked.

"Yeah. In the back." He nudged her toward the living area with the jerk of his head.

She turned and strolled down the lit, tight hallway, glancing at the random collage of framed pictures that hung along it. They were mostly family pictures, several of Zed with his niece and nephew when they were younger and some from his early days in the service. A black and white one, from a different era, which hung horizontally featured Zed and Sean's father when they were teenagers—slicked back hair, rolled-up shirtsleeves, and baggy jeans.

"Do you live by yourself, Sean?" she asked in an upbeat tone.

"Yeah," he answered quickly, almost dismissively. "How did you get my address?"

She grinned, turning her head to the side a bit as she continued down the hallway. "It's in the GSL computer system. It was pretty easy to get."

A scoffing chuckle fell from his mouth. GSL had refused to give him Jessica's address, but his *own* information was apparently up for grabs. He nearly voiced his grievance but stopped himself short, deciding not to tip his hand that he had sought her out earlier that night. It was advice lent to him by an old episode of *Simon & Simon* for dismantling someone's lies: *The less you pretend to know, the tighter they'll tie their own noose.* He was going to give her the rope.

"You want something to drink?" he asked, knowing he had nothing but a couple of diet sodas and a glass of tap water to offer.

She declined with a "No thank you."

He removed a couple of sweatshirts from an old worn-out wingchair that was close to the stove. The clothes were still unfolded and not yet put away from a laundry load two days earlier. Foam stuffing dangled from the outside of a large tear in the side of the chair's cushion.

"Have a seat," he said with forced courtesy. "Warmest spot in the house."

She grinned and said thank you, unzipping her jacket and looking to Sean to offer to take it from her. He didn't. She kept it on and took her seat.

He snatched the remote control off an end table and switched off a muted rerun of *Barnaby Jones* with the flick of a wrist.

"Did you let the Carsons know what I told you?" he asked before plopping himself down on his recliner.

Her eyebrows rose a bit. "Yes. They were appreciative. I think it was comforting for them to know that progress was being made. They're remaining hopeful. We all are."

He nodded, silently amazed at how easily the lies were pouring from her mouth. The way she delivered them was convincing, seemingly sincere. Whatever preconceived notions he had formed of her from those weeks in the plasma bank were quickly disintegrating before his very eyes.

"You look different." He nodded at her appearance. "Heading

out on a date?" He wasn't sure why that was the question that had come to his mind.

"No," she quickly answered. "I just went out with some people after work. There's usually a lot going on in Lakeland on Friday nights. I figured I'd take a couple of co-workers up on their invitation to join them for once."

He nodded.

After some uncomfortable silence slaved by, she told him how she had been talked into trying her hand at karaoke and sang a poor rendition of Belinda Carlisle's "Heaven Is a Place on Earth" in front of a room full of strangers. She laughed afterwards, and he let the ends of his lips curl a bit.

It was the kind of conversation he had dreamed of one day having with her, but Sean knew none of it was real. That made it all the harder to listen.

"So what did you want to talk to me about?" he asked, heading off a new sentence she was about to start.

"Oh, okay," she said, a little taken aback. She swallowed and nodded uncomfortably before continuing. "Earlier, when I asked you if you knew the name of the man police suspect, you said no."

"Right," he replied, curious what was coming next.

"Well, please forgive my bluntness, but I wasn't so sure you were telling me the truth."

His mouth subtly fought a grin, recognizing the irony in her statement. He said nothing.

"I mean. . ." she continued with some shakiness in her voice. "You hesitated before you answered the question, and my guess is that you might know the suspect's name but that you didn't want to tell it to me because you were afraid of getting your police friend in trouble."

It was suddenly clear to him that she was there on a mission—a mission to extract the knowledge he had of the police case. His attraction to her was going to be used as the siphon. That was her plan anyway. It was as if the two of them were back at the plasma bank, with him on the bed and her sticking a needle in his arm. Instead of blood being drawn from him, however, information was the intended acquisition.

Sean nodded, his eyes glazed over and his mind secretly running on all cylinders. *Why was the suspect's name so important to her? Why did it matter?* If his earlier theory was right, and she was indeed Andrew Carson's mistress, he could understand a curiosity over the details of the case. But the fact that she would dig into Sean's account to find his address, spruce herself up, and drive out to his home in the middle of the night to get such information didn't add up. Those weren't acts of impulsive curiosity. There was something more methodical to it—something more purposeful.

His mind whipped back to what he had seen in the GSL parking lot after Jessica thought he had already driven off—her impassioned phone conversation. He recalled the look of desperation in her face—the look of fear. As he despondently glared into her eyes as the two now sat silently in his living room, he began to observe just a hint of that same desperation and fear forming along the contours of her face.

Eye-opening sobriety suddenly struck him. He believed he finally understood what was going on. He hoped a single test would confirm the conclusion he had reached, and before he opened his mouth to speak, he held his eyes on hers, prepared to gauge whatever reaction they were about to unknowingly disclose.

"Steve McGarrett," he said. It was the name of the lead character from *Hawaii Five-O*; a name he was convinced would mean absolutely nothing to her.

That's when he saw it, a subtle sense of relief in her eyes and a deep breath drifting out of her mouth from low in her chest. She was never worried about the fate of Andrew Carson. She was worried about herself, and perhaps the suspect the police were looking for: Norman Booth.

"Ever heard of him?" he asked, remaining calm.

She shook her head. "No. I'm afraid not."

"Well, you didn't hear that name from me, okay?" he said with a raised eyebrow.

"Of course not," she said, letting a quick, nervous grin show. "Thank you. I'm sorry I stopped by so late, Mr. Coleman."

"Sean."

"What?"

"That's what you called me when you wanted inside and were making small-talk with me just now—when you wanted my help. You called me Sean. Not Mr. Coleman. You can keep calling me Sean."

"Okay. I'll do that," she said, offering a polite smile before standing up from her chair and reaching for the zipper of her jacket.

"You're not leaving, are you?" he quickly asked, wearing a contrived look of disappointment across his face. "What's your hurry?"

"I'd really better—" she started to say before Sean cut her off.

"Because I wanted to ask *you* a question."

"Oh, okay," she said.

Her jaw squared as she seemed to be fighting back the urge to roll her eyes, probably predicting he was about to ask her out to dinner sometime. She reluctantly sat back down.

He glared at her without expression for a moment, wondering if she was at all suspicious of how heavily he was judging her. "Ever hear of a town in Utah named Hanksville?" he blurted out.

Her eyes narrowed at the odd question. The mild grin vanished from her face, and she shook her head no.

"I guess there's no real reason you should have. It's a tiny little town. A speck on the map. Some shithole in the middle of the desert, surrounded by miles and miles of dirt, rock, and scrub."

Jessica's face twisted tighter in confusion.

"Not many people live there. There's only a few buildings along a highway. One diner. One gas station. A couple of rundown motels for travelers driving off the beaten path, coming to or from Lake Powell. Powell's about an hour's drive away from Hanksville."

She now looked as if she was forcing herself to appear intrigued by Sean's words. She clearly wanted to leave. "I take it you've been there?"

"Yeah. Back in high school. Senior year. Some of the other guys on the football team planned a road trip to Powell over spring break. Two days out on the water."

"That sounds like fun."

He ignored her comment. "I knew that none of them wanted me along, but I had a few bucks to spend from washing dishes at a local diner. I *imposed* myself. Told them I'd pay for half of the gas myself. I just needed to get out of Winston for a while."

She nodded.

"Anyway, after about a five-hour drive in an old, full-sized van with no air-conditioning—the last half of it through the Utah wasteland—we stopped to fill up in Hanksville. The gas station there is actually pretty cool looking. It's called something like Hollow Rock or Hollow Mountain. The building, the store, is inside of a cave that was blasted through one of these huge orange-colored rocks that you can find all around the area. I mean, they really are big." His eyes left hers and dropped to the floor before he continued. "While they were filling up, I told a couple of the guys that I was going inside to take a dump."

Jessica winced.

"When I came back out, the van was gone. They'd left without me." When his gaze returned to hers, he found her eyes wide.

"Did they do it on purpose?" she asked. "Was it some kind of joke?" She finally sounded interested.

"Who knows?" he answered. "They later told me it was an accident, but that's pretty hard to believe. There were seven of us inside that van. You'd think one of them would have noticed that someone was missing."

"When they came back for you?"

"They *didn't* come back for me. I waited there for over an hour, outside that gas station in the hot sun, feeling the eyes of the attendant inside glued to my back as I paced back and forth. She felt sorry for me. She checked on me a couple of times." A brief chuckle spilled from Sean's mouth as he recalled the memory. "That old lady at the register lived out in the middle of nowhere where she worked at a rundown gas station, had about four teeth left in her mouth, and there she was feeling sorry for *me*. I kept thinking that every moving dot that popped up over the horizon would be the guys returning for me, but it was never them. A couple of families. Groups of friends. No one by themself like I was."

Jessica now seemed legitimately invested in his story. There was sadness in her eyes that didn't appear phony. It was the sadness he'd often witnessed while watching her from afar at the plasma bank.

He continued. "One of those couples were brave enough to let a big guy who looked like me hitch a ride to the marina at Lake Powell. I knew they were heading that way because they had jet-skis in tow. By the time I got there, though, the guys had already left on the houseboat. Gone for two days."

Her jaw dropped. "Well, what did you do?" she asked. "Did another boat take you out to them? One of the park rangers?"

"No. I didn't want anyone to."

"Well, why not?"

"Because their actions spoke louder than their words. At some point, you've got to accept that you're just not supposed to be somewhere. It's not because you're a loner or a lone wolf or whatever. It's because the rest of the pack just doesn't want you anywhere near them." He could read the confusion in her eyes.

"Why are you telling me this, Sean?" she asked, sadness in her voice.

He gazed at her for a moment. "Because I can think of exactly three times in my life when I felt like the biggest asshole on the planet. That day was one of those times. Another was the day my dad walked out on me." He focused an angry glare on her uncertain eyes. "The last one was today, when I drove down to Greeley to help search for Andrew Carson's body and found that his family has no idea who the fuck you are."

Jessica's face turned completely pale, just as it had the day before in the GSL parking lot when he had first mentioned Carson's name to her. Her mouth was open but no words came out. She leaned forward in her chair, clawing her fingers into the armrests as if she was considering bolting toward the door. The doubt in her eyes signaled to Sean, however, that she didn't think she could make it past him if he tried to stop her.

She was right.

"What did you do to Andrew Carson?" he growled. He suddenly stood up.

The quick action made her leap from her chair and hold her open hands out in front of her defensively. Her body trembled as she shook her head. Tears began to build up in her eyes.

"Do you think I'm fucking stupid?" he roared, his chest tight and fists clenched. A twisted sneer etched across his face. "You show up here in the middle of the night, looking all hot, and I'm gonna blabber everything out like some love struck school kid without figuring out what you're doing?"

The tears were now streaming down her face. Her whole body shook.

"Where's Andrew Carson's body? Where?"

"I need help," she murmured.

"What?" he grunted.

"I need help!" she screamed so loudly that Sean found himself cringing and taking a step backward.

Her eyes sporadically shot from one end of the room to the other, and when she happened to turn her head to the side far enough for him to see the profile of her face, he noticed a small, clear tube wedged at the center of her ear. It didn't look like a hearing aid, at least not the kind his mother wore. It looked more advanced, like a listening device.

A loud crash at the rear of the building grabbed their attention. Sean recognized the noise as the back door being whipped open and striking the adjacent wall. His head snapped back to Jessica, quickly meeting her eyes.

Loud, rapid footsteps clanged their way down the hallway toward them. A man dressed all in black surged around the hallway corner. Sean charged him.

He wrapped one of his hands around the stranger's neck and slammed him backwards into the wall of the hallway, the impact sending several framed pictures falling to the floor in unison. Shattered glass sprayed in a dozen directions.

The man was of average height and weight, which made him considerably smaller than Sean and unable to mount an effective offense. He had short brown hair and wore glasses with thick black frames. The thick lenses made his frantic eyes look abnormally large. They grew even wider from the pressure now around his neck. He clearly wasn't Norman Booth, but the man's identity was the last thing on Sean's mind at that moment.

The man's hand rose, and when it did, Sean saw a black, shiny object gripped tightly in his fingers. He grabbed the man's wrist and pinned it to the wall where the rest of the man's body was constrained. A blue flame of light suddenly emitted from the object and reflected off of the man's glasses. It was accompanied by the loud sound of an electric charge. A taser; he was trying to shock Sean.

Repeatedly Sean slammed the back of the man's wrist against the wall, trying to jar the device loose, but the man had a death-grip on it. Sean arched his back and delivered a colossal head butt, just above the bridge of the man's nose. The back of the man's head slammed into the wall behind him so hard that it left a cracked depression in the drywall. His glasses snapped at their center. Half of the frame fell to the floor while the other half dangled from his ear.

Sean sent his thigh into the man's prone stomach, knocking the air from his lungs. He lunged backwards a couple of steps and took the man with him, yanking him from the wall. Sean quickly planted his feet and swung his body as if he were about to throw a discus. Only instead of a hurling a metal plate, he launched a human being through the air. His foot caught the phone on Sean's desk mid-flight and sent it to the floor.

The stranger landed in a heap, just in front of the stove. Seemingly fueled only by adrenaline, the man quickly but clumsily climbed to his feet. He was dazed, and without his glasses, having some trouble seeing. Sean launched forward and sent a wicked right cross directly into the man's nose and mouth.

The man's head snapped back sickly and his body flailed backwards on random footing until it collided with the cast iron stove. The stove tipped over, loudly stripping itself free of the cylinder-shaped ventilation flue that led up to the ceiling, and then crashed into the brick base below. The man landed on top of the stove, screaming out in pain as blistering hot metal and the flames from its open door tortured his body. Within two seconds, he rolled to his side.

Sean scanned the floor for the man's dropped taser. Suddenly a small object pressed against his lower back and a paralyzing electric shock ripped through his body. Every muscle in his body clenched tight and burned in agony. His eyes bulged and his mouth clutched shut. The pulsation continued for several seconds. When it ended, Sean fell to his knees, gasping for breath.

"Hit him again!" groaned the man who lay shriveled up on the floor not far from him. His mouth was full of blood, his nose appeared broken, and he was reaching into his jacket pocket for something. "Hit him again and hold it there!"

Before Sean could rebound, the pressure was against his back again, and this time the jolt sent him straight down to the floor on his chest. His body shook wildly, out of his control. He was virtually helpless. The agonizing pulsing didn't let up. He snarled, trying to pull himself forward on the floor by digging his elbows into it. The corner of his eye caught the man in black crawling over to him with something in his hand. Sean tried to get his arm up to fend off whatever was coming, but he could barely move. When the man reached him, Sean saw him lean forward. A thin, sharp object pierced the side of Sean's neck.

Almost immediately, his head felt light. His vision went blurry and he winced at the hazy sight of bright, abstract flames that abruptly lunged into the air from the floor just feet in front of him. A breath of intense heat blew against his face and he knew that the blazing stove had rolled off its base and had somehow ignited the hardwood floor.

He could hear the loud busy signal of the unhooked phone, and he felt the urge to vomit as multiple, tortuous sensations ripped through his body at the same time.

The thought of getting his hands back around the man's neck, and this time not letting go, was the last image that jerked through Sean's mind before his world went dark.

Chapter 12

It was nearly 5:45 in the morning when Ron Oldhorse saw the signal: the illumination of the narrow bathroom window along the north side of the small house, followed by a quick pulse from a lamp in the master bedroom. Though filtered through thin curtains, the brightness lit up the nearby snow-covered trees whose limbs were still drooping from the weight accumulated during the night.

Lumbergh was awake. Oldhorse wondered if the chief had managed to catch any sleep at all.

From under the concealed white tarp that served as his shelter, Oldhorse carefully removed the dark, hand-woven scarf from the bottom half of his face. It didn't come off easy. The overnight frost and wind had secured it to his unshaven jaw like opposing pieces of Velcro.

His fingerless wool gloves released the stalk of the long hunting rifle that lay beside his frigid body. He cupped his hands to his mouth and blew warm air along them to the envy of his tingling feet inside his moccasin boots. His breath lingered visibly in the air for several seconds.

The lower half of his body was covered by a small snowdrift that had formed through the night, camouflaging him well, but ultimately without purpose. The devil's kin hadn't arrived that night.

Oldhorse poked his head out from under the tarp and carefully surveyed the area before climbing from his makeshift shelter. He folded up the tarp, his legs feeling strained from the change in body position as he knelt. He then strapped on a pair of wooden snowshoes that he had made years ago from hardwood and rawhide. They were designed to leave very little of a footprint behind in the snow.

With the tarp secured under his arm and the rifle in his other hand, he made his way through the thick forest that inched up to the house where the chief of police and his family lived.

When he heard the soft snap of a twig, he quickly swung his body behind a nearby boulder. The movement was so fast that anyone watching would have half-believed he disappeared into thin air. He peered up from behind the large rock. Though it was still dark out, he spotted a young mule deer with its head buried in the thick of a pine branch. A fresh dusting of snow spotted its back, likely fallen from the branch.

With multiple layers of coats and flannel wrapped around his body, Oldhorse made his way down a steep hill to a dirt service road. There, a white and gray police cruiser was parked discreetly between a pair of warped spruces whose upper branches were intertwined. He pried open the driver's side door, shoving tree limbs aside as he did, and climbed in.

The car started hard from the freezing temperatures overnight, but it did start. He fired up the CB radio mounted under the dashboard, checked its channel, and worked the press-to-talk switch a couple of times on the handheld transmitter in a predetermined pattern. A few moments later, he received acknowledgment in the form of a similar series of breaks among the channel's background static.

He popped the transmission into drive, pulled off the road, and slowly made his way across an open meadow driving over what was left of the cruiser's tracks from the evening before.

Those unfamiliar with the area wouldn't know of the meadow north of Lumbergh's place. Thick woods surrounded it and the service road that ran parallel wasn't on any maps. The rarely used road was never plowed in the wintertime and thus was largely inaccessible during those months. The meadow it edged up to, however, received a lot of direct sunlight, and the previous day's unhindered rays left much of it only about two inches deep in snow.

When Oldhorse reached the north end of the meadow, he carefully navigated the cruiser through a collection of trees. He took his time, and a few minutes later crossed onto a wider dirt road that would have eventually branched off into Lumbergh's driveway had he turned left.

He turned right, scraping the undercarriage of the car a bit on frozen terrain after the front tires dropped off the shoulder of the road. There were no fresh tire tracks in the snow now blanketing the road. No one had come through that way during the night.

When Oldhorse reached town, he pulled into the police station and went inside. He found that Jefferson's night had been every bit as uneventful as his, though clearly more cushy. The toasty building was seventy-degrees warm and the smell of coffee wafted through the air. Indulgences never mattered much to Oldhorse. He preferred the outdoors, even at times when the elements were harsh. He relished testing his grit whenever the occasion presented itself.

Jefferson greeted him with a quick hello and offer of coffee and a ride home, but Oldhorse declined. He returned the borrowed rifle to the officer, grabbed his pack, and made his way back out the front door. He knew it was a long trek back to his cabin on foot, but he saw it as an opportunity to stretch his legs after a long night of being immobile.

He didn't own a car. He'd sold his years ago after deciding to make the mountains outside of Winston his home. He had become as much a part of the forest as the hills, trees, and rivers that carved their way along the terrain. His home was a small cabin along a slope near Red Cliff—a remote area about five miles from the town square—where he killed or raised the food he ate. The decades-old dwelling was devoid of most modern-day luxuries. No electricity. No gas. No indoor plumbing. Just access to well water a few hundred yards away.

For many years, Oldhorse's lifestyle adhered to reclusiveness. He relied solely on himself, leaving no room for others. That changed six months earlier, however, shortly after he found himself chaotically racing down a narrow mountain road behind the wheel of the car belonging to the lifeless corpse of Alvar Montoya.

Oldhorse was a man who avoided attention, but with Chief Lumbergh shot up by Montoya, the Indian stepped up and came between life and death. Once Lumbergh was at the hospital, however, Oldhorse watched from afar as doctors and nurses scrambled to save the chief's life. Lumbergh's vital organs had been spared injury, but he'd lost a lot of blood. It was touch and go for much of the night.

When the chief's wife arrived, Oldhorse watched in silence as she fought her way past orderlies, frantic to get to her husband's side. And when she did, he saw her place her trembling hands along Lumbergh's face as tears streamed down her cheeks and onto his body. Her husband was her life—her reason for living. Oldhorse could see that.

Days later, after Lumbergh was released from the ICU, Oldhorse would slip into the hospital at night, after visitation hours, to check on him. He always came late to avoid the swarm of reporters that were stationed outside prior to the evening newscasts.

Before entering the chief's room, Oldhorse would sometimes stand in the dim hallway just outside and watch the glow in Lumbergh's eyes whenever he'd look at his wife's face. She rarely left his side, spending the nights beside him on an awkwardly shaped chair. The chair was probably designed that way to be purposely uncomfortable, discouraging family members from staying for long periods of time. It didn't discourage Diana Lumbergh, however.

Witnessing their unbridled love and the way each of their lives depended on the other, Oldhorse felt something change inside him. He came to realize that the cell of isolation he had confined his heart to wasn't a necessary trade-off for independence, but rather a chosen path of emptiness that ultimately led nowhere. And when he finally opened his heart to the outside world, it found the unexpected love of Joan Parker, Toby Parker's mother.

Since then, Oldhorse had felt an unspoken affection toward Chief Lumbergh and his wife, Diana—a sense of gratitude neither of them had any clue they had earned.

It was one of the reasons why Oldhorse agreed to help when he was approached by the chief twenty-four hours earlier. Lumbergh believed that Alvar Montoya's death had spawned a new, dire threat to him and his family. The chief had shared with Oldhorse some of the alarming details of Lautaro Montoya's prison escape. Oldhorse had given the matter careful thought during his vigil.

He gnawed on a string of homemade deer jerky. It was nearly frozen from the long, cold night he had endured outside Lumbergh's house. As he walked, his narrow, hawk-like eyes carefully scrutinized a pair of tire tracks carved into the snow along the lightly used road that spanned the base of his hill.

He often referred to it as *his hill* because he was the only person who lived on it—a steep slope heavily covered with pine and aspen that kept his cabin concealed from view from the road. However, he believed in his heart that the hill, as everything, belonged to nature.

The small, rustic home sat a few hundred yards above where he stood, wedged in a rocky crevice along a small clearing.

He slowed his pace once he noticed that the tracks came to a halt just below an unmarked path he'd often use to scale the hill up to his cabin. At that point, the vehicle had performed a sharp U-turn, doubling back down the road.

A lost traveler perhaps? It was possible. The tires looked like they belonged to a compact car; most of the locals drove four-wheel drive vehicles in the winter. Once a set of footprints revealed themselves in the snow, however, Oldhorse knew whoever had come there had done so for a purpose. The driver, who looked to be a man, had exited the vehicle and made his way on up toward the cabin before turning around and coming back.

Oldhorse shoved the jerky back into his pack and pulled out a large hunting knife from a sheath at his side. He gripped it tightly in his weathered hand and doubled back down the road a ways before veering onto the adjacent slope of the hill. He disappeared behind large rocks and trees, jogging his way up an embankment with purposeful footing that sometimes brought snow up past his knees.

Though the footprints that began at the road provided clear-cut evidence that the visitor had already come and gone, Oldhorse wasn't taking any chances—not with a twisted man seeking vengeance on the loose. He climbed up above where his cabin rested, nestling his body in between the thick trunk of a snow-covered tree and a rock formation that jetted out of the ground at a largely vertical angle. He had a view of the backside of his cabin from there. Nothing looked out of place.

He cautiously made his way down to its rear, keeping his body low and sometimes slithering down snow mounds like a reptile sliding down sand. His disciplined eyes never strayed from the cabin's long back window. He looked for movement inside and saw none.

When he reached the window, he carefully peered through a gap between the pair of olive-green curtains Joan had bought for him as a gift a month earlier.

"They'll make your cabin homier," she had told him with a grin.

He skimmed the interior through the glass as best he could. Nothing seemed out of place. He quickly tapped the window with his hand, ducking down afterwards and placing an ear to the wooden wall of the cabin to listen for movement. There was none.

He slid along the side of his home and then peered around the corner to the front. There, he found the footprints that led all the way up to his front step.

The porch had largely been spared from the snowfall, thanks to the overhang of the roof where a thin row of icicles clenched onto a crude drainpipe. Still, icy footprints could be seen along the worn wooden planks, frozen flat from the moisture under the visitor's shoes that had turned solid from the overnight winds.

Oldhorse scanned the pattern they left along the wood. His heart skipped a beat when he noticed the heel-half of a print sticking out from under his front door. The visitor had entered his home.

Perhaps there was an innocent explanation. Maybe it was one of the local townsfolk looking for a custom woodcarving as a gift for someone. Oldhorse occasionally sold such creations to the general store in Winston for resale. Maybe the visitor knocked, and when no one answered, they poked their head inside to make sure Oldhorse was all right. After all, he never locked his door. He saw no need to, thus whoever came in wasn't exactly breaking and entering.

Everyone in town who knew Oldhorse, however, understood how territorial he was. The thought of one of them entering his home uninvited seemed unlikely. So when he twisted the knob and pressed his elbow against the door, he let it glide all the way open before entering, knife in hand.

His controlled breathing was the only sound heard inside the small building, that and the faint whistle of a gust of wind that pressed against the outside of the cabin for the briefest of moments. There was a very subtle scent lingering in the air, possibly cologne. It seemed slightly familiar, though he couldn't quite place where he had inhaled it before.

Initially, nothing looked out of place. Nothing appeared missing or jostled. Any wet footprints left by the man who had entered had already dried up. However, Oldhorse could tell by some matting along the long rug that covered much of the inside floor that it had been stood upon.

His steady gaze glided along the furnishings of the cabin, scrutinizing the sleeping area, the stone fireplace, and the cooking area. Everything looked just as he had left it—everything except a large, thick hunting bow that clung to a short peg sticking out from a wall in the far corner of the building.

It was hanging at a slightly different angle than how he had left it. Most people wouldn't have noticed such a discrepancy, but Oldhorse had a keen, almost eerie eye for detail. It was possible that during the night, a strong gust of wind had struck the outside of the cabin with such strength that the bow was shaken a bit and its position along the wall was altered. Yet, a sixth sense at the back of Oldhorse's mind was warning him that Mother Nature wasn't to blame for the variance.

He moved in close. Tiny, scraggly paint shavings—the color of his bow—littered the wooden floor beneath it. He dropped to a knee and closely examined the bottom of the bow. Something had been crudely inscribed on it, probably with a standard pocketknife.

EL VERDADERO HEROE?

Oldhorse glanced around the room again. His hand clasped the lower limb of the bow to turn it and see if there was anything more written. What he noticed instead was that the weapon didn't feel right. It felt heavier than it normally did.

As it occurred to him that this bow he now tugged was the same one he had used to drive an aluminum arrow right between Alvar Montoya's lungs, a high-pitched, digital noise sounding like a wristwatch alarm emitted from behind it.

Oldhorse's eyes widened when he saw a tiny red light bulb begin to flash quickly from behind the weapon. Two short, thin metal pipes were now visible as well.

The knife fell from his hand.

He spun and darted in the opposite direction. He didn't have a half-second to spare and knew it wasn't enough to make it to the door in time. With a snarl, he dove through the air, crashing through the thin glass of the window at the rear of the cabin. A deafening explosion tore through the heart of the building.

Shrapnel ripped its way through his clothes and skin before he crashed to the ground outside, hitting his head against a large rock hidden in the snow. Chards of splintered wood and shattered glass fell across his outstretched body. A dust-like residue rained down on him.

With trembling arms he crawled aimlessly along the frozen earth, instinctively putting some space between himself and the cabin. He felt faint and disoriented as blood oozed from a gash across his skull. His legs were soaked with blood as well, streaming out from the spread-open flesh beneath his shredded clothes. A torturous ringing pounded his skull, letting him hear nothing else.

Then the pain set in. His legs felt like they were on fire from the hot shrapnel embedded in them. The worst sensation came from the back of his right thigh. He twisted his body to gauge the damage and found remnants of a metal tube protruding from it. It was a piece of the pipe bomb that had gone off in his cabin.

Before another thought was allowed to cross his mind, he felt his arms collapse out from under him. He fell flat to his chest. With his head throbbing and vision blurring, he knew he was about to lose consciousness.

He struggled to stay awake but quickly found his head buried in the cold snow. Peculiar thoughts danced randomly through his mind as he drifted away. He thought it was a shame that the curtains Joan had bought him were now likely ruined. He pondered if Jefferson would now need to take his place outside Lumbergh's cabin that night. He also thought of the familiar scent of cologne he'd smelled inside his cabin.

The answer came to him where he'd smelled it before.

Chapter 13

"You told him where you were staying?" Lumbergh shouted into his office phone, slamming his elbow down across his desk and shaking his head in aggravation.

Jefferson poked his head around the corner, his inquisitive eyes silently inquiring if the phone conversation was pertinent to Lautaro Montoya. Lumbergh waved him off before reaching into his desk for his prescription bottle. He removed the lid and emptied out a couple of capsules onto his desk.

"Gary," Diana said on the other line, her voice shaking. "I was worried about you. You sent us away without explaining what was going on."

"Honey, the fewer people that know where you are right now, the better. Do you understand?"

"No!" she shrilled. "I *don't* understand. Tell me what's going on! What has you so scared? Are you in danger? Are *we* in danger?"

He could hear her getting choked up, fighting back tears. He pursed his lips and closed his eyes, forcing himself for a moment to empathize with the position he had put her in.

"Just tell me what's going on," she whispered.

His voice softened. "Listen, everything's going to be fine. I promise you. Just a couple more days of this and things will be back to normal. Trust me."

He hoped his words sounded more reassuring to her than they did to him. Besides not wanting his wife to worry, he feared if word got out that Alvar Montoya's brother was in Colorado, the chances of capturing him would be greatly diminished. If the county sheriff or feds got involved, and a media circus caravanned back into Winston, Lautaro Montoya might get scared off—but only for a while.

He knew Montoya would never let it go and the threat of him seeking retribution would forever be hanging over the head of the chief.

It was time to end things—not later but now. Only when the Montoya family tree was uprooted and fed into a wood chipper would life return to normal.

"What were you telling me about Sean?" Lumbergh asked, eager to change the topic. "He's not returning your calls?"

Diana reluctantly let the prior discussion simmer and told her husband of the conversation she had had with her brother the night before. She explained that Sean had promised to call her right back after he heard a knock at his door, but never did. The rest of the night and even in the morning she was greeted with nothing but busy signals when she called his number.

"You think a friend might have come over and they got drunk?" he asked after sliding the capsules into his mouth and gulping them down with a swig of coffee. "He could be sleeping off a stupor."

Dead silence lingered on the other end, and he could feel his wife's disapproving glare through the receiver.

"He doesn't do that anymore, Gary," she finally said. "And who would have come over? Sean's never had *any* drinking buddies."

Lumbergh smirked, fighting back the urge to suggest that Sean Coleman hadn't *any* kind of buddies, let alone *drinking* buddies. The expression on his face, however, suddenly turned serious. He felt his gut drop to the floor. His pulse accelerated as some bile forced its way down his throat.

It hadn't occurred to him until that very moment that Sean could be a target of Lautaro Montoya. No one outside of Winston should have known that the two were related by marriage. Sean's name was never mentioned in the papers or on television in the weeks following the Montoya shooting. His last name differed from his uncle's, so an outsider shouldn't have been able to make a connection to Montoya's victim either.

All along, Lumbergh had viewed Sean as a potential liability to the situation—someone who would find a way to inadvertently screw up the capture of Lautaro Montoya if he was made privy to what was going on.

Had the determined Mexican somehow figured it out? he had to wonder. *Had he followed Sean home from the police station the other day? Did he learn the truth by striking up a conversation with someone in town?*

The phone receiver shook in his hand. His knuckles turned white.

"I'll check on him, okay honey?" he said, hoping the tremble in his voice wasn't noticeable to her.

She told him that there was something else they needed to talk about—something not related to Sean or where she and her mother were staying. She tried to elaborate, but he was frantic to wrap up the conversation. He told his wife he loved her, said they'd talk more later, and slammed down the phone.

"Jefferson!" a panicked Lumbergh yelled from his office.
He launched to his feet and yanked his jacket off the coatrack in the corner of the room. His good arm went into its sleeve in no time.

He yelled Jefferson's name a second time.

His officer finally appeared in the hallway, breathing hard with half of his shirt dangling out from his waistline. "I was in the bathroom. What is it?"

"Grab the shotgun!"

Chapter 14

The side of Lumbergh's face smacked up against the police cruiser's passenger seat when his officer took a hard, sharp turn. The speeding vehicle nearly spun out of control on the slick road, but Jefferson's quick wheel work kept them from sliding into a ditch on the shoulder.

"Get us there, but get us there in one piece," said Lumbergh in as calm of a voice as he could muster. His teeth mashed a wad of gum as he reached under his jacket and pulled his Glock from its open-top holster. He quickly checked its action.

"How would he know that Sean's your brother-in-law?" asked a breathless Jefferson as he pumped the gas pedal and sent fountains of slush high into the air behind them.

"Let's hope that he doesn't, and that there's nothing to this."

Jefferson's tongue protruded from his mouth as he negotiated the twists of the snow-covered road. A trail of sweat ran down the side of his face.

Lumbergh tapped his foot nervously on the floorboard, feeling his own heart beat against his chest. "When we get there, I'll take the front and you circle around back. Got it?"

"Are you okay with your arm?"

"I'll be fine."

When they rounded a bend, the white crest of Sean's roof came into view. Once they jetted past a row of trees, the rest of the small building revealed itself. Sean's car was parked out front.

"Be okay," Lumbergh mumbled under his breath before realizing that his officer hadn't yet begun to apply the brakes.

They were coming in way too fast for the road conditions.

"Jefferson!" Lumbergh wailed.

"Shit!" cried the officer. He pinned the brake pedal to the floor with a stomp. His wide eyes consumed the sight of the rapidly nearing Nova. He grasped the steering wheel vice-like and Lumbergh braced his body as best he could. The cruiser veered at a widening angle.

Lumbergh closed his eyes and clenched his teeth before a loud collision brought the men's slowing momentum to a dead halt.

"Dammit!" Lumbergh moaned, seeing the dented rear of Sean's car pressed up against his side of the cruiser. He turned to Jefferson, whose mouth was left dangling open. The officer's wide eyes apologized profusely to his boss.

"I'm going out your side," stated Lumbergh, his mind having already moved past the wreck. "Get out!"

The two men quickly but awkwardly climbed outside of the vehicle through the driver side door. As Lumbergh circled around to the opposite side of the car, he noticed a pair of tire tracks in the snow that belonged to neither them nor the Nova.

Jefferson let out a loud cough and looked to his boss for direction.

Holding his gun out in front of him, Lumbergh motioned Jefferson around to the back of the building. Shotgun in hand, the officer disappeared from view. Lumbergh trotted to the front door. He checked the doorknob and found it locked.

"Sean?" he yelled, pounding the wooden door with the back of his clenched fist. "You in there?"

No answer.

"Jefferson?" he cried out.

He heard the officer reply after few seconds. "The rear door's busted open back here! Hang on!"

"Shit!" Lumbergh snarled. He took a few steps, training his gun on the front door and waiting for Jefferson to secure the inside.

It was taking longer than it seemed it should, and Lumbergh desperately began praying that Jefferson wasn't standing there in shock over the sight of his brother-in-law's dead body. His mind was a busy intersection of horrific thoughts and unconscionable consequences.

"Talk to me, Jefferson!" he cried out, his heightened voice trembling.

"I'm near the front door!" came Jefferson's muffled reply from inside. "He's not here."

Those three words allowed a deep breath of relief to escape the chief's lungs, but only before the officer continued.

"Something's wrong, though. There's blood, and the place has been trashed."

Jefferson unlocked and opened the front door, and Lumbergh slid in. The men quickly made their way down the hallway from the front area to the living room where it smelled strongly as if something was burnt.

"Careful," warned Jefferson, taking wide steps at the end of the hallway. "There's broken glass."

Lumbergh's eyes shifted from the shattered picture frames that lay in a clump on the floor to the overturned stove, now cold, that had left a large black singe mark across a portion of the hardwood floor. Sean's phone and its unhooked receiver were lying close by. "You said there was blood?"

Jefferson pointed to a dried crimson puddle on the floor not far from the stove. It wasn't large, likely coming from a superficial, non-life-threatening wound. Whether or not that wound belonged to Sean, Lumbergh had no way of knowing.

"Chief, I don't think Sean left here on his own," Lumbergh heard his officer state.

"Why do you say that?"

"There's a bunch of footprints and tire tracks out back. From multiple people, I think. It looks like they dragged someone out of here."

Lumbergh quickly pushed his way past Jefferson and made a beeline for the back door. He took note of the splintered frame along the doorway and carefully maneuvered his body in a way that kept him from stepping on the plethora of prints embedded in the snow. It wasn't easy with one arm but he managed once he holstered his gun.

Jefferson watched him from inside the doorway. His head was lowered and there was nervousness in his eyes. Lumbergh didn't know if his disposition stemmed from Sean's disappearance or the officer's epiphany that he had smeared away some of the prints with his own feet when he hastily entered the building.

If it was the latter, Jefferson's worries were unwarranted. There were tracks everywhere—plenty of clean imprints, though the rising temperature from the morning sun was beginning to deform them.

Two deep lines along the snow likely came from the heels of Sean's shoes as he was dragged outside and pulled into the vehicle whose tracks matched those from the front of the building. They had circled around to the other side.

Lumbergh made out two sets of footprints—one quite small and the other of average size. *Did Montoya have help?*

"Jefferson, go back through the house and out the front door. Don't use Sean's phone. It's evidence. From the car, get the county sheriff on the line. Let him know what's going on. Everything."

"Everything?"

"Yes. The conditions have changed. We need all available resources on this. A forensics team and someone who can hopefully match up these tire tracks to a specific type of car. We'll need to circulate those pictures of Montoya. Is Martinez still in town? Can you reach him on the radio and have him swing by the office, make some copies, and bring them over?"

"Yeah. I think he's still around. But aren't those pictures old and out of date?"

"They are but they're all we've got. They're better than nothing."

Jefferson disappeared back inside.

After squatting down and examining the tracks closer, Lumbergh noticed just how narrow the smaller set of footprints was. They almost looked as if they could belong to a woman. A minute later, he went back inside to better scrutinize the damage caused by the apparent scuffle.

There were no shell casings anywhere on the floor. It appeared that the fight didn't escalate beyond that of a brawl, but it was a wild brawl. Sean didn't go down quietly. If there had just been one unarmed intruder—even Montoya himself—he likely wouldn't have stood a chance against a man of Sean's size and propensity to use his fists. But with two people, it seemed they had eventually overwhelmed him.

If Montoya simply wanted Sean dead, he would have killed him there and left his body behind to be found. There had to be more to the game, and Lumbergh could only fathom that Sean was being used as a pawn to toy with him, perhaps draw him out into the open in order to fulfill his sick hunger for revenge.

Lumbergh carefully scrutinized the living area, looking for any shred of helpful evidence among the broken and overturned decor—something that could link the perpetrators to wherever they had taken Sean. Nothing immediately presented itself. He did find something that piqued his curiosity though.

The burn mark along the hardwood floor—the one left by the overturned stove . . . It was wet. Saturated, in fact. A blue rubber bucket, probably taken from under Sean's kitchen sink, was lying on its side just a few feet away.

It appeared that during the fight the floor had caught on fire and someone had put out the flames with a bucket of water. Clearly, Sean wouldn't have been in any condition to do it, so it had to have been done by one of the intruders. The big question was *why?* Why would someone who had burst into Sean's house to kidnap him bother saving his home from going up in flames? If anything, letting the fire burn would have destroyed evidence of what had happened to Sean.

When Jefferson reentered the room, he opened his mouth to speak but Lumbergh cut him off.

"When they get here, make sure they check this bucket for fingerprints. If we can identify who it is that's helping Montoya, that might help us figure out where they are."

"Got it, and the boys at County are on their way. There's something else though."

Lumbergh raised an eyebrow.

Jefferson led him around to the north side of the house, away from the road and the two entrances of the building where all of the outside action had taken place. The north side faced nothing but forest.

"There. Look!" said Jefferson, pointing his meaty finger at the snowy ground.

There was another pair of footprints that led up to the building's side window. They were definitely of a different tread than the others and were too small to belong to Sean. They came in from the forest, then led back out the way they had come.

"Who in the hell was this?" Lumbergh muttered.

He carefully made his way across the snow to the window, careful not to step on the new prints. He peered inside the window and found that it had a direct view of the small laundry room at the rear of the building—the one Lumbergh had just passed through when he stepped in from outside. He spun his head back to the tracks and began walking parallel to them as Jefferson watched on.

"Is there a *third* person mixed up in this?" Jefferson shouted, cupping his hand to his mouth so the chief could hear him as he distanced himself from the building.

Lumbergh nodded. "I don't think so," he said softly, more to himself than Jefferson.

His narrow eyes followed the tracks closely. He walked through clusters of leafless trees, where the snow grew deeper. He lost his balance a couple of times, pressing his good hand to the packed snow to keep from falling. Eventually, the footprints led him to a small clearing where he spotted another set of tire tracks that led back out to the road he and Jefferson had flown down earlier. The tracks were relatively small and close together, suggesting that they belonged to a compact car.

Lumbergh pulled a fresh stick of gum from his jacket pocket and replaced the exhausted wad in his mouth. Its wrapper, now blanketing the old piece, quickly went into his pocket.

He followed the tracks out along the road. They seemed to lead back toward town amidst numerous other tracks that were partially peeled away by the plow that came through earlier that morning. Lumbergh walked down the shoulder of the road and back to the building where a surprised-looking Jefferson spotted him.

"Where did you come from?" he asked.

Lumbergh told him where the tracks had taken him.

"I don't get it," the officer admitted. "Who do they belong to?"

The chief shook his head. "I don't know, but whoever it was doesn't appear to have been part of what happened to Sean. The tracks look just as fresh as the others though. I wonder if they saw who took him."

"And this person didn't call *us*?" Jefferson quickly responded. "I was at the office all night. Anyone seeing something like a man being kidnapped would have called that in. Don't you think?"

"You sure would think so," said Lumbergh. "Maybe they showed up right before or right after. Either way, they still might know something useful."

Jefferson shook his head, his face contorted in confusion. "But who in the hell would park their car in the woods, sneak up to Sean's house, and peep in through his window?"

Lumbergh's face tightened. His eyes glared through his officer's face.

"What? What did I say?"

"Jefferson, give me your keys," said Lumbergh. "You wait here for everyone, okay?"

Jefferson was confused. He opened his mouth to speak, but before he could utter a word, Lumbergh snatched the key ring from his outstretched hand.

Lumbergh walked quickly over to the cruiser, shoved the key into the ignition, and reached into the glove compartment. He pulled out a walkie-talkie and tossed it in the air over to Jefferson. "If the others get here before I'm back, you call me. All right?"

Jefferson nodded.

"I'll be back soon."

Lumbergh cranked the engine and drove forward slowly, peeling the cruiser's dented door away from the back of the Nova. He watched Jefferson's wincing face in the rearview mirror—his reaction to the sound of metal rubbing on metal. When Lumbergh was clear of all obstacles, he sped up and tore down the road, a single hand clutching the steering wheel in front of him.

Chapter 15

L umbergh repeatedly beat the locked door with a clenched fist, cursing under his breath as he impatiently waited. He twisted a glance back over his shoulder, taking a second look at the gray Ford Contour parked out front. He eyed its tires.

The pattern of the tread outside Sean's place wasn't legible due to some melting that morning, so Lumbergh couldn't say with certainty if they had come from the Contour. They sure looked the right size, though.

A sneer plagued his face. He could barely keep the anger stewing deep within him from pouring out and erupting into barbaric demands for the man inside to present himself. He finally heard movement from inside the home, and when the door slowly opened with a timid creak, Lumbergh pushed himself inside.

"What the hell?" squawked a wide-eyed Roy Hughes, his voice shooting up an extra octave. The dark, matted hair on his head and the redness in his eyes indicated that he had been asleep.

The owner and operator of the *Winston Beacon* was a short, trim man only an inch or two taller than Lumbergh. He normally wore circular rimless glasses that made him appear an intellectual—the academic type that might be found sitting inside of a Starbucks Coffee wearing polar fleece and sipping a latte. He sported a permanent five o'clock shadow around his chin, artificially trimmed to precision.

It was a look Hughes had most certainly worked hard to achieve as a way of compensating for his upbringing in a rural mountain town, as well as having been given the name *Roy* at birth.

"Why were you at Sean Coleman's house last night?" Lumbergh asked with fire in his eyes, directing a pointed finger at Hughes's chest.

Hughes's face tangled in confusion. Clad in a t-shirt from an Ivy League university he had never attended and sweatpants rolled at the cuffs, he blinked sporadically. "I don't know what you're talking about, Chief."

Lumbergh tightened his chin and glared through the reporter with such intensity that Hughes felt compelled to take a step back.

"Honest, Chief!" said Hughes. "I was here all last night."

Lumbergh wasn't buying it. "You wanted to snap some embarrassing photos of him, didn't you? Maybe walking around in his underwear for some bullshit *story* to print in your shitty paper!"

He threw his hand up in the air in a broad motion, casting a curse along the interior of the small workroom they stood in. Neatly clipped-out newspaper articles and columns from what Hughes's had deemed the *Winston Beacon's* finest work over the years wallpapered the room. Some of the clippings were framed. Others were simply laminated. There were even some award plaques displayed neatly and strategically, which Lumbergh could only assume had been earned during Hughes's father's tenure at the paper.

"It's an award-winning paper!" Hughes barked back, clearly offended.

"It's trash!" Lumbergh retorted. "But lucky for you I'm not here to haul you off for peeping through someone's window. I need to know what you saw last night. Was Sean with anyone?"

Hughes's eyes rolled up, and he threw both hands in the air. "I *wasn't* there, Chief! I don't know what in the hell you're talking about!"

Lumbergh continued glaring at him, his chest rising and declining as his nostrils spread open. He looked for a hint of deception in the newsman's eyes. To his surprise, he didn't see any.

"Why do you think I was at his house?" Hughes asked with a raised eyebrow, assuredly sensing a new story.

Lumbergh held his focus on Hughes for a while longer, his stomach tight from the sense of defeat that was brewing in his gut. *If it wasn't Hughes, who else could have been standing outside Sean's window?* "Roy, I'm going to ask you this one more time because it's *extremely* important. Don't fuck with me. A man's life is at stake."

Hughes's eyes widened upon hearing this. He licked his lips and his eyes scanned the small room, looking for a pencil or pen to write with.

Lumbergh continued. "I promise you that you will not get in any trouble if the answer is yes. Were you at Sean's house anytime within the last twenty-four hours?"

Hughes swallowed, his body almost trembling with the excitement he was failing to contain.

"No," he finally managed to answer before he enthusiastically added, "but what's going on? You have to tell me! A man's life is at stake? *Which* man? Did Sean beat somebody up again?" He nearly wore a full-out smile, likely envisioning big headlines.

Lumbergh's eye twitched at the reporter's opportunistic instincts. He nearly cursed him out but knew he couldn't afford to waste any more time. He turned and walked toward the front door with Hughes chasing after him.

"Oh come on, Chief!" Hughes pleaded. "You've got to tell me what's going on!"

"No I don't," said Lumbergh.

Just as he was about to leave through the open doorway, where a cold, light breeze was pushing its way in, he caught something out of the corner of his eye; a pile of papers were being shuffled by the wind across Hughes's work desk at the front of the room. The papers consisted of clipped-out newspaper articles. The top one included a large photo of a face that nearly stopped Lumbergh's heart—a face that had no sense being the focus of any current news cycle if Hughes was telling him the truth.

Lumbergh dashed over to the desk and riffled through the clippings.

"What?" Hughes asked.

There was a large manila file folder sprawled open below the articles and when Lumbergh saw that the name "Alvar Montoya" was written across its tab, his blood boiled. "Son of a bitch!"

He reached under his jacket and pulled out his Glock. He spun toward Hughes, whose eyes displayed sheer terror at the sight of the pure hatred fuming in the chief's face.

"I told you not to fuck with me, Roy!" Lumbergh's voice echoed off the walls.

He shoved his gun right between Hughes's eyes. The frightened newsman tripped backwards in an impulsive act of self-preservation. He stumbled on shaky legs before falling straight down to the floor on his butt. "What?" he cried out, hands up in the air as if he were being robbed. His face was taut with fear. "What are you talking about?"

"Why were you looking into the Alvar Montoya case?" Lumbergh screamed, unable to contain any sliver of composure. He kept his gun trained on Hughes. "Who did you see at Sean's house last night?"

"No one! I w-w-wasn't!" Hughes stammered. "I just haven't put the file away yet!"

"What does that mean?" Lumbergh demanded.

"Yesterday! He came over yesterday! He wanted to look through the Montoya archive again! He said he was doing more research! I let him! What's the big deal?"

"Who?" Lumbergh yelled savagely. "Who are you talking about?"

Chapter 16

"You can't go in there because it's a dang crime scene!" explained Jefferson. "You didn't learn that in any of your pricey college books? We can't let just any nitwit who strolls on by walk into a crime scene." He fought back the urge to smirk, enjoying a bit of a power trip at the moment.

"Come on, Officer Jefferson," replied Alex Martinez, wearing a broad smile and displaying only a hint of a Spanish accent. He had just arrived at Sean's place with the copies of Lautaro Montoya's mug shot, per Lumbergh's earlier request. "I'm not a *nitwit*. I work in the police station with you. I'm a colleague."

"A what?"

"A colleague. A coworker."

"You sure as hell ain't," Jefferson said with a chuckle. "You're an intern. A gofer. You don't even get paid. Hell, you smell too pretty to be a cop."

Martinez retained his smile. "But how am I supposed to learn about law enforcement if I don't get to do anything but odd jobs?"

"Well, I hear they need meter maids up in Lakeland. That might be a good start. They might even pay you."

"Oh. Come on," said Martinez, waving off the teasing with his hand. His short dark hair shone under the bright sun.

Jefferson suddenly erupted into a coughing fit that drew a wince from Martinez. When it ended, the officer leaned against the side of Martinez's dark-green Pontiac Sunfire and folded his arms in front of him. His grin widened in satisfaction.

"So what happened to the back of Sean's car? You know?"

The grin on Jefferson's face dissipated. "Uh, I don't know. He probably backed into a tree or something."

"Jefferson!" Lumbergh's voice blared out of the walkie-talkie clipped to Jefferson's belt.

The officer snatched it and held it to his mouth. "I'm here, Chief."

"Is anyone there with you?" asked Lumbergh, a hint of unease in his voice.

"No one important," Jefferson answered, winking at Martinez who was close enough to hear both sides of the conversation.

"Jefferson, I need to talk to you in private. It's of a personal matter."

Jefferson trained a perplexed look on the speaker. "Personal?"

Martinez widened his eyes, flashing Jefferson a simper.

"All right. Hold on," Jefferson spoke into the gadget, turning from Martinez. He walked out to the road, his stomach feeling anxious as he did. Once he was convinced he was out of earshot from Martinez, he acknowledged Lumbergh again.

"Who's all with you, Jefferson?" Lumbergh asked.

"Just Martinez. He brought copies of the Montoya mug shot. The boys from County haven't arrived yet. Why?"

"Listen carefully, Jefferson. Martinez is in on this somehow. He's been digging into the Montoya case."

"What?" Jefferson replied dismissively. "Are you kidding me?"

Jefferson turned toward the intern—a young man he had gotten to know well and had come to like over the past few months. Martinez was staring blankly back at him from across the street, leaning against the side of his rusted Sunfire.

"I just left Roy Hughes's house," Lumbergh continued. "He told me that Martinez has been asking him all about Montoya for weeks. He even came over yesterday to review the newspaper archives on the shootout."

"That doesn't mean he's tied up in what's going on," Jefferson replied. "Maybe he's doing a paper on the incident for one of his college classes."

"And he hasn't bothered to ask *me* about it?"

Jefferson sighed. He almost always trusted his boss's instincts, but he felt that this time his reasoning was thin.

Lumbergh continued. "There's more. When Oldhorse came to the office yesterday morning, he told me it didn't make sense why there weren't any foot imprints in the snow behind the building from the pig being hung."

"It snowed overnight," Jefferson replied. "The falling snow covered them up."

"It shouldn't have covered them up *completely*. The back of the building was protected from the wind. There weren't any drifts. Whoever was back there should have left foot impressions in the snow, if not detailed prints."

"I'm not following," Jefferson reluctantly admitted.

"Oldhorse asked me if it was possible that whoever had hung the pig had come inside through the front door, walked through the building to the back porch, and then done it. That would explain the lack of foot impressions in the back. I didn't see how that was possible though. I had locked both doors when I went home for dinner. They were both still locked when I came back. There was no sign of jimmying. No one broke in."

Jefferson felt his heart drop to his stomach. "An inside job," he whispered to himself.

"Jefferson, does Martinez have a key to the office?"

The officer swallowed hard. His hand shook as he raised the walkie-talkie close to his mouth. "Yeah. He does. There's a spare on the key ring I gave him for the plow truck."

"Jesus," replied Lumbergh. "He's got to be working with Montoya. He must have been the second person in Sean's house last night!"

Jefferson glared at Martinez from across the road, his complexion turning pale. Martinez was staring back. He looked emotionless as he tugged on what appeared to be a rubber band looped around his wrist. The officer forced himself to grin, hoping to conceal the anxiety he felt thundering through his veins. He turned his back to the intern again, uncertain that he could maintain a poker face.

"How in the hell could they know each other?" asked Jefferson in such a quiet, quivering voice that he had to repeat himself to Lumbergh.

"We'll figure that out later. Listen, I'm on my way back. I'll be there soon. Don't let him leave, and don't let him know we're onto him. That's the safest play right now if we want to find Sean. Got it?"

Jefferson nodded his head, glancing down at his sidearm. He fought back the urge to grab for it.

"Yeah," he muttered. "Got it."

He clipped the walkie-talkie back to his side, and when he turned to Martinez, he saw that the intern was sliding into the front seat of his car. Jefferson gasped.

"Wait!" the officer shouted out, a phony smile forced onto his face as he hustled across the street with his arm raised.

Martinez lowered his window.

"I need those mug shots from you!" said Jefferson.

Martinez squinted. "They're in your jacket pocket, Officer Jefferson," he said with a grin.

Jefferson remembered that he had indeed folded the sheets in half and shoved them in his liner pocket.

"Oh!" he said, awkwardly fumbling his hand around inside his jacket. "Yep, there they are!"

Martinez nodded politely and cranked the engine.

"Wait!" yelped Jefferson again, his mind desperate to discover the right words to keep Martinez from leaving. He placed his hand along the inside rim of the car door, obstructing the intern from rolling up his window.

A dubious expression formed along Martinez's face.

"Well what's your hurry, intern?" said Jefferson, his mouth

suddenly feeling dry. "Why don't you just stick around for a few minutes?"

"Why?" Martinez replied, the cordial smile returning to his face.

"Because. . .I was going to . . . show you the crime scene. I mean, if you still want to see it." Jefferson coughed.

"I can see it now?"

"Yeah. Sure. Why not? You brought up a good point about needing to gain some experience in this type of thing."

The plastered grin remained on Martinez's face, but his eyes went blank—dead as if there was suddenly nothing behind them. His head lowered in the direction of Jefferson's walkie-talkie that dangled from his side, seemingly examining it for a moment. When he lifted his face to again meet Jefferson's contrived, urging smile, the officer saw something different in his demeanor—something unexplainably dark and treacherous.

Martinez began snapping the rubber band on his wrist in rapid succession. His grin rose at its corners and twisted into what could only be described as an exuberant grimace that suddenly seemed larger than his face itself. It was as if he were wearing a rubber Halloween mask that was being pulled from the back of his head as tightly as possible in order to distort it into only a caricature of its original form.

Jefferson's heart stopped. His eyes exuded apprehension that he tried to hide but couldn't.

In a flash, Martinez's body went low and his hand slid in under his seat.

Jefferson instinctively went for his sidearm, but the adrenaline rushing through his body gave him trouble with his holster strap. When Martinez rose back up, Jefferson caught a glimpse of a dark gray revolver clenched in his hand. Jefferson immediately lunged toward the front of the car, dropping flat to his chest and taking cover in front of the grill.

A barrage of gunfire erupted that echoed off the surrounding hills and rocks as if it was being returned from far away. From the snowy ground, Jefferson ignored the pain of his rough landing and fumbled for his gun as bullets sliced through the air just inches above his head.

"*Mentiroso!*" Martinez shouted wildly from inside the car. "*Todos ustedes son unos mentirosos!*"

Jefferson fumbled again for his firearm as metal chards from lead entering the hood of the car sprayed in every direction. This time, the officer managed to remove the gun from its holster. He struggled to control his rapid breathing, and when the firing stopped for a moment, presumably because Martinez needed to reload, Jefferson was left with no choice but to act.

He shoved his hand up over the top of the hood and began firing into the windshield, keeping his head low and his aim blind.

He heard the transmission inside the car switch gears, and before he could process what was happening, the car sped into reverse. The tires spun quickly, but managed to gain enough traction to put some distance between the car and the officer.

Jefferson knew that he was now a sitting duck without any cover. "God-dammit!"

He rose to a knee and continued firing at the car's windshield, desperate not to give Martinez a chance to capitalize on his advantage. He saw most of his earlier shots had entered the passenger's side of the windshield. There was no one visible behind the wheel. Martinez had to be ducking down.

Jefferson continued firing his gun until it was empty. He reached into his side for another clip. Martinez's head popped up from about twenty yards out. The same sadistic smile still lined his face. He quickly cranked the steering wheel hard to the right. Brake pads squealed before the car did an almost perfect 180-degree turn along the slippery road.

Before Jefferson could switch out the clips in his gun, Martinez was already building momentum in the opposite direction. He whipped his walkie-talkie to his mouth. "Chief! Martinez knows we're onto him! We exchanged gunfire! He's headed back toward town!"

The Sunfire disappeared from view around a row of white trees. All Jefferson could do was pursue on foot, but he only lumbered forward a few steps before slipping and crashing down to his hands and knees on the road.

When he pulled himself up to his feet, he saw a small pool of red snow before him. He looked down at his stomach and found the side of his shirt around his waist saturated with blood.

"Shit! Shit! Shit!" he whimpered in panic. He placed his hand over where he believed a bullet had entered his flesh.

Lumbergh's jaw tightened when he saw Martinez's car whip into view up the road. The Pontiac tossed clumps of snow through the air behind it as it sped directly toward the police cruiser. Having heard Jefferson's panicked message over the radio, he knew the intern was armed and desperate.

He spotted something flop out from the driver side window of Martinez's car, and a second later, gunshots popped off. Lumbergh gasped and pulled his own gun from its holster. Being right-handed, he knew he couldn't swing his gun outside his window as Martinez had. He hugged the steering wheel with his thighs and began firing through his own windshield. A loud crunch accompanied each new hole that was punched through the glass, leaving a splintered mess in its wake.

Lumbergh knew he'd connected with Martinez or his car as the intern suddenly lost control. The Sunfire slammed grill-first into a large pine. Wide sheets of snow dropped from the tree's upper limbs and blanketed the car.

Seeing how demolished the front end of Martinez's car was, Lumbergh knew the intern wasn't going anywhere.

White smoke poured out from under the Pontiac's hood as Lumbergh slid the cruiser to a stop and exited the vehicle. With his gun drawn, he cautiously approached the car and ordered Martinez to raise his hands and hold them outside the window.

To the chief's surprise, Martinez did just that after groggily shaking his head.

"Slowly. Grab your gun by its barrel and toss it out onto the road, Martinez!"

The intern complied, a freakish smile forming on his face. He didn't appear hurt.

Within seconds, Lumbergh was pulling Martinez from the car and slamming him chest-first down to the frozen road. Only when the chief placed his knee deep between Martinez's shoulder blades did the intern begin to squirm.

Lumbergh used his good arm to hold the intern's wrist against his back. A switch seemed to flip on inside Martinez and he began screaming hysterically as if he were being tortured. Lumbergh struggled to slap on the cuffs.

"Mentiroso!" the intern wailed repeatedly.

Rapid footsteps suddenly approached from behind Lumbergh. Before he could turn his head, Jefferson plopped down to his knees beside him. The officer angrily yanked Martinez's wrist up to his shoulder blades, forcing an end to the intern's temper tantrum. Martinez howled in agony.

The two men cuffed Martinez's hands behind his back. Martinez moaned pathetically in either pain or defeat when they yanked him to his feet. Lumbergh opened the back door of his cruiser after a quick pat-down.

"I've been shot," moaned Jefferson, pressing his hand to his side. "I don't know how bad it is."

The chief's head whipped to his officer's scared face, then down to his side where his shirt was saturated with blood. Lumbergh snarled and grabbed Martinez by the back of his neck. He slammed

Martinez's head violently into the roof of the car, just above the opened door.

Martinez's moaning ended. It was replaced with a silent, gaping cringe and glazed eyes. The intern fell forward into the backseat. With the help of Jefferson, Lumbergh shoved the rest of Martinez's body inside and slammed the door behind him.

Lumbergh attended to his officer, peeling off his jacket and holding it to his wound. Jefferson looked at him as he did, eyes riddled with anxiety and uncertainty.

Off in the distance, the sound of sirens could be heard, growing closer with each passing moment. Knowing that officers from the sheriff's department would be there at any second brought only marginal relief.

"Let me look," Lumbergh told Jefferson, dropping to a knee and attempting to inspect the wound more closely.

"What the hell does *mentiroso* mean?" Jefferson asked, not so much directing the question to the chief but rather thinking aloud.

Lumbergh glanced up at him. "It means *liar*."

Chapter 17

"Where's Lautaro Montoya?" Lumbergh asked in the most professional tone he could muster. His eye twitched from the agonizing restraint he was imposing on himself. "Where's Sean?"

Alex Martinez was cuffed to a wooden chair in the secretarial area of the Winston Police Station, the largest room in the building. His left wrist was raw and red, not from the handcuffs, but from a rubber band he'd been wearing around it like a bracelet. It appeared that he'd been habitually snapping it against his skin, like a nervous tick. The band was removed at the station.

A uniformed county deputy stood behind Martinez with his arms crossed in front of his chest, ready to step in physically if the prisoner gave him a reason.

A dismissive chuckle dropped from Martinez's lips as a large swollen and discolored bump on his head formed a shadow along the side of his face. Clad in a t-shirt and jeans, he leaned forward a bit to look down at his feet. One of his tennis shoes had been taken from him. His big toe hung outside a large hole in his worn and dirty sock.

"Why did you need my shoe?" Martinez asked. The sly grin on his face indicated he already knew the answer. His eyes lifted to meet the deadly serious glare that Lumbergh had trained on him. The expression on the chief's face only prompted a wider grin from Martinez. "The great police chief, Gary Allen Lumbergh," the intern said mockingly. "The slayer of Alvar Montoya. Only, not really, huh?"

Lumbergh said nothing, unsure of Martinez's meaning but

feeling the need to let him get out what he wanted to say and with luck learn something from his words.

"Who's this?" Martinez abruptly asked, acknowledging a portly man who was standing at Lumbergh's side.

The man wore a brown uniform and a tightly trimmed goatee. He had dark, curly hair topped by a felt cowboy hat and his heavily browed face exuded a level of seriousness that mirrored Lumbergh.

"I'm Sheriff Richard Redick," the man answered in a deep, authoritative voice. "Now answer the chief's question if you want things to go easier on you."

Martinez's eyes narrowed but his grin remained. "Dick Reddick? Is that really your name, amigo? I bet that was a tough one growing up with. Yes?"

His Spanish accent was thicker than Lumbergh had ever heard it over the months Martinez had served under him. There had always been a trace of it, which made sense. Martinez had told Lumbergh the first time they met that he was born in Mexico, and that Spanish was his first language. It was clear now that he had spent far more time in the country than he had let on.

"How do you know Lautaro Montoya?" asked Lumbergh. "Are you related to him?"

Martinez rolled his eyes and shook his head. "No Chief. *No somos familia.*"

"Why did you go to work for me? What did Montoya tell you to do?"

Martinez chuckled again before shaking his head. An expression of disgust developed on his face. "I thought you were some kind of *super-cop*, Chief. A hero like few others. I thought you were a man who single-handedly tracked down a homicidal maniac in the Colorado Mountains—a maniac responsible for more death and pain than any of you gringos will ever know. And when you found that man, you stared him in the eye without fear and put a bullet right between his eyes."

Lumbergh said nothing. He wasn't sure what Martinez was getting at, but at least he had him talking. He felt the best move was to let him continue, and perhaps he'd hang himself with his own words.

Martinez continued. "That's the story they tell back in my village, you know? In front of fires. At night. They have murals painted of you on the outside of buildings and long walls, standing over Alvar Montoya's corpse. Only you're eight feet tall. Not the baby pig I now see standing before me."

"What's your point, Martinez?" Sheriff Redick barked, taking a step forward. His cheeks were red with vigor.

Lumbergh placed his hand on Redick's arm. His cautioning eyes pled with the sheriff to let Martinez continue. Martinez did.

"They stick thank-you letters to those walls. They leave flowers. Old women. Children. Anyone who lost a loved one to the Montoya brothers. Some fall down on their knees and thank God for you. Hell, I even once heard talk of a Chief Lumbergh comic book being made. They probably would have given you a *luchadore* sidekick."

The grin suddenly disappeared from Martinez's face. His eyes formed a scowl, one that he centered in on Lumbergh.

"If they knew what I knew they'd spit on those murals," Martinez said. "You're a charlatan who isn't worth two pesos."

"What is it that you *know*, exactly?" asked Redick, adjusting his hat.

Martinez scoffed at the sheriff's question, shaking his head before letting his gaze fall to the floor.

Lumbergh took his turn. "If the Montoya brothers are responsible for so many terrible things in your village, why are you helping one of them?"

Martinez lifted his face to the ceiling. An immense grin returned to it. His eyes glared at the above lights. "The fact that you're asking me that is only more proof you're a fraud, Chief Lumbergh. You're neither a man of great courage, nor a man of great intelligence." The intern lowered his eyes to meet his questioner before continuing. "You know . . . your brother-in-law looks very cute when he's asleep."

Aggression exploded beneath Lumbergh's skin. He clenched his teeth and lunged forward, using his good hand to grab Martinez around his throat and squeeze it mercilessly. "Where's Sean?" he screamed as Martinez's eyes bulged from their sockets and his mouth gaped open. "No more games!"

Lumbergh quickly felt Redick's arms wrapped around him, trying to pull him off of Martinez.

Lumbergh wouldn't let go.

"Chief!" Redick yelled.

The deputy standing behind Martinez grabbed onto Lumbergh's wrist with both of his hands and pried his clenched fingers from Martinez. Lumbergh and Redick stumbled backward into the desk behind them, with Lumbergh nearly falling to the floor.

Martinez coughed and gagged loudly before erupting into hideous, strained laughter.

Redick escorted Lumbergh out into the hallway and back to his office.

"What in the hell are you doing?" he snarled.

"This guy knows where Sean is!" Lumbergh snapped back. "My brother-in-law may already be dead and he's jerking us around!"

"Listen. If Montoya wanted Sean dead, he would have killed him last night and left his body for you to find. We don't know what's going on with Sean, and no one can blame you for being pissed, but we can't just beat a confession out of this guy!"

Lumbergh's chest pumped in and out with deep breaths as he stared down the sheriff. "Why not?"

The sheriff's eyes widened. "What's happened to you, Gary? When we first met, you were a disciplined law enforcement professional. As clean as a whistle. You did everything by the book. Everything! You prided yourself on it, and you were a role model for all of us." Redick shook his head, taking a moment to raise his hand and lift his hat just long enough to scratch his forehead. "Some killer breaks out of a Mexican prison, and he's been threatening you and your family, and today's the first I hear about it? If someone like that's in my county, I need to know about it! Hell, the *feds* probably need to know about it!" He threw his hands in the air. "What were you going to do, Gary? Have one of your men just shoot this guy on sight and sort out the legalities later?"

Lumbergh spoke quickly. "You don't know what this family is capable of, Richard. Alvar Montoya was as sick a son of a bitch as you could imagine. Killing was the man's hobby. You heard what Martinez said just now. We don't even know what all these brothers did in Mexico. The body count could be in the dozens!"

"It doesn't matter. We're not a lawless country like Mexico. We live in the United States!" Redick emphasized. "We have a justice system! I don't need to tell you this stuff."

Lumbergh knew the sheriff was correct, and his silence seemed to acknowledge that fact to Redick. Lumbergh also understood that the sheriff had always been more of a politician at heart than an instinctive pursuant of justice. His record meant something to him. If he felt that there was a chance of a case dismissal due to police brutality, he'd probably go as far as *personally* advising Martinez to lawyer-up.

"Listen," said Redick. "I'm certain we can get the D.A. to cut this jackass some type of deal in return for his cooperation. If he's really just Montoya's stooge, it shouldn't be a problem."

Lumbergh shot him a wicked glare. "He's far more than a stooge. He shot one of my officers! What kind of deal do you think they're going to want to give him?"

"I know that, but Jefferson's going to be just fine. The paramedics said the bullet passed right through. By now, he's probably propped up in some hospital bed in Lakeland, flirting with a nurse."

Lumbergh took exception to the sheriff's cavalier attitude toward his officer's well-being. Redick had clearly never been shot at or forced into the kind of life or death situation that Jefferson had just been through. If he had, he never would have made such a lame joke. Lumbergh worked to calm himself down.

"Richard," he began in a more mundane tone, "I'm not convinced Martinez is going to roll. He worked in this building for months. What we're dealing with today was part of a larger plan. There's clearly some kind of personal stake in this for him. I'm not sure what it is yet, but the man has clearly pledged his loyalty to Montoya."

The sheriff offered no visual reaction to what the chief said, but Lumbergh hoped his silence meant that he was letting the words bounce off the inside of his head.

"What do you want to do then?" Redick finally asked.

"Don't process him yet. Don't put him into the system. Give me some more time with him. Let me figure—"

Before he could continue, both men heard a man's voice stream out of a black police radio hooked to Redick's belt. "Sheriff, this is Chester. Come back?"

Redick pulled the radio to his mouth, its long antenna nearly poking him in the eye as he did. He turned up the volume and acknowledged his deputy.

"We've got a match on Martinez's shoeprint at the crime scene, but he wasn't either of the two people who dragged Coleman out."

Lumbergh exchanged a confused glance with Redick.

Redick spoke into the radio. "Where did you find it?"

"The tracks on the side of the house that lead into the forest, parallel to the ones Chief Lumbergh left this morning."

Lumbergh felt his stomach tighten. He reached for the radio. Redick handed it to him.

"Chester, this is Chief Lumbergh. Is it possible that one of the two sets of prints that led in and out of the house also belong to Martinez? At two different times, wearing two different pairs of shoes?"

"I sure don't think so, Chief," the deputy replied. "The size is wrong. The weight and stride look wrong, too. I think the smaller set might even belong to a woman. The larger set is from a man larger and heavier than Martinez."

"What do you think that means?" Redick asked Lumbergh.

Lumbergh thanked the deputy and handed the radio back to Redick. "It means Martinez didn't help take Sean."

"He could have been a lookout for the other two," Redick said. "You know, for headlights coming down the road?"

"No. That wouldn't make any sense. Martinez wouldn't have even been able to see the road from that side of the house. And there wasn't any interaction between him and the other two. None."

"What are you saying, Gary?" asked Redick. "That he had nothing to do with Sean's abduction? How can that be?"

Lumbergh didn't know the answer. His gaze went blank as he tried to piece together what the new information meant. His eyes finally focused back on Redick. "Even if he wasn't in on it, he saw what happened. He had to have. None of the accusations I've been throwing at him since the moment I tossed him into the back of my car has come as a surprise to him," he told the sheriff. "He's been playing up to it. That crack about Sean being asleep? I never told him that Sean was dragged outside. You know, as opposed to being forced into the car at gunpoint or something. He knows what happened in Sean's house last night. He *saw* what happened."

Redick opened his mouth to respond, but before he could utter a word, both men's attention was suddenly seized by the racket of the front door of the building being swung open and crashing into the wall behind it.

Lumbergh darted out into the hallway where he saw a breathless Toby Parker stumbling through the doorway. There were bloodstains smeared along his thick winter coat. His eyes were riddled with sheer fear and panic, and when they found Lumbergh, he screamed out.

"Ron Oldhorse is hurt bad, Chief! He's bleeding. He's out in my mom's car! Hurry!"

His words prompted a finally quieted Alex Martinez to erupt

into hysterical laughter in the next room. The sound of his deranged glee flooded throughout the entire building as he stomped his feet on the floor.

"This is perfect!" he cried out. "The *real* hero has arrived!"

Chapter 18

When a blur of light streamed in between Sean's awakening, narrowly open eyelids, he gasped and quickly spun to his back. Feeling he was still under attack, he instinctively threw a wild punch into the air above him. He connected with nothing.

The abrupt movement was followed by a wave of pain that tore through his skull, and a sense in his stomach that he might need to vomit. He held his forearm in front of his eyes, dimming the penetrating glare from the overhead light.

His throat was dry, as if he hadn't had a thing to drink in a week. He let out a heaving cough and turned to his side, realizing for the first time that he was no longer in his living room.

It wasn't hardwood that was sprawled out beneath him, but concrete, gray in color and cold to the touch. In fact, it was so cold and the air around him was so damp that he thought for a moment he was outside among the winter elements.

He wasn't. Four imposing metal walls surrounded him in a room that was probably twelve-by-twelve feet in size. A tall ceiling stared down. Its two rows of fluorescent lights began to seem less interrogatory and undefined once Sean's eyes had time to adjust. When clarity prevailed, a staggered collection of fire sprinkler heads and piping that hung from the ceiling came into view. Mounted along the upper area of the back wall was a long metal box that housed four fans. None was moving. A large metal door stood at the front of the room.

Within moments, he realized that he was sitting in an old walk-in freezer. It wasn't all that different than one he used to move stock in and out of when he worked at a restaurant in Winston for a short time as a teenager. This one, however, was stripped bare other than a thin mattress from a cot that had been tossed on the floor beside him, a large rubber bucket in the corner, and a rectangular, topless cardboard box that sat near the door. The word "peaches" and a brand name were written on the side.

There was no shelving inside. It appeared to have been taken out based on some floor discoloration and long, even scratches along the concrete that led underneath the door.

He could hear no operating sound from the fans at all. The brisk temperature inside the room, however, suggested that they had been running fairly recently. Whatever his captors had in store for him, it wasn't to freeze him to death. Still, he could see his breath.

He climbed to his knees and then to his feet, taking a moment to let his groggy body find some balance and stability. He hadn't a clue what had been injected into his body, but whatever it was had worked fast and kept him out for some time. There was a moment when he remembered gaining consciousness earlier, just for a second or two. He was sure he had been crammed in the trunk of a vehicle.

There was a small window embedded in the upper half of the freezer door. It was circular and resembled a porthole on a submarine. It was no more than a foot in diameter. The glass was thick but clear. Sean couldn't see through it, however, because something was placed over it on the other side—something of dark material. Perhaps a coat.

He reached for the long bar handle of the door, tried to push it out, but found, unsurprisingly, that it was locked. He took a couple of steps back, then lunged forward, slamming the sole of his boot squarely into the handle. The hit was solid and loud, but generated no better results. He repeated the move over and over again, sometimes edging his foot up higher and sometimes lower, looking for a weak point with any amount of give. He found none.

"Fuck!" he grumbled when his leg began to ache.

His gaze crept down to the cardboard box beside him. Sitting inside it were a half-dozen bottled waters, a couple of peaches, a bag of store-bought cookies, and a few slices of pizza that appeared to be leftovers.

"Room service," he muttered. He peered over his shoulder at the bucket sitting in the corner.

"And the bathroom."

He regulated his breathing as he carefully assessed his predicament. A dozen thoughts drained from his head like water through a colander. He thought about Jessica, knowing that she was the one who had brought him to the floor with a taser. She was involved in what had happened to Andrew Carson—either directly or indirectly. That was crystal clear. Beyond that, he understood little else. As hard as it was to believe, there was a sinister side to the quiet, attractive woman he had watched for weeks back at the plasma bank. She lived in a world of secrets.

Sean was more than a physical prisoner. He was a prisoner to the stinging uncertainty that clouded his fate. He recognized that the natural inclination of most people would be to feel fear in such a situation, but all he felt was anger. He was angry that he let himself be taken from his home. He was angry that his captors had the gall to toy with him so dangerously.

"Jessica!" he shouted. He savagely slammed his fist against the door. "Get over here! I know you and your asshole boyfriend are out there!" The truth was that Sean didn't know that, but as he'd once learned from an episode of *The Fall Guy*, it was best, even in weakness, to exude awareness and a sense that you're holding some cards. "Jessica!"

He pressed the side of his head up against the small window that still hosted a trace of frost. He listened carefully for movement while angling his eyes to try and see past the edge of whatever material was covering the window from the other side. He came up empty on both ends.

He paced the room with his hands on his hips, controlling his breathing and calming himself down. He eyed the pipes that lined the ceiling and thought about trying to dislodge one of them to use as a possible weapon. He couldn't quite reach them, however, and they were too narrow and pressed too tightly to the ceiling for him to jump up and hang from one until his weight brought it down.

He retrieved the bucket from the corner of the room and flipped it upside down. He steadied his weight on top of it, careful not to step in the center and risk an implosion. Some lingering grogginess worked against his sense of balance but he managed to stay upright.

The pipes were thin enough that he couldn't hook his thick fingers around them well with how little room there was between them and the ceiling. He impulsively searched his pockets, looking for his keys to try to use one as a miniature crowbar. They were missing. His pockets had been emptied and his belt had even been removed. This kept his pants low around his waist, being that he had lost some weight in recent months. He found himself repeatedly tugging them up while he stood on the bucket.

When it became clear that he was getting nowhere, he dropped back down to the floor. He circled to the side of the freezer evaporator that hosted the row of fans. There, he saw another pipe, this one copper, leading out from the wall. It was likely protecting the electrical wiring used to power the machine.

The pipe was as thin as those that lined the ceiling, but its horizontal mount left some space between it and the ceiling. The pipe wasn't long, possibly a foot in length. It wasn't the ideal weapon, but he believed that he might be able to use the end of it to smash through the glass of the window on the door.

He leapt into the air and wrapped both hands around the pipe.

He dangled from it before realizing that it would take more than his dead weight to pull it down. He wildly yanked on it, thrusting his hips and legs up and down to try to work it loose. He growled before planting his feet on the wall beside him and, using his newfound leverage, leaned back and pulled. He felt the pipe bend. After a few more seconds, the end that entered the wall finally snapped. Sparks flew as he fell to the floor. He managed to land on his feet before stumbling backwards to his butt. A bare, insulated electrical wire was left hanging from the wall while the pipe dangled loosely from the evaporator.

He stood up and twisted the pipe counter-clockwise until the strand of metal that had kept it attached to the evaporator snapped.

He grinned. When he turned to face the door, however, his hope quickly vanished.

Standing in the now open doorway was the man who had broken through the back door of Sean's home. He held a black revolver in his hand and it was pointed directly at Sean. A thin strip of duct tape bound his glasses together at the center and there was deep bruising and some swelling under his eyes. A gauze bandage crossed the bridge of his nose. They were all battle marks from his earlier altercation with Sean. Having switched out of his black attire, he was now wearing a navy-blue sweatshirt, jeans, and tennis shoes.

"Drop the pipe and kick it over here," he instructed Sean.

"No," Sean said brazenly.

The man's eyes widened, urging Sean to appreciate the situation he was in. "Excuse me?"

"If you were gonna kill me, you'd have done it already."

Clearly angry, he gripped his gun tighter. "Sean, no one *wants* to kill you, but let me assure you that I *will* pull this trigger if I need to."

Sean's eyes narrowed. "You will, huh?"

"Yes. I will. You've gotten yourself mixed up in some serious shit that doesn't concern you, and you've put us in a pretty tough spot."

"Good," Sean sneered.

The man shook his head in disgust and repeated his order for Sean to slide over the pipe.

Sean ignored him. "What did you do with Andrew Carson, you son of a bitch?"

He glared at Sean for a moment before responding. "He should be the least of your worries right now. Now, if you don't want to spend the rest of your time in here wearing a bullet in your gut, you'll toss over that pipe right now."

Sean returned the man's glare, unsure of what to read from his demeanor. Back at home, the man hadn't come across like a professional. He certainly wasn't someone who could handle himself in a physical situation. He was, however, clearly desperate and thus unpredictable. He might actually be willing to do what he was threatening.

He side-tossed the pipe to the man, who managed to snag it in the air without deviating his attention from Sean. The man tossed it behind him onto the floor outside of the freezer. It landed with a series of clangs.

The room behind the man was barely lit and there wasn't much to see. The edge of a wooden table. A couple of broomsticks leaning up against a wall. Beyond them all, however, Sean was sure he could make out the first few steps of a staircase leading upwards in the dark. He had to be in a basement. The man's body obscured the rest of Sean's view.

"Don't try any more of this bullshit," warned the man. "We'll know if you do."

"What's your plan here, ace?" asked Sean. "Am I supposed to *live* down here?"

"For now," he answered. "Just be thankful we didn't tie you up."

"Just be thankful *you're* still breathing," Sean retorted. "The next time I get my hands on you, you won't be." He fixed a wicked glare on the man to let him know that he meant it.

The look on the man's face suggested that he believed Sean. He began slowly inching his way backward, keeping his gun trained forward. Sean's stare continued to burn a hole right through him. Once the man was standing in the doorway, his hand latched onto the freezer door and prepared to close it.

Sean spoke again. "When do I get to see Norman Booth?"

The man froze, his eyes growing larger. "What?" He took a step forward as his hand shook.

Sean's question had clearly struck a nerve. "Booth. I know he's here. When do I get to see him?"

There was a crackle in the man's voice—an unmistakable sense of breathlessness that dropped from his mouth. He asked quickly, "What do you know about Norman Booth?"

Sean smiled at the man's disheveled demeanor. "I know that he's the man calling the shots, and that you're just his monkey."

To Sean's surprise, his words evoked what seemed to be a sense of relief in the man's posture. His lips curled at the corners. Whatever leverage Sean had earned by bringing up Norman Booth's name appeared to have swiftly disintegrated. Sean didn't understand why.

"Enjoy your stay, Mr. Coleman," the man spoke confidently. "If you behave yourself, you'll get out of this unharmed."

He exited the freezer.

As the door was closing shut, Sean was half-tempted to try and rush it, but the plan seemed too risky, especially with him being unarmed. The door closed with a click, followed soon afterwards by a muffled snap that Sean guessed was created from a padlock being secured.

"Remember what I said, asshole!" he yelled with his hand cupped to his mouth. "What you got last time was just a taste!"

The man said nothing in return. His response came in the form of the overhead lights inside the freezer going dark.

Sean's penance for *misbehaving*.

Chapter 19

O ldhorse was slumped awkwardly along the backseat of Joan Parker's car. Wrapped in a sun-bleached, woven blanket with one of his legs outstretched to the side, the desperately weak man fought through the immense pain of his injuries. He grimaced as he spoke carefully, telling the police chief in spurts of breath that it was Alex Martinez who was responsible for what had happened to him. He had smelled the scent of Martinez's aftershave just before the blast.

"It was revenge," he uttered. "He knows what I did to Montoya."

Toby nearly cut him off, out of breath himself. "Ron Oldhorse wouldn't let us take him to the hospital until we brought him here first, Chief Lumbergh. He needed to tell you about Alex."

The boy explained how they had stopped by the cabin with a dish of peach cobbler, which was Oldhorse's favorite—a fact that the boy was irritatingly adamant about. They had found his home in ruin and Oldhorse lying unconscious behind it, a bloody mess. Joan took over the telling of the story when her son got too caught up in its irrelevant details. Both Parkers' swollen faces showed that they had been sobbing most of the way back to town.

Oldhorse was barely recognizable to Lumbergh. Dried blood coated much of his weathered face. What looked to be a large, white t-shirt—stained crimson red—was wrapped around his forehead. Sections of his long, mangled hair were singed from the blast. The chief could only imagine what the rest of the rugged man's body looked like under the blanket.

Lumbergh told Oldhorse that Martinez was already in custody, then he and Redick carefully moved the injured man into the sheriff's car. Joan and Toby got inside with him.

"I'm sorry I can't see this through with you, Chief," muttered Oldhorse.

"It's all right. You've done plenty. Just get yourself taken care of." Lumbergh considered telling Oldhorse about Sean, but decided not to. He felt his friend didn't need to worry about it. He also didn't want to further upset Toby, who idolized Sean.

Lumbergh was about to close the car door when he heard Oldhorse speak his name. He poked his head inside to hear what his wounded comrade wanted to say.

Oldhorse leaned forward as best he could. "A shark doesn't let a pilot fish kill its prey."

Lumbergh squinted at the cryptic statement, letting its meaning soak through his head.

In no time, the deputy who had previously been watching Martinez was sitting behind the steering wheel of the sheriff's car. He sped through the parking lot with his three passengers inside and tore up the largely melted road toward Lakeland. Sirens howled away.

Redick received a radio call seconds later, before the men even had a chance to step inside the police station. Another deputy, Bartels, was on the other end, one that had been sent to Lakeland. He was reporting in from the motel that matched up to an orange key that had been discovered in Martinez's pocket during his pat-down.

With the possibility of Sean Coleman being held inside the room, there was probable cause to enter—along with the emphatic consent of the motel's owner who had had his own reservations about the quirky tenant.

"The guy's a nut-job, Sheriff," said the deputy from inside the motel room.

"Tell us something we don't know, Bartels," replied Redick.

"He's got a hard-on for Lumbergh. All kinds of photos of him in here. Some are from newspapers. It looks like he even took some of them himself, from a distance, probably without the chief's knowledge."

Lumbergh shook his head, angry with himself for never picking up on any suspicious behavior from the young man he had had over to his house several times for dinner and cordial conversation.

The deputy continued. "He scribbled some Spanish shit all over a bunch of this stuff. A single word with red pen or marker."

Lumbergh snatched the radio from Redick's hand. "Does it say *mentiroso*?"

"Uh. Yeah. How did you know that?" came Bartels' voice.

"Son of a bitch," Lumbergh whispered. He then asked, "What else is in his room? Anything that can get us anywhere on Sean?"

"Yeah. He's got a bunch of video tapes in here. Hold on. There's already one in the VCR. This thing's been beat to shit. I hope it still works."

Lumbergh and Redick exchanged pensive glances. A moment later, the chief heard his own voice blast out through the radio speaker.

"This is the first I've heard of this allegation. I'm certainly willing to discuss this topic with the county sheriff if there are any facts that need to be ironed out."

"It's a press conference, Chief," the deputy's voice weighed in. "You're standing outside your house in it."

"Is that where the tape was when you started it, Bartels? You didn't forward it or rewind it all, did you?"

"No, sir. Sir, I'm also seeing some building material in here, laid out on a nightstand. Pipes. Wiring. He might have been trying to make a crude bomb."

"Yeah," answered Lumbergh. "He did."

"Sir?"

"Does anything else stick out in the room, Bartels? Anything obvious? We can go through the pictures and tapes later."

"Well. . . Other than what I've already described, there's not much in here. The place looks like it was barely lived in. That's odd, because the motel owner tells me he's been staying here for months."

The deputy's statement jarred Lumbergh. He'd been led to believe that Martinez had lived in an apartment with roommates while he took criminal justice courses at a community college. He even had an address on file somewhere, which had to be fake. Being that Martinez was an unpaid intern, Lumbergh's office was never compelled to verify the address at the time of his hire.

"I've got some clothes hanging in the closet and folded in some of the drawers," said the deputy, who was continuing to work his way through the motel room.

"Anything that would fit a larger man than Martinez?" asked Lumbergh. "Any women's clothes? Is there any sign at all that more than one person was staying with him?"

After a few moments, the deputy answered. "I don't think so. The clothes all look like his. There's only one bed in the room. He's got a busted lamp here in his trashcan, along with a McDonald's bag and some candy wrappers."

Lumbergh could hear the sound of crumpling papers.

"The receipt stapled to the bag only shows a single meal. Egg McMuffin Combo. With cheese."

Lumbergh rolled his eyes.

"There are some other receipts in here," continued the deputy.

"From where?"

"A couple from a diner in Winston. A gas station in Lakeland. Wait a minute. Here's one that looks to be for the bomb supplies, at least some of them."

Lumbergh asked where the items were purchased.

"A hardware store in . . . Las Cruces?"

Lumbergh's eyes nearly bulged out of his head. "Las Cruces, New Mexico?" he breathlessly asked.

"Yes. NM."

"Cash or charge? Is there a name on it?"

"He charged it himself. *Alex Martinez*."

"What was the date of the charge?"

When Bartels answered that it was January 7 of the current year, Lumbergh tossed the radio to Redick, who was unprepared for it, fumbling it in his hands and nearly letting it drop to the snowy ground.

The chief briskly jumped up onto the porch at the front of the police station and raced inside. He snagged a clipboard off a sidewall above the reception desk and slammed it down flat. Quickly licking his thumb, he fingered through the short stack of papers pinned to its base. He soon verified that the three days Martinez had taken off earlier in the month for a family emergency spanned from January sixth to the eighth.

The sheriff reentered the station, meeting Lumbergh's enlightened glare with confusion.

"What is it?" Redick asked.

Lumbergh didn't answer. Instead, he hurried to the small, barred holding cell where Martinez had been placed. The intern was sitting on a short metal bench bolted to the cement floor; his legs sprawled out in front of him and his fingers interlaced behind his head as if he were relaxing.

Lumbergh glared at him, his chest throbbing along with his pulse, watching the hint of another snide smile begin to form on Martinez's lips. He didn't let him finish it.

"You're not working with Lautaro Montoya at all," he began.

Martinez's eyes glazed over as if his hand had just been caught in a cookie jar. The smile slowly dissipated.

"You don't know any more about where he is than I do. He

doesn't know you. You don't know him. You don't even know if he ever left Mexico, do you?"

Martinez was silent.

"Those calls I received. The threats. They didn't come from Montoya. They came from you—from a cell phone you bought in Las Cruces. That pig strung up at the back door. What happened at Oldhorse's cabin. It was all you. Nobody else."

The intern turned his face to the side, suddenly unable to make eye contact with Lumbergh. Redick watched from beside the chief, not saying a thing.

"This isn't about Alvar Montoya at all, is it?" Lumbergh continued. "It's about some sick obsession you have with *me*."

Martinez shook his head, seemingly in annoyance. A deep sigh left his mouth, followed with an unexpected giggle.

Redick cringed at the nonsensical reaction.

Lumbergh's patience had been expended. "What do you want?" he roared in a voice so loud that the two other men in the room jumped. A vein protruded at the center of Lumbergh's reddened forehead as his body shook.

Martinez's unfocused eyes nervously darted back and forth. When they stopped, they rose to meet the raw anger in Lumbergh's face. Martinez slowly rose to his feet and walked to the steel bars that separated him from the lawmen. He rested his forehead at the center of two of the bars as he glared at Lumbergh.

"I'm not the one who was obsessed with you, baby pig," he said in a tone that carried a lifetime of exhaustive torment.

Lumbergh and Martinez stared at each other intently, neither man's eyes revealing a hint of subservience.

Redick broke the stalemate. "Who was obsessed with him then, Martinez?"

Martinez's eyes narrowed. His face shifted into a sneer. "*Mi madre*," he uttered with unfiltered disgust.

The chief didn't visibly react to his words, but Redick's face tightened.

"Jesus H. Christ," the sheriff said. "Fantastic. A nut-job with mommy issues." He threw up his hands and turned his back, walking a few steps away while he rubbed the base of his skull with his hand.

Lumbergh asked Martinez what he meant. The intern took a step back from the bars, lowered his head, and clenched his forehead in his hand. He turned his back to the lawmen and placed his other hand on the back wall of the cell. He seemed to be drained of emotional energy.

"She wanted me to *be* you!" he bellowed, shaking his head. "An old woman's dying wish. She told me to go to Winston and learn from the man who slayed Alvar Montoya. *The Great Chief Lumbergh*. The legend. She told me to learn to be the man that I wasn't that day."

"*What* day?" asked Lumbergh, holding his temper.

Martinez began to sob, his head bobbing up and down. After a few moments, he regained some composure. "The day my father was killed."

When Martinez spun to face Lumbergh, his eyes were red and wet with tears. He peered at the chief with an expression that suggested he was waiting for a response.

"Are you going to make us guess on the rest of that story, Martinez?" asked Redick.

The prisoner's lower lip trembled. He used the back of his arm to wipe away the dampness from his face.

"Alvar Montoya killed him," said Lumbergh. "Didn't he?"

Martinez snarled and lunged forward, latching his hand onto the bars in front of him and showing his teeth. "Right in front of me, Chief. September thirteenth, 1993. He beat my father to death, right there in our living room, and I just stood there and watched. I couldn't move! I didn't do a fucking thing!"

Lumbergh turned to Redick, who raised his eyebrows in acknowledgment.

Martinez continued. "All my father was guilty of was selling a half-dozen joints on Montoya's turf. He was just trying to make a living to feed his family! He was just trying to put food on our table."

His chest rose up and fell steadily while the rest of him remained still. His eyes were wild and irrational.

"Before he turned to leave, he looked at me . . . and he smiled. That bastard smiled with his those big yellow teeth of his! 'Marranito,' he said. When my mother came home, she found me kneeling in my father's blood beside him."

A grimace distorted Redick's face. "Then why in the hell have you been carrying on all this shit with the chief and his family? He killed the man who killed your father, for God's sake!"

"No he didn't!" Martinez screamed out in primal fury. His face was red and twisted. He grabbed onto the bars before him and slammed his head into the steel. Four or five times his skull rattled the cage before blood from the earlier wound on his head began pouring again. "He was the same child that *I* was that day! The same baby pig! He didn't kill Montoya. His Indian friend did! My mother called me a coward for not trying to stop the man who was murdering my father, but you were no better than me. You were worse! You took the credit for what a better man did—the man who saved your ass!"

Lumbergh could feel Redick's confused gaze bearing down on him from behind. He knew he had some explaining to do, but that was the least of his worries at that very moment.

Blood drained down Martinez's face between his eyes before streaming to either side of his nose. When it reached his mouth, he continued. "I wanted to see for myself what you did when you faced the terror of another Montoya coming to hunt you down. I wanted to see if you would be the same sniveling coward that you were that day. You did just what I thought you'd do; you had Oldhorse hover over you like some parent protecting his child from monsters underneath his bed!"

The blood that had been boiling under Lumbergh's skin finally erupted. He launched forward and reached through the cell's bars, latched onto Martinez's head and yanked it hard into the steel. Martinez wailed in pain. Lumbergh kept up the pressure, trying to defy physics by attempting to pull the man's head through the bars with nothing but brute force.

Redick moved to intervene.

"Stand down!" Lumbergh snapped at him. "I swear to God, Richard, don't you put your hands on me right now!"

The derangement in Lumbergh's eyes kept Redick at bay for the moment.

Lumbergh knew the truce wouldn't last long. His head spun back to Martinez. "That's why you planted a bomb in Oldhorse's house? You were going to kill him so he couldn't help me take down some sick fuck that's not even after me?" he yelled. "All because I didn't live up to some superhero expectation you've been carrying around in that fucked up head of yours?"

Martinez screamed in pain at the bars pressed up against his temples. After a lot of squirming, he finally managed to jerk his head loose from Lumbergh's one-handed grip. His eyes bulged and his hands clutched the sides of his head.

"I don't give a shit what you think of me, Martinez," Lumbergh growled, his jaw locked as he glared at the intern. "All I care about is getting my brother-in-law back. You saw what happened to him. Your bullshit game is over. You're going to prison. If you want to catch any kind of break on the things you've done, you need to start talking! Now!"

Martinez fell to his knees, erupting into a hideous cackle that seemed to switch between laughter and sobbing. "The red fox has him now, Chief," he blathered. "She brought him back to her den."

Lumbergh leaned forward, his strained eyes blinking. "What are you talking about? What red fox?"

"You're the *legend*, Chief!" Martinez bellowed. "*You* figure it out!"

His head lifted up to face the overhead light fixture at the center of the room. He glared at it in wonderment like an infant enthralled with a mobile hanging over his bed. His lips moved, but only whispers and babble drifted out.

"Why were you at Sean's house last night?" Lumbergh yelled. "What did you see?"

Martinez now appeared to be in a hypnotic state. His eyes no longer recognized Lumbergh. Instead, they were transfixed on the ceiling while gibberish continued to drop from his mouth.

Lumbergh swore loudly and made a beeline for a nearby desk. He grabbed a chain of keys from its top, sorting until he found the one for the cell. The moment he spun back around, he felt Redick's hand wrapped around his wrist.

"I think we've already jeopardized this case enough, Gary," he said with eyes burning a hole through the chief. "You're not putting your hands on him again. Let's get this back into some realm of the law."

Lumbergh yanked his hand away. He glared at Redick, nearly choking on his own breath, fighting back the urge to shove him out of the way.

"Listen," Redick began in a restrained tone. "We've got this guy on what he did to Oldhorse and your officer. We don't want to screw that up. He poses no threat to anyone anymore. You're safe. You're wife's safe. There's no bogeyman out there with the last name of Montoya coming after either of you."

Lumbergh winced in annoyance at Redick's words, shaking his head but knowing deep inside that there was nothing amiss with the statement. "He knows what happened to Sean."

"Maybe," replied Redick. "But think about this for a minute." He nudged Lumbergh into the hallway out of earshot from Martinez before he continued. "Think about this: When you take Montoya out of the equation, what are we left with? Some nut responsible for shooting your officer and blowing up your Indian friend. That's awful, but that nut's now in our custody. Whatever happened to Sean is totally unrelated."

"Who cares if it's unrelated?" Lumbergh shot back, his face twisted in aggravation.

"Just hear me out. All we know about your brother-in-law is that something happened at his place, someone got hurt, and someone was taken out to a car. For all we know, a couple of his friends came over last night, they scuffled after having too much to drink, and then went somewhere else."

"Sean doesn't *have* any friends!" Lumbergh shouted, his fist clenched. "And he hasn't had a drink in months. Someone broke through his back door, for God's sake! These weren't people who were friends with him."

Redick held his hands out in front of him, trying to cool Lumbergh down. "Please listen to me," he said calmly. "Could some people have broken in *because* Sean didn't answer the door? Maybe they came over for a visit, saw his car was there, and were worried that he wasn't answering the door. Maybe they broke in and found him hurt and passed out so they took him to an emergency room."

Lumbergh's tilted face twisted in disbelief. "Why are you doing this, Richard? You know that's not what happened. All of your investigative training and instincts *tell you* that's not what happened."

He recognized the disingenuousness in Redick's changing demeanor as the sheriff tried to convince him that his mind had been poisoned by the fear of a man as dangerous as Lautaro Montoya on the loose and seeking vengeance. He listened to him suggest that there was likely a perfectly reasonable explanation for Sean's disappearance that had nothing to do with foul play. When the sheriff reminded him that Sean hadn't even been missing for twenty-four hours yet, Lumbergh could no longer silently entertain the display.

"I get it, Richard," he said in a composed tone that seemed to catch Redick by surprise. "In that cell over there, you've got a tightly wrapped package—a bullet point on your resume. You're not going to give that up for Sean Coleman—the town joke."

Redick's eyes narrowed angrily. "I'm not willing to let the man who injured and could have killed two men—two friends of yours—off the hook for what he did just because you refuse to do things by the book."

Lumbergh shook his head. "But you were willing to give me some leeway when you thought it might lead to a bigger fish, weren't you?"

"That's different and you know it. And if Martinez is telling the truth, and you kept Oldhorse's name out of the police file on the Alvar Montoya shooting, you've already got more than one problem on your hands."

Before Lumbergh could respond, Redick held up his hand and continued.

"Sean's house and Oldhorse's house both fall outside of incorporated Winston. That means that I technically have jurisdiction over both crime scenes. I didn't want to pull rank on you, Gary, especially with how much you've helped us with other cases—"

Lumbergh interrupted. "But you're going to, aren't you?"

After a moment, Redick answered. "Yes. Once my deputy returns, we're taking Martinez over to County. We'll get him processed and question him there. You're too close to this. I suggest you concentrate on finding your brother-in-law. If Martinez knows anything about it, we'll get it out of him."

Without giving Lumbergh a chance to protest, Redick turned his back on him and made his way to the front door. He tugged at his radio, bringing it to his lips before disappearing out the front door to the porch.

"Sure you will," Lumbergh muttered.

Chapter 20

S ean sat on the cement floor with his back flat against the freezer door. He hoped to hear movement from the outside room if anyone approached. His teeth sank into the peach he held. Its juices felt good sliding down his parched throat, as did the swig of water he took afterwards from one of the plastic bottles.

He thought hard about his captor's reaction an hour earlier when he'd mentioned Norman. The name had clearly rattled the man, but the insinuation that Booth was in a position of power put him at ease. Sean wondered if Booth was merely a bit player in a large hierarchy.

He thought about what had happened back at his home. Jessica had been wired with a listening device. The man who had busted in had heard their conversation, probably from a hiding spot in the back of Jessica's car. With Jessica wearing an earpiece, he had likely even been feeding her questions.

Maybe *he* was the big kahuna—not Booth. Maybe everything that had happened was about this man covering his *own* ass.

Sean stopped breathing when he thought he heard a faint sound from the other side of the freezer door, a couple of footsteps before things went silent again. He carefully pressed his ear to the door.

"Sean!" he heard his name called in a forceful whisper. It was a woman's voice. "If you can hear me, don't react or say anything. Just tap on the door. There's a camera inside there. They can see you, even in the dark, but they can't hear you."

Though her purposely-muted voice made it difficult to tell for sure, he believed the voice belonged to Jessica. He hesitated for a moment, thinking about whether or not he should play along. In his current predicament, he decided he had little to lose. He nonchalantly used the back of his knuckles to give the door a rattle before taking another bite of his peach.

"Good," he heard her say. Her voice was barely audible. "Listen Sean . . . I'm so sorry that all of this has happened. Believe me. None of it was supposed to happen. You were just trying to help me. I know that."

He knew then that it was indeed Jessica. He felt his chest tighten. There was no way of telling if the apparent appeal for forgiveness was genuine or if it was just another deception being played out for an unknown purpose. She had already tried to manipulate him once. Maybe this was more of the same.

"I promise you. You'll be set free of all of this," she said. "We just need another day. Two tops. After that, they'll blindfold you and drop you off somewhere just outside Winston. It will be like none of this ever happened."

He silently scoffed at the notion, taking a second to ponder the identities of "they." He placed his hands over his face and tilted his head forward, letting whoever might be watching him on a hidden night-vision camera believe that he was either resting or stressing over his fate.

"Where's the camera?" he asked, just loud enough so that he was confident she could hear him. "I won't let them see me talking."

After a few moments, he heard reluctance in her voice as she responded. "The center fan of the evaporator."

It's what he had suspected. The room was too bare for it to be anywhere else.

He slowly stood up and raised his arms in the air, stretching his back and faking a yawn before turning his shoulders to the back of the room where the evaporator hung.

"We can talk now," he said. "What the hell is going on, Jessica?"

Again, there was some hesitation before she responded. "I can't tell you what's happening. Just believe me when I tell you it's for your own safety."

"Believe you?" He placed the palms of his hands on the door and arched his back. "Why the hell should I believe *anything* you say? You lied to me about Carson, and then you showed up at my house to con me." He shook his head before continuing. "You shocked the shit out of me, tossed me in a trunk, and you and your boyfriend brought me here! So tell me again: why should I trust you!"

He took a deep breath, forcing some composure so his anger wouldn't be recognized by the watching eyes above.

"He's not my boyfriend," she replied.

"Who gives a shit? How about answering the rest of what I just said?"

After twenty seconds crept by without a response, he called out Jessica's name and thought he could hear her crying.

"Tell me what's going on," he said in a more restrained tone.

"Sean," she began through her sobbing, "have you ever had anyone in your life that you would do *anything* for? Someone who you cared about and loved so much that you would stop heaven and earth for them?"

The earnestness of her words oozed down into the depths of his soul, nearly leaving him speechless. For the briefest of moments, he forgot where he was, how he had gotten there, and to whom he was talking. "No."

Silence followed.

He regained his sense of self-awareness and told her that there was no one worth covering up a murder for, and that Andrew Carson's family deserved to know what happened to him. Holding him captive would only make matters worse for her and the people she was trying to protect.

"You don't understand what happened that night," she answered.

"Everything went wrong. Andrew Carson was an innocent man who was in the wrong place at the wrong time, and there was nothing we could have done about that."

"Don't waste time telling it to me," he said. "Let me out of here and we'll go to the police together. Tell your story to *them*. End this now."

"I can't!" she shot back, her voice trembling. "We've come too far. We've waited too long. In a day or two, all of this will be over and you'll be returned home—safely! I promise!"

He lowered his head in frustration.

"I have to leave now, or else I'll be missed."

"Wait!"

"Two days, Sean. Tops. Then you'll be free."

He growled and pounded his fist against the door. He then bit his tongue and tempered himself, worried he would alert the eyes above that he was talking to someone. He heard Jessica scurry away.

Sean hadn't been able to convince her to set him free, but the conversation hadn't been totally fruitless. He now knew that he was under surveillance. He began formulating a way to use that knowledge to his advantage.

Chapter 21

From his office window, Lumbergh watched the cloak of dimness from the early winter sunset steadily drape over the row of old family-owned shops across the street. They had long been part of his view, but he couldn't remember the last time he had taken a moment to just look at them.

Each sun-faded building had a quaint, handwritten "sale" sign inside its dusty window. Most entranceways hosted one or two decades-old gumball machines that invited young customers to nag their parents for a quarter or dime.

He watched on as Lupe Cordova, the kind, elderly owner of Winston's only Mexican restaurant, closed up shop. She was wearing a thick purple coat, and her shoulders were tight against her body. The temperature had dropped dramatically over the past hour, a sign that the expected storm was about to roll in. Snow had already begun to fall.

Cordova's place was more of a hole in the wall than a full-fledged restaurant, only large enough for one table inside. Most of her business came from her popular breakfast burritos that she made every morning. She wrapped them in foil and always had them ready for people to stop in and pick up at the beginning of their day.

As he watched the old woman fiddle with a ring of keys from her purse, Lumbergh was tormented with the undeniable reality that the rest of the outside world was carrying on as normal.

People were getting back to their lives following the 9/11 attacks. The horrific event had changed Lumbergh, as it had so many others who watched in terror the footage of men and women forced to leap to their deaths from the World Trade Center. It made him more protective than ever of the things most important to him, and it forced him to question the notion of bringing a child into such a world; Diana and he had discussed children often.

For many, the passing months and a presidential administration that seemed in control of the situation brought some ease and normalcy. At that very moment, however, Lumbergh felt contempt for that composed world, recalling that he was a part of it just a few days earlier when Alex Martinez had treated both he and Jefferson to a couple of Cordova's burritos. They had had a nice conversation about their lives that morning as they sat at a small table in the police station, chowing down and drinking coffee.

Jefferson had shared the news that he and his wife were getting back together after a months-long separation. Martinez had talked about some of the classes he was taking at school and one of his teachers. It was likely another false story from a seasoned liar, but Lumbergh planned on looking into it anyway. He couldn't remember what he himself had added to the breakfast conversation that day.

The memory was replaced with the sound of his wife crying. Her trembling voice was still fresh in his mind from the phone conversation he had just had with her. He'd delayed telling her about her brother's disappearance all day, hoping the deputies at Sean's place would find something useful—any sort of a lead to move on. After his spat with Redick, Lumbergh had even driven over to assist in the deputies' search.

Their findings were insignificant, at least from a timeliness standpoint. They took a blood sample from the floor and pulled some fingerprints from the bucket. It was better than nothing, but the evidence would take time to process and no one could know if the results would be of any help.

The deputy investigating Martinez's motel room hadn't found

much either, other than more proof of the intern's obsession with his boss. Tape after tape of news reports and interviews were skimmed through. They all pertained, in one way or another, to the Montoya shooting. There was nothing that suggested Martinez knew anything about where Sean had been taken.

Lumbergh had placed a call to Chihuahua, Mexico, to inquire about Martinez's mother. He discovered that she had passed away on January 5, which was probably what had brought Martinez back across the border for a few days.

His mother had died likely believing her son to be a coward, and that a police chief in Winston, Colorado, could be his saving grace. It was a belief she had apparently tortured her son with to the point that he had eventually snapped.

Lumbergh had also placed a call to check on Oldhorse and Jefferson at the Lakeland hospital up north. Jefferson was doing well. Oldhorse had a longer road ahead of him, but the doctors were confident he would make a full recovery except for some significant scarring. They'd successfully pulled a large piece of shrapnel from his thigh and he was now resting.

Martinez had completely clammed up. He'd lawyered-up, too, by the time Lumbergh had returned to the police station. Lumbergh suspected Redick had nudged him into it—either wittingly or unwittingly. Regardless, all Martinez had been doing for the past hour or two was staring up at the ceiling and making an occasional moaning noise. At times, he seemed to be trying to communicate with the overhead lights. It was as if whatever warped crusade he was on to torture Lumbergh through the threat of Lautaro Montoya for a perceived act of betrayal had been permanently derailed. Now he could no longer process his surroundings with any clarity or coherency.

At least he knew Diana was safe. With Martinez in custody and the Montoya threat turning out to be a sick hoax, she was no longer in danger. Lumbergh was looking forward to seeing her and holding her again, but with the storm rolling in, he'd told her to stay at her friend's house. Additionally, with the whereabouts of her brother unknown, he wasn't sure how he could face her.

The key to finding Sean was still Martinez; Lumbergh had convinced himself of that. As the police chief sat alone in mind and spirit with his shoulders hung low in the darkness of his office, he knew in his heart and gut that Martinez had seen who had taken Sean. He may have had nothing to do with the abduction, but he had seen it, and that was important.

Lumbergh felt some pain returning to his shoulder and reached into his desk drawer for his prescription bottle. When he opened its lid and found only a few capsules left inside, he realized for the first time just how quickly he had been going through the supply.

"What am I doing?" he whispered to himself.

He shook his head, and then replaced the lid and shoved the bottle back inside his desk. He decided at that moment that keeping his head clear was worth dealing with the physical pain.

When he slowly swiveled in his chair to turn to the front of his office, he took notice of the missing glass inside the door. He recalled the details of his confrontation with Sean from that day. Sean had been looking for information on the Andrew Carson case and had managed to see the prime suspect's name and mug shot on Lumbergh's computer screen.

Though Lumbergh initially resisted it, the notion that Sean's disappearance could be tied to his interest in that case began to mull within his mind. He pondered the possibility that Sean had gone looking for the prime suspect, Norman Booth. *Could he have somehow managed to actually find him?* The chances seemed small, but Lumbergh had learned in the past not to underestimate his brother-in-law when he was set on doing something, even if it was something stupid.

The premise had holes in it—big ones. There was no plausible scenario that Lumbergh could formulate that would lead to a confrontation between the two taking place inside Sean's home. Suspects on the lam typically didn't go looking for their pursuers.

The longer Lumbergh mulled over the angle, however, the more he felt that it at least deserved consideration. If anything, pursuing the lead would help pin down Sean's whereabouts earlier in the day.

He recalled Sean saying that he was interested in the Carson case because he knew a relative of the victim. It was a good place to start.

The last sheriff's deputy from Sean's house returned to the police station. Lumbergh, the deputy, and Redick removed Martinez from his cell and cuffed his hands behind his back. Martinez refused to stand on his feet, so they dragged him with his knees rubbing against the tile floor all the way to the front door.

"One more chance, Martinez," Lumbergh said, hovering over them like a watchful hawk. "Tell me what you saw at Sean's house!"

Redick flashed Lumbergh a disapproving glance.

Martinez paid Lumbergh no mind. He just hummed and moaned with his eyes glued to the ceiling.

Redick turned his head to the chief. "I'm sorry, Gary."

His eyes looked sincere, though Lumbergh had his doubts as to whether he really was.

"Listen," he added. "We've got a public defender meeting us at the station. I'm sure she'll persuade him, if anyone can, to talk."

Lumbergh shook his head in dismissal. When everyone had left his station, he retreated to his office and flipped on the overhead light.

He pulled his desk chair in front of his computer and began tapping away at his keyboard with his good hand. After a moment, he recalled the user login and password information he'd been given by his Greeley counterpart the other day. He logged into the P.D.'s mainframe and was soon looking at the Andrew Carson file again.

Carson's daughter Katelyn was listed as the primary contact in the case, so Lumbergh picked up his phone and quickly dialed her number. There was trepidation in the young woman's voice when he introduced himself, but her tone quickly changed to one of befuddlement when he explained that he wasn't involved in the search for her father.

He told her that he was looking for a man named Sean Coleman. To Lumbergh's relief, she immediately recognized the name. After some prompting, she explained how she had met Sean for the first time after he had joined one of her search parties. She said that he seemed helpful enough at first, but then became erratic when he realized that a woman he believed to be her cousin was of no relation to the Carson family.

"He didn't seem to believe us," she added.

Lumbergh asked her if she knew who the woman was. She didn't, but said that she vaguely recognized her from an earlier search party in a picture Sean had shown her.

"Picture?" asked Lumbergh. "What picture?"

She told him that she believed the picture was from an article, but she wasn't sure of the newspaper. "He said her name was Jess. No . . . Jessica!"

"Are you sure?"

"Yes."

"Did he know her last name?"

"If he did, he didn't say it."

When he asked her if she could describe what Jessica looked like, she did. "The picture was small, and I had only taken a passing glance of her when she helped us. I just remember that she had long red hair."

He nodded, writing down "Jessica long red hair" on a notepad. His eyes widened and his pencil stopped dead on the paper when Katelyn further described Jessica as "attractive-looking."

He swallowed, letting the gears in his head grind together for a moment before erratically writing under his description "THE RED FOX."

He didn't remember thanking Katelyn or fielding any questions she had about his inquiry, but he guessed he had done both as he hurriedly reached for his jacket moments later. He slid it on over his good arm and was halfway out the front door when a phrase he had heard Alex Martinez use earlier echoed through his head: *The red fox has him now, Chief. She brought him back to her den.*

"Her den," Lumbergh whispered.

He hustled back inside and snatched Martinez's timesheet. He looked at the odometer reading that the intern had recorded on the previous day. It was a number they kept track of so the police station could reimburse Martinez for any gas he used while running errands in his own car. It was the only form of compensation that Martinez ever received from the office—usually paid out from the station's petty cash drawer.

The chief repeated the mileage reading over and over again in his head while he raced down the front steps of the police station. He trampled through the snow to the side of the building where Martinez's car had been towed following its collision with the tree. It was scheduled for impound but hadn't been picked up yet.

He opened the driver side door, knelt along the front seat, and looked at the odometer. There was a discrepancy of over fifty miles. Martinez's trips back and forth to Lakeland and out to Oldhorse's cabin would have accounted for some of the distance, but nowhere near fifty miles. The intern had done a good amount of additional driving.

Lumbergh reached into his jacket pocket, pulled out a stick of gum, and popped it into his mouth, chewing ravenously.

The siren of his police cruiser was blaring loudly as he tore off in pursuit of the sheriff's car. He bit out obscenities when his tires wouldn't gain the same traction that his mind had. The snowfall was beginning to stick and the wind whistled through the bullet holes in his windshield, chilling the car's interior. He grabbed his radio and held it beside his jaw.

"Hughes. Roy Hughes. This is Chief Lumbergh. I know you're listening in on a police scanner somewhere. I need you to get back to me on channel 14," he said crisply. "Repeat. Roy Hughes of *The Windsor Beacon*. Get back to me on channel 14."

He had seen Hughes dancing around the crime scene at Sean's house when he had gone back there. The reporter looked like a kid on Christmas morning, wearing a gleeful smile and snapping pictures left and right. He was treating Sean Coleman's disappearance as his own private Watergate.

Lumbergh flipped a dial on his radio and tapped his hand on his steering wheel until a voice broke through the silence.

"Chief?" it came, riddled with a sense of puzzlement.

Lumbergh wasted no time, instructing Hughes to scour the state and local newspapers looking for a photograph from an article on the Andrew Carson disappearance.

"Andrew Carson?" Hughes asked in astonishment.

"Yes. I'm looking for a picture of people searching for his body— one with a woman with long red hair. Look closely. It's important."

Hughes asked if it had something to do with Alex Martinez and Sean, the story he was apparently already feverishly working away on for the morning edition.

"Roy, if this pans out, you'll have yourself an even bigger story. And I'll give you an exclusive. I promise," Lumbergh clipped. "Right now, I just need you to do this for me."

"Okay. When I find the picture, do you want me to bring it over to the station?"

"No. I won't be there. Just fax it to the sheriff's office."

"Where will you be?"

"Getting Sean."

Chapter 22

S ean wondered what his captors could believe a man like him was capable of doing. *They don't know me. If they bothered to do any research on the man they dragged from his home in the middle of the night, all they would have found would have been humiliating* Beacon *stories about a town drunk who never missed an opportunity to screw up his life,* he realized. *They could have killed me at any time, but they didn't. They left me with food, and offered assurances that I'd be fine. If Jessica was right, and what had happened to Andrew Carson wasn't intended, maybe they would be desperate not to let it happen again.*

He stood up from his seat against the freezer door, tossing an empty water bottle into the cardboard box he felt in the dark next to his foot. It made a hollow clunk when it landed on top of the other empty bottles.

Blindly, he paced back and forth in the dark, his shoes shuffling in uncertainty along the concrete floor. He scratched an itch at the back of his head, one that used to be persistent but hadn't bothered him in months. He was less than confident about the plan that was stewing in his head, but he'd convinced himself that it was at least worth the risk of trying. He relaxed his pace, slowing his stride. Walking to the back wall, he stood there for a moment beside it, outside of the eye of the camera. He then returned to the center of the freezer so he'd be visible again.

He repeated the routine a few more times, each time taking a longer break near the back wall, underneath the evaporator. On the fifth sweep, he reached the wall and felt his open hands along it until he found the electrical cord he had stripped loose earlier. He wrapped his hands around the end still plugged into the wall and savagely yanked on it until it tore loose. A few sparks flew as a result. He hoped the camera wasn't able to pick up the bright flickers.

The cord was longer than he remembered. Some of it must have been pulled out from behind the wall. This was good. The longer, the better.

As quickly as he could, he wound the cord up in a ball and shoved it in his front pants pocket. He then casually strolled out to the center of the room again, hoping the time lapse hadn't provoked any suspicion from "Big Brother."

He felt around in the dark for the bucket. When he found it, he placed it near the center of the room upside-down. He turned his back to the camera, facing the door of the freezer. Before sitting down, he discreetly pulled the cord from his pocket and kept it in front of his body. Slowly, it unraveled in his hands. With his head bent forward, he hoped that he would appear distraught, like a man worried about his fate in a helpless, desperate situation.

He sat there for ten minutes, sometimes placing his hand to his head; other times he interlaced his fingers behind his neck, taking one of those opportunities to slide the cord around it. He hoped the cord was thick enough to support his weight—if it came to that. A few inches from his throat, he tied the cord in a bowline knot so it wouldn't cinch up. It wasn't an easy knot to tie in the dark, but he'd practiced it and many others as a child for countless hours. Uncle Zed had been a good teacher when it came to that kind of thing.

Sean hadn't been completely sold by Jessica's concern for his well-being, but nonetheless, he banked on the notion that whoever was watching him didn't know that he was aware of their eyes. If they *did* know, the show he was about to put on would only be good for a laugh at his own expense.

He stood up. With his eyes closed, he pivoted in the general direction of the camera, holding the cord in plain view at the center of his hand while trying not to let the display appear contrived. With his other hand, he carefully performed the sign of the cross on his forehead, and then stood up on top of the bucket. He worked his fingers along the ceiling until he found one of the long pipes he had tried to pry loose before.

He carefully threaded the cord through the narrow gap between the pipe and ceiling. It took a little work, but he eventually forced it through.

He listened intently for what he hoped would be the sound of rapid footsteps from the other side of the freezer door. He heard none. The thought occurred to him that perhaps whoever was watching him had stepped away from the camera for a bit. He also considered that maybe it just didn't matter to the person what he was doing. He hoped neither was the case.

He tied the opposite end of the cord around the pipe securely, eliminating any excess slack. He stood there for a moment, listening. He still heard nothing.

It was a grim feeling—not just from the tribulation of his current situation—but also from the sense of familiarity that jetted up and down his spine. During the darkest days of his drinking and the alienation of the people who knew him best, Sean would have been lying if he'd claimed never to have thought about taking his own life. At best, it would have lifted the burden he'd become to his family and those who once felt something for him. At worst, no one would have cared. The same torment now stewed in his gut as he awkwardly stood in the dark on a bucket in a basement freezer, feeling painfully alone while waiting for someone to stop him.

Maybe they suspected that he knew they were watching. Maybe they were calling his bluff. Many uncertainties taunted the wisdom of Sean's scheme, but he had long ago stopped caring about doubts directed at him. It was time to make something happen.

"No reward without risk," he muttered to himself, reciting a line he'd heard from an old episode of *The Rockford Files*. He suspected the quote originated elsewhere.

He bent his knees and lowered his body an inch or two, until he felt his own weight mostly supported by the cord looped under his chin. He snarled and kicked the bucket out from under himself.

His eyes immediately bulged as he dangled in the air, the cord digging into his flesh. He flexed his neck and squared his jaw, keeping his body stiff and tight, and fighting back the urge to panic. Though he had been careful not to position the cord around his throat, he was quickly finding it difficult to breathe. His body trembled from the tension.

The pipe above him cried and seemed to bend slightly from his weight, but it remained attached to the ceiling. He imagined that if he could see himself in a mirror, his face would be beet-red with every vein in his forehead protruding like ropes wrapped around a rock.

With a toothy grimace across his face, drool began to slide from his mouth and the unbearable pressure under his chin nearly forced him try to grab onto the cord or pipe above to alleviate it. He disciplined himself not to, even as he felt his loose pants slide down from his waist.

He suddenly felt his body drop an inch or two. The cord was now under his throat, and his breath was cut off. The pipe had buckled.

He gasped for air but found none. He realized immediately that the game was nearing an end. If he didn't do something fast, he'd choke to death. He raised his hands and frantically forced his fingers between his throat and the cord, just as his pants slid down his legs.

The room was suddenly illuminated by the bright ceiling light.

It nearly blinded Sean as his flailing body twisted in the direction of the freezer door. Through the brilliance of the fluorescent bulbs and distress that punished his body, he saw an almost equally panicked face glaring back at him through the porthole window.

It was the same bespectacled man who had come in earlier. Seeing through the camera what Sean was doing, he now took a closer look to confirm that the act was genuine.

As torturous as it was, Sean understood he needed to further sell a situation that had already turned deadly serious. He let his hands fall to his side and his eyes roll up to the top of his head. Mere seconds seemed like agonizing minutes as he hung in the air.

The thought that the end might be near taunted his soul. *I'm gonna check out, hanging from a pipe with my pants around my ankles.*

The man disappeared from the window. The loud sound of the metal latch unsnapping echoed. Sean immediately raised his hands and wedged the tips of his fingers in between his throat and the cord again. He lifted his head as best he could toward the ceiling and pried at the cord with all of his might, frantically bucking his legs and hips.

The door swung open. The desperate-looking man sprinted inside, but only managed to take about two quick steps before his feet slid on the large puddle of water that Sean had created at the doorway from the bottles that had been left for him. The man's momentum sent him crashing forward to his knees. Sean yanked the cord up to his chin and then out from under it.

He fell to his feet, nearly losing his balance from the wave of lightheadedness that beat against his skull. He had enough presence of mind to recognize that the gun had fallen from the man's hand. He lunged for it, grabbed the man's arm instead, and tackled him onto his back.

The physical savagery picked up where it had left off at Sean's house, with him quickly overpowering the smaller man who squirmed and fought like a trapped animal. A wheezing sound poured out from Sean's swollen throat as he fought, but he bottled up the impulse to erupt into a coughing fit to clear his windpipe.

He jerked his pants back up to his waist over his boxer shorts. He straddled the man's body and twisted his wrist at a sick angle until the gun fell from his shaking fingers to the floor. He latched onto the man's collar and yanked him away from the gun before sliding his hands up to his throat.

The man's eyes turned to the size of golf balls under his glasses. He grabbed onto Sean's wrists and pried at them unsuccessfully, his legs kicking erratically along the floor.

Sean held up the pressure—he'd promised the man that he'd no longer be breathing if they tangled again.

Though raw anger was fueling Sean's desire to keep his word—something that his uncle had always said built character—the agony and helplessness in the man's eyes made him rethink his promise. He knew that even with everything that had happened, he couldn't take the man's life—not after the man had just tried to save him from killing himself.

He let go of the man's neck. He ripped his glasses from his face and immediately sent a devastating right-cross to the side of his head. The man's head snapped to the side and his body went limp. His glassy eyes peered off in a random direction. Sean could tell by his snort-like breathing that he was out cold. He tossed the glasses to one side.

He dismounted the man and reached for the fallen revolver. He quickly checked its action. A loud, delayed coughing fit left his throat as he taught himself to breathe again.

The man had to have been the only one who was watching through the camera as Sean pulled his stunt, otherwise others would have rushed into the room to assist. He searched the man's pockets and found nothing of use. He didn't even have a wallet, thus no identification.

Sean crawled over to the thin mattress that lay on the floor. He grabbed it and draped it over the man's body at an angle, hoping it looked on camera like the original captive was merely tired and seeking warmth.

He left through the open freezer door and found himself in a small, unfinished room. The concrete floor had a couple of round drain-grates embedded in it. Raw sheet rock dressed the walls. An old clothes washer and dryer sat in a corner, as did some cleaning supplies and food boxes that had probably been moved out of the freezer. At the very top of the opposite wall was a small window about three feet wide and one foot in height. There was no way he could escape through it. The outside of the window was completely covered with snow.

When he turned to close the freezer door, he found a large padlock lying on the floor beside it. A key with three others attached to a small D-shaped ring was still inside of the lock. He closed the door, snapped on the padlock, and slid the keys in his pocket. He turned off the freezer light and swiveled his head toward the staircase he had eyed earlier.

Chapter 23

Lumbergh could have radioed Redick and asked that he come back. He also could have pled with the sheriff to have his deputy pull over to the side of the road and wait for him until he got there. Lumbergh knew, however, that the sheriff would not have complied.

Redick viewed the chief as a liability to the successful prosecution of Alex Martinez—a man facing two attempted murder charges, including one for a police officer. It was a good case to have on a resume, as Lumbergh understood all too well from his career in Chicago. It was one of the things he'd noted quickly rising up the hierarchical ladder. If Redick knew the chief was coming, he would have his deputy alter his route back to County to avoid a confrontation.

Large, thick flakes of snow slapped up against the windshield of the cruiser, narrowing Lumbergh's visibility tremendously. Some snow had even managed to work its way through the bullet holes in the glass and onto the dashboard where the warmth of the automobile's defroster turned it to slush. Loud, forceful gusts of wind pressed against the driver's side of the car, keeping Lumbergh's hand clamped tightly to the steering wheel.

The storm had arrived.

The wiper blades were working like mad by the time he reached Interstate 70. It was the stretch of road where he believed he could catch up to Redick. He flipped on the flashers and sirens and sped his way down the mountain.

The traffic was fairly light in the eastbound lanes. Most people who'd come up to ski that day were surely either planning on staying the night or had already made their way back toward Denver that afternoon to beat the blizzard. The sporadic clusters of cars that did occupy the road were meandering along cautiously. Whenever Lumbergh came upon them, they'd slowly pull over to the shoulder to let him whizz by.

Lumbergh knew he was driving faster than what was safe, but if he didn't get to Martinez by the time he was processed and behind bars again, he knew he'd *never* get anything out of him.

Whenever a pair of taillights came into view through the net of whiteness in front of him, he'd pump the brakes and examine the car's make. After a dozen or so hopefuls, he finally spotted the sheriff's car winding a sharp turn in the right-hand lane ahead. Lumbergh turned off his siren but kept his flashers on.

The back of Martinez's head lit up in the backseat when Lumbergh moved in behind the cruiser and repeatedly flashed his high beams.

"Richard, it's Gary Lumbergh behind you," he spoke into his radio, hugging the steering wheel steady with his thighs. "I need you to pull over."

Even through the falling snow, Lumbergh's headlights revealed Redick's angry eyes glaring back at him through the cruiser's steel dividing grill. Martinez seemed completely uninterested in what was happening, not bothering to even turn around.

"What do you want, Gary?" Redick's irritated voice came over the radio.

"Martinez knows more than we thought. He knows where Sean is. I'm sure of it!"

"We've already been through this, Gary. If he knows anything, we'll get it from him at County with his lawyer present."

Lumbergh cursed and angrily slammed down his radio, letting it bounce off the floorboard. He took a deep breath, tightening his jaw and pressing down on the gas pedal. When he passed the county cruiser on the left, he could imagine the panic-riddled face of the deputy, whose driving suddenly became erratic as he pumped his brakes and swerved, unsure what the sheriff aimed to do.

Lumbergh continued pulling ahead of the other lawmen until the back bumper of his car was cattycorner to their front bumper. He then edged his way steadily to the right, forcing them to slow down or risk being nudged into the guardrail on the other side of them.

Once both cars came to a stop, Lumbergh threw his in park and swung open his door. He stepped outside and was nearly toppled over by the powerful blast of bitterly cold wind. The thick flakes that whisked by him were painted multiple colors by the bright, rotating flashers, almost drowning out the roadside area as they swung through the sky like volcanic ash.

The deputy opened his door and stepped out, his chest bloated with indignation. Lumbergh sidestepped him and went straight for the rear side-window. He beat his clamped fist against the glass to get the attention of Martinez who sat under the dome light. The intern wasn't responding, his blank gaze only directed at the windshield.

"The red fox's den!" Lumbergh shouted. "You saw where they took Sean! You followed them, didn't you?"

He watched for any kind of reaction in Martinez's face. There wasn't one at first, but then a snide grin slowly began to form. He leisurely turned his head to meet Lumbergh's eyes, expressing an overdue hint of clarity. His lips began moving, saying something to Lumbergh.

Lumbergh couldn't hear it through the whistling of the wind. "What?" he yelled, using his hand as a visor to try and shield out the noise.

"He said that even a man with tunnel vision has his outside curiosities!" The loud voice came from Redick who had just climbed out of the passenger's seat.

No longer wearing his hat, the wind against Redick's tightly curled hair made his head look like a thick bush with a small animal trapped inside it working to find its way out.

Lumbergh's eyes narrowed as flakes of snow pelted his face.

"It doesn't matter, Gary. He asked for a lawyer. We can't ask him any more questions!"

Lumbergh shouted back, "Sean was looking into the Andrew Carson case! The missing man from Greeley! Presumed dead. I think he found the person responsible for it and that's who took him!"

"Andrew Carson?" Redick answered with his face twisted in puzzlement. "How the hell would Sean know anything about that?"

"It's a long story. Just believe me that Sean's in danger, and Martinez knows where he is!"

The gears in Redick's skull seemed to spin for a moment, but *only* a moment. He shook his head and repeated his insistence that things be done by the law.

Lumbergh could barely contain his fury. When he felt the deputy's hand latch onto his arm to guide him away from the vehicle, he clenched his teeth and drove a sharp elbow directly into the man's face. The deputy's head snapped back, a bark escaping him. He lumbered backwards on unsteady footing, holding a hand to his eye. Lumbergh snatched the firearm from the deputy's side-holster and quickly trained it on him.

"Gary!" yelled Redick.

Lumbergh took the deputy down to the frozen pavement with a leg-trip and a shoulder-block, then turned on the sheriff.

Redick found the gun suddenly pointed at him.

"Get your hands up and get over here, Richard!" Lumbergh growled, his face stern.

Redick's complexion turned sick. With his hands slowly rising into the air, he crept out from the other side of the car. His footing was cautious due to the strong gusts of wind that intensified around them.

Lumbergh traced his aim back and forth from the fallen deputy to Redick.

"What the hell are you doing, Gary?" Redick shouted. "This is no good. Think about your career!"

"I'm thinking about my *family*! You don't give a shit about that! I get it. Now get your fat ass over here."

Once Redick grew near, Gary told him to slowly remove his pistol from its holster and toss it over the guardrail.

"You wouldn't shoot me, Gary!" Redick shouted. "You're not that kind of man!"

"*I* don't even know what kind of man I am anymore, Richard. Don't presume that *you* do. Now toss your gun!"

Redick did.

Lumbergh ordered both men to stand at the front of the car with their hands spread out along the hood. They complied, looking as if they were being placed under arrest.

Lumbergh reached inside the sheriff's car and unlocked the rear door.

"No, Gary!" yelled Redick.

"Shut up!" yelled Lumbergh, taking a few steps backwards to the door.

A couple of slow moving cars passed by them in the right lane, seemingly unfazed by the scene playing out just feet from them. Keeping his firearm aimed at the lawmen, Lumbergh opened the door and lowered his head just enough so that Martinez could hear his voice.

The intern's now alert, examining eyes belied that he wasn't sure what was coming next.

Lumbergh's gaze moved to the lawmen. "Your mother was right about me," he said to Martinez. "She knew what kind of man I am. She knew what I was capable of. If you want to see what I do to people who fuck with my family, you'll come with me now. I'll show you why murals of me decorate towns in Mexico. I'll show you why your people celebrate me. I don't need Ron Oldhorse or anyone else to put a bullet between someone's eyes when my family gets hurt. Come with me now and give me my target."

His attention slid to Martinez. It was greeted by the trademark toothy grin and the electric, eager-to-learn look that Lumbergh had come to know well.

Chapter 24

S ean carefully made his way up the wooden staircase, one step at
a time. An inactive light bulb hovered above him. He spotted a
switch on the wall, but stayed in the dark. With his arms out in front
of him and his hands gripping the revolver, he aimed the gun at the
open door at the top of the stairs. A strand of sweat slowly slid down
the side of his face. When it reached the corner of his mouth, he
tasted its salt.

About halfway up the staircase, a loud creak came from the
pressure of his weight on one of the steps. His face tightened and
he took a breath before quickly hustling up the remaining steps.
When he reached the top, he nearly hugged the linoleum floor with
his chest, swinging his arm around the corner of the doorframe,
watching for movement. All he found was a tiny, barely lit room that
housed several stacked, medium-sized cardboard boxes and an old
white refrigerator that emitted a tepid hum. The sound of fierce,
whistling wind could be heard from outside. Sporadic gusts drew
groans from the walls.

Sean saw a pair of dark curtains covering the wall beside him
and discreetly tugged on the fabric, hoping to find a window waiting
behind it. Instead, he found thick wooden planks nailed securely
into the wall, blocking whatever possible escape route existed behind
them.

It took him a moment to figure out where the room's dim light
source was coming from, but his adjusting eyes finally homed in on a

child's nightlight plugged into a low electrical outlet. It read "Barbie" in pink, cursive lettering below an image of the classic toy doll.

He looked at the boxes and strained to read their labels. He made out terms like "cast tape," "electrodes foam," and "vacutainer tubes." Some of the terms felt familiar to him, as if he'd seen them in writing before. He cautiously climbed to his feet, pointing the gun toward an open doorway at the opposite end of the room. It looked like it led out into a hallway.

Something inside of him urged him to bolt down the corridor with his gun drawn, needling his way through the building, taking aim, and pulling the trigger on anyone who got in his way. He felt justified in doing whatever it took to get outside and away from danger.

Yet, there was also a nagging voice in his head calling for a more cautious approach. There were many unanswered questions peppering his head like spitballs from an annoying school kid. Whatever moral dilemma Jessica was struggling with (as he had gathered from her comments behind the freezer door) had relevance. The fact that the people who abducted him had something to do with Andrew Carson's death, yet chose not to kill Sean, meant something. That same voice in his head told him that he should open up some of the boxes beside him and see what was inside.

Switching his attention back and forth from the hallway to the boxes, he reached his left arm over his right and tugged at the top flaps of one of the boxes that had already had its packaging tape stripped off. He opened it up without much noise and tilted it at an angle until the glow of the nightlight exposed its contents.

Plastic containers, very large ones. He was familiar with the type. Two days a week, he watched others just like them fill up with brown fluid from tubes in people's arms, including his own.

They were blood plasma supplies, just like the ones used at GSL.

At first, it seemed likely that Jessica had taken them from work, but when he stared intently at the nearly detached large mailing label secured to the box, he saw neither the name "GSL" nor "Plasma." The name appeared to belong to an individual at a post office box in Leadville, Colorado, a former silver-mining town nearly twenty-five miles south of Winston. *Is that where I am? Leadville?*

The last name on the label looked like "Robinson." Sean had trouble making out the first name.

He gently tore the rest of the label from the box and took it to the refrigerator. He guardedly opened the refrigerator door a crack, just enough to trigger the bulb inside to turn on. Through the sliver of light that crept out from behind the door, he could read the first name. Phillip Robinson.

He wedged the label into his pocket and had nearly closed the door when something from inside the refrigerator caught his eye—a unique color that he recognized—glowing from the bright bulb behind it. A very distinctive shade of pale yellow.

He opened the door wider and saw a few dozen of the same containers he'd just seen in the box, only these were filled nearly to their tops with a liquid that appeared to be plasma.

It was the kind of display he had seen many times at GSL. Whenever a donor's sitting was finished, the container their plasma was collected in was removed from a centrifuge machine and placed in a large metallic refrigerator along the back wall. The only notable difference between those containers and the ones he now saw before him was their labels. At GSL they were digitally printed with a good deal of information, including a donor identification number. All these had were patches of masking tape with handwritten dates. The ones in the front displayed the current date while the ones toward the back were marked "1/18." A week ago. There appeared to be at least four containers filled per day.

Sean carefully closed the door, letting his eyes drift to the floor as he struggled to make sense of his finding. No explanation immediately presented itself.

He shook his head and peered around the corner of the room

out into the hallway. The darkened corridor went on for a couple hundred feet. He was inside a much larger building than he had realized. Several closed doors lined one side of the hallway, while only one lined the left halfway down. The floor shared the same linoleum he stood on, suggesting he was not inside a residence, but a place of business.

The door closest to him, about ten feet away, was the only one open. A dull, quivering light from inside the doorway lit up the opposite wall of the hallway, creating a dancing projection like what would come from a television screen. *Was someone inside watching TV?* There was no sound.

Each step Sean took forward was careful and deliberate. He straightened his arms and pointed the gun in front of him, controlling his breath. When he reached the doorway, he tensed every nerve and swung inside, ready to put down anyone that jumped out at him.

There was no one there. It was a mostly empty, windowless room with a half-dozen black and white monitors mounted along the wall. All were on and each displayed a separate view. A small wooden desk was positioned below them, its chair lying on its side on the floor, as if it had been knocked over. A nearby suspended shelf with a file cabinet under it overflowed with large textbooks. Several of the book bindings displayed a red cross along their spines. On top of the shelf was a small desk lamp shining down at a sharp angle, exposing the good amount of clutter on top of the desk. It included a frosted medical jar made of glass that had what looked like milk inside it. The rest of the room was virtually bare.

Beside the fallen chair on the floor was a shattered ceramic beverage mug. It sat in a dark pool of liquid that smelled like coffee. About half of the rubble was still together in a single piece. On its face was what looked to be a hand-painted pink heart. Within its outline read the phrase "Best Uncle Ever!"

Sean guessed that the man who now lay in the basement must have inadvertently knocked the mug and chair to the floor when he saw Sean's mock suicide attempt on the monitor. He probably frantically dashed down the staircase at that point. Sure enough, he recognized the interior of the freezer displayed across one of the monitors. The man he'd knocked cold was still lying motionless on the floor, just as he'd left him, partially tucked underneath the mattress.

Four of the monitors displayed outside shots. The pictures on them confirmed to Sean that it was nighttime and also that the storm he'd been hearing about on the radio over the past couple of days had hit. A near whiteout of fast-moving waves of blowing snow overwhelmed each view. Because the snow seemed to be moving at a different angle in each of them, Sean estimated that every camera was stationed on a different side of the building.

In one of the shots, he thought he could make out a small, empty parking lot. At the corner of the screen there appeared to stand a tall business sign. It was unlit and unreadable. Another shot gave coverage to the back side of the building. At least, that's what Sean guessed from the sight of a large dumpster that sat in front of a short wire fence. He moved his face closer to the monitor when he noticed another object in the picture along the right edge of the screen. It looked like a car bumper and part of a taillight, but he wasn't sure. It really could have been anything.

Still, his lips curled into a grin. He slid his fingers into his pants pocket and pulled out the ring of keys he had taken from the freezer door. Though not labeled, one of them had teeth that looked like ones made for a car ignition. He knew he wasn't going to make it far on foot in the middle of a snowstorm. Having access to a car brightened his hopes for a successful escape. He had nearly exited the room to look for a back door when his gaze was captured by the image broadcast across the last monitor.

At first, the long object on the screen appeared to be a light-colored tarp with large lettering across it, tossed over some large boxes. Upon a closer look, however, he realized that what he was seeing was a twin-sized bed. The *lettering* across its top cover wasn't lettering at all, but rather arms—bare, human arms that overlapped a sheet or blanket.

The shape of a body hadn't been immediately decipherable below the cover because the head was concealed by what looked to be an angled tube jetting out from it.

The longer Sean stared into the screen, the more defined the image became. Beside the bed was a tall, vertical metal rod. From it hung a couple of IV containers with thin tubes running into the person's arm. On the other side of the bed stood a short table with what looked to be medical equipment. Some of it seemed to be for monitoring purposes. Most notable was what appeared to be a centrifuge machine like the ones commonly used at GSL Plasma. Whoever was lying in that bed seemed to have something seriously wrong, he decided.

He lowered his head to the raised puddle of coffee that lay unmoving on the floor. When he did, he recalled the pool of blood from the photograph on Lumbergh's computer, the one taken from the Andrew Carson crime scene. There was so much blood that Sean was certain Carson had been killed. *But what if he hadn't been? What if he had been only severely injured, and was now being kept alive by the people who took him, somewhere in this building?*

Sean thought about what Jessica had told him through the freezer door—that what had happened to Carson was an unfortunate accident. If that were true, it could explain why they didn't let him die. What it wouldn't explain was why they took him from his home instead of simply calling for an ambulance or taking him to a hospital.

The irrefutable reality was that these people were ruthless and up to something significantly lawless. The fact that Sean had been taken from his home against his will and locked in a freezer was only more proof of that. Whatever was supposed to be completed in the next day or two was worth a huge price to them—something serious enough to warrant all the deception and felonies they had committed.

If they were willing to go as far as they already have, what more are they willing to do? he wondered. *Would Carson be safe here if I escaped and went for help?* In the monitor, he made out what appeared to be some kind of restraints wrapped around the bedridden man's arms.

A jolt of anxiety suddenly ripped through Sean when the beginning of a loud song blared out from the dark. The gun nearly fell from his hand before he swung it in multiple directions, desperately searching for its source. It seemed to be coming from somewhere inside the room, which dropped his heart down into his stomach. If there was anyone else in the building, they'd likely hear what felt to him like a tornado siren echoing into the outside hallway, drawing attention to the precise spot where he stood.

"I like big butts and I cannot lie," the rap lyrics trumpeted out. *"You other brothers can't deny..."*

"You're fucking kidding me," Sean muttered under his breath, his pulse racing.

When he realized that the sound was pouring out from the desk just a couple of feet from him, he quickly yanked open the top drawer and found a black cell phone lying there among loose papers. He snatched it and backed himself into the corner of the room away from the doorway. Training his gun on the open door, he glanced down at the phone, looking for an *off* switch.

When he flipped the lid open, he pushed the first colored button he spotted. The song stopped. Sean breathed a sigh of relief, but before the air had time to escape his lungs, he heard a man's voice emitting from the phone's small speaker.

"Hello?" spoke the voice in what sounded to him like a British accent.

His eyes widened. He glared down at the small, digitized display monitor on the phone. It read, "Dr. Phil."

He froze. He'd heard that name mentioned before by his sister—

something to do with Oprah Winfrey. He was certain, however, that the two men couldn't be one and the same.

"You there, mate?" the voice asked.

Sean's first impulse was to search again for the real *off* button, and end the call. However, it promptly occurred to him that whoever was on the other end could be in on what was happening. The name Phillip Robinson hovered in his mind—the addressee on the boxes at the top of the stairs. Could he be "Dr. Phil?"

If the man was part of the ring and he didn't receive the response he was expecting—likely from the person who was now lying on the floor of the freezer downstairs—he would immediately suspect that something was wrong.

Even without fully grasping the situation he was in, Sean knew he couldn't afford that. He also couldn't afford to let the phone start ringing again.

He held the phone to his mouth and said in an altered tone, "Yeah?"

Chapter 25

"You shot out their tires in the middle of a snowstorm, Chief? Fellow law enforcement officers? That's pretty cold."

"Is that a joke?" Lumbergh replied to Martinez.

The intern now seemed eerily at ease in the backseat of the police cruiser. His broad smile could be seen from the rearview mirror, lit up by a pair of oncoming headlights. He leaned forward with his face near the grill and chuckled. "Ah. Snowstorm. Cold. Very good. Chief. No. There was no pun intended."

"I didn't want them following us," said Lumbergh, working his hardest to keep the conversation light. "They've got a police radio and a warm car in the meantime. Someone will pick them up."

Martinez asked, "So what does this mean for you now, Chief?"

"What does *what* mean?"

"This act of insubordination. How many laws did you just break? Will you lose your job? Spend some time in jail? That would be a shame to the fine people of Winston."

The comment seemed sarcastic at first, but when Lumbergh stole another glance in the rearview mirror, he recognized what appeared to be sincerity—as deviant as its origins might be—in Martinez's dark eyes.

It was above Lumbergh's pay grade to even begin to understand what was going on inside the head of someone as mentally disturbed as Martinez. He was well aware of that. In the brief conversation they had had since the moment they left Redick, Martinez largely talked as if the two of them were still friends—colleagues sharing a casual, after-work conversation. Not at all enemies.

If the awkward cordiality would bring Lumbergh to Sean, the chief was more than willing to play along with it. The limits of his compliance, however, were tested with the next query out of Martinez's mouth.

"Do you think I can get these handcuffs taken off? They're a tad tight around my wrists."

Lumbergh hesitated for a second before saying, "I can't. They belong to the sheriff's department. I don't have the keys to open them."

It was a lie, one that Lumbergh hoped Martinez wouldn't question. Being that the cuffs were taut behind his back and not subject to a close inspection, Lumbergh wasn't worried about telling it.

Martinez simply nodded.

Seconds that seemed like minutes labored by without either man saying a word. An uncomfortable sense of anxiety floated inside of the car. The cruiser's rapidly waving wiper blades emitted a persistent buzzing sound that seemed louder than it normally did due to the holes in the windshield.

Lumbergh ruminated on the questions Martinez had just asked about his career and what his fate would be once all was over. He didn't know the answer. And for a distinguished law enforcement professional who once prided himself on his stellar record and reputation for following protocol, he was stunned by his own disinterest in the possible ramifications.

The past week had taken a toll on him. It had changed him. His fear for his family had prompted him to engage in actions he would have never before considered. His deputy had taken a bullet and Oldhorse had taken far more—both because of a personal vendetta of a deluded individual.

Laws and rules just didn't seem to matter anymore.

Lumbergh drove slowly along Road 91 as Martinez directed him off the Interstate. The slippery conditions and narrow visibility tempered his thirst to go faster. The snow was like thick confetti dropped from a tall ceiling at a New Year's celebration. The wind was still strong, pushing against the front of the car in an eerie effort to keep it from their destination. The car's heater fought the chill pouring in through the windshield.

The flashers were off to avoid detection from anyone from the sheriff's department who might be out looking for him. His radio was powered off as well. He didn't want Martinez to hear any chatter blare out from the speaker that would make him think twice about taking him to Sean.

Martinez finally cut through the silence with a question that gave Lumbergh pause: "Would you really kill a woman?"

"What?"

"A woman. There was a man and a woman who took Sean last night. When we get there, are you going to kill the woman? Are you going to kill the red fox?"

Lumbergh's hand trembled and he gripped the steering wheel tighter to compensate. He wasn't sure which answer Martinez was hoping for, so he iterated what he believed would be a safe response.

"I'm going to kill anyone who stands in my way."

Martinez's face twisted into near exuberance. He grinned from ear to ear.

What a sick fuck, Lumbergh thought to himself.

The truth was that Lumbergh didn't know how he would approach the situation once they arrived at their destination. He didn't understand the circumstances under which Sean was being held, and Martinez refused to give him any hints. It was possible Martinez didn't even know.

What he *had* to know, however, was the lay of the land and the type of building they were in, if they were even in a building. The term "den" might have meant something entirely different. He might also know how many people Lumbergh would have to contend with at this den.

An endless number of possible scenarios stretched out before Lumbergh, and Martinez had no interest in narrowing that number down for him. Lumbergh's discreet attempts to draw answers were met with irritation, and he understood that if he persisted, he'd risk validating Martinez's earlier conclusion of him being a charlatan. If the state of the intern's mind disintegrated back into the zombie-like display of glazed eyes and moaning, Lumbergh would never find Sean.

What Martinez wanted was a front row seat to a brutal confrontation between his hometown's idol and very dangerous people who made men disappear in the middle of the night. As long as Martinez believed that was what he was getting, Lumbergh was convinced that he would find Sean.

There was one question that had been nagging him from the moment Martinez's footprints were confirmed at the crime scene, a question that seemed fair game because it didn't pertain to Sean's abductors. After building up some nerve, he asked it.

"Why were you at Sean's house last night?"

Martinez let a breath of air escape his lips. Though Lumbergh couldn't see him now in the darkened reflection in the mirror, he could sense some disparagement brewing in the backseat.

He nearly withdrew the query when Martinez spoke.

"I thought he may have been another Ron Oldhorse."

Lumbergh squinted and asked what he meant.

"Another of your guardian angels. Another parent."

The chief glanced in his mirror. "Why would you think that?"

A touch of somberness accompanied Martinez's words as he spoke. "I overheard the two of you talking the other day, in your office. You were arguing. He told you that you owed him for *cleaning up your shit*. Was he part of the Montoya cover-up?"

Lumbergh didn't know whether to laugh or cry. He would have felt mortified if the question had been asked by anyone other than a sick mind like Martinez, whose opinion meant nothing to him.

What the intern couldn't have possibly known was that Sean's statement hadn't been metaphorical. It was literal; an embarrassing incident back at the hospital six months earlier, when Lumbergh was recovering from the Montoya shooting, was what his brother-in-law had referenced.

Against doctors' advice, Lumbergh had changed from his hospital gown into street clothes to meet reporters and answer questions in the hospital lobby. The drugs he was on had been turning his stomach in knots all morning.

Sean happened to be visiting at the time while Diana was taking care of some long overdue errands. Lumbergh was running late for the press conference and had only taken three steps outside of his hospital room into the hallway when a horrific sound and stench from Lumbergh's pants locked both men's eyes.

In a rare show of compassion—perhaps out of a silent understanding between men—Sean helped Lumbergh change and dispose of the badly soiled clothes before anyone came back to check on the chief. Not even the nurses found out what had happened, and the two men had never spoken about it until yesterday, when Sean held it over Lumbergh's head to secure himself a favor.

Lumbergh shook his head. "God. Sean covered up nothing, and he's not my protector, Martinez. Far from it. In case you haven't noticed since you came to work for us, Sean and I don't exactly get along."

"Yet you're risking your career to save him. Your life, in fact. Why?"

Lumbergh recognized the absurdity of having such a candid conversation with a nut-job, but he answered the question anyway. "He's family, Martinez. When someone fucks with your family, you do something about it."

The mirror revealed the contour of Martinez's head as he nodded in understanding. "Take a left up here."

"Crenshaw," muttered Lumbergh, reading the small green mileage sign that sprouted out from a metal pole partially buried in a mound of snow. The sign hosted some dents and dime-sized holes from a shotgun round. Many road signs throughout the area did. The embellishments were a hallmark of mountain living.

"A little past Crenshaw," clarified Martinez.

There wasn't much in the town of Crenshaw, Colorado. Lumbergh had only passed through it once or twice before. It was really more of a rest area than a town, home to a few businesses that serviced travelers on their way down to Leadville, Granite, and Buena Vista along Highway 24. Few people actually lived there.

"How in the hell did you follow them so far without getting noticed?" Lumbergh asked before thinking to tamp down his tone.

"Impressive surveillance for a junior law enforcement officer, eh?"

Lumbergh said nothing.

"I turned off my headlights once we left the highway. Just followed their taillights from a distance. Avoided using my brakes. Did some coasting. It's a great way to conserve gas, you know."

Martinez laughed at himself and leaned back in his seat.

Lumbergh stared intently ahead.

Chapter 26

"Did you give him the last of the propofol?" asked the voice on the other end of the small phone Sean held firmly in his hand.

The sound cut in and out a couple of times, probably from the weather. The fact that any signal was getting through at all meant that Sean was likely no longer near Winston. Cell phones hardly ever worked there. He kept his eyes and his gun pointed at the open doorway of the small room.

"It's done," he calmly and quietly answered, having no idea what propofol was or who it was meant for. Still, he sensed it was the kind of response that this Dr. Phil wanted to hear. He was intent on running out the clock on the call with short, direct answers. He believed it would keep his identity from being questioned. It was a tip he had picked up from an old episode of *Nero Wolfe*.

"Good. I was worried he'd begin to stir again with us having to stretch out the dosage. What you gave him should last us at least until I get there. I'll be back soon with the replacement stock for what he knocked out of Jessica's hands. No worries. He won't be giving anyone else a bruisin'."

"Okay," replied Sean, thinking of the black eye that Jessica wore when he'd seen her in the parking lot.

"Did the wanker in the basement give you any more shite?"

Sean had no idea what a "wanker" was, but he assumed it was something other than a term of endearment. "No," he answered. "Sleeping."

"The big bugger wore himself out, eh? Good. If he acts up again, you think about what I told you. Make it look like he came at you and that you had no choice. Him or you—that kind of shite. The others will buy it. Remember . . . we've come too far to turn back now."

Sean let the man's words sink into his gut. "I will. Bye," he said soberly.

The line went silent for a moment, which made Sean nervous. He began to wonder if the reception had given out, or if the man had simply hung up. He nearly hung up when the voice suddenly returned.

"Are you okay?"

Sean winced. "Yeah. Just tired."

More seconds of silence floated painfully by. It went against Sean's better instincts to stay on the line, but he knew he had somehow aroused the man's suspicions. He had backed himself into a corner with his indecisions, both figuratively and literally. He carefully lowered the phone from his mouth and examined its face. His eyes slid across each row of buttons until he spotted a red one with a white circle and a vertical line stabbed through its center.

"Who is this?" the voice suddenly asked in a blunt tone.

Sean's heart stopped. He bit his lip and pressed the red button, cutting off the conversation. He held it down until the display light went off. "Shit."

The man on the other end had said that he'd be back *soon*. Sean didn't know if that meant twenty minutes or two minutes. Either way, it was time to leave while he could, put some distance between him and the building, and then use the phone to call in the cavalry.

With guarded movements, he briskly negotiated his way down the dark hallway. Hearing no sounds other than that of his own breathing and the discreet scuffing of his boots along the floor, he considered that it was possible that no one else was in the building. Still, there was no way to know for sure. He kept his gun pointed straight ahead.

There was only one door on the left side of the corridor. That meant that a large room was on the other side of that wall, one he hoped would lead to the outside. He twisted its knob carefully and found it unlocked. When he opened it, dim light edged the door's frame.

He peeked through the narrow opening and saw a wide area with several wooden tables staggered out across a thin, multi-colored carpet. Wooden chairs were turned upside-down across the round tops of the tables. Large, flowery portraits decorated the pale-yellow walls and some fake plants hung from hooks along the ceiling. It appeared to be the dining room of a restaurant.

A single light along the far wall, probably positioned to illuminate some now-missing wall décor, let Sean see a thick layer of dust covering the tables and much of the floor. Though shoe prints of multiple sizes spotted parts of the carpet, it had clearly been a long time since the room had been used to serve patrons.

Along the windows of what Sean assumed to be a front entrance, thick wooden planks were secured, just like he had seen in the small room at the top of the stairs. If he needed to, he'd find a way to pry them open. Because it would make for a long, noisy escape though, he'd only try it as a last resort. He quietly closed the door.

He was nearly at the end of the hallway when he heard what sounded like another door shutting somewhere ahead in the dark. It felt like it came from only a few yards away. Sean froze.

The brushing soles of someone's boots along a coarse mat and the loud clatter of footsteps soon followed it. Sean couldn't tell if they came from multiple people or just one. The hallway's overhead light suddenly flared on. Sean's body clenched with tension. He was totally exposed. There wasn't a single thing to take cover behind if the person or persons about to emerge from around the corner were armed.

He slid up against the wall beside him and felt the knob of another door press against his leg. Without wasting another second, he twisted it and felt the door release. In one quick motion, he opened the door, slid inside the darkened room, and gently closed the door behind him.

There was a single light source from somewhere inside the room and he caught a quick glance at an empty, unmade bed with colorful blankets. He heard the ticking of a clock somewhere in the room. He turned his attention back to the door. The light from under it filtered around the moving shadow of a single person whose casual pace meant it was someone other than Dr. Phil. This Phil would have surely burst through the building in a panic to confirm his suspicions from the phone conversation. It was someone else.

Sean gripped the doorknob, hoping to let the person walk on by before stepping back out and taking them down from behind. With a gun pointed at their back, he could quickly take control of the situation.

The person stopped right outside the door.

Two shadows from under the doorway, each from the person's legs, held perfectly still.

Sean released the knob and backed away from the door, feeling carpet below his feet. He hoped that the howling of the strong wind outside would cover up any noise his movements made. He gripped the gun with both hands and pointed it toward the door. Jaw tensing, his finger hugged the trigger.

The shadows suddenly changed directions and disappeared back the way they had come. With the same casual stride as before, the footsteps echoed through the hallway, growing fainter with each passing second. Sean let himself breathe.

When he returned to the door, he could hear what sounded like a faucet running somewhere from down the corridor, as if a kitchen sink had been turned on. Pipes from under the floorboards hummed with activity.

Sean's eyes detached from the door and immediately spotted

a pair of red curtains hanging along the opposite wall. They were moving with a draft from outside.

He quickly sidestepped the edge of the small, empty bed and yanked the curtains open. His eyes widened at the sight of a broad pane of glass instead of more wooden boards. At the moment, a wide view outside of heavy, swirling snow was no less appealing than that of a sunny beach in Acapulco.

He was higher off the ground than he had expected: about a nine-foot drop, he guessed. Below was what looked like an alley with a smaller building sitting on the other side of it, behind a short fence. He knew he could take the drop down to the ground. He slid the gun into the back of his pants and reached for the lower sash of the window where he found a metal latch.

When he unsnapped it, he cringed at the louder than expected noise. Almost instantly, he caught movement in the corner of his eye—a reflection in the window of something behind him. He gasped and reached for his gun, dropping to a knee as he spun around.

He took aim at the back corner of the room where a floor lamp glowed at a dim setting. In that illumination was a vision so surreal that his arms trembled in horror that he had nearly pulled the trigger.

It was a child; a totally bald child who appeared no older than six.

At first, Sean believed he'd seen a boy. When he saw the pink fleece pajamas hanging from her shoulders, however, he realized the child was a girl.

A white crocheted blanket was wrapped around her petite body. Her skin was just dark enough to make him suspect she was Hispanic. Her eyes were closed and she appeared to be asleep as she sat curled up on what looked like a rocking chair. His eyes traced the outline of her delicate features and then her body. That's when he saw something large wedged in between her and the chair.

It was of a flannel material and Sean followed it up to the shoulders of a figure behind the girl. Air spewed from Sean's mouth and his arms tightened, the gun still pointed at the hidden face belonging to the shoulders.

"Wait!" a man's weak voice wheezed out.

His hand jetted out from beside the girl, palm up in a plea for calmness. A large, opened children's book fell from beside the girl to the floor.

Sean's heart pounded mercilessly in his chest. He couldn't wrap his head around what he was seeing until his eyes finally identified the full contour of the man in the near dark. He was sitting in the rocking chair with the girl curled on his lap, still fast asleep.

"Don't shoot," his voice came again.

"Stop talking!" Sean ordered curtly, doing his best to subdue his own voice. He pointed the gun at the man's head.

The man abided, remaining perfectly still.

"Let me see your other hand," Sean instructed.

The man whispered in reply. "I can barely move it, Sean."

Sean's gut clenched when he heard his own name spoken.

"You're Sean, aren't you?" the man muttered.

"Quiet," warned Sean. "Slowly, lift your right hand up and turn that lamp on brighter. I want to see you."

The man's hand slowly rose to under the lampshade beside him. Sean noticed a wince tighten across the man's face, as if the motion caused him pain.

The bulb quickly went black for a moment before sparking back on brightly. The man's face lit up.

Below a matted mane of dishwater-blond hair was the pasty rendition of someone Sean had first seen in the photograph only days earlier, when it was displayed on the computer screen in front of Jessica as she wept.

Andrew Carson.

Sean was speechless. His legs trembled and his chest tightened. How could what he was seeing be real? The scene felt like an abstract image from a dream.

"Take it easy, Sean," Carson said softly. "I know what must be running through your mind right now."

Sean's left eye twitched. His mouth was dry. "You have no God-damned idea what's going through my mind right now."

Carson swallowed but said nothing. His eyes looked dreary, as if he had just awoken, and his complexion was pale. He seemed thinner than in his picture, but it was unmistakably him. He finally spoke as his gaze slowly lowered to the gun. "Can you put that away? You're pointing it right at this little girl."

"No, I'm not," Sean said, keeping his gun drawn. "I'm pointing it at you. What in the hell are you doing here, Carson? Are you a prisoner?"

Carson's gaze fell to the floor. He glanced at the book lying wide open before him. *A Fish Out of Water*, it was titled. When he lifted his gaze back to Sean, he looked as though he'd decided to disregard an impulsive notion to offer a dishonest answer.

"Not exactly," he stated, seemingly out of breath.

Sean's face twisted in confusion and then into anger. Before he could respond, Carson spoke again.

"It's a very complicated story, Sean—one that you're owed. I understand that you've been trying to help. Jessica told me."

"What is this?" Sean hissed. "Some sick hoax? Did you fake your own death? Was that even your blood in your driveway?"

Carson scowled. "It sure as hell wasn't a hoax, Sean. That blood was mine."

"Half the state's looking for you," said Sean. "That includes your daughter. She's about ready to write your obituary. If you're not being held against your will, why haven't you reached out to her or the police?"

Carson's eyes closed and his face shriveled into what looked to Sean to be genuine heartache. His eyes welled up with moisture.

"I k-know," he stuttered out. "I'll return to Katelyn—*my* little girl—soon, but what's happening right now is more important. I'm a part of something here. There's a lot that you don't know about."

"Then why don't you tell me *what* I don't know about?"

The girl sitting on Carson's lap stirred for a moment. She nestled the side of her bronze head against his arm. Both men said nothing until she stopped moving. Her eyes remained shut above the gentle features of her face.

"Who's the girl?" Sean asked.

"Can you put down the gun first?"

"No. Who's the girl?"

Carson took a deep breath. "She's an angel, Sean. A victim of an unfair world, and these people are trying to make things right for her."

Sean shook his head in irritation at the cryptic statement. "By doing what? Snatching people from their homes?"

Carson shook his head. "They didn't kidnap me, Sean. They saved my life."

"What are you talking about?"

"There was a man. A very bad, dangerous man who attacked me at my house. He plunged a knife into my gut and stared into my eyes as I suffered and struggled to breathe—all because he wanted to elude the police by stealing my car." There was clear bitterness in Carson's eyes as he told the story. "He would have killed me if it wasn't for them. They brought me here and stabilized me. They kept me alive so I'll be able to see my daughter again."

"Who are *they*? And why didn't *they* just take you to a hospital?"

"They couldn't! I had seen their faces!" Carson blurted out in frustration, his voice raised.

"Keep your voice down!" Sean threatened.

Carson controlled his breathing and let out a muffled cough

before he continued. "They couldn't because they needed the man. The one who stabbed me. They had been following him for some time. He's important to them."

"Why?"

"He's got something in his blood, something that most people don't have. Something that can save this little girl's life."

The cylinders in Sean's head began to fire up. His eyes drifted to the wall and his mouth gaped open as he silently lipped some of the thoughts that were rushing through his mind. He turned his attention back to Carson. "There's a man strapped to a bed somewhere in this building. Is that him? The one who stabbed you?"

Carson nodded. "He's not in this building, but he's close by."

Sean recalled seeing the smaller building on the other side of the alley when he looked out the window—likely where the man was being held. "They're drawing blood plasma from him. Plasma isn't rare at all. *Everyone* has it!"

"Not the kind he has," Carson answered quickly. "Very few have the kind he has. One in a million, they said."

"How do they know?" asked Sean. "How do they know this guy's got bionic plasma or whatever it is?"

Carson hesitated for a moment before answering. "At Jessica's work, they do tests when someone becomes a donor. They draw blood, and run tests, and they look for certain things."

Sean understood exactly to what Carson was referring. He'd been through the same process himself. "He was a donor? At GSL?"

"Almost. He came in one night, several months ago. I think it was back in the summer. He was turned away because drugs showed up in his system. However, he also tested positive for what Jessica and the others had been looking for. Some antibody."

Sean listened on.

"They approached him—privately. They told him about Anna, and they asked him to help. All he'd have to do is stay clean for a few weeks while they put him through a series of injections. The injections were supposed to enrich his platelets; I think that's the term they used. Then they'd draw out his plasma the same way they did at Jessica's work. He told them to go fuck themselves."

"Why?" Sean asked.

"He thought they were nuts. Accused them of being part of some cult. He called them vampires. When they showed him a picture of her, and he saw that she was Hispanic, he got angry. Told them there was no way in hell."

"Why would he care if she's Hispanic?"

"He's got a swastika tattoo on his arm. You figure it out. Even after they offered to pay him every last cent they had, he laughed them off. He lost his job at a casino and moved out of Lakeland soon after."

"He's Norman Booth, isn't he?" Sean broke in. "The police's prime suspect in your disappearance." He hadn't needed to ask the question. He knew the answer was yes. It explained why the man in the freezer became so alarmed when Sean brought up Booth's name. Until that moment, the captor had no way of knowing that the police even had Booth on their radar. It wasn't until Sean suggested that Booth was an active participant in Carson's disappearance that the man relaxed, realizing that Booth was viewed by the police as a suspect and not as another kidnap victim. "So Booth's the *real* prisoner. They've got him doped up and tied down, and they're sucking him dry. I saw the full containers in a fridge down the hallway."

"And they need more time to finish doing it," said Carson with coldness in his eyes. "They're out of other options. Give them that time."

Sean stared a hole through him, judging him with a black look that made him swallow and look away. "Time to do what? Kill him? When donors give plasma, they do it twice a week, for safety reasons. They're pulling at least four containers out of him per day."

"They tell me he'll live," said Carson as if the line had been rehearsed in his head.

"Oh yeah? That's what they *tell* you? Carson, I don't know what kind of sick bond you've formed with these assholes, but *I* don't owe them a damn thing. I saw Booth's rap sheet. I saw the blood he took from you. I know he's the *bad, bad* man, but no one can do what these people are doing to him. It's wrong."

"You're wrong!" Carson snapped back, wincing afterwards from the obvious pain the sudden movement caused to his body. "Booth had a choice to make something with his life and he chose a life of drugs, crime, and violence. The prick's a skinhead, for Christ's sake! This little girl was never given the choices he was. Don't take the rest of her life away from her."

"Keep your voice down, Carson!" Sean glared at him until he calmed. "This girl should be in a hospital if she needs help, not in some condemned building. Tell me you understand that."

Carson exhaled and his shoulders deflated. The girl's body drooped into his chest as he did. He looked down at her head. "There's nothing more that the hospitals are going to do for her, Sean," he said. "Rules, regulations, liabilities; they've handcuffed too many doctors. There are risks they can't take. They can't do what needs to be done, but I bet if it was their own daughter whose life was on the line, they'd figure out a way. That's all this family is guilty of: figuring out another way."

"Family?" Sean asked.

Carson glared at him. "Yes, Sean. Family. Why don't you try looking them in their eyes and telling them that what they're doing is *wrong*?"

Sean's eyes narrowed.

"He's in here!" Carson abruptly shouted out, his voice straining from the volume. "In Anna's room!"

Eyes bulging, Sean lunged forward and placed his hand over

Carson's mouth. The girl on his lap stirred again, starting to wake. Adrenaline pumped through Sean's body in rhythm with his racing heart as he frantically slid around to the side of Carson's chair, knocking the lamp to the floor as he did. It crashed loudly and its bulb exploded. The room went dark.

"You stupid son of a bitch," Sean growled.

With Carson's chair positioned between him and the door, he went down to a knee and kept his hand pressed tightly to Carson's face. Carson was too frail to put up much of a fight. Thunderous footsteps from down the hallway sprinted toward the room. Sean aimed his gun toward the door as the wind outside howled wickedly.

"Andy?" the little girl asked from the dark in a dainty, confused voice. "What's happening?"

Sean felt Carson's teeth sink into the flesh of his fingers. He absorbed the pain and kept his gun on the door, waiting for the quickly approaching moment when it would spring open.

Chapter 27

L umbergh made his way across the off-ramp leaving the highway. He could barely see ten feet in front of him as he slowed down to about fifteen miles per hour. The mesmerizing, dizzying snow lit up by his headlights came down in sheets. Driving any faster would have surely sent the cruiser skidding off the shoulder and into a ditch. He carefully straightened out the wheel once he pulled onto a much narrower road, proceeding slowly and cautiously.

He switched back and forth between his high and low beams, hoping one setting would give him an advantage. Neither did. He was dealing with a virtual whiteout.

In the backseat, Martinez whistled a long, meandering tune that Lumbergh didn't recognize. The intern seemed to be enjoying himself, eager to witness what he had come to see.

A single set of tire tracks was the only blemish on the snow-covered road. Someone had come through not much earlier, likely driving a truck or a van, based on the width of the tracks. The driver looked to have been in hurry with some of the wide, reckless corners it had taken.

"How much farther?" asked Lumbergh.

"Not much, Chief. Maybe another mile or two."

The incline of the road grew progressively steeper and the cruiser's tires began to struggle to find traction. They spun helplessly a couple of times, but some shifting of gears and some second attempts kept the cruiser moving in the right direction. The painfully slow pace Lumbergh was forced to travel frustrated him, but not half as much as the increasing volume of Martinez's whistling.

Martinez abruptly stopped and began stomping his feet on the floorboard like an excited child on a school bus. "What are you going to do to them, Chief? Come on! Tell me!"

Lumbergh said nothing, trying to ignore the growing sense of sickness in his gut.

Martinez snickered. "*Mi madre*. She would be so pleased right now. The two of us working together. Me learning from the best. Once we get there, Chief, I'll stay behind you. I won't get in your way. I'll just watch and learn. Right?"

Lumbergh forced himself to nod.

Chapter 28

"What is it? What's wrong?" a woman's panicked voice darted out from the corridor a half-second before the door flew open and the flip of a light switch chased away the darkness.

The imposing brightness nearly blinded Sean, but through the narrow slits of his eyelids, he recognized Jessica's loose red hair whip inside the room.

Sean yanked his hand from Carson's teeth and placed both hands on his gun to steady it as he stood. "Let me see your hands!" he barked out like a police officer.

"Mommy!" the little girl shouted in terror. Her confused eyes looked up in horror at the large stranger hovering over her with a drawn pistol. She slipped from Carson's lap. He tried to latch onto her arm, but he was too weak. She fell to the floor with a thud.

"Anna!" Jessica screamed.

"Your hands!" Sean yelled. "Let's see them!"

Jessica wore a mask of sheer terror. Her empty hands shot to the ceiling and she spread her fingers. Sean ordered her to turn around. When she did, his eyes examined her for weapons. No bulges. She was dressed in jeans and a loose t-shirt. The jeans were wet at their ankles, suggesting that she had been walking around outside. Her feet were bare.

Sean told her to close the door and she did. "Who else is here, inside this building?" he roared.

Out of the corner of his eye, he could see the frightened little girl crawling across the floor toward Jessica. She moved in an awkward motion along the carpet in her pink nightgown, only using her hands and arms. It was as if she was partially paralyzed from the waist down, though she did manage to tuck a knee into the floor a couple of times.

"Tell her to stay where she is!" Sean demanded, nodding the gun at Jessica.

"Let her go to her mother, for God's sake!" Carson snapped angrily. "You aren't going to shoot anyone!"

"Shut up!" warned Sean. He backhanded Carson across the scalp, drawing from him a sharp wince.

Jessica lowered her head to meet the girl's wide, fearful eyes. She forced a calming smile and said, "Stay where you are, Peanut, okay?"

The girl stopped and nodded. Her eyes were wide with fear and they quickly filled with tears. Her body shook as she cried.

In no logical world should Sean have felt guilty for how he was handling the situation; still, the child's tears drew remorse from him. He had never known that Jessica had a daughter, let alone a sick one. Yet, the revelation made strange sense. While watching her at GSL all those weeks, he'd seen a nurturing, maternal side to her. It cut through her otherwise cold exterior whenever she attended to donors. Her gentle, warm touch served as a ray of comfort, the way it would to an anxious child. It was one of the things that attracted him to her.

What also became quickly apparent was the source of her emptiness and detachment over that time. He had noticed it from the first day he had met her. The standoffishness; the expressionless gazes; the apparent absence of happiness or even a stray moment of contentment. They were all driven by the hopelessness of a mother who was living with the agonizing trauma of watching the health of her young, precious daughter deteriorate. Her daughter was dying. There was no room for joy in Jessica's life.

It was her daughter, Anna, that Jessica had referred to from the other side of that freezer door in the basement.

"Have you ever had anyone in your life that you would do anything for?" she had asked him. *"Someone who you cared about and loved so much that you would stop heaven and earth for them?"*

She wasn't talking about covering up a crime for some boyfriend, as he had believed at the time. She was talking about crossing the moral and legal boundaries of kidnapping—a kidnapping in which the hostage's body was his own ransom. Her rationale was her daughter's life.

Sean forced himself to breathe and again asked Jessica if anyone else was inside the building.

The request triggered the expression on her face to suddenly melt back into panic.

"Oh my God," she said in an appalled whisper. "Where's Adam? What did you do to Adam?" Her head shook as she spoke.

"Who the hell is Adam?"

"My brother!"

"How the hell would I know your brother?" Sean yelled.

"The man from your house, dammit! The guy you beat up. What did you do to him?"

Anna peered up at Sean through large, drained eyes and asked, "Did you hurt my Uncle Adam?"

The innocent tone of her voice again pulled guilt from Sean's heart. He recalled the broken coffee mug on the floor of the other room. *"Best Uncle Ever."* It was likely a gift from an adoring niece.

"He'll be fine, honey," he answered with a reassuring wink. He offered her a cordial, calming grin and added, "He's just taking a nap. Probably dreaming of tasers."

Jessica censured Sean through narrowed eyes.

"Is anyone else inside this building?" he asked again, this time in a more restrained tone.

"Just us and Adam," she replied.

Sean raised a brow and asked, "And not the man of the hour, Norman Booth?"

Jessica's eyes shifted to her daughter as Carson shook his head sourly. Anna questioned her mother with a confused look, the name clearly foreign to the little girl. Sean could see she likely had no idea that a man was being held against his will somewhere nearby.

"No. Not here," Jessica muttered in answer to Sean. She raised her finger to her mouth to pre-empt the barrage of questions she anticipated coming from her daughter.

"Is that who gave you the shiner?" Sean asked, eying the bruise she still wore on her face. "He woke up, didn't he?"

She didn't answer.

Carson did. "He got an arm loose. Wacked her good."

"Someone hit you, Mommy?" asked Anna, her eyes flowing with concern. "You said you fell down."

"It was just an accident, Peanut."

Jessica turned to Carson and asked him if he was okay. When he nodded, she queried, "Did he drag you in here?" She nodded toward Sean.

"No," replied Carson. "Anna couldn't sleep because of the wind. I had finished reading to her when *he* came in."

"Let's save all the chitchat for the next barbecue," said Sean, reciting a line he'd once heard Telly Savalas speak on an old episode of *Kojak*. He'd always liked the quip. He turned to Jessica. "Why didn't you just leave me at my house last night? Why did you bring me here?"

"Because you knew who I was," she quickly answered, visibly uncomfortable that the sensitive conversation was taking place in front of her daughter. "You would have told the police about my connection to Andy's disappearance. We needed you out of the way for a few days."

"Until this was over," Carson broke in. "Then you and I would *both* go home."

Sean's eyes leapt to Carson. "Are you sure about that?" he asked, holding his stare.

Carson's face tightened. "What do you mean?"

"Who's Dr. Phil?" Sean asked the room before turning his attention back to Jessica.

Carson and Jessica exchanged anxious glances.

"Come on. Who is he?" badgered Sean.

"From *Oprah*, Mommy?" asked Anna in a whisper.

Sean fought back an impulsive smirk.

Jessica ignored Sean and replied directly to her daughter. "He's talking about Uncle Phillip, Peanut," said Jessica.

"Another uncle?" asked Sean.

"*My* uncle," Jessica reluctantly responded. "My father's half-brother. He's a doctor—an extremely good one. A specialist. He came halfway around the world to save her, a little girl he had never even met before. He's *going* to save her. He's convinced us that he can."

Sean lowered his gaze to Anna, watching her delicate face stiffen as she struggled to wrap her young mind around the words being spoken by the adults around her.

"If you'll let us," Jessica added.

Her pleading eyes pulled at Sean's heart, but he didn't let her see a hint of emotion. He kept his gun drawn. He understood how desperate the family was to save their little girl's life. A million thoughts spun through his head.

Jessica's reaction outside the GSL parking lot a day earlier now made sense. When Sean had approached her there, claiming to know about her *uncle*, she wasn't thinking of Andrew Carson. The panic in her eyes came from the belief that Sean knew about *Dr. Phil*—her real uncle—and the connection he had to Carson's disappearance.

It was a wonder she didn't have a heart attack at that very moment, believing for a few seconds that Sean had somehow figured out *everything*. By the time Sean had finished explaining himself that day, she had come to understand that her secret was still safe. Posing as Carson's niece was a good way to pacify any suspicions

Sean may have had from their conversation, or so she thought. She couldn't have envisioned that he would further pursue Carson's disappearance, meet Carson's family, and discover that she wasn't who she said she was.

Just why she was at Carson's house and helping with the search for his body that day the newspaper photo was taken was still unclear. Maybe she was trying to determine how much the police and family knew about Carson's disappearance, and if they had linked him to Norman Booth. Maybe she was trying to clean up some evidence left behind from the night they snatched the two men. Or maybe she was just curious about the people whose lives had been affected from what she and her family had done. The empathy she felt for Carson's daughter was clearly what drew tears from her eyes the night Sean confronted her in that back room at GSL.

He thought of Norman Booth—a lifelong violent criminal who viewed life as cheap, stabbing a stranger for getting in the way of something he wanted. What was *his* life worth? Could Booth ever *willingly* give a gift more positive and meaningful to the world than the one he could give to Anna—even if that gift came at the expense of his own free will and, also, his life?

Sean wondered what kinds of terrible things he could somehow convince himself to do if it meant saving the life of someone he loved. What would *he* do to a man like Norman Booth if it meant he could bring Uncle Zed back from the grave? Sean had been taught throughout his life, growing up in a rural mountain town, that the sanctity of life was a precious thing, and it was something he truly believed. He had trouble at that very moment, however, determining which argument that belief more accurately favored: Booth's life or Anna's life.

He had only been around the girl for mere minutes, but he read nothing but innocence and reverence in her eyes. It was clear that Carson had grown tight with her in a relatively short period of time.

He seemed to look upon her like a daughter, perhaps longing for the old relationship he once had in happier times with his own daughter.

It was possible that Carson was right about Booth. Maybe the thug would recover from the dangerous quantities of plasma being drained from his body. Perhaps as Carson and Sean had each been promised, he'd be dumped on a roadside somewhere and go on to live the rest of his life however he saw fit.

That scenario, however, seemed like pure fantasy to Sean. He couldn't envision Booth remaining silent about what happened to him. Booth knew his captors and could put every one of them in jail by simply pointing a finger. That was the best-case scenario. With Booth having his own troubles with the law, he'd more likely choose to settle the score himself.

Either way, a freed Norman Booth could easily result in Anna being left without any family—possibly even losing her life as well, depending on how sick of a man Booth was. Sean was convinced the family would never let that happen, especially not Dr. Phil, who was fine with taking out the one guy who was an innocent party to the whole mess. In all likelihood, Booth would never make it out of that building alive. Sean glanced at the man in the rocking chair.

Carson seemed he had some doubts about his own fate. "What did you mean by that? When you said, '*Are you sure about that?*'"

Sean glared at him. "Good old Phil wanted good old Adam to kill me if I didn't behave myself down there in the basement. These people aren't as harmless and noble as you think they are, Carson."

"That's not true!" Jessica said angrily. "Those were empty threats! Adam only made them to scare you!"

"It wasn't Adam who made them!" Sean snapped, spinning his head toward Jessica. "They came right out of the doctor's British ass."

"Australian," corrected Carson.

"Who gives a shit?" Sean dug his fingers into his front pocket and held up the cell phone for her to see.

Jessica was speechless. Her daughter watched her face, shaking her head in the confusion of it all. Seconds dragged by without anyone speaking.

"He could be right," said Carson to Jessica. "The things Phil's said. How angry he was when Adam wanted to bring me here. Phil's the doctor, yet Adam was the one desperate to keep me alive that night. Part of me's been wondering if Phil . . . if Phil would have preferred that I died on my driveway. Anna's life might be the only one he values in this at all."

Jessica closed her eyes, seemingly trying to dislodge Carson's words from her head before they could sink into her psyche. When her eyes opened, their intensity burned a hole through Carson. He looked away, making him look like a child who was being scolded by a parent. She focused the same glare on Sean.

Sean didn't look away.

"What are you going to do, Sean?" she asked somberly. "You're the one holding the gun. You're calling the shots. You can either let us finish what we've started or you can end it all right now by blowing the whistle on us. If your decision is the latter, I want you to look into my daughter's eyes and tell her that you've made the decision to sign her death warrant."

He stared bitterly at Jessica. The notion that he was being put in the position of a judge over blood rights—deciding who lived and who died, whose blood would be traded or sacrificed for whose life—infuriated him. His eyes soon dropped to Anna, whose aura of innocence now tugged at his soul like a magnet. The girl didn't understand any of what was being said. She couldn't possibly understand. Her wide eyes and her slightly opened mouth made that painfully apparent.

There was no fairness in the situation for anyone. Not an ounce. There was no fair trade for life-saving blood.

Sean felt his blood boil under his skin. He was angry at himself for ever pursuing the path that had ultimately brought him there. That path began with what he thought was a harmless crush on someone he hardly knew and was fuelled by a lust to honor his uncle's life.

Now he found himself sitting on a jury of one. He, the man who stood before Anna—the man who she now looked up at with heartbreaking fear—was the sole decider of her very fate.

If Norman Booth had been a willing participant in what Dr. Phil was doing, the decision would have been easy, even if laws had been broken. But he was far from a willing participant. For Anna to live—or even have a shot at living—Booth had to die. Maybe it would be from his body shutting down. Maybe it would be from a bullet to the head.

Anna swallowed and turned. "Mommy?" she said.

"Don't look at me, Peanut," Jessica answered, keeping her eyes on Sean. "Look at him."

Anna did, and Sean's gut tightened as his gaze traced her bald head. She had to have already been through so much. Chemotherapy. Long hours in hospital beds, undergoing tests. Probably surgeries. The emotional turmoil alone had to be unbearable, not just for her, but clearly her entire family.

His gaze fell from her head to her damp eyes. They glistened from the lights above and penetrated his conscience. Despite the chemo, her skin looked as soft and pure as any other child her age. Her small nightgown hung from her petite shoulders and went down to her knees. She looked like a doll that a healthy girl her age might play with. Sean's gaze dropped to the floor, much the same way Carson's had only seconds earlier.

"Tell her, Sean," Jessica persisted relentlessly.

He wondered if it was the same technique that had been used to turn Carson to the family's line of thinking. He understood that guilt could be just as effective of a weapon as a gun or knife, and

Jessica was wielding it with precision. She had no other choice. Her daughter's life was on the line.

However, he did have a choice. If he walked away and never spoke a word of what he knew to anyone, Anna might live, though there would certainly be no guarantees. Norman Booth, however, would assuredly die. As bad of a person as Booth undeniably was, wasn't only God Almighty justified in making such a decision? Did they have a claim to serve as his executioners?

Sean pondered again what he would have done to save his uncle's life if he could have. But when he thought of Uncle Zed, he remembered a phrase he'd heard him utter a few times over the years. The words spoke to him just then as if the old man was standing right beside him, whispering them in his ear.

"The darkest places in hell are reserved for those who maintain their neutrality in times of moral crisis."

He was sure his uncle wasn't the originator of the quote. It likely came from the mouth of some historical figure or perhaps some self-help guru with a dozen books under his belt. But Zed never spoke of things he didn't believe. It was that quality that earned him integrity in the eyes of every single person who'd ever met him.

Those words repeated themselves in Sean's skull. He had already spent years of his life immersed in his own personal hell. He had no intention of returning. And walking away from the present situation sure seemed liked a clear act of neutrality.

"I'm sorry," he muttered aloud. "I can't let his happen. There has to be another way."

When he lifted his head to meet Jessica, he expected to watch her crumble to the floor and hear the sound of her bellowing in despair. Instead, he found dryness in her face, as if the intense expression was chiseled in rock. Only her eyes were animated, darting back and forth neurotically between him and Carson. It was if she hadn't heard a word he had just said and was instead engaging in some covert communication that she didn't want him privy to.

He turned his head and saw that Carson was doing the same thing, though he looked far more tormented than she did. Carson's eyes targeted Sean. His mouth hung a bit open, and he looked as though he wanted to tell Sean something but couldn't quite bring himself to speak.

"What?" said Sean.

When Sean saw Carson's eyes hurtle toward the window behind him, Sean spun around and found a small red dot illuminated at the center of the glass.

Jessica launched herself forward, throwing her body over her daughter protectively.

"No!" Carson yelled in warning as Sean's eye caught a thin red beam flash directly across it.

Sean slung his head to the side just as the window loudly exploded from the center. Burning pain tore along the back of Sean's skull as he lost his balance and toppled to the floor.

Fierce, freezing wind howled into the small room as gunfire popped off, muffled by the rough weather. It sounded like fireworks in the distance, but its proximity was surely close. Sparks flew from the ceiling, and then the room went pitch black.

Anna screamed in panic.

Sean scrambled along the floor amidst the chaotic screaming. The wind peppered him with blowing papers and other loose objects. The bitter cold air made it hard to breathe.

The gun was no longer in his hand. He didn't know where it was. The room was black, and there was a sick moaning sound to his right. He believed it was coming from Carson.

When Sean's hand went to the back of his own head, he felt moisture. Warm blood. Seemingly a lot of it.

"Sean!" Carson called out from the dark, sounding very weak and resigned.

"What?" Sean snarled.

"Run!"

The word was spoken with such dejection that it came across like a dying request. *Had Carson been hit by one of the bullets?*

It had to have been Dr. Phil who'd fired the shots, Sean rationalized. He must have gotten back, seen Sean through the window with a gun in his hand, and tried to take him out. Feeling warm drops of blood tapping the back of his neck and not knowing the extent of his injury, he feared the doctor might have been successful.

A splintered thought darted through Sean's mind as he crawled toward the door. Carson had tried to warn him of the laser sight. Jessica hadn't. She'd decided at that moment that not only was Norman Booth's death worth the life of her daughter, but so was Sean's. Like Dr. Phil, she was now *all in*.

He could hear Jessica whispering words of comfort to her daughter in the dark. He knew she was fine. He also knew *he* wouldn't be fine unless he heeded Carson's advice. The doctor was likely on his way inside the building to finish the job.

A small ray of light from the hallway beamed in through a half-inch hole in the door sliced open by one of the bullets. Sean yanked the door open and stumbled out into the hallway. He heard a loud thud from somewhere near the stairs. He ran in the opposite direction, down the hallway toward the room where Jessica had come from earlier. His shoulder knocked a plaque of some sort from the wall as he rounded a corner and found himself at the edge of a small landing area where he saw some loose boots and a utility sink. The sink's faucet was pouring water.

He spotted a door at the side of the landing as the sound of someone jogging along the tile floor echoed from down the hallway. Sean was through the door in no time, entering a large, dim room that was so cold and full of clutter that he knew it had to be a garage. The ticking sound of a recently killed car engine confirmed his speculation.

He desperately ran his hands all over the wall beside him, his fingers raking through filth and grime as he cursed for a light switch. He found a mounted plastic box that felt like a garage door opener and pressed its center. He let out a gasp of relief when the loud sound of grinding metal gears fired up.

A dull light from above snapped on, the bulb embedded in the garage door operator. He saw bare sheet rock walls and Jessica's car. Large blue tarps hid a big object beside the car. The Chevy Cavalier was covered with an even layer of snow except for the windows where beads of water drained down them.

He lunged to the car and looked through its side window. He found no key in the ignition. He remembered the keys in his pocket. He dug them out, but knew he didn't have enough time to test them out on the car. He didn't even think he had enough time to look for something to use as a weapon, even a crowbar or shovel. He was convinced that his pursuer would bust through the door behind him at any second, brandishing his *own* weapon—whatever piece that laser sighting was mounted to.

Sean bolted for the slowly opening garage door. When he heard a commotion break out behind him, he dove to his chest and slid under the door. It was a hard landing and he felt something crack beneath him, but he rolled until he was outside. There he was immediately engulfed in the savage, biting wind and heavy snow. The elements pounded him mercilessly and he was almost knocked to his side as he scrambled to his feet. The keys were no longer in his hand.

A gunshot ripped out from somewhere back in the garage, and the sound of tortured steel competed with that of the howling wind. Sean let a wicked gust of air dictate in which direction he ran. There were no lights outside the building, at least none turned on. The night and the dense snow gave him some cover. He took advantage of it as best he could, working himself into a full-fledged sprint away from the front of the building and off in the direction he thought was east.

Chapter 29

"Just another hundred yards," said Martinez in near exuberance. "It will be on the right. A building."

When the police cruiser rounded another bend, the land flattened out and the road widened. Lumbergh watched Martinez's broad, bloodthirsty smile gleam in the rearview mirror. The chief quickly pulled over to the inside shoulder of the road. He positioned the cruiser under the broad, overhanging limbs of a drooping pine and popped the transmission into park.

"What are you doing?" asked Martinez, his eyes narrowing.

"Did you think I was going to drive right up to their front step and let them see a police car?"

The intern's face was riddled with confusion. "I . . . I guess not."

Lumbergh reached into the glove compartment and began pulling out shotgun shells. He shoved them into his jacket pocket.

The smile returned to Martinez's face. "Can you fire a shotgun, Chief? You know, with your arm?"

Lumbergh reached under his jacket, wincing as he did, and awkwardly peeled the sling from his shoulder. He tossed it to the floor mat in front of the passenger's seat. "I can now," he replied, trying to convince himself it was true.

He wasn't sure he could effectively grip the forestock of the weapon with his left hand, but with his arm free of the sling he believed he could at least steady it. If not, he still had his Glock holstered at his side. He loaded some extra clips for the handgun into a pocket as well. After he killed the engine, he jammed his keys in with the clips. He turned on his police radio and fiddled with the channel.

"What are you doing?" Martinez yelped out, pressing his face against the grill. His frenzied eyes flashed back and forth from the mirror to the radio.

Lumbergh ignored the question, speaking into his radio instead. "This is Police Chief Gary Lumbergh of Winston calling for Sheriff Richard Redick. Please come back."

"Chief!" Martinez screamed. "Why are you calling him?"

"I'm telling him where we are."

Martinez slammed his forehead into the grill twice. "No! You said you were going in alone! You said you didn't *need* anyone's help! You promised me!"

"I *am* going in alone, Martinez," said Lumbergh. "I'm not waiting around for them to get here."

"Then why?" Martinez cried, leaning back and repeatedly kicking both of his feet against the grill.

"Because if I don't come back, I don't want you freezing to death in the car."

Martinez stopped kicking. He leaned forward, pressing his nose to the grill. His eyes were crazy and he was desperately out of breath.

"That's right, Martinez. You sure as hell aren't coming with me."

"No!" Martinez bellowed as if a rockslide was crumbling down on top of him. "Liar! *Mentiroso! Mentiroso!*"

When Redick came on the air, Lumbergh ignored the temper tantrum going on behind him. He let the sheriff vent out his anger over what Lumbergh had done to him. Lumbergh then raised his voice and spoke over Martinez's ballistic shrieking, giving the sheriff detailed directions to his location. He provided no other information.

"What in the hell's going on in the background? What's that noise?" questioned Redick, frustrated over Lumbergh's refusal to elaborate on the situation.

Lumbergh turned his head to Martinez and watched the wiry, unhinged little man bounce off the back of a car like a rubber ball.

Lumbergh held the radio close to his mouth. "The squeals of a baby pig."

Chapter 30

C lusters of tall, wavering pines heavy with snow were barely
visible. They bordered the open, fairly flat ground Sean ran
along. It could have been a dirt road below his feet, but it was hard
to tell in the snow. He saw no tire tracks. The doctor must have come
in from the opposite direction.

There were lots of hiding spots. Trees. Snowdrifts. Sean knew
he was leaving tracks though, and even with the snow coming
down as hard as it was, they wouldn't be immediately covered up.
Anyone with a flashlight could effectively pursue him. Though he
was freezing cold and felt lightheaded, he knew he had to put more
distance between him and the building before he stopped running.

He glanced back over his shoulder; the wind instantly brought
tears to his eyes. He could no longer see the building or anything
beyond blowing snow. He felt his pants sliding down from his waist
and he tugged them back up.

His hand then went to his head and he cringed when he felt the
burning of an open wound. His fingers searched for a bullet or an
entry wound. They found neither. It had to be a graze, albeit a bad
one considering the amount of blood he had lost. The back of his
head still felt warm from whatever was oozing out, so he pressed the
palm of his hand tightly to it. He hoped the pressure would end the
bleeding.

After a minute, he jammed his other hand into his front pocket,
limping along as he did. His fingers were already turning numb
from the cold, but he managed to detect the edge of the cell phone

he'd taken from the desk. He pinched it in his grip and yanked it from his pocket. It fell to the ground in multiple pieces.

"No!" he moaned, halting and falling to his knees.

He sifted through the snow and found jagged pieces of plastic and some exposed wires. The phone must have been demolished earlier from his dive under the garage door. He wasn't sure if it was fixable, but the weather and the darkness made it impossible to even try. He picked up every piece he could find, hoping he had them all, and shoved them back into his pocket.

He climbed to his feet and pulled his pants up again. It was then that he saw a single light cut through the night from a distance away. It was in the direction he'd come from. It looked like a pinprick at first—so small that he had almost missed it. It quickly grew larger, however, and took on the shape of a rectangle. Whoever had the light was moving along at a good pace.

It was possible that it didn't belong to the doctor, but it likely did. The doctor's actions had made it clear that he wanted Sean dead. If Sean got away, everything he and his family had been working toward would be brought to an immediate end. As far as they were concerned, a free Sean Coleman meant a dead Anna. It was obvious how they stood on that ultimatum.

He pressed his hand back to his wound and continued running. He tucked his head low between his shoulders, enduring the weather as best he could in just a sweatshirt, loose jeans, and hiking boots.

A humming noise began to filter its way through the whistling wind, and when he spun his head to look for its source, he found that the light had grown much closer. It was approaching so quickly that he discounted the possibility that it was a flashlight. It had to belong to a vehicle, and the hum that was loudening in volume was the sound of its engine.

He was certain he hadn't been spotted yet. The falling snow was too dense. Visibility was too limited. That would change at any second. The vehicle was just about upon him.

He had no more time to think. He clenched his teeth and darted for the shoulder of the road. He leaped over a snow bank sandwiched by two trees. He expected to find ground on the other side, but there was nothing but air. He fell ten feet before his legs sank into the side of a snow-covered hill as if they were two large lawn darts.

The vehicle flew by on the road above him, its single headlight flaring up the night for a moment. Even before he could force his legs from the snow and climb to his hand and knees, he heard a reduction in the engine. It had to belong to a snowmobile. The sound was too distinct. The driver likely stopped accelerating once the footprints he was tracking came to an abrupt end.

The slope he was on was steep, but the older, crunchy snow below the fresh powder gave him some traction to keep from falling down it. He worked down the incline quickly but deliberately, sliding on his chest at times and moving his arms in a swimming motion. Once a couple of large pines were between him and the view from the road, he clung to a bare aspen and positioned himself behind a long snowdrift covering an overturned tree.

Though the ridge above gave him some marginal cover from the wind, his body felt frozen. He could barely feel his fingers and his toes were getting there as well. The hair in his nose had turned to ice and his face felt tingly. He struggled to breathe.

The light above the ridge grew brighter as the driver of the snowmobile positioned the vehicle so that the headlight pointed in the direction where Sean had leapt from the road. Due to the steepness of the slope, Sean was still hidden in the dark. Only the tops of the tree he clung to were illuminated. He kept still, poking his head just slightly above the drift.

A man's shadow crossed in front of the beam of light before his silhouette came into view. He was bundled up tight, wearing a fat winter coat with a hood pulled firmly over his head. He appeared to wear ski goggles. The fur-trim of his hood was so dense that he looked like a lion whose mane was fluttering wildly in the wind, a predator stalking its prey.

He stared out over the ridge for a moment before disappearing and quickly returning with a flashlight. Sean ducked down as its beam methodically traced the area. His teeth began to chatter and he wrapped his arms around his chest to try and keep the rest of his body from shaking.

The beam swept over Sean's head a few times, never staying in one spot long enough to make him suspect he'd been spotted. When the small red dot of a laser sight accompanied the beam in its search, he held his breath.

"You must be freezing down there, mate!" the man's voice called out in the thick accent Sean recognized from earlier on the phone. It was barely audible above the weather, but Sean managed to make out what he was saying. "Come on up here and we'll sort it all out back inside! I'll throw a billy on the stove!"

Sean held still. His eyes rolled in his head. He knew there was zero chance that Dr. Phil was going to let him live. If he popped his head up, it would be shot off in half a second.

"You'll die out here, you bloody bastard!" the doctor screamed, his voice raising a couple of octaves. "Don't be stupid!"

Sean knew the doctor could very well be right. If he didn't die from being severely underdressed in sub-zero temperatures, covered only in a sweatshirt and jeans, he'd certainly acquire frostbite—the kind people didn't recover from without losing parts of their limbs.

The doctor was counting on desperation prompting a desperate move, but Sean knew that a slim chance of survival was better than no chance. The one thing he had going for him was that he was sure the doctor wasn't going to try and come down the hill. The drop-off from the road and the slope below it were terrain that couldn't be negotiated well with a gun in one hand and a flashlight in the other, especially with the weather. For now, the two were stuck in a stalemate.

Sean gazed hypnotically at the partially lit landscape below him, blowing warm breath into his cupped hands. He made sure to completely trap it with his fingers tight together, aware that the doctor might otherwise see a virtual smoke signal rising from his hiding spot.

Heavy, crowded flakes whipped by almost horizontally between trees and the large, protruding rocks that rested under the frosty white blanket. His mind wandered to the snowstorms that he and his sister used to watch in wonderment as kids from his bedroom window. It was back before his father had left. Seemingly happier times. Simpler times for sure. Snowfall like that would mean a day off from school. Diana and he would spend it building forts in the snow and even the occasional snowman, though Sean always thought they were corny.

Perhaps it was those memories that urged him to believe just for a moment that if he could just last until the morning, everything would somehow be all right. His adult sensibilities quickly kicked in, however, and chased youthful naivety off into the night.

The doctor continued to call for Sean to show himself, shouting above the unrelenting wind. Sean could barely make out what he was saying at times. The doctor's rants altered between impassioned pleas and angry tirades as his frustration grew. Sean grew confident in his belief that his pursuer was too afraid to come down the hill after him.

A quick flash of light from further down the slope suddenly triggered Sean's attention. It appeared between two large trees that jetted out from the hillside. Before Sean could make out what it was, it disappeared. It did so in accordance with a change in direction of the doctor's flashlight, suggesting it was a reflection.

He kept his eyes trained in the direction of the now hidden object and he waited for the flashlight to expose its outline again. When it did, Sean saw what looked like a thin, horizontal metal rod. It was pretty far down the hill, which made it look small, but he was certain that it wasn't merely part of a fence. It belonged to something larger. A building perhaps. The edge of a rooftop.

He hoped it wasn't a mirage brought on by wishful thinking, like an imaginary oasis in the middle of a desert as portrayed in cartoons. The doctor either wasn't interested in it or couldn't see it through the blowing snow. He kept reflexively pulling his beam away before Sean could get a good look at it. If it was a building, maybe it was a home. Maybe someone lived there—someone with a phone. Maybe even with a gun.

Sean's instincts told him not to stray far from the road, even with what was happening. If it wasn't a building below, what would he do then? The road was the only other sign of civilization he had seen since leaving the restaurant. He had no way of knowing how remote of an area he was in, so if he lost track of the road or couldn't get back to it due to the incline of the hill, he might never find his way out of the area alive. He also thought about the possibility of a snowplow or ranger driving by. He wondered if he could somehow get a driver's attention, even with Dr. Phil hovering above like a vulture.

"Come on, Sean!" the doctor yelled in anger. "Get your ass up here! You'll die if you don't!"

Leaving his hiding spot was a risk, but it was a risk Sean decided he had to take. He waited until the flashlight beam and its laser shadow swung away from his position before making his move. He lunged forward, crawling quickly on his hands and knees through the snow. Lumbering downward at what felt like a sixty-degree grade, his hands soon collapsed in front of him, their numbness making them unwilling partners in his escape. He switched to his elbows.

He scurried around trees and over snow mounds until the hill grew too steep to continue on headfirst. He swung his legs in front of him and began sliding down on his butt.

The glow of the flashlight suddenly whipped onto Sean. When he saw his own shadow cast along a thick tree a few yards in front of him, he knew the doctor would open fire. He snarled and lunged forward, leaping through the air as the shots rang out. They sounded like they came from a cap gun under the brutal wind that pressed against Sean as he dropped back to earth.

When he landed, his momentum put him on spontaneous footing. He did his best to maintain his balance, ducking and weaving around tree after tree to put as many obstacles as possible between him and the doctor.

Shots continued to fire.

Sean heard a couple of bullets split through wood. One sounded like it ricocheted off a rock.

When one of his feet dropped into a patch of unevenly deep snow, he lost control and he went down hard. He tumbled forward, crashing through limbs and bouncing off trunks and rocks. He managed to get an arm up in front of his face to protect it, sparing him some stiff shots that otherwise would have broken his nose or done worse.

He plunged down the slope for what seemed like an eternity until he finally came to a rest on his back along an unexpectedly flat patch of land. He held still for a moment, realizing that he was still alive and in one piece. He lifted his head and carefully looked over his shoulder, scouting for the doctor's position. The doctor still hadn't left the ridge. The distant glare of his flashlight swiveled back and forth erratically. He had lost track of his prey.

Sean slowly started to climb to his feet, but a sharp pain jolted up from his side. He winced as he raised his shirt and wiped his sleeve along the tender area to check for blood. It was too dark to tell for sure, but he didn't see any. He also felt no bulge. It didn't look as though he'd been shot, but he wondered if he'd suffered a cracked rib from the fall.

Other aches and pains could be felt throughout his body. They would slow him down, but he could walk, and that's all that seemed to matter now. With his face twisted in discomfort, he surveyed the area and spotted the building he had seen from the hill. It stood just about twenty yards away. It wasn't someone's home. Far from it. It looked to be a small storage shed with thin, weathered walls made of wood and an arched tin roof. A blanket of snow covered the wall that faced the wind. Behind the shed was an open area, perhaps a small meadow for grazing livestock or a patch of land for farming.

He heard a faint buzzing sound in the distance, and when he looked back up at the ridge, the beam from the flashlight was gone. He traced the headlight from the snowmobile for a second as it glided along the ridge, back in the direction from which it had come. It soon disappeared from view. The doctor had left, but Sean doubted he had given up the hunt.

He tugged at his pants, circled around to the opposite side of the shed, and found its door. A faint bulb from a light mounted at its side gave Sean hope that the shelter was equipped with electricity. Unfortunately, a closer look revealed that it was nothing more than a solar-powered landscape light, the kind people bought for a couple of bucks at a hardware store to use as decor in their yards along a pathway or garden. It served as a makeshift porch light, barely bright enough to reveal a padlocked metal door latch at its edge.

A hard boot from Sean made short work of the lock, splintering the frame as the door flung open. He trudged onto plank flooring inside and quickly ran his arm along the wall beside him. His elbow bumped up against some hidden shelving and he knocked small items to the floor as he searched for a light switch. He found none. He stepped back outside just long enough to yank the light from the wall. It came off easy. Pinning it between the palms of his hands because his frozen fingers were having trouble gripping it, he looked around inside.

Being out of the wind let him catch his breath and wipe the tears from his eyes. He was still freezing and shaking uncontrollably, but the elimination of the wind helped him think straight. The light was so dim that he couldn't make out which items were what in the shed until he was just a few inches from them. He found some grease guns and aerosol cans along the shelves, accompanied by some old rolls of duct tape, twine, and a box of cloth rags. The layer of dust that covered everything suggested that it had been a long time since anyone else had been inside.

He crossed over to the other end of the shed, his shins and knees knocking up against solid metal items that felt like equipment. When he felt the corner of a table press into his side, he twisted his torso in what narrow space he had and found a workbench. There wasn't much across the top of it. Some small stain cans, a metal coffee can filled with nuts and bolts, and an anchored vice. On the pegboard mounted above it, he found a number of dangling hand tools including a small hammer, and a few wrenches and screwdrivers. There were also a few bungee cords.

He'd hoped to spot a hatchet, a knife, or something else that he could use as an effective weapon if needed, but an oversized, open-ended wrench was the best available. He managed to lift it from its hook and slide it under the waistline of his pants. It dropped down into one of his pant legs.

"Come on," he grunted, angry that his loose-fitting pants wouldn't let him store the weapon. He lifted his leg and let the wrench spill out to the floor.

There were some smaller plastic items arranged along the pegboard. A few paint brushes, some zip-ties, and an item that widened Sean's eyes the moment he realized what it was.

He initially thought it was just another screwdriver, but it was a utility lighter. Mostly made of plastic but with a metal nose, they were built to ignite a small flame at the pull of a trigger. It was the kind people typically used to light outdoor grills, but Sean planned on using it to bring his shivering body some warmth.

He dumped the coffee can upside-down and let all of the nuts and bolts inside fall to the top of the workbench in a loud heap. He then placed the empty can on the floor and filled it with some wadded rags he grabbed off of one of the shelves. He sorted through the collection of aerosol cans until he found some WD-40. He dropped to his knees and depressed the nozzle with the palm of his hand, thoroughly dousing the rags.

Getting the lighter to work was the toughest part. There was barely enough room to squeeze one of his deadened fingers through the trigger. After he finally got it hooked, he cursed as he worked on the complicated safety switch on top. Matching the pulling of the two levers was a challenging task in eighty-degree weather; doing so with numb fingers was nearly impossible. He eventually got his flame and wasted no time holding it to the rags.

The rags lit up like an inferno, nearly knocking him backwards. He leaned forward and held his open hands over the blaze. The fire brightened the inside of the room, its flames casting dancing shadows along the walls. He couldn't feel its warmth at first, but his hands soon sensed the burn of being thawed out. He held them in front of him for a moment, inspecting, and found no blackness. He breathed a sigh of relief.

The walls of the shed continually creaked from the strong winds outside. There was a decent draft pouring in between the wooden boards and the flapping door where he'd broken off the latch. It wasn't strong enough to put out the fire, and he hunched over it, greeting the warmth that brushed against his face.

With the inside of the shed now almost entirely illuminated, he raised his head and took stock of the items around him. He found some farming equipment sprawled along the floor, including a walk-behind tractor and a sickle bar mower. They didn't appear to be there for storage, but rather to be worked on. Both were turned on their sides amidst loose parts. There was thick, coiled rope hanging by a nail in the wall, as well as an old, rusted bow-rake hanging from two nails. A couple of gas cans sat in a corner. A lot of clutter lined a second set of shelves, including random cuts of wood, boxes of nails and screws, and more paint cans.

When Sean saw what appeared to be a blanket or a thick tablecloth hanging off the corner of a shelf, he climbed to his feet. Cringing with each movement, he pulled the cover down and wrapped it around his shoulders before returning to the fire. He added a few more rags to the can and fueled the flames again with more WD-40.

After ten minutes or so, his body stopped shaking and he eyed the large wrench lying on the floor. He climbed to his feet and snagged a bungee cord from the wall. He laced it through his belt loops and hooked the ends together in front of the top button of his jeans. With his pants now snug, he slid the wrench into the back waistline, and this time it stayed in place.

He understood that there was no way he was going to make it back up the hill to the road—not at night in the middle of a snowstorm anyway.

With the meadow outside likely some type of farmland, he wondered if the property's owner might live somewhere nearby. He had seen no other buildings around, but that didn't mean one didn't exist somewhere, hidden among the trees. There at least had to be another road, some way of getting to the meadow and the shed from the outside world.

His thoughts scattered when he heard a distant buzzing sound trickle in from the gusts of wind that howled outside of the shed. He gasped, and then made his way to the door, still wearing the blanket, and poked his head outside. He saw the single headlight of a snowmobile blistering though the snow along the meadow.

"Shit!" he barked.

He plodded back inside, letting the blanket fall from his shoulders as he grabbed the bow-rake from the wall. He kicked over the coffee can, knocking the rags inside it to the floor, and stomped out their flames with his feet. If the doctor hadn't already seen the light from inside the shed, he wasn't going to let him.

He looked outside again and saw that the snowmobile hadn't

grown much closer. It was advancing in the general direction of the shed, but it was moving extremely slowly, possibly even at idle speed. The doctor was being very cautious in his approach.

Sean realized that staying inside a small building with thin walls would make him easy pickings for a man with a gun. He choked up on the rake and exited through the door, slipping around to the opposite side of the shed. Suddenly the front of the building lit up from the vehicle's headlight.

Shuffling backwards on his feet, Sean gripped the rake as if it was a lifeline. The engine of the vehicle steadily purred without deviation as it grew closer. He watched in confusion as the beam of the light moved on past the shed and began exposing the landscape at the bottom of the hill he'd fallen down. The vehicle came into view, and to Sean's shock, no one was riding it.

A second beam of light suddenly flared up from directly behind him. He spun around in terror. The dot of a small red laser was pinned directly on his chest.

"Bang!" a man's voice shouted out from the night, his silhouette unclear from behind the center of the blinding light.

Sean recoiled, anticipating the next sound he heard to be the blast of a gun as a bullet pierced his sternum.

Instead it was the man's voice again. "Back inside the shack, mate. It's fucking cold out here."

Chapter 31

Lumbergh carried the shotgun low as he slowly crept his way up the side of the road. He kept constant surveillance of the land around him as he did. The freezing wind forced fresh tears from his eyes when he faced it. He wiped them away with his shoulder. A Mag light dangled at his side, switched to the off position to avoid detection. The radio in his pocket was powered on, but the volume was set at zero.

The further he walked without finding anything resembling a building, the stronger the nagging feeling stewed in his gut that Martinez had steered him wrong. He prayed that what the intern had told him wasn't simply part of another game, another deception. When Lumbergh finally heard the eerie groans of metal swaying in the wind, his doubts subsided.

There was a wide sign mounted to a tall pole eight feet high just a few yards away from him, wobbling from the weather. It was worn down and some of its panes had fallen or been blown off. He struggled to read it without any light. The only word he could make out with any confidence was "Grill."

It appeared to belong to a restaurant. He shuffled passed it, raising his shotgun and cringing when his tender arm felt the weight of the forestock. He told himself that he was a fool for proceeding on his own, especially in the shape he was in, but he was convinced that he couldn't afford to relinquish command of the situation to Redick. The stakes were too high.

He heard the wind whipping up against a solid object somewhere in front of him, and mere seconds later, the outline of a large building presented itself. It was a long, single-story building. He jogged to the side of it, ducking. When he reached what he believed to be the front of the building, he pressed his back to the wall. As far as he could tell, the windows had all been boarded up, as were the doors a little further down. The doors appeared to be the main entrance to the building. There had to be another way inside.

He was about to swing around to the back when he noticed a faint light spread out across the east end of the building. He carefully made his way along the front side, keeping low and trying to listen for movement or voices inside the building—an impossible task with the rough wind.

The closer he got, the more it became apparent that the light was from an open garage or service door. By the time he reached the spot, his heart was pounding through his chest.

The light exposed a driveway that led up to the open garage. The snow along the driveway showed signs of a lot of activity; multiple trails of footprints spread out into the night. Among them were what appeared to be snowmobile tracks.

Lumbergh wondered if whoever was inside had somehow seen him coming and had taken off. He deemed that unlikely. When his eyes found crimson-colored splatter in the snow, he swallowed hard. Whatever lingering doubts he'd had about being in the right place quickly scurried off in the wind.

He clenched his teeth and swung inside the garage with his shotgun pointing in front of him. He held it close to eye level, controlling his breathing while he cased the inside of the room. He saw a Chevy Cavalier parked inside and a bare area where the snowmobile had likely been parked under a tarp (now wadded up in a heap to the side). The light from above was coming from an automatic door opener. That meant either the door had just been opened or that someone had very recently tripped the sensor line along its base.

He spotted a door at the back of the garage and made his way to it. He twisted the knob and found it unlocked. Cautiously, he pressed open the door and slid inside.

He found himself in a small landing area where the fluctuating sound of running water came from behind a near corner. He moved forward, twisting himself around the corner with his finger hugging the shotgun trigger.

Water poured from a faucet into a large, unattended sink. Lumbergh negotiated his way around it, his adrenaline pumping. When he reached the end of a bright hallway, the frantic sound of a woman screaming suddenly echoed through the interior of the building. It came from very close by.

"I'm sorry!" the woman wailed repeatedly, amidst what sounded like a child crying.

The urgency in the woman's voice and the subsequent sound of a man moaning brought Lumbergh down the hallway quickly. *Could the man be Sean?* He glanced back over his shoulder twice as he made his way toward an open door where all of the action seemed to be coming. Anxiety tore through his veins at the sight of the many doors that lined the hallway of the unfamiliar building. There were lots of hiding spots for someone to get the jump on him. He was a sitting duck.

When the painfully loud creak of a floorboard gave away his presence, he bit his lip.

"Adam!" the woman's voice called out. "Did you find Phillip?"

Lumbergh darted forward and swung inside the entryway of the room with his gun drawn. He was greeted by an unexpected blast of wind that tore through the room from a large shattered window at the opposite end.

The first person he saw under the light of a single table lamp on a small nightstand was a young girl. She was huddled in a corner of the room in a nightgown, her hands pressed against her ears, and she had no hair. Her wet eyes met Lumbergh's, then the gun in his hands. She screamed in horror.

His eye caught movement at the other end of the small room, and he immediately swung his gun toward it. There he saw a woman with long red hair that twisted in the wind.

The red fox.

She knelt on the floor beside an overturned rocking chair. She spun to meet his glare and the barrels of his shotgun, and shrieked.

"Police! Let me see your hands!" Lumbergh yelled.

With her eyes already red and filled with tears, she quickly whipped her hands into the air. The blood that laced them was nearly as bright as her hair.

He gasped. His gaze dropped to a man's pair of legs that sprouted out from behind the toppled chair.

Lumbergh felt the floor beneath him bend and twist. Lightheadedness sank in and his stomach dropped to his ankles. The shotgun nearly fell from his trembling hand.

"Sean," he whispered, fearing he had arrived too late.

Just as a building rage began to boil from under his skin, the woman's voice pierced through it.

"Let me keep helping him!" she pled with desperation in her voice. "I have a medical background, and he's in bad shape!"

He was still alive.

Lumbergh lunged forward. He kicked the fallen chair and a smashed floor lamp out of the way before dropping to his knees, letting his gun fall beside him. He reached for the bloodied man whose shirt was partially peeled from his chest. The frightened, conquered eyes that he found staring up at him took Lumbergh's breath away, but they didn't belong to his brother-in-law.

Lumbergh glanced at the blood that streamed from a hole in

the man's neck just above his left trapezius. Some had pooled beside him on the floor. He then looked up at the woman before him. The two acknowledged a mutual understanding with their eyes, and Lumbergh instructed her to continue helping the man.

Lumbergh edged backwards on his knees, pulling the shotgun along the floor with him. Broken glass crackled below his body.

The woman pressed a bloody, wadded up towel against the wound and held it firmly in place.

"The bullet's still in there," she said.

"You're Jessica, aren't you?" he asked, his voice shaky.

Though she kept her focus on her work, the increased tension in her body signaled to him that she was stunned that he knew who she was. She nodded.

"Who else is here inside the building?" he asked, pulling his radio from his side. "Who's Adam? Who's Phillip?"

Before she could answer, the man on the floor spoke. Lumbergh was unsure until that moment that he even could, due to his injury.

"They went after Sean," he weakly gurgled out. His mouth was the only part of his body that moved. "They're going to kill him."

"What?" Lumbergh barked, sitting up on his knees.

"They're not!" lashed out Jessica, keeping her eyes focused on her work. "I let Adam out to stop Phillip. To bring him back here. He's a doctor; a surgeon. He can better help you, Andy."

Lumbergh squinted at the sound of the name. He traced the contour of the wounded man's face. His eyes widened upon recognition. "Are you Andrew Carson?"

"Yes," Jessica answered before Carson could.

"Listen to me," muttered Carson, his eyes floating in disarray. "Phillip's going to kill Sean. He tried to kill me."

"No," she moaned, shaking her head in denial. "He shot you by accident." Her defensiveness suggested she was trying unsuccessfully to convince herself that what she was saying was true.

"No accident," muttered Carson, a tear rolling down his cheek. "He set his sight on me right after he shot at Sean. No accident. Sean was right. Two liabilities. Flies in the ointment."

Jessica didn't react to his words, seemingly fighting back her emotions from spinning further out of control.

"Which direction did they head in?" asked Lumbergh.

"I don't know," she answered.

"Please," groaned Carson. "Don't leave me alone with her."

Jessica lifted her confused eyes to meet his.

"I don't trust her anymore," he said as more tears poured from his eyes.

Hearing those words, Jessica pursed her lips and her own tears began sliding like rivers down each side of her face. She kept the pressure on his neck and begged understanding from Carson with her dreary gaze. He looked away from her.

Lumbergh couldn't possibly conceive what kind of bond the two had seemingly formed while Carson was a captive, but it was clear whatever foundation it had been built upon had just come crumbling to the ground. It was also apparent, to the chief's immense frustration, that he couldn't take off after Sean. Not now. He couldn't leave a direly wounded Andrew Carson—who was asking for his help—alone at the hands of one of the people who had abducted him.

Lumbergh cursed and pulled his radio to his mouth. He got Redick back on the air and told him to call for an ambulance. Redick pushed back, demanding more details.

"A man's been shot, Redick! Now get me that ambulance and get your fat ass out here! I need you to take my place!"

As the lawmen argued back and forth over the radio, Lumbergh's eyes drifted to the gaze of the little girl who sat in the corner of the room. She was sitting perfectly still, clearly too frightened to do much else. She took shallow, labored breaths. The purity and innocence in her face provided a surreal contrast to the chaos that was ensuing around her.

He could only imagine the emotional damage the scene being played out caused her, adding to whatever ailment she was dealing with physically.

"Anna," said Jessica. "If you need your oxygen, it's under your bed, okay, Peanut?"

The girl shook her head.

"Sir," Jessica said to Lumbergh. "Can you put something under his feet? They need to be raised up again."

Lumbergh waded up some small blankets and used them to elevate Carson's legs. It was then that he noticed for the first time that Carson had been treated for an older injury. He had large bandages and gauze wrapped across his stomach. They were poking out from under what was left of his shirt.

"Are you touching me?" Carson unexpectedly asked. "My legs?"

Lumbergh nodded through narrow eyes.

Carson's eyes drifted up to the ceiling. He looked utterly defeated. "I can't feel them," he stuttered. "I can't feel my legs. Not again."

Lumbergh and Jessica exchanged sober glares.

When Jessica turned her head to Carson, her eyes bulged and she screamed out, "Oh, Jesus!"

Carson's eyes were rolled up into his head and his body began to seize.

"What's happening?" Lumbergh shouted.

Chapter 32

Sean couldn't believe he had fallen for the doctor's stunt with the snowmobile. It was a common ploy used in countless television programs and movies in the 1980s, and thus he should have known better.

Lock the accelerator down and let the vehicle drive on its own. Misdirection 101.

"We've never been properly introduced, mate," said the doctor with some gruff in his voice.

Both men stood facing each other inside the small shed as the weather wailed outside. The doctor was a small man, much smaller than he had looked from the road. His back was to the door. Sean's arms were raised. The flashlight beam trained on his face by the doctor kept him partially blind while the red laser light pasted to his chest kept him still. Sean could barely make out the features of the doctor's face and he couldn't see the gun well. All he knew was that it was definitely a handgun, not a rifle. The sound of the snowmobile's engine buzzed steadily, somewhere in the background. The vehicle was probably pinned up against a tree, still in gear.

Sean said quickly, "You're Dr. Phillip Robinson, Australian asshole."

The doctor said nothing for a moment. Sean's brazen words seemed to leave him stunned. He finally let out a snort and a snicker. A wide grin formed on his face from behind the glare of the flashlight.

"Well, they told you who I am, did they?" he said.

"They told me enough. They think you're some kind of hero. An angel sent from above to save a little girl's life."

The doctor nodded. "But you don't think so?"

"No. I think you're the first doctor I've met who doesn't care about life at all."

The doctor's body tensed and he angrily snapped the laser beam from Sean's chest to his forehead. Sean fought back the urge to turn away. If he was going to die, he was going to go out with dignity. He glared forward, nostrils flaring.

"You ignorant bastard!" the doctor growled. "What I'm doing, I'm doing to save *many* lives!"

"Bullshit!" Sean fired back. "Someone smart enough to have come up with a cure for cancer wouldn't have to treat a patient in some backwoods, boarded-up restaurant."

The doctor's body shook in rage. Sean expected his finger to pull the trigger at any second.

"She doesn't *have* cancer, you bloody toad!" he screamed out.

"What the hell does she have then?"

"It's called amyloidosis. I wouldn't expect you to have heard of it!"

The term was completely foreign to Sean, but he recognized that the doctor's contemptuous need to validate his actions might buy him some time. He half wondered if that was all that had kept him from getting shot outside.

"What is it?" he asked, remembering the wrench wedged in the back of his pants. His shirt was pulled down over it, so the doctor hadn't seen it when they were outside.

The doctor scoffed. "I'm not going to waste my time explaining concepts like amyloid protein, blood marrow, and platelets to a man of your limited intellect, Mr. Coleman. Not to some mall cop."

"I ain't a mall cop, asshole."

"Whatever. In commoner terms, let's just say that it's a rare disease that leads to a person's organs shutting down. Most people who have it are much older than Anna, but that's what the girl has nonetheless."

"Why is she bald if she doesn't have cancer?" Sean asked.

"Oh Christ, you imbecile," the doctor sneered in condescension. "Chemotherapy isn't just used for cancer patients." He was about to continue when Sean interrupted him.

"So you think you can take whatever's in Norman Booth's blood plasma and use it to cure amy-loid-whatever it is?"

"Amyloidosis," the doctor pronounced in irritation. "No. I don't *think* I can cure it. I *know* I can."

"And you're going to do it here? Instead of in a hospital?"

The doctor's shoulders lowered. "My methods are considered too controversial for the medical community; not just in the States, but also in my country."

"Is there *any* country in which kidnapping someone, strapping them to a bed, and sucking their insides out *wouldn't* be controversial?"

The doctor cackled and shook his head. "You narrow-minded buffoon. You and the rest of the reactionary sheep. . . You never think about the big picture. You never think *outside of the box,* as they say. Every genius of his time was considered too unorthodox—too abstract for what society was comfortable with. Darwin. Tesla. . ."

"So you're a genius now?" Sean asked with a forced chuckle. "*Dr. Phil* is the next Einstein?"

The doctor glared at him coldly. "No, Mr. Coleman. I don't presume to be one of the historical greats, but I do aspire—at the very least—to acquire the recognition of James Harrison."

"James Harrison? The president?" asked Sean.

"You bloody moron!" the doctor sputtered. "You're a Yank and you don't even know your own bloody history! William Henry Harrison and Benjamin Harrison! *They* were your bloody presidents!"

"Thanks for the history lesson. I'll remember that next time I'm on *Jeopardy.*"

Something outside caught Sean's attention, something just

around the edge of the broken door. It was a streak of light that lit up the blowing snow for the briefest of moments. It went unnoticed by the doctor who still had his back to the door. The light didn't seem to have come from the snowmobile. The beam was too thin and the direction was wrong.

"James Harrison is an Australian bloke," continued the doctor. The comment drew Sean's eyes back to him. "He's the most famous plasma donor in the history of the world. *The man with the golden arm*, they call him. Harrison has an unusual plasma composition. So unusual that it is used to treat Rhesus disease. He's been donating regularly for years, and it's estimated that his plasma alone has saved around two million unborn babies from the condition."

The light flashed through the air outside again. This time it was broader in scope. Someone was approaching the shed. Sean shifted his focus back to the doctor. "How can you compare *yourself* to Harrison?" he asked. "If Norman Booth's the one with the super-plasma—the plasma that's gonna save lives—isn't *he* the next James Harrison?"

"He could have been," the doctor answered quickly. "And that's what Jessica and Adam told him when they met with him. He didn't care. He didn't want to be a part of history. So I'm afraid he won't be sharing the spotlight now. His sacrifice, however, will be preserved in the work that I'm doing. Just as Anna's will."

Sean's heart skipped a beat. His eyebrows shot up in shock. "What do you mean by that? Anna's sacrifice? What sacrifice?"

The doctor hesitated before continuing. "I'm afraid it's too late for the girl. If I had gotten to her sooner . . . if Booth would have agreed months ago to work with us . . . I possibly could have saved her."

Sean's mouth hung open. He couldn't form the words to speak.

The doctor continued. "Her organs . . . her heart . . . Her body's going to shut down regardless of what I do. It's too weak, too damaged. She's on a transplant list, but she won't reach the top of it in time. People with amyloidosis aren't prioritized due to the systemic nature of the disease. The postoperative mortality is high as well. Many doctors believe a transplant is a waste of time." He took a breath before continuing. "What I learn from her before she dies is going to save many others who suffer from amyloidosis, or *will* suffer from amyloid heart disease in the future. How her body reacts to what I pull from Booth's *super-plasma*, as you call it, will provide every answer I need. The others will live because of her, and I will never forget that she gave me the tools I needed to make that happen."

"That's what all this is about, you son of a bitch?" Sean shouted. "Your *legacy*? That girl's family thinks you can save her! They think that every single thing they've done has been to keep Anna alive!"

The doctor remained silent.

"You lied to them! You told them that she was going to live!"

"Yes, I lied!" shouted the doctor, his body shaking with anger. "Because this work is more important than them. It's more important than Norman Booth. It's more important than Andrew Carson. And it's sure as hell more important than Sean Coleman."

Sean watched over the shoulder of the enraged doctor as the door directly behind him was slowly pulled open—not by the wind—but by someone.

"I was *meant* to do this!" screamed the doctor in a tantrum. "Do you understand that? I was meant to! Just weeks after I explained my theories over the phone to Jessica, she miraculously found the very type of donor I needed! Do you have any idea what the odds were of that? Do you have the foggiest notion of how rare and valuable a man like Norman Booth is?"

Sean said nothing. He held his eyes on the doctor.

"Anna's death won't be in vain, I assure you. Others will live because of her. And before *you* die, Sean, you should know that your sacrifice will be equally appreciated as well."

"Phillip!" a man's voice rang out from the dark.

Sean's forearm instinctively covered his own face.

The doctor lunged against the wall beside him and spun around, keeping his gun pointed at Sean while he directed the flashlight in the opposite direction from where the voice had come.

Adam's wet glasses and swollen face were suddenly lit up like that of a monster from a climactic scene in a horror movie. Blood from the beating Sean had given him earlier stained his upper lip. He wore a thick jacket and strands of his otherwise matted hair were swaying in the wind. He held a flashlight, pointed at the floor. He held something else in his other hand. His intense eyes scorched a hole right through the doctor.

"Adam!" the doctor said nervously, flipping his head back and forth between him and Sean. "I got him. He didn't get away!"

With no beams now directed at him, Sean carefully lowered his right hand, inching it toward the swell of his back.

"I heard you," said Adam in a hoarse, bleak voice. His head shook ever so slightly. "I heard it all."

The doctor said, "I don't know what you think you heard, Adam, but—"

"You used us, you son of a bitch!" Adam howled. "She's going to die. Anna's going to die and you used us! You told us she would be all right!"

Thick tears rolled down Adam's cheeks from under his glasses as the expression on his face leapt between despair and rage.

Sean's hand gripped the large wrench wedged in his jeans.

"Take it easy, mate," said the doctor. "Listen, there are things I can do for her. Things to make her more comfortable."

At those words, Adam's face recoiled, twisting into something that nearly didn't look human. A mask of pure fury. His arm rose quickly, and in his hand was the gun Sean had lost back in Anna's room. The laser sight left Sean's chest. Sean gripped the wrench tight and lunged at the doctor.

Two deafening gunshots rang out in the small building, each lighting up the entire room for a fraction of a second. The flickers of light granted Sean a flash of visibility just long enough to deliver a stiff shot into the side of the doctor's neck. Both sets of flashlights fell to the floor, as did all three men.

The crackle of broken glass and plastic left only one flashlight operable. It rolled across the floor and came to a hard stop against something. Its beam projected the haunting shadow of an equipment blade across the wall opposite the men.

Among a pile of moving limbs and loud moans, Sean saw the reddened sight of the doctor's handgun he'd dropped. Sean grabbed the weapon, then went for the flashlight. Once it was in his hands, it felt like a Ruger 9mm. He swung it toward the men just in time to see the doctor stumbling out the door with his arm favoring the back of his neck. Sean squeezed the trigger of the gun, but all the bullets caught were the door quickly swinging shut from the wind.

Sean quickly climbed to his feet. He was about to take off in pursuit of the doctor when the beam of his flashlight exposed a pool of blood swiftly spreading across the floor. Sean found Adam. He was alive at the moment, but his face was already turning pale as his wide, scared eyes scoured the ceiling.

Sean fell to his knees, setting the gun on the floor as he held the flashlight between his legs. He unzipped Adam's jacket and peeled it from his body. His shirt was saturated with blood. A fountain of it poured up through a hole in his chest. Sean placed his hand over the wound, trying to control its flow with hard pressure. He knew it wouldn't do much good.

The loudening buzz of the snowmobile engine cut through the wind. The doctor was escaping. Blood streamed from between Sean's fingers as Adam breathed his last, shallow breaths. Sean lifted Adam's head with the cup of his hand. In Adam's eyes, Sean saw defeat.

"It's okay," he said out of instinct, hoping his words brought a little bit of peace to the man who had gone to such great lengths to save the life of his precious little niece.

Sean didn't know what else to say. He didn't know what else a man could possibly want to hear on his way out, even though he'd imagined a thousand times what last words he might have uttered to his uncle had he been there with him the day he was killed.

In the end, it seemed to make sense that just not being alone would likely be the final wish of a man about to leave this world. So Sean held Adam's hand, even as the snowmobile sped off into the night. He nodded at the man who lay on the floor, hoping that the realization that he'd see his niece again soon, healthy and in a better place, might be of some last possible comfort to him.

Chapter 33

Anna crawled out into the hallway, dragging her weak legs behind her as her tears fell to the floor. She couldn't take it anymore. All the blood. The shouting. She prayed to God that her mother and the policeman would save Andy.

She loved Andy. She loved him for his kindness, and had come to think of him as a father. Just before she had fallen asleep in his arms, he had read to her a story of a fish that wouldn't stop growing. When finished, she'd heard him whisper that he loved her, too.

"Please, God. I want Andy to read to me again."

She couldn't breathe well without her oxygen, but she hated wearing the mask. It made her feel like a kitten wound up with a ball of yarn. It also made her feel closer to the end of the journey—the one that would put her in God's arms.

The farther down the hallway she crawled, the less she could hear the angry voices. She glanced at her Barbie nightlight that was plugged into the wall. She always found Barbie's smile to be warm and fresh. Her mother sometimes called the doll an optimist because she "didn't have a single care in the world." Anna wished she could be like Barbie.

As she slowly progressed down the hallway, she saw that her Uncle Adam's office door was open. She decided that he must have left it like that when he took off outside after the big man who swore so many times. She was sad that her uncle was in such a hurry and had not said goodbye.

She wasn't supposed to go into his office, not without knocking first. But with the door open and him not there, she thought that it might be okay this time. She slid along the floor until she was through the doorway. There before her was the coffee mug she had given him. It was broken. The sight made her sad. She pulled the wet pieces of the mug together and closely examined them. She was sure she could fix it with a little glue, and she hoped that she and Uncle Adam could do it together as a fun project.

When she looked up, she saw that all of the small television sets above his desk were turned on. She smiled. They had been off whenever she had been in the room at other times. Her uncle didn't want her to know what he was watching on them. She never understood why.

After watching what was on the screens, her grin went away. The shows were boring. Blowing snow. No sound. There was something happening in one of the screens, though, on the television farthest away from her. She climbed up onto her uncle's desk chair to take a closer look. It wasn't easy. Her arms were weak, but they worked better than her legs. Out of breath, she wished she had brought her oxygen after all.

She pushed aside a glass jar of white liquid sitting on the desk that was in her way. She found a sticky note underneath it, and she smirked. She liked sticky notes and the way they wrapped around her fingers when she played with them.

She stuck the note on her index finger and looked at the television again. On the screen was a man sitting up in his bed, looking around the room he was in. She didn't recognize the actor. He seemed angry and confused, and pulled at some of the tubes attached to his arms and chest. She figured he must not have liked having tubes around his body, either. He looked like an angry puppet that was mad at his strings. The man suddenly slid off the side of the bed and crashed down to the floor. She grinned, as she did every time she'd seen someone fall down on a television show.

The man crawled to his feet and pulled himself up on his bed.

He looked weak and wobbly. She wondered if he had amyloidosis, too; he was wearing the same kind of gown that she'd worn while in the hospital.

She played more with the sticky note and noticed some writing on it. Her lips moved as she tried to read it.

Hook up propofol before 10:30 or he'll wake up!

Chapter 34

Alex Martinez screamed and snarled in lunacy, repeatedly tucking his knees to his chest and then launching both feet into the car door that faced the forest. With the front of his shirt sopping wet from the slobber that poured from his mouth, he dropped to his back and dealt out the same punishment to the door's window. As hard as he connected with each blow, the glass would neither break nor even grant him the sympathy of a crack.

He needed to see what Lumbergh was doing. It consumed him to his very core. He needed to watch the chief kill those people who'd gone after his family. It's what his mother demanded from the grave.

He let out a piercing howl when he heard something crack in his ankle and felt crippling pain jet up his calf. What started out as desperate crying transformed slowly into hideous laughter as he succumbed to the binds that kept him trapped in his cage.

"Lumbergh!" he wailed with all of his might. His body arched like a bridge with his pelvis pointed toward the ceiling.

When he collapsed back to the upholstery, he lay there for a moment, sniveling and mumbling to himself. He choked a little on his own phlegm as his warm breath lingered in the air. He soon found himself glaring at the dome light that hovered above him. Though it wasn't on, it seemed to cast a peculiar radiance.

Martinez tilted his head, examining the glow and wondering what it was trying to tell him. Lights spoke to him every so often. Sometimes they were a beacon of hope and comfort when he felt lost and afraid. Sometimes they scorned him, mocking him for his weaknesses and torturing him for his incompetence.

This light was something different. Its luminosity was inviting and forgiving. It was calling on him to do something. It was a red light—a dancing red light that became more pronounced as the seconds ticked by. Its glow widened beyond the plastic cover and began spreading its way along the entire ceiling of the car.

Martinez lifted up his head and twisted his neck, and saw that the light had somehow moved outside of the window. It lit up the falling snow, making the flakes look like hot, glowing lava dropping to the earth from the mouth of a volcano.

A wide grin spread across Martinez's face. "You're beautiful," he breathlessly told the light. It was drawing him to it.

He spun on his butt and faced the opposite door. Like the other, he had tried several times to force it open to no avail. But it looked different now—flared up in the almost neon blanket cast by the red light. The light was begging him to try the door just once more. He was sure of it.

He cocked his uninjured leg and heaved it into the center of the door. When it connected, the sound of a loud snap and the clatter of metal pieces dropping to the bottom of the door panel bought new life to Martinez's eyes. He kicked the door again and it flew open, helped by the strong wind that then held it wide.

The entire area outside was aglow in red, fluctuating with passion while the wind reached inside the car and pulled at him. Unbounded exuberance bubbled up from his legs to his neck and he lunged for the door. With his arms still bound behind his back by cuffs, he scrambled to get outside. When he did, he understood that the light wanted him to follow Lumbergh and bask in the fury of his vengeance.

He bolted across the road, limping as he did. "I'm coming!"

A half a second later, nearly two tons of metal moving over thirty miles per hour smashed into his body. He felt his spine snap before he was pulled to the frozen ground and dragged underneath the monster he had not seen. Through the immeasurable pain of crushed limbs and flattened organs, he heard the monster's victorious roar, and then heard nothing else.

Chapter 35

Booth snarled as he crashed down to the cold cement floor for the third time. It was as if the large man couldn't remember how to walk, and the small room he knelt in seemed to taunt him over the deadness he felt in his limbs as its spinning walls and bright lights whirled. His hands went to his face and he felt a straggly beard he didn't remember growing.

Where was he? What had happened to him? He was wearing a hospital gown but he was definitely not in a hospital.

He tried again. On shaky legs, he stood and straightened his back. He took another couple of steps before he felt his bare right foot drag. He grabbed onto something with his hand to maintain his balance, realizing that it was the handle of a refrigerator. When its door swung open from his weight, he nearly went down again. A second later, he found himself glaring at several rows of clear containers that sat inside. Each was filled nearly to the top with a rust-colored fluid.

"Those motherfuckers," he muttered. His nostrils flared and his dark eyes burned a hole through the wooden door he spotted at the far wall.

A stiff shot with his shoulder splintered the door's frame and he crashed through. Falling to the white, frozen ground, what felt like an arctic windblast quickly tore his gown from his body, leaving him naked and prone to the brutal elements. Yet, the rage that scorched its way through his soul kept him warm.

When he pulled himself back to his feet, his eyes narrow and tearing from the wind, he saw a white van parked just yards away, outside of a large building. He hobbled his way toward the van, cursing and growling until he reached the passenger side door. He yanked it open and pulled himself inside. There weren't any keys in the ignition, and his visible breath filled up the cab and steamed up the windshield as he searched for them. When he popped open the glove box, he found what looked to be a handheld taser. He snatched it out and pushed its button. A wicked blast of bright blue light lit up the interior of the van. He'd found himself a weapon.

The people that had done this to him were somewhere inside the large building. He couldn't leave without settling that score. They had to pay. But just as he opened the van door, a small, intense light in the distance near the corner of the building pierced its way through the night. He closed the door.

The light sped closer for a few more seconds before it went dark. It had to belong to a vehicle. Perhaps a snowmobile. Seconds later, the figure of a bundled up man emerged, running toward the van.

Booth grinned and clumsily climbed over the seat and into the back of vehicle. He hunched down behind the driver's seat, waiting like a stalking predator.

The van door swung open and the bundled up man slid into the driver's seat. He quickly reached across the cab for the glove box, his body freezing at the sight of it already hanging open with the taser gone.

"What the blooming hell?" he said with a thick accent.

When he spun his head to look behind him, Booth lunged forward and drove the taser into the temple of his head, lighting up his face with its blast. The man's body convulsed violently. The frozen, horrified expression on his face made him look as if he wanted to scream, but couldn't. All the man could do was listen helplessly to the haunting words that suddenly poured out from behind him.

"Your blood won't save lives like mine, shitberg. But I'm going to have fun taking it anyway."

Booth kept the juice turned on until the man looked to be on the verge of passing out. When he finally let up, the man's limp, weakened body fell forward. Booth dropped the taser and latched onto the man's head with his bulky hands. He screamed with effort as he slammed it repeatedly into the van's steel dashboard. Warm blood oozed down through Booth's fingers, widening the sadistic grin that stretched across his face as he continued the man's torment.

With insane glee, Booth shoved him into the dashboard with such malevolent force that the knobs and levers quickly whittled away, along with the doctor's face.

Chapter 36

Lumbergh stood bent over at the waist. He was holding both of Carson's legs at a sharp angle to try and drive more blood back toward his brain, while Jessica placed her ear near Carson's mouth to listen to his breathing and check his pulse again. Carson had stopped seizing.

The chief's head spun when he thought he heard the sound of an automobile engine fire up from somewhere outside in between gusts of wind. He grabbed the overturned rocking chair behind him and dragged it close enough to drape Carson's ankles across it. He then raced to the shattered bedroom window. Jessica glared at him in confusion.

Lumbergh pulled his Mag light from his side and swept its beam back and forth across the blowing snow. Across the alley behind the building he saw the outline of another smaller building that looked like it could have been used for storage. A door at the front of it was flapping open from the wind.

A pair of brake lights suddenly lit up at the far end of the building. Lumbergh's head swiveled toward it. "There's a car back here!" he yelled. "Whose is it?"

"It's got to be our van," answered Jessica, not moving her head from Carson.

"Who would be driving it?"

"I don't know. Phillip maybe. He had the keys."

Lumbergh whipped the radio to his mouth. "Redick! I need you here now! Right now!"

Redick didn't answer. The van began moving around the corner of the building.

Lumbergh breathlessly raced for the bedroom door, stopping for a moment before he reached the hallway. "If you let him die, I'm going to do everything in my power to make sure you spend the rest of your life in prison. Do you understand?"

Jessica nodded, only lifting her eyes to Lumbergh for a moment before returning them to Carson, whose glazed eyes swam in disarray.

With shotgun in hand, Lumbergh ran down the hallway.

Some radio air cleared before the chief finally heard Redick's voice emit from his side. "We've got a situation here, Chief."

"I've got a situation *here!*" Lumbergh yelled out, knowing that Redick couldn't hear him with his hand off his radio.

He ran out through the garage and into the storm. He saw the flashing red lights of the sheriff's car rotating down the road, close to where he thought he'd left his police cruiser. The lights weren't moving in closer and he didn't understand why.

The van was steadily heading in the opposite direction, traveling up the snow-covered road with its headlights turned off. Lumbergh could only see the vehicle when the driver tapped the brakes.

"Dammit!" he roared.

He threw the shotgun in a mound of snow beside him, knowing it would only slow him down. He still had his pistol in his holster. He took off after the van on foot, reaching for his radio while doing his best not to slip and fall.

"Redick, get up here! The culprits are getting away. They might have Sean with them!"

"I can't!" Redick yelled back. "We . . . We ran over someone, God-dammit. They're mangled under the car!"

Lumbergh's eyes bulged. A gasp whizzed out his lips. "Is it Sean?"

"No. I . . . I think it's Martinez. He came running right at us! Why isn't he with you?"

"Shit!" grunted Lumbergh. "I left him locked up in my car! How in the hell did he get out?"

"How the hell would I know?" Redick screamed back defensively. "You stole him from us, remember?"

Lumbergh cursed, slid the radio back to his side, and yanked out his Glock. He clenched his teeth and ran as quickly as he could, lunging with every stride as the frigid wind and snow pounded his small body. Another flicker of the brake lights showed that the van was now far away and moving too quickly to catch up to on foot.

Lumbergh dropped to the snow on one knee and steadied himself to fire. He knew almost instantly, however, that he couldn't take the shot. Even after the van's headlights switched on and gave him a more definitive target in the distance, he couldn't risk sending the van off the side of the road by blowing out a tire or hitting the driver. Sean might be inside.

Lumbergh crumbled to the snow, falling to both knees, and cursing the world as he turned his head to the sky. The haunting words that Andrew Carson had uttered back in the building floated to the top of his thoughts.

"They're going to kill him."

Though it was possible Sean was in that van, the notion didn't seem likely. If his pursuers were intent on killing him, they wouldn't have bothered to take him to another location first. They would have put him down where they found him.

A reluctant tear began to slide down Lumbergh's face as he holstered his gun. He told himself that it was drawn from the wind, but he knew that wasn't the case. He held his radio to his mouth as his hand shook and told Redick to have his men find out where the road came out and to get some deputies there.

"Head up the road on foot and you'll find the building," Lumbergh added. "You're not that far out. Andrew Carson is inside.

He needs medical attention. There's a woman in there, too. Take her into custody once the ambulance gets here. I'll explain later."

"The ambulance is pulling up right now!" Redick shouted excitedly. "Wait! Andrew Carson from Greeley? He's there?"

Lumbergh switched his radio off. He wasn't in the mood to explain it all. He climbed to his feet with his head hung low and began making his way back toward the building. He clipped the radio to his side and pulled his Mag light from next to it.

When he flipped the light on, he noticed that there had been a lot of activity along the road. Footprints, tire tracks, and even what appeared to be the ski lines of a snowmobile. Most were faint, having been covered with fresh snow, but he saw a more recent set of skis that led over the shoulder of the road and down a hill.

Lumbergh scoured the side of the hill with his beam and traced the tracks downward until they disappeared behind some trees. The hill was steep. He probably shouldn't have tried to navigate down it with only one arm to balance himself, but he did. He slipped along the snowy, frozen terrain repeatedly, sliding on his butt when he needed to. It was becoming dangerous, but he didn't allow anything to discourage his descent.

Whenever his light lit up new ground, he feared he'd find the large body of his brother-in-law lying face down in the snow. Each overturned tree and narrow boulder seemed to resemble that frightful image until his mind let him accept otherwise and allowed him to take a new breath.

The further down he climbed, the more isolated Lumbergh felt both in his thoughts and his soul. How would his family move past what had happened?

On wobbly legs, he ducked between two sagging trees. That's when his eyes widened at the sight of a thin red laser dot pinned to his chest. He froze in his tracks.

"Bang!" he heard a man's voice shout out from the dark over the whistle of the wind.

The sound jolted Lumbergh's body. His mind raced through the process of dropping his light and replacing it with his Glock, but he knew it would take the hidden man in the woods only a fraction of that time to fire off a shot.

"You've thrown your last shrimp on the barbie, mate!" the voice shouted.

Lumbergh recognized the bad humor, but more importantly, he now recognized the man's voice.

It was Sean.

The corners of Lumbergh's mouth slowly curled into a relieved grin.

Chapter 37

L umbergh watched the beginnings of a new morning flourish out from beyond the distant, snow-covered horizon. Billowy orange clouds with yellow streaks hugging their edges hovered over the crisp outline of a curved mountain range. The crest of treetops resembled goose bumps from so far away.

It would have been an even grander, awe-inspiring sight had it not been viewed from behind the metal grill of the sheriff car's backseat. He sat there in the warmth of the vehicle's heater as the engine purred along, waiting alone for the return of one of the deputies who would drive him to Redick's office. There, multiple charges would be filed against him.

Lumbergh had never had his rights read to him before. It was a somber, surreal experience.

The wind had died down dramatically and the snow was no longer falling. The turbulent weather had left with most of the squad cars and the ambulance that had taken Andrew Carson to the hospital. Carson was going to pull through. He heard one of the EMTs say the injury looked "purely vascular." The same paramedic got Carson to feel finger-pressure against his toes—a good sign that if there was damage done to his spine, it wasn't permanent. It was even possible the numbness Carson felt earlier may have stemmed from an old leg injury that was acting up. Regardless, the bullet from his neck still needed to be removed. Carson was likely already in surgery for that.

Carson would soon be reunited with his daughter. Katelyn was said to sound ecstatic over the phone when she heard the news that he had been found. Lumbergh had witnessed the ear-to-ear grin on Carson's face, in between winces, when he briefly spoke to her from the top of a stretcher as he was lifted into the ambulance.

Jessica and Sean were still being questioned by the sheriff's people inside the restaurant. Lumbergh expected Jessica would be taken away for processing at any moment. Her life was a world of hurt: a daughter who was still dying, a brother she learned had been killed, and the knowledge that she was the only one left to go down for everything her family had done.

Dr. Phillip Robinson's mutilated body was discovered in the abandoned van near Leadville. His legacy would not be to live on as a hero in the medical world, but rather as a man with a twisted mind who was murdered by perhaps an even more twisted person. Norman Booth was still on the loose.

Lumbergh lowered his gaze to his freshly wrapped sling before turning his head and peering down the road through the back window at the mob of reporters being held at bay by a few strands of yellow tape and uniformed officers. He couldn't hear the reporters from that distance, but they looked to be shouting over each other, snapping off pictures, and panning the area with video cameras.

He hoped Redick would at least have the decency not to drive the two of them through that crowd on their way out and let the police chief of Winston be shown as a common perp. Broadcasted on the evening news and in papers with pictures of him humiliated in the back of the sheriff's car wasn't the way Lumbergh wanted the public to learn of what he had done.

He knew his days as the police chief of Winston were over. He'd broken serious laws and the man he'd illegally taken into custody was now dead. Martinez's body had left with the county coroner an hour earlier, after deputies worked for twenty minutes to pry it out from under the car.

Lumbergh understood that he was likely going to serve time, and the accomplished law enforcement career he'd built over the years wouldn't count for anything once he got out of prison.

At least he could still face Diana. His wife understood that everything he had done, he had done for her brother. He felt the warmth and unconditional companionship of her voice over the phone when they spoke. Their marriage would remain strong. He felt as though there was more she wanted to tell him, but he told her they'd get to talk in person at the sheriff's office. He couldn't wait to see her face again.

He lifted his head when he felt the passenger door open. He was expecting it to be Redick or one of the deputies. Instead he found Sean taking a seat in front of him. The car creaked under the added weight. A large gauze bandage was fastened to the back of his head.

"What are you doing?" asked Lumbergh.

"Just checking in. You warm enough?"

"I'm fine."

"Listen, uh . . ." Sean began with a humility in his tone that Lumbergh had never heard before from his brother-in-law. "I want to thank you. I want to thank you for coming after me." He turned his head to meet Lumbergh's attention with the corner of his eye. With a chuckle, he added, "I didn't know you cared."

Lumbergh blew air from his nose, subtly shaking his head. "A lot of good it did you," he said. "I didn't end up helping you at all. You got away on your own."

"Don't give me that shit," said Sean. "You saved Carson's life. He was dying on that bedroom floor. Jessica couldn't have kept him alive on her own. You got the paramedics here in time."

Lumbergh lifted his shoulders in concession. "Fine."

"It's more than *fine*," said Sean.

Lumbergh took a deep breath. "Unfortunately, it's not going to do me any good. I'm going away, Sean. Martinez is dead and I'm to blame for that."

"Martinez," Sean grumbled. "I never liked that guy."

"It doesn't matter. His death is my fault."

"Actually, it's Jefferson's fault."

Lumbergh's eyes narrowed. "What in the hell are you talking about?"

"I talked to old Jeffrey on the phone a little while ago. In the hospital. I think I interrupted his sponge bath. He said he crashed the side of the police cruiser into my car yesterday—which he'll be paying for by the way. He fucked up the door somehow. The lock wasn't working right. That's how Martinez escaped."

"Shit," Lumbergh moaned, leaning back in his seat. "Don't tell anybody that. Don't drag Jefferson into this."

"I won't. It's got to be hard enough for him just to be . . . you know . . . just to be Jefferson."

"Be nice, Sean. He'll be the acting Winston Police Chief now."

"Christ," Sean breathed.

Neither man spoke for a while. Lumbergh stared out the side window while Sean did the same out his window.

Lumbergh finally broke the silence. "When I'm done answering for all of this, I'll be lucky if I can find a job as a security guard." Upon digesting his words, he winced and added, "No offense."

"None taken." Sean twisted in the seat until he was looking Lumbergh directly in the eye. A sly smile slowly formed on his face.

"No, Sean. I don't want to be a security guard with you," said Lumbergh, dead seriousness in his eyes.

"Like I'd even ask," said Sean, shaking his head in dismissal. "Gary, what if I told you that you're going to stay Winston's police chief?"

Lumbergh let his head tilt to the side. A less than amused expression lined his face. "I'd tell you to stop fucking with me."

———

Sean chuckled. It was the reaction he was expecting. He then told his brother-in-law that Sheriff Richard Redick was willing to overlook every illegal act Lumbergh had committed under one condition: Redick was to get sole credit for using Martinez to track down and find Andrew Carson.

Sean watched his brother-in-law's face twist in confusion and audacity as he listened. "Andrew Carson is a huge story, Gary. No one was expecting to find him alive. A politician like Redick knows better than to waste that kind of press and celebrity on you. I think the fathead wants to be the governor someday. Something like this might actually get him there."

Lumbergh shook his head and opened his mouth to speak, but Sean cut him off.

"Don't say anything. Just think about this for a minute, Gary. Everyone knows that you're *the man*—the guy who took down Alvar Montoya. You're a rock star. If this story is played legit, Redick will be the man who put a hero cop behind bars. And for why? Because that hero cop defied Redick's shitty judgment and found Andrew Carson all on his own."

"And?"

"My point is that all of that will come out in court, and it would be best for everyone if it just went away."

"Oh Jesus, Sean!" Lumbergh cried out. "That's not going to work!"

"Yes it will, Gary! But only if you let it. Redick's not going to cut you totally out of the picture. He knows he needs you here at the scene for the timeline to work out right in the report. You just need to be working under his toota . . . Um . . ."

"Tutelage?" Lumbergh jumped in.

"Yes!" Sean said, snapping his fingers and pointing. "That's the word he used. He's just has to be the one who compelled Martinez to talk and bring you all here."

"And, of course, Martinez is not around to explain otherwise," said Lumbergh with his eyes bearing down on Sean.

"Right. In his escape attempt, he accidentally got run over. That's the truth anyway, isn't it? No one's going to question that."

Lumbergh leaned forward, placing his elbow on his knee and his outstretched hand on his forehead. He used his palm to press his right eye wide open. "I can't believe this," he muttered. "All of that bullshit lecturing Redick gave me about following procedure and being a professional. . . What an asshole!"

Sean smiled. "I won't argue with that. Still, he knows you're a good cop, and that all of that Montoya bullshit was what fucked with your head."

Lumbergh swung his body back into his seat and stared up at the ceiling.

"If you're on board, I just need to let Redick know and we'll get you out of the back of this car."

Lumbergh closed his eyes and took in a deep breath.

"Listen Gary, I know you're a man of integrity. It's one of the things that irritates the hell out of me about you. But tell me what kind of justice would be served if you went to prison because some loon who nearly killed Oldhorse and Jefferson got what was coming to him. Tell me what justice would be served if the man who killed Alvar Montoya, saved Andrew Carson's life, and has been a good husband to my sister was put behind bars."

"Enough!" Lumbergh sputtered out, opening his eyes. "I hear what you're saying, but . . ."

"There's something else, Gary."

"What?"

"You can't be a good father to your baby if you're behind bars."

Lumbergh's eyes immediately shot open and his posture snapped forward. He breathlessly glared at Sean with his mouth gaped open. "Are you serious?"

"Yeah. Diana's been waiting for the right moment to tell you. She didn't want to do it while you were acting all loony. You scared the shit out of her when you sent her and Mom away."

"I'm going to be a dad?" he whispered to himself once his eyes slid from Sean's face.

"That's right. Don't tell her I told you, either. She wanted it to be a *precious moment* or whatever, but you didn't give me any choice. I know you don't want your kid visiting you in the clink in between bang sessions with some of the guys you put away over the years. The decision should be an easy one, Gary. I need you to make it right now."

Lumbergh furiously shook his head, then laughed out loud as a broad smile lifted his cheeks. "You know," he said with a chuckle, "you're an asshole for not telling me about this when you first got in the car."

"I know," said Sean with a smirk. "I just wanted to let you sweat it out for a few more minutes. *Prime you up* for the big decision." *Prime you up* was a term he had once heard Dennis Franz say on *NYPD Blue*. He'd always wanted to use it himself. His face slowly turned serious. He waited for Lumbergh to look at him before he spoke again. He then told his brother-in-law that the truth needed to be stretched just a little bit more—not for Redick but for Sean himself. "Jessica was an unwilling participant in this," he said. "Do you understand?"

Lumbergh stared right through him. His smile disappeared and he seemed to be fighting back the urge to launch into a tirade. "Sean," he said calmly. "I know what you're doing, but it won't work. The story just won't work." He reminded Sean that Martinez only knew about the restaurant because he followed Jessica and her brother back to it.

"Who knows that it was Jessica?" asked Sean. "Who knows that Martinez saw a *woman* that night at my house? Redick sure as hell doesn't know. He just knows that two people took me. I already told him that those two people were Adam and Dr. Phil."

"You what?" said Lumbergh with wide eyes and a gasp.

"You heard me."

Lumbergh's mouth gaped open for a good five seconds before he spoke again. "Sean, once I have time to think straight, I know I'll be able to give you a dozen reasons why that story just won't fly."

"And I'd give you a dozen reasons why it will. I'd start with telling you that Jessica and Anna don't even live here. They have a place in Lakeland. That's a fact. This old restaurant is owned by her brother, Adam. As far as anyone needs to know, Jessica's involvement was limited to discovering Norman Booth's *super-plasma* at GSL last summer and telling her family about it."

Lumbergh shook his head, but Sean continued.

"Adam and Dr. Phil did everything else on their own. Understand? Adam was very close with his niece and was desperate enough to do anything to save her. Dr. Phil just wanted to make a name for himself. They put this all together themselves. They kidnapped Norman Booth, brought him back here, and invited Jessica and Anna over just last night to tell her what they had been up to. She told them she wanted no part of it. She even helped me escape."

"Why would you even be here, Sean?" exclaimed Lumbergh. "Why would Adam and Phil even know who you are and what you were doing? Jessica's the only link between you and them!"

Sean answered quickly, having formulated the answer in his mind earlier. "Jessica helped search for Andrew Carson on her day off from work. She was just being a good citizen, having heard about Carson's disappearance on the news. After I saw her picture in the *Denver Post* and decided that I was going to try and impress her—this woman I knew from GSL who I'd been building up the nerve to ask on a date—finding Andrew Carson was my way of impressing her."

"Oh give me a break!" Lumbergh shouted out. "This sounds like the plot line of an old John Cusack movie! You had a crush on her, so *this* was your way of impressing her?"

Sean glared angrily at Lumbergh, deciding not to tell him that